Angel

Richard Brautigan

Other Works in the Angel Series:

Angel

A CHANT OF PARADISE

R.E. BRAITHWAITE

ARCHWAY
PUBLISHING

Archway Publishing books may be ordered through booksellers or by contacting:

Archway Publishing
1663 Liberty Drive
Bloomington, IN 47403
www.archwaypublishing.com
1 (888) 242-5904

This is a work of fiction. All of the characters, names, incidents, organizations, and dialogue in this novel are either the products of the author's imagination or are used fictitiously.

ISBN: 978-1-4808-4851-1 (sc)
ISBN: 978-1-4808-4849-8 (hc)
ISBN: 978-1-4808-4850-4 (e)

Library of Congress Control Number: 2017910556

Print information available on the last page.

Archway Publishing rev. date: 7/18/2017

-For Chanel-

Dartmouth College, 1970

After the assassinations of MLK and Bobby Kennedy—and The Democratic Convention of '68—and The Bobby Seales Trial—and the invasion of Cambodia—and Kent State—and the college strikes—and the March on Washington.

Supple and Turbulent, a ring of men
Shall Chant in orgy on a summer morn
Their boisterous devotion to the sun,
Not as a god, but as a god might be,
Naked among them, like a savage source.
Their chant shall be a chant of paradise...
They shall know well the heavenly fellowship
Of men...

From Sunday Morning by Wallace Stevens

Chapter One

Friday October 30, 1970
Boom Boom (Boom Boom)
Setting: Colby Junior College for Women

ANGEL LEANED AGAINST GROUCHO'S IMPALA AND STUDIED
the sky. It was too early for snow, but that's sure as shit what looked to be coming
their way. He took a hit of the joint and shivered. An early winter wouldn't be a
bad thing. Cold could be purgatorial, too, and Angel's soul begged for chastening.

Shit.

Angel smiled. He was in a mood. Pussy, he told himself.

He exhaled and watched the smoke dissipate into the breeze. Snow would mean
that Cassie couldn't drive up to Hanover for the weekend. That would be sweet. He
didn't need her pursed lips and look of disapproval every time one of his friends said
something stupid, which was pretty much all the time.

Angel remembered when Cassie loved coming to Dartmouth and found his
friends witty. He remembered when the two of them could go to parties and enjoy
the company of others. Now, they cloistered themselves in Angel's room for sex and
talked of a future that grew increasingly improbable. They had become one of those
couples who knows a break-up is coming soon and tries too hard to make their last
days together seem convivial.

Oh, Cassie. His first real love.

Shit.

The joint tasted good. It was from Groucho's new stash, and the leaves were
tightly bunched and smelled fresher than his last batch. Angel wondered if Groucho
had taken his advice and begun buying from Gandalf, Angel's freshman advisee.
Whatever the case, it was turning Angel's head into mush too quickly, so he cupped

1

it in his hand and slowed down. Angel looked upwards again. The first flakes of winter began to flutter past him, and he smiled.

A car door slammed nearby, and two girls passed him. He could hear the disapprobation in their voices. "That guy is smoking pot." They peeked at him as they passed. Angel gave them a sweet smile and exhaled upwards into the leaden sky. One smiled back, despite herself, and then hurried away.

That's right girls. Angel was a desperado, a born rules breaker.

God, he loved Colby girls. He loved their cheerful anti-intellectualism and their perpetual good will. They seemed throwbacks to another age, sent to Colby by their antediluvian mothers to meet Dartmouth men and get married or some such nonsense.

Not that he wanted a girl with bubble-gum for a brain. No, he much preferred Cassie's intellect and ambition. Cassie, with her dark hair and slow, sly smile and the endlessly surprising knowledge of things she couldn't possibly know. Ah, Cassie, why did love die? Or did it simply wear out because it burned too hot for too long? Yes, he would be glad if it snowed, and he got a reprieve from Cassie for the weekend. It was exhausting being forced to smile and kiss and cuddle all the while worrying that the next thing the other might say would begin with the words, 'we need to talk...'

Angel was tired of his part in this game, too, but the Colby girls with their child-like good humor brought out his paternal side. Besides, he was the only one who did it well, so, here he was. He glanced at his watch and surveyed the campus. In a couple of minutes, the bell in the clock tower would toll, and class would be over. The buildings would empty and chattering girls would crisscross the quad in small packets of female energy. That always made him happy. Girls always looked so excited when they traveled in bunches. Guys at Dartmouth rarely walked in groups and didn't speak to each other even if they did.

Sure enough, the bell sounded and, in an impossibly short space of time, noisy little groups began to emerge. The classroom buildings were on opposite sides of the campus, and the girl groups took off in seemingly random directions, like spooked birds fleeing a feeder. Angel liked the way their flight destroyed the too perfect symmetry of the Colby campus. He enjoyed trying to discern a mathematical pattern to their campus crossing. It was like chaos math. The only constant was the groupings of three, four, or five. Like acceptable packets of energy in quantum theory.

Angel saw Cane enter the periphery of the quad and begin his hunt, so he put the joint out on the heel of a boot and pocketed it for later. He would need it. That and a half bottle of aspirin, a pint of rum, and an ice-filled towel.

Game time.

Unlike Angel, Cane seemed to take entirely too much pleasure in his job. Cane was perfect and knew it. He was six and a half feet tall but looked much bigger from most of the girls' perspectives, and he had an insouciant look which seemed, somehow, more dangerous than if he had looked malevolent.

Cane opened a beer and chugged half of it. He shook his locks, and it appeared from Angel's perspective as if he actually growled. Cane started deliberately towards a five-some of girls on the far side of the quad.

Game on.

Cane had chosen an interesting group. It was led by a brunette who walked ahead of the other four. Her followers were all varying degrees of blonde, and they fanned out in a rough V formation behind their brunette Alpha. The blondes laughed with each other and hugged their books against their chests. They brimmed with life and looked to be headed to one of the dorms across campus. Class was over for the week, and their body language shouted 'party time.'

The Alpha, though, was the one who interested Angel. She paid little interest to her acolytes. Her face revealed that her brain was occupied with something other than boys and free beer. She clearly interested Cane, too, because he bore directly down on her from an oblique angle, swigging beer as he stalked his prey.

When he came within their range, he registered on the girls' radar, and they detoured slightly to avoid him. All except for the brunette. She wasn't moving for anyone. This was her campus and her universe.

Angel smiled. Time for him to go to work. He strolled through groups of girls, smiling at those who smiled at him. His boots crackled on the gravel path, and his adrenaline began to kick in. His smiles grew broader, and girls looked at him and chattered to each other as he passed them.

Cane had engaged the Alpha. Angel couldn't hear their words, but he could imagine the general drift of their conversation. It would go something like:

Cane: "How are you girls doing today?"

Girls: Silence. Avoidance. Don't make eye contact. He's a brute.

Cane: "Fucking bunch of snobs."

Alpha: "Leave us alone."

Cane: "I'll fucking leave you alone. I wouldn't fuck any of you if you begged for it. Maybe the little chubby one, but the rest of you can go fuck yourselves."

Cane was fairly profane.

Angel saw the Alpha try to push past Cane, only to have him block her path. Consternation began to grow among the followers as they looked at each other and tried to discern an escape route if things turned uglier. The Alpha bridled, though, and stared defiantly up at Cane. More words were exchanged and Cane poked her in the chest, knocking her backwards a step.

The brunette's eyes lit up, and she got in Cane's face and let him have it.

Cane put a finger against her breast bone and shoved her backwards. This time, he followed his push and moved towards her. He raised his can of beer and began shaking spurts of beer on her.

Angel could hear, "Fucking bitch" loudly repeated and saw the first glimmers of fear on the brunette's face.

Angel began to jog towards the group.

"Hey," he shouted. "Hey, asshole."

Cane turned towards Angel.

"Who the fuck are you?" Cane asked.

"Leave the girls alone," Angel said.

Cane cackled. He turned back to the brunette and poured beer over her head.

Angel grabbed the brunette's wrist and pulled her behind him, shielding her from the giant.

"Just chill," Angel said. "Leave the girls alone."

"Or what, you little dick?" Cane wanted to know. Cane looked him up and down. "What are you?" he said. "Some kind of fairy cowboy?"

"Come on, girls," Angel said and began to push past Cane.

Cane wasn't having any of it. He grabbed Angel's shoulder and spun him.

"Those are my chicks," Cane said. "They're hot for me."

Angel confronted Cane. It was time.

Cane stared at Angel. He chugged the rest of his beer and bounced the can off Angel's chest.

"Fuck you," Cane said.

"No," Angel said. "Fuck you."

Cane glared at him for a second, and then he raised a fist. Angel didn't back down, and, for a moment, they had a staring contest.

Angel could feel his adrenaline really kicking in. What a rush.

Then, Cane clubbed Angel on his left cheek. Angel staggered backwards and went for Cane, but Cane hit him again, in the mouth this time, and Angel dropped to the ground. His eyes watered, and Cane seemed a giant blur, but he rose and put his fists up.

Cane looked taken aback. He did nothing for a second, but then he began to laugh. "You should see your face," he said. "You look like shit." He burped loudly and made his exit, cackling as he left.

Angel stood for a moment and then sagged to a knee. His head felt like it was exploding, as if a glass ball had blown up in him and was sending shards into his face and skull. He didn't even examine his nose. He knew it was broken. He had broken it often enough before to recognize the symptoms.

Shit. His nose and his ribs. Why were they always the parts which broke? Well, at least noses were better than ribs. He wouldn't breathe well for a week or so, but that was better than trying to sleep or fuck with broken ribs.

He did feel his mouth, though, to see if any teeth were loose or broken. Nope, everything seemed relatively intact. When he looked at his hand, it was covered in gore, so he knew he must be bleeding pretty badly.

He raised his head to the group of girls. The blondes were frozen in horror, but the brunette knelt in front of him.

"Are you all right?" she asked.

Angel laughed.

"You're kidding, right?" he asked.

She smiled slightly and touched his nose.

"Your nose is broken," she said.

"You think?" he said.

Someone produced a bandana, and alpha girl began to wipe his face. And then came the part he hated. As his adrenaline ebbed, the nausea burbled in his throat. Angel gently pushed the girl's ministering hand aside and leaned over. His stomach heaved twice, but then it calmed. He waited for the feeling to recede and sucked in air. He raised his head again to see the girl looking sternly at him.

"Come on," she said. She helped Angel to his feet.

Then Groucho and Blake arrived.

"Angel, what the fuck happened to you?" Blake asked.

The blondes began describing the ordeal to Groucho, but the brunette led Angel resolutely away.

"Where are we going?" Angel asked.

"My dorm. We're going to get you cleaned up," she said.

"I'm fine," he said.

She looked at him ironically and smiled again. She shook her head. 'Men,' her expression seemed to say.

When they reached her dorm, she led him to a set of back stairs and took him to her room. Angel plopped in a chair. The girl disappeared, and Angel tilted his head back, holding the bandana to his bleeding nose. He looked around her room. It wasn't what he expected. For one thing, she had no posters or any of the other decorations most girls deemed necessary. Instead, there were books everywhere. He got up and went to a shelf. Biology. Chemistry. Lots of science. Lots of history, too. Interesting.

Then, she returned and firmly ordered him to sit back down. She wiped his face with a cold, wet towel. She was gentle, and, although his face hurt like hell, her hands felt like magic.

It gave him an opportunity to study her face. She had gray eyes and light freckles on the tops of her cheeks. She looked smart, and Angel could feel himself getting hard. He liked smart girls. Even better, he liked getting attention from smart girls.

"What's your name?" he asked.

"Maggie," she said.

Maggie, he repeated to himself. Maggie the Cat. His stiffening dick told him that he wasn't Brick to her Maggie. She left the room again, and he watched her go this time. Nice ass. And she moved well. An athlete or dancer or something like that? He loved the way her hips moved when she walked.

She came back with another towel and knelt in front of him, making sure the bleeding had stopped before she dabbed again.

Angel wanted to tell her what a lovely body she had. Her breasts weren't large, but her tight sweater showed their perfect shape. Not as perfect as her ass, but fine, nonetheless.

But he settled on saying, "I'm Angel."

She stopped dabbing for a second and looked at him. "Really? I heard that boy call you that but thought I'd misheard."

"Yep."

"And what brought three Dartmouth guys to Colby on a Friday afternoon?" she asked.

"What makes you think we're from Dartmouth?"

She eyed him scornfully. "Seriously? You're Angel, and one of the other boys was named Groucho? All of you Dartmouth guys have nicknames. It's ridiculous." She stopped. "So, what's wrong with the other one? Blake? He didn't rate a nickname?"

"How do you know his real name isn't Gustaveous, and Blake is a nickname?"

"Touche," she laughed.

They were quiet. It felt nice. He liked this girl.

"We came to invite girls to a party at our fraternity," he said.

"What fraternity?"

"Phi Psi," he said.

"Never heard of it," she said.

Angel smiled. "It's a shitty fraternity. You wouldn't like it."

"I love your approach," she said.

Angel looked perplexed.

"Your line is 'come to a party at our shitty fraternity. You wouldn't like it,'" she said. "Does that usually work?"

"Picking up girls is Blake's job. He does have a nickname. We call him Smooth."

She sat back and looked at him. "You're done. That's the best I can do," she said.

"I know. Not much to work with in the first place," he said.

"Nope. But now your face matches your beat-up cowboy boots."

Angel rose. He was still wobbly. Great. That meant a concussion.

"You're really not going to hit on me or invite me to your party or anything?" Maggie said.

Angel smiled. Okay, this girl was unfairly pretty and unfairly funny.

"Would you like to come to a party, tonight?" he asked.

"How come you're having it tonight instead of tomorrow night?"

"The good fraternities get to host the Halloween parties," he said. "So, we get the night before. But we're having a band and everything. True, it's a bunch of high school guys who are playing for beer, but it's a band. And I've heard them. They do a good version of *House of the Rising Sun*. So, want to come?"

"So, this is a personal invitation? I would be your date?"

"No. I have a girlfriend. Sort of. She goes to Smith, and she won't come if it snows, which it will. And she doesn't like me anymore."

"You're inviting me to a party, but it isn't a date because you have a girlfriend who won't be there?"

"Something like that." He smiled. "Well?"

"No."

"No," he laughed. "After you practically begged to be invited? You are Maggie the Cat."

"Does that make you Brick? You don't like girls? Is that the real reason your girlfriend isn't coming? All boots and no boner?" She blushed as she said that, but they both laughed. "No, anyway. I have a boyfriend, a real-life Brick, and he'll be here in about an hour. He's taking me to a Dartmouth party at *Tabard*. He has a high school friend who's a member. They have a band, too."

"Ah, a real band at a real fraternity. I may crash their party and steal you away."

"I'd like that. It's a Halloween party. You'd have to wear a costume, but, with that face, you could come as Frankenstein."

"What are you going as?"

She laughed. "A cat. Maggie the Cat."

Shit. She was too much. A reader on top of the fine ass and great sense of humor. This girl even knows her Tennessee Williams. Be still my beating heart. And my throbbing member. Angel stood to leave. This was fun, but it was, after all, a business trip. "I'm sorry about your towels," he said, gesturing to the bloody pile on the floor.

"No biggie," she said. "I stole them from the girl next door. She's a total bitch." At the door, she put a hand to his cheek. It was a tender gesture. "Take care, Angel. Don't play hero again this weekend. Let this heal. It's a nice face." She traced the scar above his right eyebrow with her finger. "An interesting face."

Angel went back down the way they had gone up. He knew men weren't allowed in the girls' rooms, but the house mothers often looked the other way. He was grateful this one had.

Downstairs, Angel found a happy chaos. Blake and Groucho were entertaining the girls. Lots more had appeared, and everyone wanted to hear about the big fight. When the crowd saw Angel, they treated him as a conquering warrior.

Angel grimaced. Everyone was so excited. Blood had a way of doing that, he knew. He was glad he had made their day, though it didn't seem fair that Groucho and Blake were being treated as fellow warriors. What had they done?

Shit. He was getting too old for this.

The three of them walked outside into what was already a steady snow. As they crossed campus, the flakes adorned Groucho's hair. They looked like decorations in a bush.

In the car on the way back to Dartmouth, Groucho drove and Cane rode shotgun. Blake sat in the back with Angel, who smoked the rest of his joint.

Angel lay back and listened to their happy chatter.

Cane turned around and handed Angel a beer. "Sorry I hit you so hard," he said. "I meant to hit your cheek, but I caught you kind of flush with that first one."

"And the second shot?" Angel asked.

"You nose didn't bleed right away, so I went for the mouth. I didn't figure you would mind a busted lip, and lips bleed a lot."

Angel thought that over. He knew Cane was right. If Cane hadn't drawn blood, the girls wouldn't have been so excited.

"That fairy cowboy line was pretty fucking funny, wasn't it?" Cane asked.

"Hilarious," Angel said. "How many girls did we get?"

"A shit load," Blake said. "Practically that whole dorm."

"Good," Angel said. He sipped the beer and held the cold can to his face. A bevy of beauties meant a lot of walk-ins from the dorms and the other fraternities. That meant he needed to hit Moe's for an extra keg or two. Being Social Chairman was wearing him down. That's all the guys wanted from him: blood, bands, babes, and beer.

"Cane said you didn't even flinch this time," Groucho said. "You two are getting really good at this."

"Yeah," Cane said. "That was probably my best performance, yet."

"Yeah, well that may be my last time," Angel laughed. "Your performance, my ass."

Cane turned to him. "I do all the work," he said. "All you have to do is stand there and get hit. How hard is that?" He turned back around and cracked another beer. "Fucking pussy. That was epic. Just admit it."

Angel smiled and closed his eyes. The pot was tasty and the cold can felt good against his face. Not as good as the memory of Maggie, though. She was fine.

Angel stared out the window at the snow and let a fantasy form in his mind. This time, when Maggie was examining his face, he took her hand and kissed her palm. She looked at him and read his eyes. Her gray eyes told him 'yes,' and he kissed her. She tasted, for some bizarre reason, like fresh apples. He put his hands on her cheeks and drew her to him to kiss her again. Maggie melted against him and sighed.

Angel could feel himself getting hard again.

God, he loved women.

And Cane was right.

It had been epic.

Chapter Two

That Same Friday October 30, 1970
At Phi Psi (The Shitty Frat House)
Setting: Dartmouth College

GROUCHO DROPPED ANGEL OFF AT MOE'S. ANGEL STOOD patiently while Moe finished ringing up a crabby old townie ahead of him in line. Moe waited until she left the store, then he pointed at her with his thumb and said, "Mrs. Hutchinson. I don't know why she comes in here. All she does is complain that my prices are higher than at a grocery store."

"Some people like to complain," Angel said.

"Yeah," Moe groused. "They're called women."

Angel smiled. Moe complaining about complainers. That was funny.

"What happened to your face?" Moe asked.

"I was at Colby recruiting chicks for our dance tonight," Angel said.

Moe nodded as if he knew what that meant. "You know your nose is broken?"

"Yeah, no big loss," Angel said. "I need to double my keg order for tonight. Do you have enough?"

Moe disappeared into the back. He returned nodding. "Yeah, I'm good. Budweiser is restocking me tomorrow anyway. Halloween's always good for business."

Angel signed for the beer and trudged down the alley to Phi Psi. His face was really beginning to hurt. He bent to the road, made a snowball, and pressed it against his lip and nose.

When he walked up the driveway to Phi Psi, he saw a girl sitting on the steps clutching an overnight bag to her flat chest.

She had the saddest face he had ever seen.

Angel looked around but didn't see a guy or a group of girls to explain her plight. A crying girl wasn't exactly an anomaly. There were always fights and break-ups going on, but it was early in the day for either. Besides, he thought he pretty much knew all the Phi Psi girlfriends, and he had never seen this chick before.

He nodded at her as he mounted the steps and went inside. He shook off the snow and hung his jacket in the coat room under the staircase. He bought a bag of peanut M&Ms and a Coke from the vending machines and checked the message board to see if Cassie had called. Of course, she hadn't. He held the cold Coke to his face and began to climb the stairs to his room but stopped halfway up.

Shit.

He descended and went outside, praying the girl would be gone, but there she sat, a mute bundle of agony covered in tears and snot and snowflakes.

Don't talk to her. Don't get involved. You know this always ends up shitty for you.

But, he sighed and sat on the step next to her. He didn't speak at first, being content to observe her. She glanced at him suspiciously and wiped snot on the sleeve of her jacket and sniffed.

"Aren't you cold out here?" he asked finally.

"What do you think?"

Okay. Just as snotty on the inside as she is on the outside.

He rose to leave, but she looked up, and he could see pain in her blurry eyes.

"Want to come inside?" he asked. "It's warmer in there."

"No. I'm fine." Then, "I heard there's a dance, but no one seems to be here."

"Yes, well the dance doesn't start for a few hours. Really, don't you want to come inside? Look, the snow is falling harder again." He opened his Coke and took a meditative sip. He tore open the M&Ms and ate a red one. He held the bag out as an offering, but she shook her head.

She glanced at the sky and then at him. It was the first time she had made eye contact. She seemed to be sizing him up.

"What would I do inside until the dance?"

"I'll put you to work."

She rose as if she were doing him a favor and went inside. Angel followed. He showed her where to hang up her coat and took her into the Blue Room where, together, they lit a fire.

"Here," he said. "This will warm you up." He pulled two chairs from the wall, and they sat. "What's your name?"

The girl stared into the tentative fire. She seemed determined not to look at him. "Jane," she said finally. "What's yours?"

"Angel."

That elicited a slight turn of her head, but, after a curious glance, she went back to the fire.

"No, it's not," she said.

"Yep," he said. "Since I was a kid." Her nose still ran, so Angel handed her his handkerchief. She blew her nose and wiped her eyes.

"This is a big room," she said. "Why is it painted this hideous color?"

Angel laughed. "Years ago, we started having spaghetti suppers before dances. That's how toga parties began. We wore sheets so we could have food fights. Well, the story goes that after an epic night, the walls were covered in spaghetti. The guys scraped the walls, and someone found gallons of this blue day-glow gunk in the basement. We've been using the stuff for years."

Jane finally looked up at him. "Is there a bathroom I can use to clean up?"

"Upstairs," he said.

Jane seemed suspicious but followed him up the broad staircase.

"This is where the guys' rooms are," he said. He pointed to a door. "That's mine." Her eyes grew even more suspicious.

"I'm not having sex with you," she said.

Angel smiled. No, you're certainly not. "Good to know," he said. Just then Groucho came out of the bathroom with a towel around his middle.

"That's Groucho," Angel said. Groucho smiled brightly at her.

"Are you one of the Colby girls?" Groucho asked.

"No. What's a Colby girl?" Jane asked.

Angel waved Groucho away with a nod of his head. "Colby is a college for girls near here. We met a bunch of them this afternoon who said they were coming to the dance." He opened the bathroom door and glanced inside. It was empty. "I'll guard the door for you. You need anything? A towel? Soap?"

She looked baffled. Angel had been pretty sure it was a simple question. Jane didn't seem to be too sharp. "A towel and some soap would be nice," she said. She disappeared in the bathroom. Angel ducked in his room and got her the things she wanted plus a brush. He picked his and Cassie's hairs from it and dropped them in the trash. He knocked on the bathroom door and then cracked it. Jane accepted the items mutely.

Angel sat on the floor outside the bathroom and cursed himself. He knew better than to pick up strays. Good deeds had a way of backfiring when women were involved. Then, he brightened. At least she was unattractive, and he wouldn't be tempted by her.

When Jane came back out, though, she looked completely different. She had cleaned her face and pulled her hair back into a pony tail. Without runny makeup, she didn't look half bad.

She held out Angel's things and actually smiled. The smile tumbled her over the line into reasonably attractive. Angel smiled back.

He put his things away and showed her his room. She stood in the doorway as if afraid to enter.

"Well, this is where all the magic happens," he said.

"By magic you mean sex?"

Angel laughed. "No, I meant this is where I read and write. I'm supposedly a nascent novelist."

She took a step in, looked around, and set her bag down. "Are all these books yours?"

Angel nodded amused.

"Are you ever going to ask me why I was crying?" she asked.

"I know why. You're unhappy. I figured that if you wanted to tell me anything more specific, you would have done so. If you wanted me to help, you would have asked. I assume a guy made you cry."

Jane nodded and sniffed. She shook her head angrily. She didn't want to cry anymore.

"One of our guys?"

"No," she said, "He's in a real fraternity."

Angel smiled. He didn't really want to know, not unless she had a grievance which he and the guys could redress. "Anyway," he said cheerfully, "You can come up here any time you want. It will be safe. You can even sleep here if you don't have a place to go. I'll sleep in the bunk room."

She looked confused, so he took her hand and they went up another flight of stairs. He opened a door and showed her the bunk room, two rows of bed stretching from the front of the house to the back.

"You sleep up here?" she asked.

"Uh huh. Unless I'm sleeping with a girl."

She pointed to the huge leaden glass oval at the far end of the room. "The glass is broken. Don't you freeze up here?"

"Pretty much," he assented. "Come on, I'll show you around. Then, we need to begin to set up for the dance. The band should show up pretty soon." He led her down a hall and up yet another half-flight of steps. "This is the pool room."

Jane stroked the length of the table, rubbing her hands on the felt. "It's huge," she said.

Angel opened a set of windows and led her out onto a flat balcony. They were directly over the step she had been weeping on. "If it weren't snowing, we could see the White Mountains." He put an arm around her waist and pointed. They went back inside.

"I like your house," she decided.

"I do, too," he nodded and took her back downstairs. He showed her the tube room and the card room. "These rooms will be filled with socially maladjusted morons soon," he said. They went back to the kitchen. "I'm going to make a ton of spaghetti as soon as I get the band situated. But, right now, let's go downstairs to the bar and tap a couple of kegs.

Their timing was perfect. Fast Eddie and Sandman had just lugged two snow-chilled kegs in and were wheeling them into position.

"Angel," Sandman exclaimed and came around the bar. "Let me see the damage." He held Angel's face up to the dim light and examined it. "Your nose is broken."

"Yes," Angel laughed. "I know it is. I was there when it happened. I straightened it as best as I could."

Sand turned to Eddie. "Eddie, does his nose look straight to you?"

Eddie came around the bar and peered at Angel. "I don't know," he said. "I haven't ever examined his face before." He put a thumb and forefinger across the bridge of Angel's nose and jerked it to his left. Angel heard a cracking sound. "There," Eddie said. "That's better."

Sand took a look. "Just a bit more," he said.

Eddie put his hand back to Angel's face, but Angel backed off laughing. "All right, you assholes." He turned to Jane who had been watching the whole thing with wide eyes. "Jane, this is Fast Eddie. He thinks he's some kind of minor mafia figure and a bad man. This is the Sandman. You don't even want to ask how he got the nickname. They are both Viet Nam vets, so be respectful. All you have to remember is Sand's nice. Eddie isn't."

Sand and Eddie shook Jane's hand. "Please tell me you're not with Angel," Sand said.

"I'm not with anybody. Well, I'm supposed to be, but the asshole I'm supposed to be with…" She stopped and her lip trembled.

Eddie saw her reaction and led her to a bench. He sat next to her and said, "Tell Uncle Eddie what happened. Maybe we can help."

Angel rolled his eyes at Sand. "You guys tapping the kegs?" he asked.

"Yeah," Sand said. "We got them."

"Good," Angel said. "I'll get the band set up. Jane, if you get tired of these two with their Viet Nam stories, come to the Blue Room. I'm going to meet the band."

"Some band," Sand said. "A bunch of high school townies playing Beatles and Stones."

Angel shook his head and climbed the stairs. He smiled as he heard Jane ask, "Were you guys really in Viet Nam?"

The band still wasn't there, so Angel headed back to the kitchen and began to chop onions and tomatoes and mushrooms. He put six pounds of ground beef in a frying pan, and turned the stove to medium high. He scooped up all the onions and dumped them in with the browning beef and garlic. When all that began to sizzle nicely, he put in the mushrooms and covered it. He opened six large cans of spaghetti sauce, pouring Tabasco and pepper in liberally. After draining the grease off, he mixed the sauce in with the meat. He turned the stove down, and went to the Blue Room. There, six long-haired teens accompanied by a pair of bell-bottomed girls were warming by the fire and unpacking their gear.

Angel shook hands with the apparent leader, a guy named Zach.

"Where do you want us?" Zach asked.

Angel pointed to a corner next to the fire. "That's the stage leaning against the wall. Just put it down over there. There are plugs all around the room. Do you need extension cords or anything?"

"Nope, we got it," Zach smiled.

"Zach, I'm going to trust you and pay you up front in case you don't see me later, but I need to go over the house rules." He took an envelope from his pocket and handed it to Zach who handed it to one of the girls.

"I know," Zach smiled. "No cursing, no drinking, no drugs, and our chicks have to leave. We've done this before."

Angel smiled, too. "Not at Phi Psi, you haven't. Cursing is encouraged. Have fun. The more fun you have, the more fun the crowd will have. Do your drugs before you begin, and do them outside. Your girls are welcome. Hi girls," he said and flashed his best smile at them.

"Hi," a lanky brunette giggled.

"Drinking is cool, too, but don't take drinks from anyone but me or a guy named Sandman. I don't want a narc or an undercover cop to bust you. Drink outside during breaks. Out back is best. And, this one is important, no fucking the college girls. If one of them is here for sex, my guys get first dibs."

Zach gave a thumbs-up to his guys. "Got it. We're going to kill for you."

"Come find me if you need anything," Angel said and left.

He went to the kitchen to find Jane stirring the sauce for him.

"Hi," she said.

"Hey," he said. She held the spoon to him and he tasted. "Not bad. Okay woman, you're in charge of this. You don't have to watch it. Just leave it uncovered on low. Check it every five or ten minutes. Pasta is on the counter. Scrub this pot before cooking pasta in it." He smelled it. "I think it had mushroom tea in it."

"Where will you be?" she asked.

"Floating around, making sure things are ready. Lots of toilet paper and paper towels in the bathroom. Putting out the trash cans. That sort of thing."

Jane went to him and held her face up to him.

"You're really not going to hit on me, are you?"

"Probably not," he laughed. "I have a girlfriend. Well, sort of. And you're here because a guy was an asshole. So..." he trailed off.

But she didn't move her face and beamed at him. Shit. She was kind of attractive in an 'I'm not too bright and my life is miserable' kind of way. Not his favorite type. He sighed inwardly and kissed her. Once. Lightly.

She just smiled and left her face there. He poked her nose and said, "That's all for now, woman. Get back to work."

Jane laughed and picked up a cup of beer from the counter and sipped.

"Where did you get that?" he asked.

"Eddie and Sand tapped the keg. They poured me a cup to taste it. They're gentlemen."

"Ha," Angel said.

"I'll do toilet paper and towels," she said. "Where do you keep them?"

"There's a closet in the hall just outside the bathroom," he said. "Hey." She turned. "Don't go getting all cute and sweet on me. I have too many women as it is."

Jane crossed her chest and said, "I won't. Scout's honor." She gave the pot a stir and bopped off to do her chores.

Angel stood for a second. God, he really needed a joint. He followed Jane up the stairs and went to his room. He had pre-rolled several joints for the night. He selected a fat one and took it downstairs with him. The band was warming up, so he peeked in to watch and listen. Shit. They weren't bad. He made a note to grab some extra cash in case he wanted them to play longer than they were scheduled.

He went to the front porch and lit the joint. The snow was falling even harder, which might discourage some of the Colby girls from driving. That would be crappy, a busted face for nothing. He heard a voice call from above him. He went into the yard and peered up.

Groucho stood on the roof. "I thought I smelled something. Bring that up to the pool room."

Angel nodded and went back in, taking the steps two at a time. He almost knocked down Jane as he turned the corner to go up another flight to the pool room. They both laughed.

"Eager to see me again?" she asked.

"I was," he said. "Bathroom ready?"

"Bathroom ready," she said and saluted. "I was just going to check the spaghetti."

"Take this to the pool room and flirt with whoever's up there, instead," he said. "I'll cook."

She took the joint and bounced up the stairs, waving her butt at him. She was one of those girls who don't have much chest or hips, but her butt still managed to be cute.

Stay away from that butt. You have enough problems, and Maggie the Cat may show up.

He nodded 'yes sir' to himself.

Guys were emerging from their rooms by then, and when Angel went in to take a leak the showers were full of love warriors. He went back downstairs to check the spaghetti. One of Zach's girls was stirring it. She saw Angel and licked the spoon seductively. Angel smiled.

He poured in a cup of sugar. "Secret ingredient," he said. "Tell anybody, and I have to kill you."

She stirred again and tasted it. She smiled appreciatively. "I think it's ready," she said. "Want me to start the pasta?"

Angel recognized her as the girl who had pocketed the band's money. "And you are?" he asked.

"Wanda."

"Are you Zach's girlfriend?"

"No, Zach's my brother. I'm the band's manager. I'm completely unattached."

Down boy. She's in fucking high school.

Yeah, but she's pretty fucking sexy.

High school.

All right. Nag, nag, nag.

"Yes, Wanda, start the pasta," he smiled.

He went back to the Blue Room to find a dozen Phi Psi guys listening to the band and drinking beer. Sand came in carrying a wooden Coke box with a dozen cups of beer. He stopped in front of Angel who took one.

"These guys are good," Sand said. "And I like your new chick. She's not your usual type, but she's a good girl."

"She's not my chick, and what do you mean 'my type?'"

"Smart, rich, curves," Sand said.

Angel nodded. That sounded about right.

He checked the tube room and, sure enough, a bunch of nerds were watching *Jeopardy*. Art Fleming was shaking his head at a contestant's answer, and the tube room crowd howled with him. Treat saw Angel and nodded at him. Treat was always about five seconds ahead of even the smartest contestant.

The poker room was stirring to life, too. Four guys played in a desultory fashion. A girl Angel recognized from Smith sat on the arm of a chair and leaned against Jake Johnson, one of only three black brothers in the house. She saw Angel and smiled. He nodded and smiled back. She turned to Jake and whispered something in his ear. Jake turned to Angel and back to the girl laughing. Angel was glad he could provide so much amusement for so many. He sighed.

He went to the phone under the stairs and fished in his pocket for four quarters. He inserted them and dialed the number of the phone in Cassie's dorm. A girl answered.

"Hi, could you get Cassie Anderson for me?"

"Sure thing," the girl said and let the phone dangle. He could hear her clop down the hall and bang on a door. He heard voices, and she returned.

"I'm sorry. She just left."

"Do you know if she was coming to Dartmouth tonight, by any chance?" Angel asked.

"No, Agnes said Cassie was headed to the library."

Agnes was a friend of Cassie's and would know where Cassie was or wasn't going. Good. Not good that she wasn't coming. Good that, at least, he knew for sure. If Maggie showed up, he didn't want World War III.

He climbed the steps and plopped into his desk chair. He pulled his notes from Stone's class and the draft of the Joyce essay he was working on. Well, sort of working on. He had thought about it for two days, almost nonstop, and had made a kind of outline and a list of pages of the quotations he knew he would need.

He heard the door open, and he turned to see Jane peeking in.

"Am I disturbing you?" she asked.

He smiled. "No."

She moved behind him, put her hands on his shoulders, and snuck a look at what he was doing.

She frowned. "James Joyce?"

"Yes. Have you read any Joyce?"

His tone must have sounded as snotty as her face had been, because she said quickly, "Yes, I'm not illiterate. I go to Northeastern."

Angel gave her a blank look, and she said, "It's in Boston. It's a good school. You are such a snob."

He swiveled his chair and pulled her into his lap. "I'm sorry," he said. "I didn't mean anything. It's just that I was pretty deep into this shit. I tend to lose myself when I work."

She regarded him and then kissed him lightly. "Apology accepted."

"Jane, can I ask you something? You don't have to answer. When we first came up here, you were afraid to put foot in my room. It seemed like you were scared. Did your boyfriend hurt you somehow?"

Jane darkened. "I can't tell you everything, but I came to Dartmouth this weekend because he invited me, and right now he's with some slut. She'll probably go up on the wall, too."

Okay. That hadn't helped much.

"Do you have a way to get back to Boston?" he asked.

"I have a ride, but she doesn't leave until Sunday."

"You can stay here," he said. "And I'm not hitting on you. I'm really not."

"I know. You don't even like me very much," she said.

"What do you mean?" he asked.

"A girl can tell," she said. "It's okay. I don't feel very likeable right now."

A bamming on the door interrupted them. "Angel," Groucho said, "The girls are starting to pour in. Party time."

"The girls?" Jane asked.

"Angel got about forty Colby girls to show," Groucho said and left.

Jane touched his battered lip and nose. "Do these have anything to do with the girls?"

Ah. Perceptive wench. Maybe there was more to Jane than Angel had thought. He smiled at her.

As they went down the stairs, the music began, and the crowd let out a guttural cheer. Shit. How many people were here?

He took Jane's hand and pulled her back towards the kitchen.

"We have to eat if we're going to drink," he said.

In the kitchen, Wanda had already served portions to Groucho, Blake, Treat, Sand, and Eddie. She made plates for Jane and Angel. As he ate, Angel observed Wanda. She seemed to be one of those girls who is happiest when doing something. She was pretty and obviously smart, (with a light spattering of freckles which reminded him of Maggie) but she was going to be a wild one, a keeper for some lucky guy. She caught him watching her and smiled slyly at him. He smiled back, and Jane elbowed him.

"She's jail bait," she whispered.

"I know," he said.

"This is fucking outrageous," Sand said. "You've outdone yourself."

"It's hot as hell," Blake said.

"Pussy," Eddie said with his mouth full. It sounded like 'fussy.'

When they finished, Groucho stayed to help Wanda scrape plates and put things away.

"Thank you, Wanda," Sand said.

"Hey," Angel said. "I made the stuff."

"Shut the fuck up, Angel," Eddie said.

Good grief, there were a lot of people for nine o'clock. The Blue Room was more than half full of drinking, cheering, dancing people. Angel laughed. The Colby girls had all worn costumes and looked cute as hell. He searched the room for Maggie but didn't see her.

Sand came by with his beer box, and Angel grabbed two, one of which he gave to Jane who took it and pulled him into the small sea of dancing people.

The geometry was primal: the Colby girls danced with each other while the boys circled on the outside, looking for an opportunity. "It's like an old-fashioned May dance," Jane shouted to him. Wow, she was way smarter than he expected.

He nodded. "Or the girls are the protons and the guys are the electrons."

"What are we?" she laughed.

"We're together, so I guess we make up a neutron," he said. She laughed again and broke away from him and danced wildly. The band was playing *Layla* and doing a pretty good job of it. They even had a pimply boy playing steel guitar. A young Duane Allman, Angel thought.

People kept pouring in. Angel counted forty-two girls who seemed to know each other. If they were all Colby girls, he and Cane had smashed their old record by a lot. One of the girls saw Angel dancing and let out a shriek. Jane was pushed aside and watched smiling as half a dozen girls mobbed Angel, kissing his cheek and hugging him. Angel smiled idiotically and tried not to spill his beer. Girls turned to other girls and said things excitedly. 'It's Angel,' they seemed to be saying, 'the hero who confronted the giant.' A girl Angel recognized from the dorm kissed his nose and lip in the 'let mama heal you' manner and leaned close to his ear. "Maggie has a hard on for you," she said. Angel shouted back, "Is she coming tonight?" But the girl didn't seem to know what he had said and was pulled back into the happy melee.

Then the band slowed, singing *Sitting by the Dock of the Bay*, and Angel found himself holding Jane. Her hair smelled faintly of cinnamon.

He let himself go for a few moments and actually enjoyed dancing. His mind drifted, and he fancied he was holding Maggie. He danced with mental Maggie happily, wondering why she wasn't mental Cassie. Were he and Cassie finished? She was the only girl he had dated for so long, and their two and a half teen years together seemed a lifetime. His high school crush. The girl who had skipped her senior year at the super snobby Mrs. Porter's School to go to Smith and be near him. She would have been Valedictorian, something which would have soothed her stubbornly competitive nature. Ah, Cassie. What did we do wrong? That she had not even called to tell him definitively she wasn't coming spoke volumes. She was angry with him. Or hurt by him. Or probably both. Shit.

Angel could feel his mild social panic kicking in, so he broke free from Jane, who smiled and raised her beer, cheering for the band as the song ended. He wove through the crowd and looked over his shoulder. Jane was dancing again. She didn't even seem to know he was gone.

Good.

He climbed the two and a half flights to the pool room. Eddie was kibitzing two guys Angel had never seen before while Blake leaned against a wall. Angel climbed through the window onto the roof and breathed in the cold air. The snow had stopped, at least for a while, and Angel fancied he could see snatches of stars through the leaden clouds. He pulled a joint from his pocket and drank and smoked in peace.

He began to shiver, and when he went back inside, he found Eddie schooling one of the strangers in straight pool. Eddie, as always, talked all the way through each shot.

"Two ball cross side," he said. "The leave will be lined up for the six. Shit. Over-hit it. Now I've got to take the fourteen. If I miss that, though, and the angle's shitty, it will leave you three easy shots."

Angel smiled, picked up someone's beer and headed back down the stairs to check on the action at the bar.

He found Sand tapping a new pair of kegs. "Moe just delivered these," Sand said. "Good call. We're going through them fast. We've never had this many people. Sweet job on the chicks."

"If we run low," Angel said, "I'll take Cane and Longbow to steal a keg from SAE."

"Already on it," Sand said. "Cane is partying at Sigma Nu and knows to bring us a keg around midnight."

"Cool," Angel said.

Just then a bottle crashed to the floor and a groan went up.

Shit. Angel hated bar bottles. It was the dumbest game on the planet. Two guys stood at opposite ends of the bar and slid empty bottles towards each other. If one hit the floor, the guy who slid it had to chug a beer. People got way too drunk way too fast. Plus, Angel usually ended up cleaning up the glass the next day. Well, the chick who was with him did.

Angel peeked into the chapter room. There were a handful of guys playing beer pong. Their dates sat on the couches which ringed the room, staring at painted images depicting the fall of Rome and the pagan pleasures which ensued. Cartoon men banged women all over Rome, usually in a burning building. Nobody even knew who the artist was. It had been there long before any of them got to Dartmouth. It was a beauty.

Okay, he had done his duty. The party was on its way to being a smashing success. He went upstairs to his room and closed the door. He put Muddy Waters on his stereo and sat at his desk trying to finish an elusive chapter of his novel. Why was the girl doing what she was doing? Angel didn't know. She perplexed him. He loved writing about her, but he didn't understand why she was so self-destructive. He wrote doggedly for an hour, hoping he would write into comprehension.

His door opened, and he turned to see who it was. Jane stood there, looking pleasantly drunk.

"Hi," Angel said. "Having a good time?"

"Yes," she said. "Angel, when are you going to try to get me into bed?"

He smiled. "I'm not. I told you you're safe here."

She frowned and sat on the edge of his bed. "You think I'm ugly, don't you? That's what Nelson said. 'Get away from me, you ugly slut.' And he went off with that whore of his." She began to cry.

Shit. Not again.

He sat by her and pulled her head to his chest. He held her and let her sob. "You know what I do when I want to stop thinking about something?" he asked.

She shook her head.

"I smoke a joint and take a shower. A hot as hell shower."

She looked at him. "Only if you'll shower with me."

Angel hesitated, but he knew deep down that he was already screwed with this one.

"Okay," he said. "Let me check to see if anyone's in there." He left briefly. The coast was clear. When he returned, Jane stood clad in only her panties. Angel's heart sank. Was he really doing this? Apparently so. He kicked off his boots and took his shirt off. Jane watched mutely. He took off his jeans and his underwear. He hung there, half-erect. Jane studied him briefly, but he couldn't tell what she was thinking at all. Just like the girl in his novel. An enigma.

He wrapped a towel around his middle and tossed her one. She turned away from him and pulled her panties off. She bent as she did so and confirmed his suspicion that her rear end was by far her best feature. Jane and Maggie. It was double bubble weekend.

He hung a 'girl in bathroom' sign from the outer door knob and turned the water on in his favorite shower. He tested with his hand until it was burning hot. Jane leaned against him, a still, mute, cipher. He took her hand and pulled her into the water.

"Oh, no," she laughed. "It's too hot."

But he was persistent, and, soon, he could feel her relax and begin to enjoy the pounding water. He stood behind her and shampooed her hair. He rubbed her scalp hard with his fingers.

"I've never had anyone do this for me before," she said.

He soaped her back, including her cute butt, and knelt and washed her legs. He turned her towards him. She covered her middle with a hand and braced against the wall with the other, lifting one foot at a time for him to wash. When he finished, he rose and handed her the soapy cloth to wash her front. She turned away from him and washed. When she rinsed everything, she stood aside and let him enter the spray.

"Do you want me to wash you?" she asked.

"Do you want to?" he asked.

She nodded shyly. He turned to her, and she soaped and washed his chest and his stomach. She looked up at him questioningly before going any farther. He dared her with his eyes, and she moved to his hardening mid-section. She washed him awkwardly with the cloth but then put her hand tentatively on his dick and looked up at him again.

"It's pretty big," she said.

Angel said nothing.

She turned him around and perfunctorily washed his back. She avoided his butt.

Angel took the soap from her and finished washing himself. When he put his face in the water, his nose and lip burned fiercely. The pain had been earned, though, and that always felt good in a masochistic sort of way. He stood under the pelting water until he no longer felt any ache on his face. He turned off the shower and smiled at her.

They dried, and Jane scampered down the hallway to Angel's room. Angel laughed and followed.

When he entered, Jane lay on the bed, waiting for him.

He laughed but sat and caressed a breast. She was practically flat, but her nipples were nice. He leaned over and kissed her.

"It's not going to happen, Jane." He tapped her forehead, "I have a girlfriend. Besides, I don't do anything with women who have been drinking."

"I'm not drunk," she said.

Angel began to dress, and Jane pulled the covers over her and sulked.

"Meanie," she said.

He frowned and left her there. He went downstairs, running his hands through his hair to comb it. His good mood had dissipated in Jane's self-pity. Was it his job to make every woman feel good about herself?

He sat on the steps midway down and watched the partiers through the stair rails. Wanda saw him sitting there and joined him. She handed him a beer. He reached into his back pocket and handed her an envelope.

She looked at him questioningly.

"Ask the guys if they'll play an extra hour or two," he said.

"They would have done it for free. They're having a blast. This is the biggest crowd they've ever played for. And see the two girls on the stage?"

Angel nodded. Two topless Colby girls sang into beer bottles as if they were mikes.

"I guarantee the guys have never seen that before. It's like Woodstock or something."

Angel took a sip of his beer and pulled a roach from his pocket. He lit it and offered it to her. She shook her head.

"I don't want to get you in trouble," she said.

Fair enough.

"Can I ask you a question?" he said. "I know you're in high school, but why do you seem so much more mature than most of these people?" He waved in the general direction of the dancing mob.

"High school?" she laughed. "I'm a junior at Boston College. I'm probably older than you. Zach's my little brother. I'm babysitting him tonight because my mother doesn't trust Dartmouth fraternities."

Angel looked at her anew. Well, shit.

"But, yes," she said, "Ask away."

Angel thought. "There's a girl upstairs lying naked in bed who wants me to, you know. But she doesn't really want me to. She just thinks she's supposed to be grateful to me because I took her in when she was having a meltdown. I don't know her or particularly like her. Plus, I have a girlfriend I think I'm breaking up with, or she with me. I mean, I guess it's mutual."

Wanda chuckled and put her hand on Angel's arm. "First of all, there wasn't a question anywhere in that disjointed ramble. And, secondly, you don't talk about your feelings much, do you?"

Angel hung his head and smiled. "No. I don't think I actually have feelings. Not like normal people, anyway."

"Oh," she said. "A tough guy, huh? That's why the cowboy boots and the banged-up face? Been in a fight recently? Over a girl?"

He laughed and leaned back against the stairs.

Wanda touched his nose and pushed sideways. "Does that hurt?"

"Yes," Angel smiled.

"But you didn't flinch, did you?"

"The hurt doesn't bother me," he said. "It's just pain. That's what I mean about feelings. Things don't bother me the way they should."

"I see," she said, but she clearly didn't. "Back to your question. You were asking me whether you should have sex with that girl? The one you were dancing with?"

"Yes."

"Would it hurt you? Would it help her? Answer those, and you'll know what to do."

Hmmm…Wanda was seriously cute.

"That's a highly moral position to take about cheating on one's girlfriend," he said.

"Your sarcasm is noted, Angel. Is that really your name? I heard all those girls in costume practically chanting your name as if you were the high god of something or other."

"Are you a psychology major or a religion major?" Angel asked.

Wanda laughed hard at that. "Psychology with a minor in primitive religions, but I'm pre-med. How in the world? Never mind. So, you're a lot smarter than you look?"

"Is that a compliment?"

"Are you in need of one?" Wanda asked. "I highly doubt it, Mister 'Should I charity bang that poor girl or should I stay faithful to one I no longer cherish?' Woops, here comes door number one, and I'm out of here."

She bounded off, and Angel turned to see Jane descending the steps. She sat by Angel.

"I'm sorry," she said simply.

He put his arm around her.

"Who was that?" she asked.

"She's the treasurer of the band."

"She likes you," Jane said.

"How do you know that?"

"She was so animated, and her body language was all flirty," Jane said. "You can go after her if you want."

He squeezed her shoulder, and she lowered her head to his chest. "Nope, I'm with you tonight." He raised her face and kissed her.

She sighed. "I think I might go to bed. Would you mind?"

Angel shook his head.

"Check on me later?" she asked.

"Of course."

She hugged him and climbed back up the steps to his room.

Angel went to the tube room. Johnny Carson was doing his Art Fern routine with a busty blonde Angel didn't recognize. There were girls in the tube room. Perhaps a first in Phi Psi history. He smiled and checked in on the card game. Sand was staring down a guy from *Tabard* and slapping his thigh in time with the music. Angel smiled at that, too. That was Sand's tell. He had a good hand. *Tabard* guy didn't seem to know what it meant. The pot was huge, but the guy pitched his chips in and Sand pounced with a boat, fives over threes. *Tabard* guy had a dead man's hand. Those fuckers never seemed to win.

Angel clapped Sand on the shoulder. Sand raised his cigar and his glass of bourbon in salute.

Angel stopped in the cloak room and checked the message board. Still no message from Cassie. He was getting pissed. That she didn't come was fine, but to not even call? That was her new thing, being passive aggressive. Before, she was always so direct, but now?

He bought a Coke and some M&Ms and clung to a wall in the Blue Room, watching the melee. Wanda was the lone girl on stage with the band, and she was a hell of a dancer. She made eye contact with Angel and danced the rest of the song straight at him. Shit. He needed to get her number.

Or not. What was he thinking? Cassie, Maggie, and now Wanda. The last thing he needed was another woman. But, dear Lord, she was a fox.

The band was playing what Angel could only describe as a Jimi Hendrix version of *Wild Thing*. A trio of girls jumped on the stage, crowding off a laughing Wanda, and led the dancers' chants of 'Wild thing, you make my heart sing,' every time it recurred in the song. Pandemonium reigned. Someone threw a beer which splatted on the wall next to Angel who laughed and ducked. The Colby girls had adopted Phi Psi brothers like pets and had them dancing wildly in the center of the room. Guys he had never seen move, much less dance, were gyrating wildly with the girls, most of whom were only partially dressed by that point in the evening. What was with this new topless craze? Women's Liberation or the pill or better drugs…he didn't care what had caused it. He approved wholly. A girl he recognized as one of Maggie's friends shook her breasts in Groucho's dazed face.

The nakedness of woman is the work of God. Yep, William Blake knew his shit.

A group he recognized as football players stood on the periphery and began to try to infiltrate the Colby ring. Angel didn't like the looks of that.

Sure enough, a scuffle broke out on the dance floor. The dancers parted and made space for the combatants who swung wildly at each other. Angel put down his Coke, shoved the bag of M&Ms in his pocket, and waded through the crowd. When he got there, Eddie had dragged one of the guys away and had him in a choke hold. The other guy got off the floor and lunged at his adversary. Angel tackled him, and the two fell to the floor. The guy attempted to get up, but Angel was quicker and hit him in the mouth, causing the guy to fall back on his butt. By then, Sand was there, and he and Eddie escorted the two combatants outside and threw them in the snow, where they lay cursing. The smaller of the two began to vomit what seemed to Angel an excessive amount of bile and beer. The big guy looked as if he wanted to re-enter the party, but Eddie and Sand blocked his path. Treat had joined them, so the guy sulked and cursed his way down the driveway and into town. Angel went back inside to make sure order had been restored.

The music and the dancing began again, and Angel tried to locate his Coke. Crap. Someone had kicked it over. He went and bought another one and saw a girl, naked from the waist up, in the library. She swayed drunkenly to the music and perused the books. Angel recognized her as the Smithie who had been dancing earlier.

"Hey," he said. "Looking for a particular book?"

She smiled boozily and wobbled. Her breasts shook as she sought to re-establish her balance. Angel put out a hand to steady her.

"*Our Mutual Friend*," she said.

"Pardon?"

"You asked what book I was looking for," she said.

"Oh, that's upstairs in my room. And that's not a line. It really is. But my date is sleeping up there."

"Oh," she said and smiled. "I didn't really want it, I was just noticing that it was missing. All the other Dickens novels are here. But not *Our Mutual Friend*. Isn't that funny?"

"Hilarious," he said and helped her sit down in a reading chair.

"I lost it," she said.

Angel looked blank.

"My shirt," she said. "I took it off to dance, and I haven't seen it since. Do you like my chest?" She arched her back to display her wares. "They're bigger than Cassie's, aren't they?" she asked.

"Oh, you're Marjorie," he said. "I knew you looked familiar."

"Marianne," she said. "Yes, I am. Why didn't Cassie come? This is a wonderful event."

"I have no idea," he said, "And, yes."

"Yes, what?"

"I like your chest, and they're much larger than Cassie's."

"That's one 'yes' for each breast," she said. "But everyone's bigger than Cassie. Poor Cassie. Why do you have a date upstairs? Is Cassie here?"

Shit.

"Marianne," Angel said, "Do you have a ride back to Smith."

"Yes, I drove," she said. "But I know I'm too drunk to drive home. One of the other girls can drive."

"If it's still snowing, I can find a room for you and your friends," Angel said. He imagined her friends being as smashed as she was. "Wait here, I'll get you a shirt. Did you have a coat?"

"Hanging up in the cloak room," she said and pointed.

"Good. Just wait here, I'm getting a shirt for you."

Angel ran up the steps and went to his room. The light was still on, and Jane was reading at his desk.

"Just getting something," he said. "A girl lost her shirt." He rummaged through his dresser and found a tee shirt he never wore.

"Angel," Jane said. "This is good." She held it up. It was one of the early chapters of his novel.

He beamed and left.

But Marianne was nowhere to be seen. He put the shirt on the Coke machine and tried Cassie again. This time, no one even answered, which was shitty because the phone was right outside Cassie's room. It was after midnight. Where the fuck was she? Surely, she wasn't still in the library. Shit. He checked his internal temperature. He was more pissed than jealous or worried. It should have been the other way around. Yep. Their relationship was on last gasp.

Sand walked by and handed him a cigar. "Rooftop in ten minutes," he said.

Angel nodded.

He felt a hand on his shoulder and turned. Maggie? Nope, it was Wanda.

"Me, too," she said.

Angel looked blank.

"Take me to the rooftop."

Angel took her hand, and they climbed the stairs together. A new crew was playing pool. They didn't look very good. He and Wanda stepped out on the roof and breathed in the clean, cold New Hampshire air. The snow had stopped, and the sky had cleared. They couldn't quite see the White Mountains, but the stars were out.

"Do you know the constellations?" she asked.

"Yes," he said and lit his cigar.

"Point them out."

"Nope."

"Why not?" she asked.

"Don't want to," he said and puffed contentedly.

She laughed. "You shit." She punched his arm. He pulled her to him, and they watched the heavens together contentedly.

"I have a boyfriend," she said.

Angel nodded. "Me, too."

"You have a boyfriend? You told me you have a girlfriend, already. Now, you have a guy, too? My, you are a busy man."

Angel laughed. "You knew what I meant. Why did you say, 'I have a boyfriend?'"

"Because we've both been thinking, we could be good together, haven't we?" Angel gave her a stony stare. "Oh, shit. You didn't think that, did you? Now, I'm embarrassed," she said.

"You're not my type," he said.

"Oh?"

"I don't like smart, beautiful, sexy, funny, empathic women," he said. "They're high maintenance."

She huddled against him. "Why thank you, sir. That was a sweet compliment."

He squeezed her and said, "Now shut the fuck up and let me enjoy the moment."

She laughed but shut up.

Eddie and Sand joined them soon after.

"Did you see those bozos?" Eddie asked. He sounded pissed.

"Who?" Angel asked.

"Those guys shooting pool. Guys like that shouldn't be allowed on our table. They can't shoot for shit," Eddie said.

"How outrageous," Angel mocked him.

Sand lit his cigar and looked at Wanda. "Have we met? Every time I turn around, Angel has his arm around a different woman."

"I'm Wanda. I'm Angel's home town honey. I can't believe he's never spoken of me. We're pre-engaged. I want to get married before the baby comes, but, you know Angel. Everything has to be his way."

Sand peered at her, trying to decide if she were being serious or jerking his chain. Wanda broke into a laugh. Sand just nodded. Pretty fucking funny.

Below them, three members of the band ran into the front yard and began to puke.

Wanda laughed and disengaged herself from Angel. "Guess I have to get the kiddies home. Good night Angel." She stood on tiptoe and kissed him. "Do you want my number? Just in case?"

"I know how to find you," Angel smiled. "I have your brother's number."

"Call when you're single," she said and kissed him again.

The men watched her climb through the window and, a moment later, saw her going to the snowy pukers to check on them.

Eddie looked at Angel. "You're such a douche." Angel and Sand puffed on their cigars.

By about three, the only people left were the Colby girls, a few hangers on from dorms or other fraternities, and the Irish crew. Phi Psi had nine Irish guys, and they ended every late night down in the bar singing ballads.

Angel sat on a bench, and the Colby girls acted as if he was the Pope. Each sat by him for a moment requesting an audience. Every conversation sounded something like, 'Thank you for inviting us here. We had a great time. We had never heard of Phi Psi before. We'll be back again,' and so on. They all ended with a version of 'I hope your face is okay,' and the ceremonial touching of his lip and nose, which, clearly, had become relics in some obscure church of testosterone. He must have had twenty girls touch his face that evening, counting Jane and Wanda.

Jane crept down the stairs and lay on the bench with her head in Angel's lap.

Michael Robartes led the singing. Groucho's voice was among the sweetest. Even Eddie sang. The men stood in a circle with their arms on each other's shoulders and sang verse after verse of songs Angel had never heard. That wasn't true. He had heard *Danny Boy* before, but the rest were new to him. He leaned against the wall and stroked Jane's hair. His face hurt. The various forms of anesthesia had worn off, and the dull ache of bruised bone had set in. He felt his teeth again, but nothing wobbled too much or fell out. He could only breathe through his right nostril, but that was okay. He would live.

Wordlessly, he took Jane's hand and led her upstairs to his room. He stripped nude and undressed her slowly, kissing her breasts and her stomach as he took things off.

They climbed in bed, and he lay on his back, holding her. He kissed her again, and she sighed and curled against him.

Angel stared at the ceiling until he could make his mind bend to his will and go blank. Then he closed his eyes and dreamed of Maggie.

Maggie sat in his desk chair. She looked thoughtful. She put down his work and turned to him. Slowly, she rose and took off her clothes. He liked her body. He especially liked the way her waist gave way to the curve of her hips. She glided across the room and lay beside him. 'Oh, Angel,' she whispered in Lauren Bacall's voice.

That was as far as he got. The real-life Jane lay next to him, beginning to snore softly.

He smiled at her and kissed her forehead.

It had been an epic day.

Chapter Three

Saturday October 31, 1970
Reconnaissance

ANGEL WOKE AND STRETCHED. HE FELT GROGGY AND DIS-
combobulated. Why? He hadn't drunk that much the night before.

Shit. Jane.

Please, let her be gone. Her bag was still by the door, though, and the clothes she had worn the night before lay over it. He went to his desk and checked his watch. It was after noon. He walked naked to the shower with his towel over his shoulder. He did his purgatorial scalding and looked in the mirror. Nope. Too lazy to shave. He poked at his nose. That was as straight as it was going to get.

He threw on jeans and a tee shirt and went downstairs. No one was around, but he heard laughter from the kitchen and went back to explore. There, he found Jane holding court for Sand and the guys. Jane and Sand's girl Linda were fixing eggs and bacon. Linda saw Angel and poured him a coffee.

"Oh, here we go," Sand laughed.

They all watched as Angel spooned six huge sugars into his coffee and poured in some Hershey's syrup. He pulled the milk from the fridge, poured a dollop in, and stirred.

"Seriously?" Jane asked, her eyes wide.

"I'm diabetic," Angel said. "I need a lot of sugar."

"Really?" Jane asked.

"No," Eddie said. "He's just a pansy."

Jane put her face up to Angel's and gave him a quick kiss. "I'm going to shower." And she ran off.

Angel followed her with his eyes. Why did she suddenly look so much better? Was it because she seemed happy? He hadn't thought her capable of the emotion.

"That shit's not gonna fly," Eddie said.

"What shit, and why won't it fly?" Angel asked.

"Jane didn't tell you?" Sand said.

"No, we didn't talk much."

"This *Boar's Head* guy Nelson fucked her over pretty bad," Eddie said.

"Nelson, huh? And by 'won't fly' you mean we are going to do something about that?" Angel asked. But he already knew the answer. He sighed. "You guys go. Take Cane and some of his friends with you. Start a rumble. I don't care. I'm not going. I have too many friends in *Boar's Head*. They're good guys."

"Never generalize about the goodness of a group of men," Eddie said.

"Eddie, when you want to start a fight, why do you always sound like a bad translation of *The Art of War*?"

"Hey, don't knock *The Art of War*," Eddie growled. "You know what I mean. *Boar's Head* may be overflowing with goodness and light, but there can still be a few shitheads."

Angel nodded. "Lord knows we have plenty of shitheads."

Sand chuckled. Eddie glared.

But Angel knew he would go to *Boar's Head* with Eddie and Sand that night. He knew they would start something. Couldn't they at least wait for his nose to heal? Go next month, maybe?

"Okay," Angel said, "But first, Jane and I are going to go over there and talk to Nelson. What a puke name. Sounds like a polo player."

"No, you aren't. Why would you do that?" Eddie hissed.

Angel stared at him and drank his coffee. He piled the remaining bacon on a plate and began to munch on it.

"Because," Angel said as patiently as he could, "We don't know that Nelson has done anything wrong. We just know Jane says he has. She may be a stalker or something. She probably is."

"Oh, we know he fucked over Jane pretty bad," Eddie said.

"What exactly did she say he did to her?"

"She didn't go into specifics," Sand said.

Angel laughed. "Well, there you go."

"Angel, if you go over there, it will fuck up the entire operation," Eddie said.

"How will talking to Nelson mess up your grand plans for retaliation and revenge? I assume you have a plan."

"Oh, we have a plan," Eddie said. "But it won't work if you take away the element of surprise."

"Fuck you, Eddie," Angel said. He put the last piece of bacon in his mouth and went back upstairs.

He sat at his desk and waited for Jane. He didn't have to wait long. She came in chuckling.

"Groucho walked in and peed right in front of me," she said. "He jumped when he saw me. It was pretty funny."

"Groucho can't see without his glasses," Angel said.

Jane sat on the bed. "Someone's in a mood."

"Get dressed," he said.

"Where are we going?"

"To talk to Nelson," he said.

Jane looked dumbfounded, but she nodded. "Okay."

"I'll be downstairs."

Angel took a quick tour of the house to assess the damage. The Blue Room looked fine. The lack of sticky spots meant that someone had mopped. Who would have already done that? He ducked downstairs. The bar looked okay, too. It smelt of sour beer, but the broken glass had been swept into a pile in the corner. A new keg stood behind the bar waiting to be tapped. He felt it. It was icy cold. Sand must have just brought it in from the snow. He pulled the old keg out, put the new one in, and screwed on the tap. He tested the pressure and poured two mugs of foam then dumped them. Ready to go.

He went back upstairs and found Jane with her coat on and carrying a bag.

"What's the bag for?" he asked. "Are you leaving?"

"I thought you were getting rid of me," she said. "You seem so angry."

Angel felt like shit. "I'm not angry with you, Jane. I'm angry with Sand and Eddie and Nelson and stupid guy code."

"I cleaned the whole house for you," she said. "I wanted to thank you somehow for last night."

Angel's anger softened. Great. Now, she was turning out to be a good kid.

Jane stood awkwardly. She clearly had no idea what he was talking about. Angel took her bag and put it in the cloakroom next to the Coke machine.

"You and I are just going to talk to Nelson," he said kindlier. "I want to know how pissed we should be at him."

"We?" she asked.

"Sand and Eddie and me. We need to assess the situation."

Jane nodded. She still had no idea what he was talking about. Well, that made two of them.

Shit.

The snow pelted them as they began their trek. The ground snow crunched beneath Angel's boots, meaning it was below twenty degrees. They walked in silence until they got to The Green.

"You've been here before, so I guess Nelson has given you the tour," Angel said.

"No, not really."

"Well, this is The Green. That's Baker Hall, the library. It's the exact same plan as Independence Hall, only bigger."

Jane looked.

"And we're walking on part of The Appalachian Trail," he said.

"What?"

"The Appalachian Trail. It goes all the way to Georgia."

"I know what it is," she said. "This is part of it? This road?"

"Yep," Angel nodded. "It comes from over there." He pointed. "And it goes down that hill and across the Connecticut River."

Jane took his arm and squeezed. They walked the rest of the way in silence. Jane seemed happy. Well, for her, anyway. Angel doubted she was capable of sustained happiness. There was something either tragic or pitiful about her, depending on her mood. And her moods seemed evanescent.

But why wouldn't she be cheerful? She was going back to see a guy she liked on the arm of another guy. If Nelson was a jerk, she had Angel. If Nelson was jealous, well, victory.

They stood outside *Boar's Head* for a few moments.

"Ready for this?" Angel asked.

Jane nodded. She looked nervous but excited.

They went in. It was early afternoon, but a pretty good crowd was already there. Girls were everywhere, decorating the place for the big Halloween bash that night. Angel saw Will Macy, a buddy who was on *Palaeopitus* with him, and asked for Nelson.

"He went somewhere," Will said. He nodded oddly at Jane. "His roommate Spencer is down in the bar, though. Maybe he knows where Nelson is."

Angel thanked Will, and he and Jane descended into the bar which ran twice the length of Phi Psi's. It had booths and didn't smell of stale beer. Jane pointed to a boy carving a pumpkin, and Angel squired her over to him.

"Spencer?" Angel said.

Spencer glanced up and made a sour face when he saw Jane. "What the fuck are you doing here?"

"Where's Nelson?" Angel asked.

Spencer ignored Angel and said, "Get the fuck out of here, you little whore. Nelson told you not to show up. He's with Emily this weekend."

"Spencer," Angel said, "Look at me." Spencer looked up at him. "Where's Nelson?"

"Who the fuck are you?"

Angel clenched his teeth but smiled. Eddie was a psychopath, but he was invariably right about these things. Spencer was a piece of shit, Nelson was probably a piece of shit, and Angel should keep his mouth shut. Element of surprise and all that tactical crap.

He looked at Jane. Her face showed nothing, but she turned and stiffly climbed the stairs.

"Nice talking to you, Spencer," Angel said.

"I don't know what you're doing with that trash, but I'd get a penicillin shot if I were you."

"Good to know," Angel nodded and left.

He found Jane outside. She stood under a giant fir tree with tears running down her face. Angel pulled her to him and hugged her. His whole body felt coiled, as if it needed to strike something. He pulled out his handkerchief and dried her tears. "Stop it," he said. "He's not worth it, and, besides, your tears will freeze in about ten seconds. When you try to get them off, skin rips and bleeds. Then the blood freezes, and, well, so on."

Jane sniffed, "Really?"

"Yes, really," he said. "Actually, no, but it could happen."

He took her arm and walked her around Sphinx and up the hill towards the Bema. They stood on the top of the little hill by the observatory and searched for the faint outline of the White Mountains through the snow. It was quiet and profound.

"Jane," Angel said quietly, "Who is Emily, and what happened?"

Jane sounded like a zombie. "Nelson and I had a date this weekend. He invited me nearly a month ago. He came to Boston last week, and we had an argument. I thought we could fix things this weekend. I guess not."

"Jane, look at me. Did Nelson tell you not to come this weekend?"

She nodded. "But Angel, I thought we were in love. I know I was."

"Jane."

"No, I know what you think. It wasn't like that. Nelson and I met last year at a dance in Boston. He was a gentleman. He came to Boston twice to see me before I ever came to Dartmouth. He told me he loved me. He was my first, and he was sweet and kind. I don't know what happened."

Angel sighed. Now he knew why she was so snotty and pathetic. It was the old 'I lost my virginity to him' thing again. Why was that such a big deal to women? Jane's next words, though, gave Angel a chill.

"But up here," she said, "In front of his friends, he made me do things."

"What kind of things?" Angel asked.

"I can't tell you," she said. Tears formed in her eyes. "It's too embarrassing. Bad things. That's what we fought about. I told him I wouldn't do them anymore."

He took Jane's arm and walked her back to campus. The Baker Tower bells played *Inna Gadda Da Vida*. That was fitting. Angel could feel the blood surging through his body. Shit. This was going to happen. Sand and Eddie and he, and anybody else who wanted in, were going to come back to *Boar's Head*.

When they got back to Phi Psi, Jane crept back into bed and huddled under the covers. Angel found Sand and Eddie in the pool room and performed his *mea culpa*. "You were right, Eddie," Angel said. "Nelson is a shit."

"I told you," Eddie said.

"You two can have Nelson. I want the roommate," Angel said. "He insulted Jane right in front of me."

"Did she tell you what they made her do?" Sand asked.

"No," Angel said. "Did she tell you?"

"She told Linda. Linda just told us."

"Why didn't Jane tell me?" Angel asked.

"Because she likes you," Sand said. "And she's ashamed."

Angel went to his room. Jane was sleeping soundly, so he got his writing stuff and crammed it into a satchel. He blew her a kiss, tiptoed out, and went to Sanborn, the English Library, where he sat in his chair facing out over The Green. Mrs. Sellers apparently expected him, because the books he had requested were neatly stacked next to his chair, and she appeared almost immediately with coffee and chocolate chip cookies. She smiled benevolently at him. He sipped his coffee.

"Perfect," he said and smiled back at her.

Why did women treat him so well?

When he finished, he took his coffee mug and plate back to Mrs. Sellers. It was dark, and the street lamps glowed orange as he trudged through the snow to Phi Psi for dinner and to set up for the night's shenanigans. They weren't having a big party. That had been the night before. The big houses got to host on Halloween.

Jane was up when he got back and was sitting at his desk reading a Donne essay he had written his freshman year. She looked up and smiled, "So, this was the freshman Angel. Not bad."

How did she manage to smile cheerfully and look tragic at the same time? For he could still see sadness under the veneer. He wondered if she would ever be rid of it.

"Got anything green in that bag of yours?" he asked.

"I do."

"Put it on," he said. "Football time."

"You're taking me to the game?"

"Of course," he laughed. "What did you think? I was going to leave you here with all these maniacs?"

She laughed and got up. "Turn your back while I dress."

"You do know I've seen you naked?"

"Yes, but you turned me down. I wasn't good enough for you," she said.

"Ha," he said. "Do me a big favor."

"What?"

"This will sound terrible, but don't wear the bra with the falsies. Your body is perfect without them."

"I'm completely flat without them," she said.

"Come here," he said.

She looked suspicious but went to him.

Angel pulled her sweater over her head and unbuttoned her blouse. He removed her bra and stood back. He bent and kissed each nipple. "Now those," he said, "Are perfect. They match the rest of you."

Jane blushed and shooed him out of the room. Angel went down the hall and knocked on Groucho's door. Groucho stuck his head out. Someone was in the room with him, and the smell of hash flooded the hall.

"Give me back the football ticket I gave you," Angel said.

"I thought Cassie wasn't showing up," Groucho said.

"I'm taking Jane."

"Oh, righto," Groucho said. He disappeared in his room and came back with a bent-up ticket.

"The hash smells primo," Angel said.

"It is. Want some?"

"Later."

He knocked on his door, and Jane opened it. She had on a green skirt and a tight white sweater. Her nipples poked through.

"Nice," he said.

"I thought you might like that," she said. "It's scratchy, but nice men get what they want."

"Oh," he said. "I'll have to try being nice sometime."

She laughed and brushed past him, heading for the bathroom.

"Want me to guard it for you?" he asked.

"No. I'm just doing makeup. I don't mind seeing boys peeing."

Angel flopped on his bed and waited for her, but, almost immediately, he hopped up and went to the bathroom. "Hey," he said, "I'm going downstairs to make a call."

Jane nodded in the mirror, and Angel went to the cloakroom and fished out a handful of quarters. He dialed and listened to it ring three times. He was about to hang up when Cassie answered.

"Cassie?"

"Hello, Angel."

Silence. Shit. She already sounded pissed, and he hadn't even said anything yet.

"Just wanted to hear your voice," he said. What he wanted to say was, 'where the hell were you last night when I called,' but he didn't.

"I talked to Marianne a little while ago," Cassie said. "She said you had a date."

"No," he said as casually as he could. "We kind of gave sanctuary to a crying girl."

"She also told me you had a whole host of girls chasing after you. Did you do that Good Angel, Bad Angel thing with Cane again?"

"Yes."

Her tone became colder, if that was possible. "You know that demeans women, don't you?"

"Oh, as if mixers don't. They're like cattle calls. Buses of girls show up, and guys line the sidewalk rating them as they step off the bus. Then, the women stand around the gym hoping some guy will deign to find her attractive enough to dance with him."

"At least that's honest," she said.

"Honest? You want honest? I let Cane hit me in the face twice in front of a group of five women. It doesn't get any more honest than that. Those girls wanted to come to Dartmouth to party. Would you rather they showed up and just waited to get drunk and be hit on, roaming from party to party, or come to Phi Psi, where, though you think we are all lowlife jerks, you know they would be safe?"

"I think it's disgusting."

"I called over and over last night. Where were you?"

"At the library," she said.

"At midnight on a Friday night?"

"Yes, at midnight on a Friday, as difficult as that might be for you to understand. Goodbye, Angel," she said and hung up.

Well, fuck you very much.

He turned and Jane was standing there.

"I'm sorry, Angel," she said.

"It's fine," he said. "And you look really nice. I hope we see Nelson and that fuckwad Spencer at the game. The drool from their mouths might freeze. They might lose body parts."

"You are a ridiculous man," she said, but she blushed again and ducked her head.

"So, I've been told," Angel smiled.

The snow was taking a hiatus, and the game was as free of weather problems as a late autumnal game in Hanover could be expected to be.

Cornell looked bigger and stronger than Dartmouth's team, and they had twice as many players on the sideline. Bob Blackmon's genius, however, was on full display.

Dartmouth scored on the first series on a sixty-six-yard pass play.

"Did you see that?" he asked.

"Yes," she said. "It was a tight end reverse pass."

Angel stared at her. He looked over her head at Sand who had heard her. Sand shrugged. "The chick knows her football," Sand said.

"Both of my brothers played," she said. "I was raised watching football."

"Growing on you, isn't she?" Sand said. Jane laughed.

It was twenty-eight to nothing at halftime, and Angel was curious to see what the Dartmouth Band had cooked up for Halloween. Cane had intimated that he was involved, somehow.

As if on some unseen cue, the band members raced from all over the stadium to the middle of the field and formed an untidy group. Their uniforms didn't even match. In the middle, Cane stood, dressed in white and holding a tuba.

"Cane doesn't play tuba, does he?" Eddie asked.

Angel shook his head. "Just watch. Cane said this would be epic."

For three songs, there wasn't much to see. The band pretty much stood still while going through *Monster Mash, Satisfaction*, and the first half of *Why Don't We Do It in the Road*. But, towards the end of the third song, they moved into a formation which looked like a sideways six. As the song finished, the top curve of the six began to straighten. The crowd began to laugh.

"Oh, my God," Jane said. "It's a penis."

At the climax of the song, Cane ran the length of the formation and shot out. Immediately, the penis began to droop until it was in its original formation. Cane stood alone in white and raised his tuba to the skies and blew a mournful note. The crowd roared.

After the game, everyone ate pizzas from Jake's. They lit a fire in the blue room and gradually thawed. The hot pizza and cold beer from the bar soothed their souls, and they chattered about the game and their plans for the *Boar's Head* invasion. Jane said nothing.

Groucho joined them, and he was blasted. He grinned cheerfully and nodded at whatever anyone said.

"This is the best this room has looked in years," Sand said, glancing about him.

"You would know," Angel said. He turned to Jane. "Sand and Eddie are on the six-year plan."

"Because they went to Viet Nam?" she asked.

"Sort of. They went to Viet Nam because they dropped out of school," Angel said.

"As I was saying," Sand continued drily, "Jane and Linda did a nice job cleaning the house."

"Thank you, John," Linda said.

"Your name's John?" Angel asked.

"Yes, thank you, John," Jane said.

"Did you girls clean the kitchen and the bar, too?" Angel asked.

"Who'd you think did it? Groucho?" Eddie asked.

Groucho beamed idiotically.

They chatted happily for an hour, but they all knew that soon it would be time for the evening's main event.

Later, Angel lay on his bed with Jane. They stared at the ceiling and talked about school. "Pre-law," Angel mused. "I never would have guessed that."

Jane turned on her side and smiled at him. "And what would you have guessed?"

"I don't know. Maybe sociology, with a thesis on 'How to Annoy Men.' Something like that."

Jane laughed. "And how am I annoying?"

"Well, this is the fifth time you've played *Maggie May*," he said.

"I like it," she said. "I like you." She paused. "Angel, why don't you let Sand and Eddie do the tough guy stuff tonight? You're already banged up enough."

"Cowboy existentialism," he smiled. "As John Wayne might have said," he dropped his voice an octave and did his best John Wayne impersonation, "'A man's gotta do what a man's gotta do.'"

After that, they lay silently until it was time to prepare for battle.

Jane warned them that the *Boar's Head* party had a vampire theme, so the guys scrounged up dark attire.

Angel owned a tails jacket, courtesy of his days as an SDS spewer of Communist crap his freshman and sophomore years when he had aspired for an Abbie Hoffman look. He had worn an Uncle Sam top hat and the tails jacket when standing on a stage and delivering communist tirades. Sand looked like Elvis with his sideburns and his shiny black suit. Eddie looked like a saxophonist in a blues band. He had mutton chops anyway, and with the dark suit and the sunglasses, he looked like the guy in the back of the band who snaps his fingers to the beat while strung out on heroin. All three men had their hair slicked back with huge dabs of Brylcreem. Linda had liberally applied hair spray, so their hair glistened but was hard as concrete.

"Let's rock this joint," Eddie said, and the avengers were off.

As they crossed campus towards *Boar's Head*, their boots crunching in unison, they were in high spirits.

"Angel, none of my business, but is Jane any good in bed?" Eddie asked.

"What the fuck, Eddie?" Sand said.

"You're right, Ed" Angel said. "It's none of your business, but we didn't do anything."

"No shit?" Eddie asked.

"No shit," Angel said.

"Why not? You don't like her?" Eddie persisted.

"She's all right. She's not really my type," Angel said. "Why, do you dig depressed and depressing chicks?"

They stopped outside of Sphinx. Eddie lit a cigarette, and Sand bummed one from him. It was cold as shit, but, otherwise, it was a fine night.

"Pretty funny what Cane did." Sand said.

Everyone nodded. They became quiet.

"So, if I make move on Jane, you're cool with that?" Eddie said.

Angel thought it over. He couldn't see why not.

"Not a good idea, Eddie," Sand said.

"Why not?"

"She digs Angel," Sand said.

"So what? Angel doesn't exactly reciprocate her affection," Eddie said.

"What if Eddie tries," Angel says, "But he just flies in low? You know, be subtle. If she responds, cool. If she doesn't, he backs away gracefully."

"She's not a baseball card you trade. The girl is fucking nuts right now," Sand said. "We're going to beat up a scumbag who shat on her pretty bad. So, she does the whole transference thing to Angel, her white knight. Give her some breathing space. You know Angel is going to shit on her too."

"Hey," Angel said.

"Oh, like you're going to fall for that chick," Sand said. "What about Cassie?"

"Okay," Eddie said. "How about Angel gets her number, and after a week or two I call her?"

Sand looked dubious. It didn't sit right with Angel, either, but he had no idea why. Jane wasn't his property.

"Ed, we've seen this shit before. Remember that chick, Lois?" Sand said.

Eddie nodded glumly. He turned to Angel, "Lois and I were dating for, like, almost a year. We broke up, and Art asked her up for a weekend. She came up and hung around me the whole time. Art didn't take it well."

"Let's just play it by ear," Angel said. "We may never see or hear from her again."

They nodded. Good plan. Sand and Eddie stubbed out their cigarettes.

"Game on," Eddie said.

"Game on," Sand said.

"Is there a plan?" Angel asked.

"Yeah," Ed said. "We go in there, isolate Nelson somehow, and beat him until his parents won't know him."

"Great plan," Angel said.

"Hey," Eddie said. "We don't need your snotty attitude. You got a better plan?"

"Just thinking, maybe we should have a plan to isolate him," Angel said. "Maybe an exit strategy would be a good thing, too."

"Hey," Eddie put a finger in Angel's chest, "In country, we make do with whatever we find."

"This isn't Viet Nam," Sand said.

"Same shit," Eddie said.

"No, Ed, it isn't," Sand said.

"Fuck you guys," Eddie said. "And you both look ridiculous. Sand looks like a fat Elvis vampire."

"Asshole."

"Asswipe."

"Okay, girls," Angel said. "Quit fucking around. Let's get this show on the road."

"Only thing to remember," Sand said, "is don't hit them on bone with your fist. Go for the face or the kidneys. The side of the jaw is okay, because there's lots of horizontal give, but the point of the jaw will break your hand. Same with the forehead."

"Good to know," Angel said.

"You're a boxer," Eddie said. "You should already know this shit."

"We wear gloves," Angel said.

"Oh, yeah."

The crowd flowing into *Boar's Head* was steady and thick, so it looked as if they would be able to slip in easily. Angel was glad he didn't see any of his friends. They weren't going to like having one of their brothers messed up.

Boar's Head was a good house. It didn't have the snob prestige of an SAE, but, unlike Phi Psi, it actually held rush and turned down people.

A guy and a girl sat outside the front door turning away underage townies. They were asking five bucks each.

"Pay the guy," Eddie told Angel.

Angel shook his head and paid for the three of them.

It was wild inside. The big party room housed the band, and it was a hopping affair. *The Swinging Medallions* were playing, and the room was almost filled with dancing chicks. Clusters of guys leaned against the walls, smoking cigarettes, pounding beers, and bobbing their heads in time with the music. There was a bar set up in each corner, serving blood red drinks from giant urns. The lighting was definitely ghoulish. A cluster of stage lights hanging from the ceiling painted the walls in dripping colors and shapes, making them look as if they were melting. A revolving strobe light caused visual chaos by turning one wall at a time into a neurotic mess. It was pretty cool.

Angel dug it, but he knew that if he was tripping, the strobe would give him a stroke.

"Eddie's the only one who got the memo," Sand said.

"What memo?" Eddie said.

Sand pointed to a pair of guys who walked by them. Nearly every guy in the place was wearing shades.

"It's cool vampire night," Sand said.

"What's with all the Elvis vampires?" Angel asked. "I don't get the connection."

Sand shrugged.

A cute girl wearing a peasant blouse and skirt offered them the red drinks from a tray. She had bite marks drawn on her throat. Cute.

"What is this?" Eddie asked.

"Something with Vodka is all I know," she said. "It might just be 7-Up with grenadine. It's pretty tasty."

Angel took a drink and leaned towards her. "We're looking for a guy named Nelson."

"Sure, I just saw him down at the bar," she said. "You can't miss him. He's the only blonde Elvis vampire in the house."

They watched her sashay off, her cute butt wiggling as she walked.

They descended to the bar and took stock of the situation. The jukebox blared *Radar Love*, and Eddie's head bobbed to the beat. "I really dig that song," Eddie said.

"Me, too," Angel said. "Cool beat. Did you recognize the band upstairs?"

"Yeah," Eddie said, "*The Swinging Medallions*. Why?"

"When I was in high school, those guys played a lot. We had these giant city-wide dances."

"You must have gotten a ton of ass from those things," Ed said.

"We can't start anything down here," Sand said. "Too many guys and only one exit."

Angel pointed to a guy who had to be Nelson. He was indeed a blonde Elvis and held court with Spencer and a number of good looking women.

"He is pretty," Sand said.

"I'd definitely do him," Angel said, "if I didn't know he was a shithead."

"Wouldn't hurt to blow him and then beat the shit out of him," Sand said.

"You two are a laugh riot," Eddie growled. "I'm shooting pool until he leaves. We need him upstairs."

Eddie had only taken two turns when he handed his stick to a drunk sitting on a bench.

"Finish for me," Eddie told the guy.

Nelson and Spencer were on the move with a blasted blonde in tow.

Emily. That had to be Emily.

Nelson and Emily headed up the stairs towards the guys' rooms, but Spencer patted Emily on the butt and veered off towards the dance.

Angel followed Nelson up the stairs, and Sand and Eddie trailed him.

Angel saw Nelson steering Emily into a room, and he grabbed Nelson's arm. "We need to talk," Angel said. "In private."

Sand put his arm around Emily's waist and escorted her back to the stairs.

"We need to talk to Nelson," he said. "Drug deal stuff. Go dance. He'll catch up with you in a minute."

Emily nodded and giggled. She put a finger to her lips, "Shhh, super secret," and wobbled away.

Angel pushed a protesting Nelson into the room and looked around. Yep, this must be Nelson's and Spencer's place all right. There were posters of naked women everywhere. An expensive looking Polaroid camera and tripod stood in a corner.

"What the fuck?" Nelson squawked, but Eddie grabbed his face and pushed him against a wall.

"You don't speak," Eddie said, "unless we ask you a question."

Sand opened his wallet and flashed a badge in Nelson's face. "You've got two choices, son. Either you answer our questions, or we beat you silly. Your call."

Nelson had a 'this isn't happening' look on his face, but he stammered, "What do you want?"

Sand snapped his wallet shut. "Show us the Wall of Shame."

What the fuck?

"All right," Nelson said. "But I didn't take the pictures. My roommate Spencer did, and every girl was cool with what we were doing."

"Show us," Eddie said.

Spencer opened a closet door and stood back. There must have been forty Polaroids taped there. In every shot, a girl was being fucked or giving a blowjob. Emily was one of the girls. She cheerfully vamped for the camera with a dick in her mouth. And there was Jane, prominently displayed. There was a standard shot of Nelson over her in the missionary position. There was one of her giving Nelson a blowjob. Unless he was tiny, his dick was deep down her throat. Farther down, there was one of Spencer fucking her from behind and one with him in her mouth. There were also two with guys Angel had never seen. They weren't *Boar's Head* guys.

Angel knew the look on her face. It was that of the sad, snotty girl he had met on the steps the day before.

"That's a good one," Eddie said, pointing.

"Yeah," Nelson said. "That's Spencer fucking her ass. She was really into it."

"Looks like it," Angel said. "Who took that shot?"

"I guess I did," Nelson said, "But that girl was all over our shit. She's a serious slut."

"And who's seen these pictures?" Sand asked.

"Everybody." Nelson said. "If you try to arrest me, you'll have to arrest everyone I know."

Angel ripped the photo of Jane blowing Spencer off the wall. "He's all yours. I get the roommate," he said and went to the door. He turned to hear Sand say, "Okay Nelson, one more time. We beat the shit out of you, or we arrest you on about thirty charges including pornography and rape, and you spend twenty years getting ass-fucked. Like I said, you get to choose."

Angel saw Eddie putting on his gloves and left. He went to the ballroom and found Spencer in front of the band, pulling Emily's sweater over her head and holding her breasts up for inspection to the cheering crowd.

Angel smiled in anticipation. He wished he had gloves. He took off his tails jacket and hung it over a bannister and waded through the crowd towards Spencer.

Emily recognized Angel first and gave him a bleary smile. Man, she was messed up. Angel briefly wondered what kind of shit they had talked her into taking.

Angel pulled her away from Spencer and pushed her aside.

"What the fuck, man?" Spencer said. "You made me spill my drink." He began to wipe at his shirt, but, when he looked up at Angel, recognition flickered in his eyes.

That was when Angel hit him first, flush on the side of the jaw. Spencer went down as if he had been shot, collapsing in an awkward heap. He got his hands and knees under him and began to straighten up. Angel hit him with an uppercut just under his ribs, and Spencer's face turned into a mask of agony. He sagged, but Angel held him up. Spencer gasped for air, but Angel hit him in the face again. Spencer fell hard. The look he gave Angel was one of horror. Then, the screaming began. Spencer's face was covered with gore, and his aquiline nose lay sideways. Angel held the photo of Spencer and Jane in front of his face.

"Remember this?" he said. "Yeah, that's Jane, the girl you called a slut earlier today. Right in front of me, you called her a whore. I gotta say, Spencer, that's a pretty fucking insensitive thing to say to girl who's with a guy. I know I felt disrespected. Look at her expression, Spencer. Look at it."

Spencer turned away and spat blood. Angel grabbed his hair and jerked his head up. Angel felt hands grabbing at him, but he angrily shrugged them off. "Look at her, Spencer. Does she look like she's enjoying herself? Like this is voluntary shit?" Angel pocketed the picture. "I'll hold onto that in case you sic the cops on me. I'll have you charged with so many things you won't ever get out of jail again, you sick, pathetic fuck."

Angel hit him one more time, and Spencer went down again. He didn't move after that.

Angel turned to the crowd who circled him.

A pair of hysterical girls bent over Spencer, screaming inchoate inanities. Their voices meshed nicely with the strobe lights and the lava lamp walls.

Angel found himself staring directly at Jason, a friend from his freshman dorm. Angel held the picture up to Jason, who shook his head and said, "I didn't know anything about this." Angel growled and pushed his way through the crowd. Amazingly, no one tried very hard to stop him.

When he got outside, the cold air hit him like a punch. He leaned against the fir Jane had wept under earlier and tried to slow his racing heart. He felt like a walking stroke.

He headed up the street towards The Green and was almost there when the nausea hit him. He sat in front of Dartmouth Hall and put his hand in the snow. It felt like it was broken. Sand and Eddie had told him not to hit bone, but he hadn't listened. He threw up in his throat and lay back in the snow. As he cooled, the nausea left him, and his face lit up in a huge grin. That's how he was when Eddie and Sand picked him up.

"This yours?" Sand asked and tossed Angel his tails coat. "Never leave evidence behind."

"What's wrong with you?" Eddie asked. "You should be happy. Tonight, you were a warrior."

"I beat the snot out of Spencer," Angel said. "I mean I messed him up bad. He'll remember this day every time he breathes for the rest of his fucking life."

"Shit, Angel," Eddie said. He looked somberly towards Sand. "Tell him, Sand."

Angel looked from Eddie to Sand. What was wrong with these two? They looked as if they'd been lying on a couch watching football all day. And here he was, a total wreck.

"Tell me what?" Angel asked.

"Shit man," Sand said. "I don't how to tell you this, but Spencer's dead. You killed the fuck."

Angel looked from one to the other, but Sand couldn't keep a straight face and soon both men were laughing.

When they got back to Phi Psi, Jane was sitting on the steps shivering. Sand and Eddie patted her on the shoulder as they passed. She stood when Angel approached. He smiled and raised a triumphant fist. Jane went to him and put her arms around him. She buried her head on his chest and wept.

Angel took her to the Blue Room where Sand lit a fire, and Eddie arranged a semi-circle of chairs. They sat Jane down, and Eddie handed her a stack of photos.

Jane looked through them. Her face was stony, and her back was rigid.

"Did you look at these?" she asked Angel.

"No, Sand wouldn't let me," Angel lied.

She threw a photo on the fire, and it burned in bright oranges and greens. She threw another and another. Then she threw the whole pile on the flames.

She turned to Sand and Eddie. "Was that all of them? They didn't have any others stashed away somewhere, did they?"

"No," Sand said. "Eddie asked Nelson that same question, and, let's just say, we're convinced he was telling the truth."

"Did you hurt him?" Jane asked.

Sand hesitated. "Yeah, we did," he said. "I'm pretty sure his pornography career is over for a while. But I think Angel messed up Nelson's roommate a lot worse."

"Spencer? You went after Spencer?" Jane asked Angel.

Angel nodded.

"Our little Angel is being modest," Eddie said. "Spencer's probably at Dick's House with a fucked-up face."

Jane didn't react for a moment, but then she nodded her head definitively, "Good. I'm glad. Did you see Emily?"

"Yes," Angel said.

"What was she like?"

"I think they had her pretty drugged up," Angel said. "Nelson was taking her to his room when we intervened. She saw what I did to Spencer. Maybe she'll think before doing things for those asswipes."

They were silent.

Eddie broke their reverie. "You're being awful quiet. Are you okay?"

Jane thought. "I don't know how to say this, but I don't think I've ever had men go to bat for me. I don't think I've ever had anyone do that, not even my parents." And she burst into tears again. Sand and Eddie rose to leave. Eddie patted her on her shoulder again, and Jane and Angel were left alone.

Jane took Angel's battered hand and kissed it. "Let's go get some ice on this and bandage it," she said. She stood and held her hand out to Angel. He took it, and the two went to the kitchen, put ice cubes in a rag, and wrapped his hand in it.

They went to Angel's room, and, there, after letting it ice for a while, Jane bandaged his hand and wrist. Then, she undressed him slowly. She pulled his shirt over his head and ran her hands over his chest, stopping each time she came to a scar.

"How did you get this one?" she asked as she touched the scar which ran down his right shoulder.

"Motorcycle," he said.

"And this one?" she traced her finger under the right side of his rib cage.

"Motorcycle."

"And this bullet hole looking thing?"

"That one's from skiing. A doctor had to cut a hole there to insert a tube. I broke a bunch of ribs in a fall, and one of them punctured a lung."

She unbuckled his belt and jeans. He sat on the edge of the bed and she pulled his boots and jeans off. She knelt and removed his socks. They both stood, and Jane looked up at him. He just smiled, and she bent and pulled his underwear down for him to kick away.

Angel stood before her, hard and ready. Jane went to him, put her hands on his chest, and looked into his eyes.

"Angel," she said softly, "Make love to me."

"I have a girlfriend," he muttered.

"No, you don't," she said firmly, "I heard you talking to her, remember? Besides, I'm not asking you to marry me. Nelson made me feel cheap, and you make me feel, I don't know, like I'm a real person. Sand and Eddie, I don't know how to thank them. But you are the one who took me in and treated me as if you'd known me forever. I'm so ashamed of those pictures. But you and Sand and Eddie, you don't care what was on them, do you?"

"No, we don't," Angel said.

"And now they're gone."

"And now they're gone."

Jane turned on the stereo with a sly smile. *Maggie May* began to play, and Angel laughed. He lit two candles and doused the overhead light.

"Tell you what," he said. "I'll turn away while you undress. I'll get under the covers and wait for you to come to bed."

"Oh," she said. "We're playing sweet, are we?" She waited for him to turn his back and then undressed quickly. She laughed and beat him to the bed, leaping under the covers and pulling them up. Angel sat on the edge of the bed and stroked her hair.

"Now, I know you've never done this before, so I'll be slow and gentle."

"Angel, what are you talking about?"

"You're about to lose your virginity, aren't you?"

Jane giggled. "I am?"

"Sure, Sand and Eddie gave it back to you. And now you'll give it to me."

"My God," she said. "I wandered into a pack of romantics."

"That you did," Angel said, and he slipped under the covers." He took her hand and placed it on him. "Now this is what we men call a penis."

Jane stroked it, "I like it. What on earth will you do with it?"

"I'll show you," he said, and he kissed her. Jane sighed and closed her eyes.

His hand ran to her mid-section, and she shivered when he touched her.

And show her he did.

Afterwards, Angel lay with a sleeping Jane on his shoulder. Well, now he'd done it. He had cheated on Cassie. He was the one who really lost his virginity. Shit.

He watched Jane's shallow breathing and crawled quietly from the covers. He pulled a half-smoked joint from his dope box and lit it. He sat at his desk and contemplated Jane.

He knew he should feel guilty, but, try as he might, he couldn't find a shred of pity for Cassie. She would have been angry the whole weekend. She would have disdained the dance once it started getting wild, and she would have hated what he and his friends had done that night at *Boar's Head*.

That sank in. Cassie didn't like him, the actual Angel. She loved some version of him she had in her head, but she didn't much like the real Angel.

He bet Maggie would have enjoyed the party. And Maggie would have been proud of his valor at *Boar's Head*. She had certainly dug watching him get clobbered by Cane, so she must be turned on by blood. Shit, she would probably have gone with them to watch and cheer.

He took a towel and went to shower. His right hand was virtually useless. That was going to be a pain in the ass, trying to write with a busted hand. He got under the hot water and let it soak into his still sore face. He soaped and washed himself as best he could with his left hand.

When he got out, he felt human again. He threw the towel over his shoulder and re-lit the joint.

He sat naked at his desk and tried to find a way to grip a pen in his wrapped hand. Nope. That wasn't going to work, so he opened his T.S. Eliot and turned to *Sweeney Erect*. The language was simple and crisp, and Angel could picture the barbaric Sweeney standing at a sink, razor in hand, patiently waiting for the woman down the hall to stop screaming. Sweeney knew that 'they all stop wailing eventually,' which absolved him of his guilt for not going to her rescue.

Angel knew he could never do that. He could never let a woman be hurt. He looked at Jane and knew he had, indeed, picked up a stray.

He felt bad for her. Most women he knew struggled to be happy, but Jane had it worse: she struggled not to be unhappy. Lying in his bed, though, she looked peaceful and almost cute.

He smiled and went to her. He slid under the covers and pushed her gently towards the wall. He lay on his back and tried again to fantasize Maggie's being next to him instead of Jane.

But he couldn't. He even tried to think of Wanda, but the live girl lying next to him kept drawing him back to her.

He kissed her on the forehead, and she smiled and said, "Angel." He lay back and smiled, too.

Surely, Edshu, the trickster god, had brought Jane to him to tempt and punish him for his sins.

And Angel had learned never to disobey the gods.

$$\mathcal{C}hapter\ \mathcal{F}our$$

Wednesday November 4, 1970
WDCR (Dartmouth College Radio)

ANGEL PICKED THE NEEDLE UP AND TURNED HIS MICRO-phone on.

And that was the original version of Summertime from Porgy and Bess. I first heard it sung at the St. Louis Opera House when I was about eight. The whole operetta moved me, but, when I heard Summertime, I understood longing and suffering. At eight years-old. That's some fine music. Contrast that with the Janis Joplin right before it, and you can see how tightly the white Rock scene is tied to rhythm and blues. Pull your old Stones albums and listen to each song. Try to decide which ones are original and which ones come from the Mississippi or Chicago blues scenes. Pretty cool, huh?

I have to sign off in a minute, but I wanted to leave you with an imprecation: look around you. See those female types all over campus? Those are our co-eds, and they deserve our respect. Most deserve our obeisance. Remember, they had to be just as strong intellectually as we did to get into Smith or Radcliffe or Bryn Mawr or whatever Seven Sisters Schools they transferred from. And then they had to fight with each other for our paltry two hundred transfer spots. You know why it seems as if every co-ed was Valedictorian, Student Body President, and first violin? It's because they were. So, talk to them with respect.

More importantly, I'm sick of the way some of us treat women in general. Some friends and I had to go to the defense of a girl who had been used as pornographic fodder for the entertainment of a couple of perverts. We confiscated and destroyed a series of photos those guys took, and, when they objected, we convinced them forcefully that they were scrotum lice.

Have some of us missed the prime command of hippiedom? Thou shalt not give drugs to unwitting people and then make them do disgusting things.

Put more plainly: you want to get laid? Do it the old-fashioned way. Charm a woman.

I'll go further: make the girl ask you for it. I don't ever initiate anything unless the girl, in a sober and straight condition, has indicated her desire for said action. It works for me. Try it. Romance a woman. If that doesn't work, be friends with her or try someone else.

Sigh.

This isn't rocket science. Be a fucking human being, not a walking, slobbering turd.

You worry that the FCC will toss me off the air for that language, don't you, as if the government doesn't have better things to do than monitor a college radio station in the middle of nowhere. And the college will give me a stern warning, but they will approve my message, so they, too, will let it slide.

Not that being on the side of goodness and light will always protect you. It didn't work out for Shelley when he ran off with Mary Godwin to practice her father's famous open marriage theory.

But, if this is my last show, I leave you with a beauty, Jimi Hendrix singing and playing Voodoo Child.

Well I stand up next to a mountain, and I chop it down with the edge of my hand.

Doesn't get more macho than that.

I doubt Jimi drugs his women to get them to do things.

Peace out, boys and babes. This is Angel's Blues signing off on a brisk Wednesday night.

Angel put the needle back down and clicked off his mike. Scottie banged on the glass for Angel to leave. Angel leaned back, sipped his Coke, and gave him the finger.

Chapter Five

Thursday November 5, 1970
Dryhten Ana Wat

ON THURSDAY, THE SNOW FINALLY CUT THEM SOME SLACK.
On his way back from Professor Stone's class, Angel turned down Main Street to the fire station and slipped ten bucks to the guy who ran the snowplow. After the first heavy snow, the driver carved a huge oval in Phi Psi's backyard which, after Sand and Fast Eddie watered it each night, turned into a hockey rink.

Class had rocked. Stone was Stone, and he suffered Angel to dominate another class arguing about whether Stephen Dedalus was being serious or humorous during his harangue on aesthetics and the ascendancy of drama. Angel argued that Stephen was lecturing tongue in cheek. It was like the library scene in *Ulysses* when Stephen was asked to prove by algebra his ridiculous Hamlet theory.

That was a funny, fucking scene.

"I mean," Angel said, "Stephen's spinning his theory about Anne Hathaway to AE and thinking simultaneously 'AEIOU' because he owes AE a pound. How often do we hear linguistic jokes about vowels? He even cracks that awful pun about Anne Hathaway's hold on the young bard, 'Where there's a Will, Anne Hathaway.' He's being facetious the whole time."

"That's in *Ulysses*, though," Stone argued. "When Joyce was asked about Stephen in *Portrait*, he called Stephen a 'prig.' He has no sense of humor in *Portrait*."

"Oh,"" Angel said, so you're arguing that after *Portrait* ends and he goes to Paris and is summoned home because his mother is dying, he suddenly becomes light-hearted and witty. I'm not buying it. Even his friends think he's being funny. Hence, the 'sitting in the balcony trying to pare his nails out of existence' mockery of him."

The other seven students in the class feverishly flipped back and forth between *Portrait* and *Ulysses* trying to keep up.

Stone was a good guy to let Angel continually get away with hijacking his class, and he obviously enjoyed their battles.

As Angel walked back to Phi Psi, he could feel an idea trying to solidify. It was about Molly Bloom's soliloquy. He couldn't see it, but it was worming its way to the forefront of his mind. There was a thesis there, somewhere.

Stone was going to get a kick out of the essay Angel had just turned in on *Portrait*. Stone was going to give him a citation for it, the first one Angel had gotten since his series of essays on *Paradise Lost*.

The house was quiet when he got home. Guys were probably still on their way back from the slopes. This was the first time the Dartmouth Skiway had been open this early in years. Angel was pissed he had classes all afternoon.

Angel went to the snack machine under the staircase and got two packs of peanut M&Ms. He ripped open a bag and popped a handful in his mouth. He fished out another quarter and got a Coke. It was cold and tasted like heaven. On the bulletin board above the house's pay phone, he saw a note which read: 'Angel, call this number. Some chick called asking for you.' Of course, there wasn't a time or a date or the name of the chick. His friends were worthless.

He dropped a quarter in the phone and dialed.

"Hello," a voice said.

Angel perked up.

"Maggie?" he asked.

"Yes. Angel?"

"What's left of him after the beating Cane gave me and the carnage of the weekend," he said wryly. "What's up?"

"Are you an English major?"

"I am."

"I thought so from the Tennessee Williams stuff. I need a favor," she said.

"Shoot."

"I'm studying for a huge lit test and could use some help. How are you with American lit?"

Shit. He was better at British or Russian or Irish or just about anything else.

"It depends," he said. "Whom have you guys read?"

"Hemingway, Fitzgerald, Whitman, and some Emily Dickinson. Oh, and Dreiser."

"Yuck," he said.

"You don't know any of them?"

"No, I just detest Dreiser. I'm cool with the rest. Where are you?"

"At Colby."

Angel smiled. "So, you want me to drive to Colby to help you study? Why can't you drive here?"

"If you don't want to help, that's okay," she said coyly.

Minx.

"I'll be there in an hour. I need to finish dinner and shower."

"What's for dinner?" she asked.

"M&Ms."

Maggie laughed. "It figures."

Angel went up the stairs three at a time and undressed in his room. He sat naked at his desk, chewing M&Ms and jotting down his Molly idea. He took a swig of Coke, grabbed a roach, and headed down the hall to the shower.

He turned on the water and lit the roach. He felt with his hand, and when the water was no longer icy, he climbed in. Soon, it was scalding him. He put out the roach and leaned out of the shower to put it on a sink.

Fast Eddie walked in. "Is this for me?" he asked and re-lit the roach.

Angel shampooed his hair and rinsed.

"Hey Eddie," he said. "You still out there?"

"Yeah."

"That girl I told you about? The Colby chick that Cane hassled?"

"Yeah."

"She just asked me to drive to Colby to tutor her in American Lit."

"So?"

"Is she hitting on me?"

"Definitely. That's at least a two-hole invitation."

Angel thought it over. He soaped and rinsed again and got out of the shower regretfully. He loved hot showers.

"Yeah," Angel said. "I think so, too."

He wrapped a towel around him and went back to his room.

This called for clean clothes. He scrounged up some fresh underwear and jeans. He chose a thick, white shirt and put on his vest. Buttoning his shirt left-handed was an adventure. His right hand was better and the bandage was gone, but it was still swollen and clunky. He pulled on his cowboy boots and combed his hair with his fingers. He glanced in his tiny mirror. His face looked better, better being a relative term.

He hopped in his car and drove down I-91 listening to the tires sing 'you're going to get laid.'

His relationship with Cassie posed a moral and ethical dilemma, but their fight over the phone on Saturday had left him dour and pissed off. If that was their future, count him out. He didn't do arguments. They never helped, and shitty things got said that stuck forever. Still worse, when they began, they never stopped. They started a cycle of recriminations and self-pity that seemed to have a life of their own. Yep, his Cassie days were toast.

But, he would see her at Christmas. Maybe if they didn't see each other for a few more weeks, Christmas would be medicinal.

Somehow, he didn't have much faith in the whole 'absence makes the heart grow fonder' crap.

When he got to Colby, the dorm mother waved him over to her. She handed him a log to sign and called Maggie to let her know her boy had arrived.

The woman looked askance at his scribbled 'Angel' and made a face at him. "We need a real name," she said.

Maggie came happily down the stairs and laughed. "That is his real name," she told the woman. She took Angel's hand and pulled him towards the stairs. The woman said nothing.

Angel followed Maggie up the steps, marveling at her sweet round butt. He stayed a couple of steps behind her to soak in the view. Maggie glanced over her shoulder and smiled. She knew what she was doing to him and thought it fun.

Once in her room, Maggie put a stack of books and a notebook on the floor and flopped beside them.

Angel sat, too, and leaned back against her bed.

"Did you make it to Dartmouth Friday?" he asked.

"No. Jeffrey and I just stayed here and sulked for two days. It wasn't pretty. I'm tired of it. We're pretty much done."

"Sorry," he said.

"How about you? Did what's her name show up?"

"Cassie," Angel said. "And no. I was a bachelor all weekend." He didn't mention the phone fight. Angel was repulsed by men who complained about their women.

"Cassie," Maggie said, "Is that short for Cassandra?"

"It is."

"So, does she know all of the future but no one will listen to her?"

Angel smiled. So, Maggie knew mythology, too. She was growing on him quickly.

"Can we begin with Whitman?" she asked. "It's easiest for me if I study chronologically."

Angel nodded and picked up her volume of Whitman. "Which poem?"

"*Song of Myself*," she said.

"Cool," he said. "We'll sound our barbaric yawp across the world."

"What does that mean, anyway?" she asked, "Barbaric yawp?"

"It means he isn't trying to be pretty. He knows he's a primitive. Let's start with the lonely woman watching the men bathe nude."

"You would begin with the sex part."

Angel grinned at her, and they waded in.

Two hours later, Maggie finished writing a note on *The Sun Also Rises* and closed her notebook with a flourish.

"Done?" he asked.

"Done."

Maggie rose and began putting books away. She tossed her notebook on her desk.

Angel rose, too. "Guess I should be heading back to Dartmouth."

"Oh," Maggie said. They both stood awkwardly. Angel wasn't sure what his move was supposed to be. Maggie decided for both of them.

She sat on her bed and patted to a space next to her.

"Don't go yet. I told my roommate not to come back until later."

Shit. This was looking like sex, and Angel felt ambivalent about the prospect. He didn't want to cheat on Cassie, at least not so soon after Jane, but Maggie was pretty tempting.

Angel sat next to her. Her bed was against a wall, and Angel slid back until he was leaning against it.

Maggie did, too.

They were both silent. Finally, Angel broke the silence.

"What are you doing here, Maggie?"

She laughed. "This is my room."

"No, why are you at Colby? You're smart. You didn't need my help tonight. I mean, it was a blast to study with you, but you already knew enough to make an A on a test. I'm not knocking Colby, but what are you doing here?"

"Says he while he knocks Colby. Well, my mother went to Colby and my father is on the Board of Trustees. So, we cut a deal. I do my two years here and then get to go anywhere I want. I'm thinking Dartmouth. I hear you're co-ed, now."

"We are. So, you're rich? Where do you live?"

"Long Island. And yes, my father makes a ton of money. Is that a disqualifier? You don't date rich girls?"

Angel chuckled. "Cassie is a millionaire in her own right. Her father owns something like sixty banks. I just meant you don't act rich or snobby. Cassie doesn't either. It's one of the things I like best about her. And I'm not exactly poor. My dad is an engineer who makes good money, and I go to every free debutante party I get invited to."

"Where are you from?"

"Florida," he said.

"Florida? I thought Texas or something. What's with the cowboy boots? Do you always wear them?"

"No. I take them off when I go to bed. Or to the shower."

"Florida, huh? I thought you were some kind of dashing, wild west ruffian? I mean, what with the vest and all, you look kind of like a pirate."

Angel laughed. He got that a lot.

Maggie touched Angel's face. Her touch was gentle and felt good. His groin began to stir.

"Your face looks better than it did the last time I saw it," she said. Her eyes shyly asked Angel to kiss her.

He pulled her to him and kissed her softly. It was funny: she tasted just as he had imagined. When he withdrew, she kept her eyes closed for a moment. Then, she sighed and opened them.

"I wish Jeffrey kissed like that," she said.

"Who's this Jeffrey guy?"

"My boyfriend. Well, my ex-boyfriend. I don't think I'm going to be seeing him anymore." She twisted and pulled a small frame from her headboard. "That's Jeffrey." She pointed to an almost pretty young man with great hair. Jeffrey wore a turtleneck and looked like a gentleman except for the headband he wore.

"Yep," Angel said. "He looks like a Yalie."

Maggie laughed. "And what does a Yalie look like?"

"Like that," Angel said and pointed. "I'll bet that orange bandana is color co-ordinated with the rest of his outfit."

"Just with his sash and socks," she said, and they both laughed. "Do you have a picture of Cassie?"

"No."

Angel was confused. If this was supposed to be a seduction, it was moving in the wrong direction. Maybe he had misread the situation. Maybe this was just a study session. Why keep him there after they finished working, if that was the case?

He studied Maggie. She seemed to be having some sort of internal struggle.

His struggle was simple: To fuck or not to fuck?

Angel pulled her towards her and kissed her again. This time, he let a hand graze her breast, and she shivered. She didn't withdraw from the kiss or do anything to stop his hand. He could feel the stirring in his trousers. Someone was ready. But was Maggie?

On a hunch, he withdrew and asked her, "Maggie, why did you ask me to come here?"

Maggie's face became sad.

"I don't know," she said. "I've been thinking about you since Friday."

Okay. Angel had been thinking about her, too, sort of. But the way she said it still didn't sound like sex was in the air.

Once again, she stroked his face and studied it, as if memorizing each small scar or irregularity.

"You are nothing like Jeffrey," she said.

Angel waited.

"Thanks for saving us the other day. I couldn't get the sound it made when that big guy hit you out of my head. It was primal."

"Oh, Cane," he said. "I'm sorry he scared you."

"You know him?"

Oh, shit. Had he just given their ruse away? Angel inspected the light freckles on her cheeks and almost fell into her eyes.

Shit. He liked this girl.

Angel took a chance and told her the truth.

"Yes, he's a friend of mine."

"He's awful," she said.

"Well, he was supposed to be awful," he said. "He wouldn't have harmed anyone. He was just supposed to set the stage for me to be a hero."

Maggie stared at him.

"I don't understand. He hit you. Was he supposed to do that?"

"Yes."

"And you came to protect us, knowing that Cane, or whatever his name is, would hit you?"

"Yes."

"So, what? So, you and your friends could pick up girls for your party?"

"Yes."

"Have you done this before?"

"Yes."

"And you get hit every time?"

He nodded.

"And this works?"

"We got forty girls to come to our party," he said.

"It's barbaric."

"Yes."

"You guys are morons."

"Yes."

And she burst into laughter. Angel smiled, too. Score one for truth. Maggie grabbed his face and kissed him. She got off the bed and practically danced around the room laughing.

"That's the stupidest and funniest thing I've ever heard."

Angel was relieved. "You're not mad?"

Maggie sat back beside him. She poked his nose.

"Ow," he said.

"You got your nose broken to meet me," she said.

"Well, to meet you and your dorm mates."

"Don't spoil it. I've never had a man get hit for me, before."

"Well, I'm glad you're enjoying it. Any time you need someone to take a punch for you, I'm your guy."

"Jeffrey would have run like a scared rabbit," she said and paused. Her eyes drifted away.

Angel watched her. He was surer than ever that something was on her mind.

"Angel, can I ask you something?"

Was this it? The real purpose of his visit?

"Do you have any homosexual friends?" she asked.

Okay, he was officially confused. He looked at the lump in his pants. Down boy.

"Yes," he said. "Not a lot, but that's partly because most guys won't admit they are. Most don't even tell their families. So, I'm sure I have more friends like that than I know of."

She thought for a moment.

"Do some have girlfriends?"

"Yes," he said. "A girlfriend is a good cover if you don't want to explain things to friends or family? Maggie, what's this all about? I thought you called me for, well," and he pointed at his all too obvious hard on.

Maggie's eyes widened. "Is that for me?"

"Well, it's not from looking at Jeffrey's picture or talking about him."

"How long has that been there?" she asked.

"It's permanent. I carry it everywhere I go. It's actually attached."

"No, I mean, how long have you been hard?"

"I don't know. Since our kiss. Since I brushed your breast. This is the strangest conversation I've ever had."

She reached gingerly and touched it.

"You are completely hard."

Angel laughed. "Yes. Completely."

"I can't get Jeffrey hard. That's what started our latest fight."

"Sweetheart, you got me hard while you were tending to my face on Friday. I got hard thinking about you on the way home. I don't know what's wrong with Jeffrey. What are you saying? That he's into guys or something?"

"Not, 'or something,'" she said. "That's exactly what I'm saying. I think I'm his cover. Do you know I have to give him a blowjob to get him hard? I mean every single time. And sometimes even that doesn't work."

Angel laughed. "That doesn't mean anything. There are a lot of reasons a man might not respond. Maybe he satisfied himself before he got here. Maybe, I don't know. There are other explanations, though. Maybe you don't make him feel like you want him. Maybe lots of things."

"Angel, you said you got hard the minute we sat on the bed. Long before you kissed me. And, when we were walking up the stairs, I could practically feel your eyes burning a hole in my rear end."

"Well, you happen to have a particularly nice rear," he laughed. "I'm sorry about that."

"No, I was turned on, too. That's what I mean. Jeffrey and I don't turn each other on."

"Are you turned on now?" he asked.

Maggie blushed. "Maybe."

"Does this feel good?" He stroked her face. She nodded. He moved his hand to her breast. "And this?" She nodded again. He put his hand under her sweater. She sucked in her stomach at his touch but didn't demur. He moved his hand to her back and unsnapped her bra. His eyes never left hers, and he moved his hand up until he held a breast. "How about this?"

"Oh, yes," she said.

Angel pulled her sweater over her head. She put her arms up to help. She removed her bra and flung it.

Angel pushed her back until she was lying on the bed. He lay next to her and kissed her again. She put her arms around his neck.

"You taste so good," she sighed.

"I was just thinking the same of you." Still kissing her, he ran his hand down to her chest. She sighed again. He raised his head and looked at her breasts. He bent and took a nipple in his mouth and sucked lightly. Maggie shuddered. His mouth went back to hers, but he ran his hand up insider her skirt. Maggie sucked in her stomach again and opened her legs slightly. Angel ran his hands under the elastic band and sought her pussy. He slid a finger along it.

He took his hand away and stopped kissing her. He leaned on an elbow and looked down at her, a smile on his face.

"You were being truthful," he said. "You are definitely turned on. And, no, there's nothing at all wrong with you." He gazed down her body. "You are truly beautiful. I may never go soft again."

"Angel, you don't have to stop. I mean, if you don't want to," she said.

"Yes, I do," he said. "You asked me here to talk about Jeffrey, not to make love to you. My ego misread the signals. So, talk to me."

"No," she said. "We can talk afterwards." She pulled his face back to hers.

"Why me?" he asked. "We barely know each other."

She lay back. "I know you," she said. "You're Angel, the blues guy. I listen to your radio show every Wednesday night. The minute I heard your voice, I knew it was you, even before your friends called you Angel." She put her arms behind her head and looked at him. "Angel, what were you talking about last night on your show?"

"The porn stuff?"

"Uh huh."

"A girl showed up at our house Friday night. Some guys in another fraternity had done stuff to her. A couple of friends and I corrected the situation."

"Corrected it? What does that mean?" she asked.

Angel looked at her. "We hurt a pair of guys and let them know their shit stinks."

"So, English nerd by day and vigilante at night, eh? Very eighteenth century French."

Angel laughed. "*The Scarlet Pimpernel*, huh? I hoped you were thinking more Zorro or Superman."

Maggie smiled and then grew quiet. Angel bent and kissed her belly button and ran his fingers over the tiny blonde hairs on her belly. He glanced up. She had drifted a million miles away and looked sad. First Jane and now Maggie. And probably Cassie, too, if he could see her face. Sad girls all. Why was that?

Of course, Maggie had called him. Who better to talk with? She couldn't talk to her friends at Colby. That would be cruel to Jeffrey. They would look at him strangely thereafter.

"I don't get blowjobs," Maggie said.

"Of course, you don't," he said. "You don't have a dick."

"Funny man. No Mister Grammar Police, I mean, why should women have to do that for men? Dicks are unattractive, and I hate when that thing's staring me in the face. Like a Cyclops. I don't like giving them."

"Maybe you prefer women," Angel said and blew a farting sound on her stomach.

Maggie hit him on the back. "You're mean, but really, what do I do about Jeffrey?"

"Well, if you like him, then you support him, and if you don't, you break up."

"Yes, but how do I support him? I can't accuse him of being that way. If he is, you know, homosexual, it would crush him that I know, and if he's not, that would be even worse."

She sounded miserable.

"He must be so lonely if he is," she said mournfully. "Can you imagine, having to sneak around? Not even being able to tell his family. And the boys at Yale would be so cruel to him."

Tears were forming in her eyes.

Angel sat up and unzipped her skirt.

"What are you doing?" she said.

"Taking off your clothes," he said. "I want to see your body. Don't worry, I'm not going to do anything. I just want to look."

"You are insane," she said half laughing. But she let him slide her skirt and panties off. He tossed them in the general direction of her bra and ran a hand up her leg.

"Have you been to Italy?" he asked.

"No, why?"

"But you know *The Pieta*, the Michelangelo one?"

Maggie nodded.

"Describe it," he said.

She looked at him for a moment. "Mary is holding Jesus across her lap."

"Right," Angel said. "Why did Michelangelo sculpt that exact moment?"

Maggie shook her head.

"Because," Angel said, "He was a Renaissance man. 'Man is the measure of all things' and all that. You know what he was depicting with that sculpture?"

"No."

"He was showing us our almost infinite capacity to suffer for another. He was sculpting our compassion for others. Yes, Christ was God and Mary would become Queen of Heaven and all that good Catholic stuff, but, at that moment, Mary was a mother lamenting a dead child. She suffered because Jesus suffered. We suffer because we know her pain."

"What are you saying, Angel?"

"You and Jeffrey. You had that look on your face a moment ago, Mary's expression. You were suffering for Jeffrey. You could be irate that he's using you as a shield. You could be embarrassed that your boyfriend is not really a boyfriend. But all you felt was sorrow for Jeffrey's plight. Then, you went beyond that." She turned on her side facing him, and he traced a line from just above her knee over her hip and down again to her waist. Maggie shivered. "You went past Jeffrey and felt compassion for every other man who feels lonely and hides from himself. I love the way your hip flares up and creates this incredible curve." He ran his hand over her hip again. "You are so amazingly beautiful. You have no clue how lovely you are. Lying as you are now, that's how every sculptor and painter has evoked female beauty, but all of that pales in contrast with the beauty inside of you, your sorrow for the woes of another person."

Tears welled in Maggie's eyes.

She was there for the taking, Angel knew, but he withdrew his hand from her side and wiped tears from her eyes. Much better to leave now and let her have her sorrow.

Like Gabriel Conroy at the end of *The Dead*.

He wondered if compassion would die out if women ceased to exist.

He looked at Maggie and marveled. She was rich; that was obvious. But she had none of the snobbery and Long Island hauteur she could have had.

Yes, this was a beautiful, sexy woman, and she was lying nude by his side.

Angel kissed her eyes. They tasted of salt.

"I'm going now, Maggie," he said and rose.

Maggie returned from whatever planet she had been traveling on and looked at him confused.

She made as if to get up, but Angel put a hand on her.

"No," he said quietly. "Let me have this image of you as I leave."

"Don't go," she said.

"I have to, Thor is threatening to break out of my pants, and, unless I go, he will. And I don't want him to."

"Oh, I see. Either I'm not attractive enough to tempt you, or you don't like girls either."

Angel took her hand and placed it on him.

"Do you have a third theory?" he asked.

"Yes, you are a sweet, gentle man and a good listener."

Angel laughed and removed her hand.

"I don't think I've ever been mistaken for any of those things, but I'll let you hang on to the illusion."

He went to the door, but her voice stopped him.

"Angel, this isn't over."

He turned to her. She lay in that pose so beloved by Henri Moore, Picasso, Matisse, and every other artist who had a chick-centered dick. He looked over her body and sighed.

Maggie laughed.

"All right," she said. "Go. But there better be a next time."

He nodded and sighed again.

When had he become such a pussy?

Chapter Six

ANGEL FELT PINNED DOWN, AND HE LOVED IT.

"I think you just prefer Whitman because he's a man," Cara said caustically.

Cara was one of the first wave of Dartmouth women. She had come from Vassar, and she had come with both purpose and attitude.

Angel dug it.

"No," he began. He paused to find a measured tone. He was used to dripping acid on his enemies in English classes, but, clearly, doing so to Cara would paint him as anti-women. Life was going to be interesting from now on.

"I like Dickinson," he said. "When I read her, I find myself subconsciously adopting her measured tone and thinking with her pauses. I admire her, I really do."

"But Whitman goes on and on," Cara said bitingly. "That's what you like about him, his largeness, his scope." Cara was the one dripping sarcasm.

"Yes, but."

"That's the beauty of Dickinson," she argued. "She is quiet. She is reflective. She is everything loudmouth Whitman isn't. He brays like a jackass about everything. He uses a hundred words where ten would suffice for Dickinson. Isn't that what good poetry is about? Saying things in a compact way?"

"No, I'm pretty sure you're thinking of math," he said. The class laughed. Not good. He didn't want to embarrass Cara. She was fierce enough already.

"Cara, my problem with Dickinson isn't that I don't appreciate or understand her. Nor is it that she is concise."

"Men write more. That's just a fact," Cara said. "You like big, bold, and wordy. That's why you don't like women writers. They're not blabbermouths like Tolstoy."

"Please tell me you're not putting Dickinson on a level with Tolstoy," Angel said.

"No, she's better than he is."

Okay. Now he was pissed. Time for some truth-telling. "Dickinson didn't write sparse prose because she was a woman," Angel said. "That's just bullshit. She wrote that way because her mind, her peculiar, shy, introverted mind, worked that way. Women don't use a lot of words? I love Jane Austen who pumped out novels at an alarming rate. I read and re-read all the Brontes. I may write my thesis on Virginia Woolf, and she was wordy. In fact, there was no action at all: just words. And how about George Eliot? Huh? *Middlemarch* is brilliant. I put it easily into my nineteenth century top ten. She makes Whitman seem economical. It takes her ten pages to get a character out of a chair. And I love her. Explain that."

"I have only read *Silas Marner*, so I can't argue Eliot, and I confess I haven't read Woolf," Cara said.

"So, what is your problem with Dickinson?" Professor Dannings asked.

"I'm not sure," Angel confessed. "I have a simple test of great literature. It's kind of like Holden Caulfield's."

"You want to run right out and meet the author?" Dannings said.

"No, I want to sit down and read the book again," Angel said. "Not right away. It's like eating a great meal. You want it again, but you have to let it digest. When I first read *Bleak House*, I knew I was hearing straight from the old horse. Truth without varnish."

"What old horse?" Jaime said.

"Sorry," Angel said. "That's from *The Horse's Mouth.*"

"Which is?" Jaime asked.

"It's a novel by Joyce Cary," Dannings said.

"Second greatest comic novel of all time," Angel said.

"What's the first?" Dannings asked.

"*Tom Jones*," Angel said. "No, wait, I guess you'd have to count *Ulysses* and probably all of Dickens."

"No *Don Quixote*?" Dannings asked.

"Oh, okay, scratch my entire comment. Maybe it's number two in the twentieth century, though."

"Get back to Dickinson," Cara said. Her tone had changed. She sounded more curious than combative.

Angel looked at her. She seemed a shit load nicer when she wasn't being defensive.

"My point," Angel said, "Is that when I read *Bleak House* or *Hamlet* or *Absalom, Absalom* for the first time, my mind felt overpowered, as if a great battle had just begun, and I was losing. I knew I needed to read them again. And probably again and again after that. You spoke of the point of poetry. For me, it's truth, straight from some divine source, as if the poet had stepped over the edge and reported on what he saw before he was annihilated by its power. The poet is just a lightning rod. The truth comes straight from the ineffable source."

"And Dickinson doesn't speak truth?" Cara asked.

"No, she does," Angel said. "It's just that I don't feel the urge to re-read one of her poems the way I do a passage by Virginia Woolf or Joyce."

"My problem with Dickinson is that she's bloodless," Angie said.

Angel looked around. That was the first time Angie had spoken all quarter.

"Bloodless?" Dannings asked.

Angie colored and stammered, "She's sexless."

The class erupted.

"No, I know what she means," Angel said. "So is Woolf. George Eliot writes like a virgin, but at least her characters have passion. She's a lot like Thomas Hardy, only more intellectual."

"I find it offensive that you would find a woman writer to be sexless," Cara said to Angie.

"I mean she writes as if she has never experienced life," Angie said.

"She writes as if she's never been laid," Monk said, which cracked the class up.

Angel found it interesting. Angie, the shy Angie, laughed at that while Cara, the class terror, his nemesis, frowned.

Angel played peacemaker. "Cara, I'm not trying to argue that Dickinson isn't a major poet. She is. I may prefer Whitman simply because he was the great innovator. I mean, he's writing in stream-of-consciousness long before Freud unleashed Joyce et al. Dickinson's dashes are innovative, too. They tie poetry to musical cadences in a completely new way, the first real sound innovation since rhyme and meter were invented. I think Whitman and Dickinson are the two best poets in the nineteenth century, better than any two you could put up from any other country."

"What about the French symbolists?" Danning asked.

"Trash," Angel said. "All feeling. No brain. Dickinson has them beat by a mile, and Whitman was only the third writer to really utilize stream-of-consciousness."

"The first two being?" Dannings asked. "No, wait. I want to read the Angel mind. Hmmm. Shakespeare's soliloquys and, okay, I give up."

"*Tristram Shandy*," Angel said.

"Ah, yes, the wild Mr. Sterne," Dannings said. "And unfortunately, *tempus fugit*. That, children, as they say, will be all for today."

Angel waited until Cara had loaded all her things into a leather valise and followed her out.

"Hey," he said. "I apologize for Monk. That was a tad crass."

Cara turned. Her face was softer when she wasn't doing battle, but she still looked guarded.

"A tad?"

"I hate to say this, but that's pretty much what all Dartmouth classes are like," he said. "We're pretty much the intellectual lumberjacks of the Ivies."

"I know that. My father went here," Cara said. "I practically grew up coming here for reunions and weddings and skiing trips."

"Anyway, I just wanted to tell you how much I enjoy sparring with you," he said.

She smiled. "Sparring. Classes at Dartmouth are warfare. I'll remember that. That I can do."

"Yes," he nodded. "You certainly can." He nodded and walked away.

Cara, however, trotted after him. "Angel, back there, when you waited for me after class, you weren't hitting on me, were you?"

"No," Angel said. He was confused. Had he done or said something to indicate that?

"Good," she said. She smiled and left.

He watched her walk away and shook his head.

Oh, brave new world. This co-education shit was going to be more complicated than he thought.

He cut across The Green and went down Main Street. He stopped in the alley at Moe's and wrote a check for Phi Psi's Halloween weekend. Moe was in his usual surly mood and nodded curtly.

Angel walked down the hill to Phi Psi trying to puzzle out Cara's attitude. Was it good he wasn't hitting on her because she didn't like him? Or was it good because she liked him but didn't want to misread signals?

"Howdy cowboy," a voice said from the Phi Psi porch. Angel looked up, and there sat Maggie, rocking in a chair and grinning at him.

Angel smiled and sped up. Maggie came off the steps and leapt into his arms. Angel dropped his books in the snow and spun her around.

She laughed happily when he put her down. Angel could feel the familiar heaviness come over him. He looked into her eyes for approval, and, when he saw it, he kissed her.

When he withdrew his lips, Maggie said, "Wow. That was nice. I need to drive here more often."

Angel could barely speak. He felt himself getting hard and knew he had to defuse the situation.

"What are you doing here?" he asked. "Are you playing hooky?"

"No, silly," she laughed. "It's Mountain Day."

"Mountain Day? Colby doesn't have Mountain Day. That's a Smith, Mt. Holyoke thing."

"We do now," she laughed. "A siren sounded and word went around quickly. We're off tomorrow, too."

Shit. Mountain Day. Did that mean Cassie was on her way to Hanover?

"Your face just changed," Maggie said. "I should have called first, shouldn't I?"

Angel smiled and kissed her lightly. "No, I couldn't be happier to see you. Don't get all puffed up, but I have been thinking about you constantly."

"Uh huh," she laughed. "I'll bet."

"No," he confessed. "I was just wondering if Cassie might show up, too."

"Who's Cassie? Oh, your girlfriend," she said.

"Come on in," he said. "The guys are going to love you."

He took her hand, and they went inside. He gave her a quick tour and found Sand and Eddie watching *Jeopardy* in the tube room.

"Shit," Eddie complained. "Sanskrit. It's fucking Hindu. 'I am become death.' How could he not have known that? Every moron in the world knows that."

"Ed," Angel said. "This is Maggie. Maggie, Ed. And this is Sandman. Sand is the nice one. Ed, not so much. But you can count on him if you need back-up."

"Ooh, a bad man. Well, Eddie, I was planning to knock off the Vermont State Liquor Store later tonight and could use some help," Maggie said.

"I like this chick," Eddie said. "I'm in. I've even got the firepower."

"You like every chick Angel shows up with," Sand said to Eddie.

"Fuck you Sand."

"Douche."

"Asswipe."

"This is the girl who ministered to me after Cane hit me," Angel said.

"Oh, shit," Sand said. "He hasn't stopped talking about you. You're right, Angel, killer eyes."

"I only heard him talking about her ass," Eddie said.

"No, you prehistoric douche, her eyes, her grey eyes," Sand said.

Maggie laughed. "So, Sand, is it? He didn't say anything at all about my rear? I think it's my best feature."

Both men looked at her dumbfounded.

"I'm taking a shower," Angel said. "These two can entertain you. Good luck." And he left her there.

"Can I get you a beer?" Eddie asked.

"Or some of Groucho's new weed?" Sand asked. "It's supposed to be killer."

"I'm fine," she said.

Angel went to the cloak room and dialed Cassie's dorm. A girl answered. Angel didn't recognize her voice.

"Hey, is Cassie in her room?"

"No, she's doing a lab. Can I take a message?"

"Doing a lab? Isn't it Mountain Day?" Angel asked.

"No, we had that a month ago. It's November. The leaves changed a long time ago," the girl said.

Angel hung up. Shit. Smith had Mountain Day and Cassie hadn't even bothered to call him. She had come up his freshman and sophomore years.

And how had he not noticed a flood of girls on campus? Because there were already co-eds there, he guessed.

He bounded up the stairs.

He had to admit, he was excited. And he hadn't been kidding: he had been thinking about Maggie a lot.

He stood under the hot shower for what seemed an eternity pondering the ethics of Maggie's arrival. Her presence wasn't as big a betrayal to Cassie as his excitement at seeing her was. He knew it was wrong to use Cassie's recent coldness as an excuse to philander, but, shit, he was drawn hard to Maggie. He toweled off, having resolved little, and walked naked back to his room to cool. He put on fresh underwear and jeans and searched his drawer for clean socks. He pulled socks, jean, and boots on and picked out his best shirt and began to button it when he heard slow clapping and turned to see Maggie standing in the doorway.

"That was fun," she said. "Like a strip-tease in reverse. I was beginning to think I'd never see you naked."

Angel smiled and finished buttoning his shirt.

"How did you get away from Sand and Eddie?"

"I told them I wanted to get up here before you were fully dressed. Sand walked me up the stairs and pointed out your room. He told me not to be too disappointed."

Angel grinned. "Were you?"

"Quite the opposite," she said and blushed. She looked around his room. "You know, you can tell a lot about a man from his environment."

Angel nodded and watched her circle. She sat in his desk chair and spun around to face him. "And what can you tell from mine?" he asked.

"Lots," she said. "You have a ton of books."

"So, do you. Is that a good thing?"

"Books are good," she said decisively. "But I don't have a fraction of your collection. This looks like excess."

Hmm. That was faintly Oscar Wilde-ish.

"Yep," Angel said. "I'm just showing off. Best way to seduce women in the world, lots of books."

She turned back to his desk. "And your desk is messy, but I'll bet you know where every sheet of paper is."

Angel went to his desk. He pointed to a stack of folders. "Those are things I'm working on, essays in folders marked E and fiction and poetry in folders marked F or P."

She ran her fingers across the folder marked F. "Mind if I peek?"

Angel smiled. "Look at anything you want. The only confidential thing is the stack of letters in the drawers. Those are off limits. If you wrote me, you'd appreciate my protecting your privacy."

"Indeed, I would," she said primly and opened the F folder. She picked up a story and began to read. She glanced over the pages at him and said, "So you think we might have the type of relationship which entails letters? That's sort of sexy."

"I like letters."

"I do, too, but I've never gotten one from anyone besides my parents," Maggie said. "There's something delightfully old-fashioned about you." She smiled slyly, waved him away, and went back to reading.

Angel put his keys and wallet in his jeans pocket and brushed his hair with his hand. He reached over Maggie, got his pot box, and kissed her lightly on the hair.

He put a Sinatra record on the stereo and turned it down low. He sat sideways in bed, leaning against the wall and rolled a joint on the record cover.

He watched Maggie as he smoked. She read intently and, periodically, smiled slightly. Once, she glanced up at him and nodded, only to immerse herself again in whatever she was perusing. Angel went to her and peered over her shoulder. It was the one about his two seventh grade lovers, Dee Dee and Serena. He held the joint for her, and she took it without looking at him and kept on reading.

"My, my," she said and made a 'tsk tsk' sound. "You were a bad little boy, weren't you?" She handed him back the joint. She put the manuscript down and stood to face him. "Please tell me that's not autobiographical."

Angel smiled and took a hit of the joint.

"Really?" she asked. "Seventh grade? With two different girls? And they were friends?"

"Best friends."

"I don't remember ever sharing a boy with anybody, let alone my best friend. And, I repeat, seventh grade? I didn't lose my virginity until my senior year in high school."

Angel put the joint in an ashtray and held her in his arms. "Grey eyes," he said.

"What?"

"I told Eddie and Sand you had the most amazing grey eyes, and that you had these sexy, sexy freckles," Angel said and kissed her. "I would never discuss a woman's derriere with my friends."

"Oh," she said. "So, you weren't impressed by my rear end. You were certainly drinking it in as you followed me up the stairs."

"Drinking it in," he said. "Sensual turn of phrase." He slid a hand down her hip and around to the curve of her ass. "I didn't say I wasn't impressed, just that I wouldn't talk about it to others."

"Because that would be, what, un-chivalric?"

"Because that would be un-chivalric." He kissed her again, a real kiss this time.

He took her hand. "Let's take a walk," he said.

"Scared to be alone with me in your own bedroom?" she purred.

"Yes," he said. "I am. Come on. This will be fun. I promise. I'll even let you buy me dinner."

"Oh," she said. "Lucky me." She arched her eyes at him. He knew how to read that expression. It was her 'this is going to be a challenge' look.

Angel grabbed their coats from the cloak room and helped Maggie into hers. He took her hand and led her up the hill to Main Street. It was getting dark quickly, one of Angel's favorite times, and the gas lamps had come on. The snow was light but steady enough to make the whole campus look romantic.

He gave her the quick tour. As Jane had been, Maggie was fascinated by the Appalachian Trail stuff. The clock in the Baker Tower chimed five and played *Purple Haze*. Maggie stared open-mouthed at it and laughed.

"We get to program the bells," Angel told her. "There are two full octaves of bells, so we can play almost anything. It's computerized." Maggie held his arm and looked charmed. Angel felt a warm rush through his chest and throat.

Whoa boy…he knew this feeling. Slow the fuck down.

Angel walked Maggie through Baker Library and took her to the top floor which was carved completely out of wood. "We matriculated here," he said. "We wound all the way up the stairs. President Dickey sat there." He pointed. "And he spoke to each of us in turn. I don't know how he did it."

"What did you talk about?" Maggie asked.

Angel laughed. "He asked me if Florida was populated entirely by retired Yankees."

He took her hand again and led her to the basement, the entirety of which was furnished with old tables and chairs. A handful of students were studying and looked up briefly when they appeared. He held his hands over her eyes as they entered. When they reached the middle, he took his hands away.

Maggie gasped and turned slowly, trying to drink in the three hundred foot Orozco mural which depicted the entire history of the Aztecs and their conquerors.

"Angel, it's amazing." She practically ran to the Creation scene and then walked the entire perimeter of the room, gazing in wonder at the brutality and the boldness of the images. "It's so…I don't know."

"Honest," he said. "It's what I believe about art. Orozco had a vision, and he evoked it completely honestly. He didn't pull any punches. It's called *The Epic of American Civilization*."

"It's devastating."

He took her up a stairway into an adjoining building.

"This is my favorite building," he said. "This is Sanborn House, the English library." He led her to his chair. "I read for hours here every day. Mrs. Sellers, she's the librarian, puts my books on the floor around two each afternoon. When I arrive, she magically appears with coffee and chocolate chip cookies. It's like heaven."

Maggie flopped into his chair and ran her hands over the smooth leather. She sighed. She leaned forward and looked out the window. "You can see the entire Green." She looked up at him. "Angel, this is wonderful. I want to go to Dartmouth next year. I want to steal your chair."

He took her hand and led her up a pair of half-stairways and down a hall. He pulled a latch on a smallish door and opened it for her. He leaned in and switched on a light. Maggie took a half-step into the room and looked around.

"Angel, this is so 1700's." She sat at one end of the ancient wooden table and looked about her. "Does that fireplace work?"

Angel nodded. "We light it almost every class. This is where I have most of my English classes. I love the beams and the lead glass windows."

"And the low ceilings and slate floor. This is amazing. Colby classrooms are so antiseptic."

They walked back out into the swirling snow and went down the hill towards Occom Pond and the golf course. They skirted the pond. Maggie picked up a rock and tried to skip it, getting laughed at by Angel for her efforts. They walked across the eighteenth green of the golf course and went carefully down the slope to the fairway. They crossed an old wooden bridge and wandered down the fifteenth hole. Angel pointed up a steep hill.

"See the flag?" he asked.

"Uh huh."

"That's the green on this hole. We're standing on the tee."

"You have to hit the ball way up there?" she asked. "What's this wooden monstrosity over us?"

"You can see it better from up above," he said and pulled her towards the hill. It was steep and icy, and it took them several minutes to make their way to the top. Soon, they stood on the green and looked back over the course.

"Oh my," she said. "You can see forever. That's a ski jump, isn't it?"

"Uh huh," Angel said. "A lot of Winter Carnival events take place here. The races are at The Dartmouth Skiway, but the ski jump and the cross-country stuff are here."

"On your golf course," she laughed. "Where's the skiway?"

Angel pointed. "About ten minutes that way."

She turned to him and leaned against him. "I've been to Dartmouth before," she said, "But I had no idea how beautiful it is."

Angel kissed the freckles on the bridge of her nose and under her eyes. He pulled her head backwards and kissed her throat. He picked her up in his arms and took her to the middle of the green where he dumped her unceremoniously and knelt beside her. Maggie unzipped her jacket, and Angel helped her squiggle out of it. When he took his coat off, she sat up and unbuttoned his shirt, kissing his chest and stomach as she did. She pulled her sweater off, revealing her bare breasts. Her nipples stood hard against the cold. He sat her on his coat and pulled her boots and jeans off. She crossed her arms and shivered.

"I have never," she began, but Angel shut her up by kissing her. He kissed her throat again and moved to her taut nipples. "Oh," she gasped as he took one in his mouth. He kissed his way down her stomach, and he kissed her mound through her panties. She lay back gingerly. Angel adjusted his coat so her back and butt were on it. Her hair flopped into the snow as he kissed her. She arched her back and shivered again while he slid her panties off.

"Are you freezing?" he asked.

"Shut up," she said and pushed his head down on her.

She spread her legs wide and he knelt between them. He reached between her legs and held a butt cheek in each hand. He lifted her to his face and licked the inside of each lip.

"Oh, dear Lord," she whispered.

He licked up and around her clit and then down and into her. He shifted until his arm encircled her waist, holding her rear end off the snow, and he inserted two fingers into her while he tongued her. She grabbed and twisted his hair as her body writhed. He felt the voltage go through her body as she spasmed and came.

"Oh, Angel," she said over and over, like a mantra.

When she stopped convulsing, he licked her lightly. She shivered.

"Sensitive," she muttered.

"I know," he said.

He lowered her ass onto the snow, and she lay there a moment, oblivious to the cold.

Then she sat up, looking fierce.

"Now, you," she said. Her hands fumbled with his belt and his zipper. He was still kneeling and allowed her to pull his jeans and underwear down. He was as hard as he ever remembered being.

She grasped him in both hands and began to stroke him. She looked up at him with wild eyes. She lay on her stomach and kissed the tip of his dick and took it into her mouth. Angel suffered her to suck and stroke him for a moment, but then he withdrew.

"That's all you get for now," he said.

She rolled off her stomach and sat. "What do you mean?"

"Just that."

"You can't just stop," she said.

"Of course, I can," he laughed. He pulled up his jeans and zipped them. "In about ten seconds, I would have come."

"Well, that was the general idea," she said.

"And that might have been it for the night. This was just foreplay."

"Foreplay?" she laughed. "I'll foreplay you, you sadistic man," and she tried to unzip his jeans.

Angel grabbed her hands and twisted her over onto her back. He lay full upon her and crammed a handful of snow into her mouth.

"Want to play, do you?" he said.

Maggie twisted her face and howled with laughter. Angel began to rub snow on her breasts and stomach.

"Stop it," she howled. "Stop it. You'll make me pee."

Angel sat back smiling. Maggie was having a laughter attack, and she couldn't stop. Angel began to chuckle as he watched her.

She was like a different species from Jane. Her happiness and laughter seemed to possess her so completely.

When she caught her breath, Angel helped her back into her sweater. Maggie pulled her panties and jeans back on. She was damp from the snow, and it was difficult. When she had them halfway on, she collapsed on her rear again and began laughing.

Angel helped her stand and pulled up and buttoned her jeans. Both then sat on their coats and wrestled socks and boots onto their frozen feet.

Fully dressed, they donned their jackets and embraced. Maggie kissed Angel hard.

"How do I taste?" he asked.

"Like me," she smiled. "No one's ever done that for me before."

"Done what?" he asked, daring her to put it into words.

She blushed but got out, "No one's ever eaten me before."

"Eaten what?"

"My pussy, you asshole," she shouted at him and pounded him on the arm.

They laughed and walked hand in hand back to the clubhouse. When they were safely on pavement again, Angel put his arm around her, and they re-traced their steps past Occom Pond and up the road to campus. By the time they got to Phi Psi, they were thoroughly soaked and completely chilled.

They laughed all the way up the stairs and into Angel's room where they stripped and raced to the shower. It seemed to take forever to heat up, and Maggie pushed Angel against the cold tile wall and kissed him frantically.

When he drew her under the hot water, she screamed and pulled away from him, but he was stronger and won. She danced and laughed as the hot water scorched her.

It was Angel's turn to kiss her, and Maggie responded, mouthing "oh dear Lord" between kisses.

He soaped her body, and for the first time, paid attention to her magnificent ass. He got his hand soapy and worked them between her cheeks and across her rear opening. She shuddered and jumped as he touched it, but he kept exploring until his hand was completely between her legs. She spread them and leaned forward until her hands could have almost touched her ankles. The water bounced off her back and she moaned as Angel entered her again with the fingers of his left hand. He reached around her and rubbed her sensitive clit with his right hand. And, for the second time that night, Maggie shuddered and screamed as she came. The bathroom door opened and shut almost immediately, and they heard a shouted "sorry," but Maggie's orgasm wouldn't seem to stop. She straightened and leaned against the wall under the shower head. Angel knelt and kissed every square inch of her ass, which quivered at each touch from his lips. He smiled and stood. That should do her for now.

She turned and stared at him. Tears sprang to her eyes, and she began to beat him on his chest.

He grabbed her hands and laughed. "Are you okay?"

"No, I'm not all right, damn it," she said sobbing and laughing simultaneously. "What have you done to me?"

Her face became fierce again, and she pushed him against the shower wall and knelt. He was at full Thor, and she engulfed him and took him deep into her throat until she almost gagged. She withdrew, gasping. "You're so big," she said. She held him in her hand. "And it's so beautiful."

Angel disengaged himself and, laughing, pulled her to her feet. "I told you," he said. "Later. I don't want to come during foreplay."

"Foreplay? Foreplay! You keep saying that after I've almost had an epileptic seizure. I thought I'd had orgasms before, but oh my God. I thought I was dying on the golf course."

"It's not the same when you're by yourself, is it?" he asked.

"You shit," she laughed and began to hit him again.

"Stop, you violent wench," he said and climbed out of the shower. He grabbed both towels and left her there.

"Angel," she shouted. "Angel, you get right back here." She stood indecisively under the water. "Shit," she said. She turned off the water and made a run for his room. Groucho was leaving his room but saw her and made a U-turn and closed his door.

Maggie turned the knob on Angel's door. It was locked.

"Angel," she shouted, loud enough for everyone in the house to hear, "I'm going to kill you."

The door opened, and she ran inside where he held a towel for her. He wrapped her in it and kissed her.

"Why are you so mean?" she asked.

"Just thought you could use a little discipline," he said.

"I'll discipline you," she said and flew at him laughing. He caught her in his arms. The towel dropped and they clung together.

But Maggie began to shiver, so Angel let her dress. He sat on the bed, clad only in jeans, and watched.

Maggie pulled her panties on and looked helplessly about. "My jeans are wet."

Angel laughed and rummaged in his closet for a flannel shirt. "Didn't you bring a change of clothes?"

"No, I didn't think a madman would attack me in the snow."

"I meant a change for tomorrow," he laughed.

Maggie got serious. "You want me to stay the night?"

"Oh, I'm sorry. I guess I was being presumptuous."

"Shut up, you big butthole," she said and went to him and put her arms around him. She put her face up, and he kissed her.

"You're really not going to make love to me, though?" she asked. "Is it a first date thing or something?"

"No, I told you, the other was just play. The main event is later, after I've gotten some food. I'm famished, and I've decided to let my rich chick take me to dinner."

"Oh, you have, have you?"

"No dinner, no love-making," he said sternly.

She smiled. "Dinner it is."

Angel took her clothes downstairs to the dryer and borrowed sweatpants from Groucho, who was the slenderest guy in the house. Maggie looked silly in Groucho's pants and Angel's shirt, but they went to The Hanover Inn, nonetheless.

Maggie was embarrassed but smiled so sweetly at the waiter that he smiled back at her.

Angel sipped coffee and watched Maggie devour the bread and soup she ordered. She looked up over her soup spoon and smiled at him.

"You look like the cat who caught a mouse," she said. "Very self-satisfied."

"I'm just marveling at you," he said. "Tell me something, Maggie. At Colby, you said dicks are ugly, and you detested blowjobs. But today, I was fearful for my life."

Maggie laughed. She licked her soup spoon provocatively. "Well, assuming that's a real question and not a pathetic cry for a compliment, I would have to say that I was truthful both times. You, sir, have a lovely cock. It just screams, 'take me in your mouth,' and it tastes divine."

"So, you've been blowing the wrong people?"

Maggie blushed. "Apparently."

Angel smiled. "I like to make you blush. It makes your freckles stand out."

"I don't blush," she said.

"And you don't like dicks," he said.

She waved the spoon at him. "You are a very dangerous man. You might be addictive."

Angel smiled and leaned forward to kiss her, but the waiter said 'ahem' and put their dinners in front of them. They ate in silence, eyeing each other like adversaries and smiling conspiratorially.

Back at Phi Psi, they climbed to the pool room and watched Eddie dispatch Groucho at straight pool.

"I don't get it," Maggie said. "What's the string of beads above the table?"

"Each ball you sink just counts a point," Angel said. "Eddie has run seven straight balls. When he misses, he'll rack the points."

Eddie missed and glared at Angel. He pushed seven beads to his column with his cue.

"You didn't leave me anything," Groucho said.

"That's the fucking point," Eddie said.

"You look a little shaky, Ed," Sand said. "I may make some money tonight." He searched for a straight cue and began to chalk it.

"This game's not over," Groucho said and played a safe. The cue ball rolled farther than he meant for it to and left Eddie a shot.

"You're a dead man walking," Eddie chortled and ran the rest of the rack.

Groucho looked long at Maggie, and then said, "Hey, are those my pants?"

Maggie laughed. "Angel fucked my pants right off me. They actually caught fire."

"I like this chick," Eddie said and broke the new rack. "Dead man walking, Groucho. Dead man walking."

"My education at Colby has been woefully incomplete," Maggie said.

"Yeah," Eddie said. "You didn't know there were any dicks as short as Angel's." He made three more balls and tossed his cue on the table. "Pay up, Groucho."

Maggie laughed. "No, I meant I didn't know what stimulating intellectual conversations men have in the wild."

"Yep," Sand said, "We're a bunch of fucking Voltaires."

"Don't you men ever talk about anything? Or do you just insult each other all day?"

"What would you have us talk about?" Sand said.

"I don't know? Politics, women, your thoughts or feelings," Maggie said.

"No politics," Groucho said. "That was pretty much burned out of us the last two years."

"It would be wrong to talk about our women," Angel said.

"And we don't have thoughts," Sand said.

"Or feelings," Eddie added. "And if I did have them, I wouldn't waste them on this bunch. I mean, look at them. Pathetic waste of space, all of them."

Groucho looked hurt.

"Not you, Groucho," Ed said.

Angel took Maggie's hand and led her out of the room and down the stairs to his room.

She sat at his desk and shook her head. "You guys are a mess."

"That we are," Angel nodded.

She stood and went to him, "But you are the most romantic man I've ever met."

He kissed her. "I've told you before, you clearly need to meet more men."

"Angel, do you think my clothes are dry. I've really got to get back to school."

"You're not staying with me?"

"You haven't invited me," she said. "I just kind of showed up today."

Angel sat her on the bed and took her hands in his. He looked long and sternly at her. She looked disconcerted.

"Maggie," he said.

"Yes?"

"Would you please stay with me this cold, snowy eve? If you say 'no,' I fear my heart might crumble from anguish. Have pity on me and stay."

"Well," she said, "Since you asked so nicely, I think I just might."

"And may I fuck your lovely brains out?"

She laughed and stroked his face.

"Now you're talking my language," she said.

Angel took her into his arms and lay her down.

And he proceeded to fuck her brains out.

Chapter Seven

Wednesday November 18, 1970
WDCR: Angel's Blues Hour Ramble

ANGEL GROUND OUT A ROACH AND OPENED A NEW BAG OF M&Ms while Muddy Waters sang. Muddy's sentiments seemed pretty antediluvian to a chastened Angel. When the song ended, Angel lifted the needle and removed the record.

And that was my main man Muddy Waters singing Mannish Boy on Dartmouth's own WDCR, the voice of peace and sanity in the Upper Valley. I love that song, but it gives me pause in light of some of my recent misadventures, and you know what that means: yes, it's time for another pedantic ramble by your verbose Angel.

Where to begin? I think I'll start with the state of co-education on campus and then move to moral misgivings.

I have a wonderful adversary in my Modern American Poetry class named Cara. She and I do battle daily. I have two qualms, though. One: I find myself having to bite my tongue before I speak. Speech is not free when you have to censor yourself before speaking. But too many of my opinions sound male and chauvinistic when they pop out. It was awkward last week when I tried to explain why I prefer Whitman to Dickinson. Esoteric stuff? Yes, I know. But the gender of the poet had never occurred to me before, and, suddenly, gender warfare broke out. But my second worry is greater. After class, she seemed to think that by merely speaking to her, I might be hitting on her, so I asked the two girls we have in Phi Psi, my fraternity for juvenile delinquents and other types of misfits. Both told me they were never sure if a guy was asking, for instance, what the reading assignment was, or if he was asking them to drop to their knees and perform fellatio. Imagine living like that? Never knowing if the person talking to you is sincere or just a horndog?

More on that another day, but I want your opinions to the following: what steps could we take to facilitate a truce between the sexes on campus and make things seem normal? Send notes or letters to Jerry Davenport courtesy of WDCR. He hates it when I do this, so make sure to say something to piss him off further.

And now to the confessional booth. I learned, to my surprise, that our signal carries to Colby. I learned because a fine specimen of Colby-ism named Maggie said she and her friends listen to my show on a regular basis. Oops. That made me think back and wonder what awful things I have said over the past two years on air. As one of my favorite philosophers says, "Oh, well."

So, before we go any farther, everyone, wherever you are, raise your glass or toke your joint and say, 'Hi Maggie.'

Well, the amazing Miss M and I have struck up a rather spirited friendship. What's wrong with that? My regular listeners will know the answer to that question. I have a long-time girlfriend who lives far enough away that I haven't seen her in two months and won't see her again until Christmas. Lots of us are in that situation, both guys and chicks. How many out there, especially you poor sodden freshmen who usually date your own hands, have home-town honeys or home-town boyfriends? Lots, I imagine. So, in these fine days of the sexual revolution, what's the protocol? Where are the battle lines drawn? Do you date? Do you cheat on that honey or that poor schmuck back in Winnebago, Wisconsin or wherever? Did you catch the fine alliteration of that last question?

Is there a new standard to cover these situations? Or is there still but one solution to the problem of the distant lover: chastity and its ensuing insanity? My Edwardian self is quite clear on the matter, but my more modern self tells me that Edwardian mores were only designed to destroy fun.

This is, of course, a question without an answer. I ask you to think about our co-eds and about the changing mores the modern age has wrought. And, of course, I encourage you to flood Jerry with letters and thoughts. Long, long missives are encouraged. I'll discuss the results next week.

But back to Muddy Waters. When I first heard Mannish Boy, I thought the line 'I can make love to a woman in five minutes time' meant that he was a victim of premature ejaculation and was, for some reason, boasting about it. I realized later that 'making love' means 'seducing.' So, the boast is 'I can get into a woman's pants quickly.' Is that our Dartmouth credo? Really? Is that our definition of manhood? Because, if it is, we need to do some attitude adjustment tout de suite. That's French, you cretins, and I've never met a self-respecting Frenchman who wouldn't disavow Muddy's boast. To the French, seduction is an art best done slowly, subtly, and, as a result, successfully.

Sorry Muddy, but I like to take my time. Don't I Mags?

So, to my sweet new friend and all her Colby dorm-mates, I dedicate the next song, my last of the evening. Goodnight Hanover and environs. This is your Angel signing off with Muddy redeeming himself in Baby Please Don't Go.

Goodnight Mags. Goodnight Cara and all the wonderful new co-eds. I love all of you.

Angel put the needle down and leaned back. He removed his headphones and clicked off his mike. He re-lit the joint to make sure that TJ, who followed him, would complain of the smell to Jerry the next day. Angel, of course, would feign innocence and everyone would be happy. Angel would get to be a pain in the ass, TJ would get to be a tattletale, and Jerry would get to rant and remonstrate, his favorite things.

To each his own, another of Angel's mottos. It went beautifully with the wonderfully fatalistic 'oh, well.'

He ground out the joint and pocketed his M&Ms. He shook his Coke can, but it was empty.

Well, he was just the lean, mean motherfucker to remedy the Coke situation.

He left Muddy to himself and, grinning at TJ, exited the booth.

Ah, the life well lived…

Chapter Eight

ANGEL AND SANDMAN WERE THE LAST TWO PHI PSI GUYS left in the boxing tournament. One of them needed to get through to the Sunday semi-finals. Phi Psi needed the points. They had a real shot at the Intra-Fraternity Athletic crown. They had already won the flag football title and would cruise in Bridge. Freak would win chess, too, unless some fraternity had gobbled up Pitkoff, the Russian weirdo who was a big deal internationally. Angel would love to see Freak play Pitkoff. That would be cool. He should arrange it as a weekend's entertainment later in the year. They could sell tickets and have a dance afterwards. Maybe in the spring. After the big match, everyone could go to Union Village Dam and skinny-dip.

Angel had a better chance of winning his bout than Sand did because the guy Angel was fighting was three inches shorter, and he had the reach on him. Sand was fighting a black dude who was a friend of JB, Angel's freshman roommate, and he was supposed to be a badass. Besides, Sand was in the light-heavyweight division which meant more punching power and more weight to drag around the ring. There was no way Sand was in the kind of condition needed to fight more than two fights.

Angel was pleased he had gotten past his first opponent without re-breaking his nose (which was still sore from Cane's ministrations). He had a raging headache, and his neck was stiff, but, otherwise he was intact. Not bad for a guy who trained by smoking pot every night and seldom slept.

Angel looked around the gym, but, other than the small knot of fraternity brothers behind Eddie in his corner, he didn't recognize anyone. There were some girls there, which was nice. Nothing like waving your dick in front of women to help keep the adrenaline up.

When the bell sounded, Angel took a deep breath and advanced cautiously. He hadn't seen his opponent, Hector, fight before, but he had heard he was a tough son of a bitch. Supposedly, Hector had a rough first bout, so Angel expected him either to conserve strength by boxing technically, which would have suited Angel's conditioning and fighting style, or to charge like a bull and try to end things quickly.

Hector opted for charging. Angel let him come at him and stung him on the side of the face with a jab. Thump. Sweat flew. Hector shook his head angrily but kept coming, and, soon, they were in a clinch.

Shit, Hector was strong. Angel hung on and took a few body shots, most of which glanced off harmlessly. It was hard to generate much power from that close.

The referee parted them, and Angel flicked a jab at Hector as they broke, which was borderline illegal. That was just to piss Hector off. He could hear Eddie in his corner saying, "What the fuck are you doing? Don't irritate him. Stay away and box." Angel smiled slightly and nodded at Eddie. Hector saw the smile and interpreted it as cockiness. He bull-rushed Angel again and, this time, got in a good kidney shot before Angel could wrap him up.

"Dance and jab," Eddie shouted.

Angel tried, but his dancing seemed more like an eighth-grade two-step with a reluctant virgin, so he settled on moving clockwise and landing jabs on Hector's forehead. A slight cut opened on Hector's brow, and the ref stopped the fight to check him. The bell interrupted the break, and Angel flopped on his stool and pretended to listen to Eddie.

"Two more rounds, and you're done for the day. You can do this. Jab and move. I just bet fifty bucks on you. If that guy beats you up, I'll beat you up worse later. Got it?" Eddie wiped Hector's blood off Angel's gloves and pounded him on the back.

Angel smiled and nodded.

"You can do this," Eddie said.

Yeah. You fucking do this, Eddie.

Eddie had lost his first bout. He had gone berserk and attacked some poor fucker in his own corner and been disqualified. That was the same Eddie who expected Angel to be cool and collected.

The bell rang. Angel took a swig of water and went to meet Hector. Hector was more cautious and tried to box with Angel. Dumb idea. Angel just kept his distance and jabbed Hector's cut back open. Again, the fight was halted to check Hector's eye, but he was ruled all right and the ref signaled for them to engage again. Angel tried to do as he was told, but he was having a tough time moving. His shoes felt like concrete pads.

"Hit him," Angel heard a voice yell. He looked out of the corner of his eye. It was Cane.

"Hit the bum, you pussy," Cane yelled again.

A group of Hector's friends didn't seem to appreciate Cane's pugilistic commentary, and they yelled back.

"Let's go Hector. Hit the pretty boy," one yelled.

Hector glanced aside and nodded. He waded back into Angel with renewed ardor.

Thanks, Cane.

Hector swung a combination of lefts and rights at Angel's midsection, but Angel blocked them with his arms and jabbed again with his left. Hector's eye was almost closed, so Angel knew he couldn't see the jabs being thrown.

Hector withdrew and circled. He was clearly confused.

That's right, Hector. If you come for my body, your hands are down and I punish your face. Raise your hands and come at me again.

"Watch his jab, Hector. He's got nothing else."

Yeah, Hector, listen to your buddy.

Hector obediently raised his hands in a classic boxing position. Angel looked at Cane who raised his eyebrows in the universal what-the-fuck-you-gonna-do expression.

Blake sidled up to Cane accompanied by a cute brunette Angel didn't recognize. Whomp.

Angel felt his head explode, and he staggered back. He could hear Cane and Blake laughing and Eddie yelling some kind of instructions.

Angel staggered back and covered up. Almost by reflex he met Hector's advance with a series of jabs, all of which Hector parried easily.

"Pay attention, douche," Cane offered with a cackle.

Hector's fans were pushing towards the ring excitedly.

Angel circled Hector warily.

Get your head back into this.

Hector nodded at Angel as he advanced. He looked more confident and less tired.

Angel stopped moving left and flicked a slow jab at Hector's eye. When Hector raised his gloves to parry, Angel hit him in the ribs with a right hook. Hector's mouthpiece fell from his mouth again, and he bent over in pain. Angel moved in to take out the bloody eye, but the bell rang, saving Hector.

As Angel went to his corner, he heard a commotion and looked to see Cane, Blake, and Groucho engaged in a shoving match with some of Hector's fraternity brothers. Insults flew fast between the factions.

Angel plopped on his stool and closed his eyes. The cold, wet towel felt welcome, and he relaxed by listening to the 'fuck you's' and 'eat me's' fly back and forth. Eddie was in his ear, "One more round to survive. All you got to do is keep from getting knocked out and you've won. No stupid stuff."

Angel nodded. It felt good leaning against the turnbuckle.

When the bell rang, Hector waddled towards Angel. He didn't look happy and protected his ribs with an arm.

Well, let's give him something to really feel unhappy about. Three more minutes and I'll be back at Phi Psi showering and spending a woman-free night partying and working.

Angel got off his stool. His back had tightened. That would kill the pop on his jabs. He heard a female voice call his name. It sounded like Wanda. He quickly scanned the crowd but didn't see her. His adrenaline kicked in for the first time that afternoon. Cane and the guys were still shoving and shouting at each other, and Hector came out acting all tough. Show-off time. He did a nifty dance as he left his corner and shuffled towards Hector's right side. That was the eye which puffed bloody and black. Angel flicked three quick jabs, all of which hit. He danced backwards as Hector swung wildly. He closed again and got under Hector's guard and hit him again with a right in the rib cage. Hector went to a knee, and his eyes had that startled look a man gets when he knows he's really hurt. He got back to his feet even before the ref got to him, so Angel closed again and hit him with a hard hook. Hector's mouthpiece flew again, and Angel saw his eyes go dead, a sure sign that he was done. Angel put his hands up in the air and did his little dance again. The crowd noise surged, and he thought he heard Wanda's voice again and raised his hands to the crowd while doing his Ali shuffle.

"Back off," Eddie admonished. "He's finished. Don't do anything stupid."

But Angel didn't listen and when Hector got up, Angel backed him across the ring, peppering him with jabs and body shots. Hector tried to clinch with Angel, but he slipped and fell directly into Angel's legs. Angel's left knee gave way, sending a shot of pain up his whole left side. Angel tried to step around Hector, who grabbed at Angel's legs to steady himself. Angel tried to wrench free, but he slipped and fell, crashing face first into the turnbuckle. Angel stood, dazed, and turned. Hector was on his feet, his face a mask of blood, but the ref was pushing him towards his corner. Angel advanced to the middle of the ring and waited. His right eye couldn't focus. He felt with the back of his wrist, but his nose was still intact. There was blood on his glove, though, so something was bleeding. He hoped it was Hector's blood, but his right eye wouldn't focus, and he had a feeling it was his. The ref went to Angel who had a fleeting moment of panic. Was he disqualified for something? But the ref raised Angel's right arm. Fight over.

The crowd erupted again.

Everything else after that was as blurry as his eye. Eddie dragged him to his corner, and a doctor climbed through the ring to examine him.

"What day is it?" the doctor asked.

"Saturday."

"Where are you?"

"Intramural boxing tournament. Quarterfinals. I fought a guy named Hector."

The doctor squirted something on his forehead and then pressed gauze against it.

"Hold that in place," he commanded.

Angel held up his hands. "Can't. Gloves."

Eddie grabbed the gauze and pressed.

"What's going on?" Angel asked.

"I'll know in a second," the doctor said. He dabbed at Angel's eye and then shone a light in it. "Well," he said. "The eye looks fine. You cut your eyebrow on the turnbuckle. Your buddy said you hit it pretty hard."

Angel nodded.

"Let's get him to the locker room. I need to stitch him up."

Eddie helped Angel up. Blake unlaced Angel's gloves and pulled them off. When he tried to walk, Angel was surprised how unsteady he was. He looked about for Wanda but didn't see her.

He was allowed to shower before the doctor stitched him, which was amazing. Even the scalding on his eye seemed medicinal. He couldn't imagine how Hector felt.

He saw the doctor talking to Eddie and writing something down. Eddie just kept nodding.

Eddie flashed a wicked smile and waved the prescription in front of Angel's face. "We have pain pills for the evening. This is going to be epic. And I have fifty bucks to blow, thanks to my little Angel. I'd kiss you if you were a girl and weren't so ugly. Doc's going to stitch you up. Sand's up next, so I've gotta go. See you back at the house."

"Nice Eddie. How about 'How do you feel, Angel? I'm so sorry you're so banged up, Angel.'"

"Yeah, yeah. Waah. Cry me a river," Eddie laughed and then split.

The doctor bent over him and wiped the brow clean of blood. "I've seen you before, haven't I?" he asked Angel. "I think I've even stitched you up before."

Angel smiled.

"Okay, young man, do you want to go to Dick's House where I have topical anesthetics or just go for it here."

Angel smile grew bigger. "Go for it." He lay back on the training table and closed his eyes. He sighed. He was surprised how sharp the pain was when the needle went through his skin. Brows must have a lot of nerves. But he settled in to enjoy the experience, and, before the doctor finished snipping off the tied ends, Angel was nearly asleep.

"Done," the doctor said. He put his things up and patted Angel on the shoulder. Angel sat up grudgingly.

"No alcohol tonight," the doctor said. "You may have a concussion, and I want to make sure. You hit that post pretty hard."

Angel nodded.

"And no fight tomorrow. Sorry, but that's the rules."

"What?" Angel said. "I can see just fine. You allowed Hector to fight with a cut brow."

"His was farther from the eye, and Hector didn't have a concussion."

"But, I'm fine."

"Go home. No fight tomorrow."

He patted Angel again and left.

Angel and Blake went back into the gym and watched Sand getting pounded. The other guy was just too skilled, which meant, of course, that Eddie would be racking up on pain pills.

The bell rang and Sand practically fell onto his stool. He saw Angel and raised a glove. Angel made a fist and smiled. Good stuff. Man stuff.

Angel left and trudged to Phi Psi in a light snow. The cold air felt good but made his stitches burn. His back and knee were giving him fits, though. He would need to ice them when he got back.

God, it smelled better out in the snow than it had in that stuffy gym. The world was a cold, clean miracle which didn't give a shit about man and his petty quarrels.

At the same time, the smell of sweat and blood had been exhilarating. All the gym lacked was a rank odor of sawdust, beer, and urine. Then, it would have been straight out of a Hemingway story. Boxing. What a great sport. No excuses. No pity. Just some guy and you, face to face. It made his confusion over Cassie and Maggie seem silly and vain.

His head was beginning to boom like the bass of a speaker. He listened for the rhythm of the pain. He could set down a bass line with it and write a song. 'Man, this mo-fo hurts my head, boom boom boom boom.' No, The Animals had already written that song. Maybe the doctor was right. Maybe it was good he wasn't fighting the next day. That meant he could work late and sleep in on Sunday. That sounded heavenly.

The thought gave him the urge to re-read *Sunday Morning*. Wallace Stevens was on his way to being Angel's new favorite poet, and *Sunday Morning* had all the ghastly beauty of a bloody sunrise. He pictured Maggie as the woman in the poem, a tall, lanky brunette, slow of gesture and speech. Elegant. A brunette Veronica Lake with a better ass. Her peignoir fluttered faintly in the morning breeze, raising goosebumps on her thighs. Or was it her consecration of the moment and the flight of the descending birds which thrilled her all the way to her loins? Sex and religion and blood: they formed a mysterious nexus. Angel sighed for so much beauty. He smiled. That last was stolen from Stevens, too, from *The Idea of Order at Key West*.

He smiled at himself again, but this time for his hyperbole. Yeah, Stevens was his new favorite, after Blake and Shakespeare and Dante and Eliot and Yeats. Angel chuckled. He was a dumbass. His thoughts bounced around like a ping-pong ball in a tornado.

Angel descended to the bar and filled a plastic bag with ice for his knee. He climbed to his room and flopped on his bed. He put half the ice in a towel and lay on it to freeze his aching back. The rest he put over his knee. Shit. He had wanted to make it to the finals, though that would have probably meant taking a pretty good beating. He was pretty sure he would have been fighting Jaime Needham, the guy who had beaten him the year before, and he didn't like the smug fuck. How would he have fought him this year? He didn't know. Well, it didn't matter now.

He bounced a baseball off the wall and thought of Maggie and Cassie. Cassie would be pissed that he was beat up again. Maggie would have probably dug it. He closed his eyes to nap. A whole Saturday night with nothing to disturb his equanimity, followed by a long, lovely Sunday. He would have time to read and to begin work on the Maggie story he had in mind.

He kicked off his boots and tossed the baseball towards his desk.

He thought of the line in the William Carlos Williams short story of the frustrated doctor. Angel hadn't realized it, but fighting today had been exactly what he had needed. How had Williams put it? He had 'a longing for muscular release,' and he had gotten it. He could still feel his fist hitting Nelson's roommate two weeks before. Wham. Like hitting a side of beef. Better than sex at getting rid of *angst* or sorrow.

He pitied women. Fighting had to be better than crying for soothing the savage soul.

Had he just thought that fighting was better than sex? That was going a tad bit too far.

He touched his forehead and ran his fingers over his stitches. An image of Wanda standing in his doorway flickered through his head.

He sat up, ready for the night.

He felt damn fine.

Chapter Nine

Tuesday November 24, 1970
Blood, Sweat, and Tears

ANGEL DUMPED THE TRUCK OFF IN THE ALLEY BEHIND
Moe's and tossed the keys to Moe.

"Did the Vanderbrughes pay you?" Moe asked.

"No," Angel said. "They said to put it on their bill."

Moe nodded curtly. "We have a bunch of kegs tomorrow for an alumni party.
See you around noon."

"Or shortly thereafter," Angel laughed and left.

Moe shook his head.

Angel's back and shoulders still ached from the boxing tournament, and lugging
kegs didn't help at all. He didn't know how Lester did this all year. Lester was a
skinny little fuck, but he must be strong. Kegs were heavy as shit. Lester, though, had
taken a well-deserved break and split for Thanksgiving, so Angel subbed for him.

Blake and Cane were pretty much the only friends Angel had hanging around
campus over break. Blake was from La Jolla and couldn't afford to fly home, either.
Cane, well, who knew?

Angel went to his room and stripped off his shirt and lit a joint. This was going
to be sweet. Almost an entire week to read, write, and earn a few extra bucks working
for that cheap bastard, Moe.

He took off the rest of his clothes and went to the shower where he soothed his
muscles and readied his head for linguistic battle with a story he was working on.

Angel heard someone call his name and stuck his head out of the shower. It
was a girl's voice.

He wrapped a towel around him and went to the hallway. He heard the front door close, so he bounded down the stairs and opened it. He saw a girl walking towards town.

"Hey," he said. "Looking for me?"

And the lovely Wanda turned and gave him a brilliant smile.

"You didn't have to take your clothes off for me," she said with a laugh.

"Get in here," he laughed back. "I'm freezing."

Wanda took her sweet time climbing the driveway and the steps. Angel laughed and held the door for her. She followed him upstairs to his room and sat on his bed.

"Turn your back," he said.

"Really? I had you pegged for an exhibitionist."

"Okay," he said. "You weren't bull-shitting at Halloween? You really are in college."

"Cross my heart," she said.

"And you have seen a man naked before?"

"Indeed, I have," she laughed.

So, Angel toweled, taking his time to find clean underwear and pull on his jeans. Wanda smiled appreciatively. He turned his desk chair to face her and sat. "I almost asked what you are doing in town," he said sheepishly.

"Thanksgiving," she laughed. "Why are you here?"

"I can't afford to fly home," he said.

"Ah," she said. "A poor Angel."

"No," he said. "My dad has plenty of money. I just like to pay my own way."

Wanda touched his forehead. "What happened to you?"

"Boxing tournament. Believe it or not, I won the bout."

They sat awkwardly for a moment.

"I've been meaning to call," Angel said.

"Sure, you have," she said.

"No, I want to hire Zach's band for a pre-Christmas party. Plus, I wanted to tell him how much everybody loved him and his guys."

"He knows," she said. "They've gotten a ton of business since that night. Zach said you even mentioned him on your radio show."

"I did."

Silence.

"I thought you meant you've been meaning to call me," she said.

Angel smiled. "That thought crossed my mind, but I quickly quelled it."

"Why?"

"You know why, you minx. You aren't dating material."

"What? There better be a compliment hidden in there somewhere," she laughed.

"You know exactly what I mean. I'd fall for you hard. You are totally addictive, and I've got girl problems all over the place."

"That's your technique, isn't it? You say something that sounds mean and then follow it with something that melts a girl's heart."

Angel smiled and ran his hands through his hair. He got up and began putting on a shirt.

Wanda rose and went with him. She began to button his shirt for him. Slowly. The silence became excruciating.

"Well, I just came by to see if you were here and to tell you I'm in town." She looked up in his eyes. "Call if you want to talk. Or something."

Okay. Hold yourself in check. And down boy. Behave yourself for once in your fucking life.

And, of course, he heard the front door open and a female voice call out, "Angel. Anybody home?"

Maggie? What the fuck?

"And that must be door number one, again," Wanda said.

"No," Angel said. "You haven't met this one."

Wanda laughed and left, saying, "I'll send her up." She peeked back in and held an imaginary phone to her ear. "Call me," she mouthed.

Angel smiled and finished dressing.

His door opened, and there was Maggie. She took off her coat and put it on the bed.

"Am I interrupting something?" she asked.

Angel sat in his desk chair and pulled on his boots. God, Maggie looked amazing. She was wearing a short skirt and a tight sweater, and her makeup and hair were impeccable. She had put some effort into how she looked.

"You look beautiful," he said.

"And you are dressing just after a girl left your room," she said. "I think I better go."

She turned again before Angel could protest and said, "Wait, was that Cassie? Oh, God. I'm sorry. I should have called. I mean, I tried to call, but no one answered all day long, and I…" She stopped and sat on the bed.

Angel sat by her. He turned her chin up toward him. "No, that wasn't Cassie. I haven't seen Cassie since you were here. That was Wanda. She's the manager of a band I'm hiring for a dance in two weeks. That was business."

"You were dressing," she said.

"She came in looking for me while I was showering," he said. "The reason you couldn't get anyone is because everyone is gone. I'm that last person here. Well, and Smooth, but I haven't seen him for days. He's been staying with a co-ed a lot."

"So, you weren't…" she stopped.

Angel smiled and shook his head. "Nope."

"I feel so stupid," she said.

"Good, that gives me a strategic advantage," he said.

Maggie frowned and touched his forehead, just as Wanda had done.

"Boxing tournament," he said.

"What a shock," she said and smiled slightly.

"So, my lovely Mags, what are you doing here, as if I didn't know already?"

"Yes, Angel, you should know. You haven't called me. I haven't seen you since Mountain Day."

Angel sighed.

"And you know why I haven't. Maggie, we both know what's going on. I need to deal with Cassie before I can see you. You and I don't seem to be able to keep our hands off each other."

"Or our mouths," she mumbled.

"Excuse me?" Angel smiled.

"You heard me. When you did that to me, I don't know. It was like, for the first time a man really likes me. He's not just trying to put his thing in me and get off."

Angel put his arms around her and rocked her. "I do like you Maggie. Too much. But I have to be fair to Cassie. And you don't strike me as the type who wants to be 'the other woman.' Look, I see Cassie in a couple of weeks. It will either be over or, I don't know what. Purgatory. I can't see it ever going back to how it was."

"You still could have called me, even if just to tell me that."

"You're right. I should have. I think about you all the time. I hope that counts."

"I know. You talk about me every Wednesday night on your show," she smiled. "I sound pretty amazing. It gives me chills. I'm sorry I came here. I'm going home in the morning, and I couldn't stand not seeing you."

"I'm glad you did. And you made that awful Wanda girl leave," he said.

"Yeah," she said drily. "She looked unbearable."

"Unbearable," he said and kissed her throat.

She put her head back and sighed. "Will you talk to Cassie at Christmas?"

"Yes, between shifts at the paper mill. I won't see her much, unless her dad flies us to New York to do Christmas shopping, but I will definitely talk to her."

"Wait, Cassie flies you to Manhattan to Christmas shop?"

"On one of her dad's private jets."

"And what's that about a paper mill? Your father is an engineer, isn't he? Why do you work at a paper mill over Christmas?"

"I pay my own way," he said quietly.

She touched his face. "That explains a lot. I was going to ask you to come to Long Island with me for Thanksgiving. I guess you would have said 'no,' wouldn't you?"

"I would have said 'no,' but not because of money. I need to see Cassie before you and I can do anything." Angel caressed a breast through her sweater and said, "My, my, my. How I have missed you." He held her face in his hands and kissed her.

She threw her arms around him and pulled him down on the bed. Angel pulled her sweater up and kissed her stomach. He tickled her belly button with his tongue. She arched her back and moaned. Then, he put his lips to her stomach and blew, making a farting noise. Maggie doubled up and laughed.

"What are you doing?" she asked.

"That's all you get," he said.

"You always do this," she laughed. "Why do you tease me? You're such a booger butt."

"A booger butt, huh?" he smiled. "My, I'm so glad we studied literature together. You have such a way with words."

Maggie laughed and hit him on the arm and put her face up to be kissed again.

"I'm serious Maggie," he said. "No more until I see Cassie. Despite all evidence to the contrary, I'm not a cheater."

She flushed and pulled her sweater down. "Can we just talk? I'll take you to dinner."

"No," he shook his head. "Wouldn't work. How does your body feel right now? Mine feels like a giant electro-magnet inside your panties is pulling on my dick. I'd love to hang out with you, but I can't."

Maggie stared at him. "You're serious, aren't you?"

He nodded.

"Maggie, when I'm free from Cassie, I'll talk to you. I'll be yours whenever you want me and however you want me. Scout's Honor."

Maggie rose and put on her coat. She looked at him for a long time and went to the door. She walked stiffly.

"I might not be available," she said.

Angel frowned. "Then I wish you well," he said.

Maggie frowned, too. "Goodbye, Angel."

"Goodbye, Maggie."

And she left. He heard her go down the steps and out the front door.

Shit.

He flopped on his bed with his hands behind his head.

Had he handled that correctly? Probably not, but then, it was almost surely one of those no-win situations.

He tried hard but couldn't shake off the feeling that, of the two, Wanda was the more pleasant. There was something needy about Maggie he hadn't noticed before.

He sighed, hopped off the bed, and ran down the stairs. Maggie was pulling out as he got to her car. She stopped but didn't roll down her window right away. When she did, he could see she was crying.

"Mags, get out of the car," he said.

"Why?"

"Mags."

She wiped her eyes with her sleeve and did as he bade. He held her to him and stroked her hair.

"Maggie, Maggie the Cat," he cooed. "I could fall for you. Please let me do this the right way, the right way for both of us." And he held her face and kissed her. Maggie collapsed against him and cried. He smiled and raised her face to him and kissed her tears and her lips. She was salty, but she tasted like apples.

She shuddered and sighed and relaxed against him.

Angel heard a familiar voice hail him, "Yo, Angel, is that the chone from Colby?"

Angel looked up to see Cane striding towards them.

"You aren't going to believe this," he told Maggie.

Maggie sniffed and turned to see Cane. Her eyes brightened, and she laughed. "Cane, is it? I believe we've met."

Cane cackled. "You dog," he said. "Are you banging this chick, whom, if my memory serves me, met you under false pretenses?"

"Actually, he's turning me down," she laughed.

"Ah. Because of Cassie?" Cane asked.

"Uh huh," Maggie said. "Pretty weak, huh?"

"Angel's a pussy, anyway. If you want man-size, call me," Cane said. He reached down and pecked her on the cheek. "I'll leave you lovebirds alone. I just came by to trade manuscripts with Angel." He handed Angel a folder. "This is my newest one. Stenders hates it, so it's probably pretty good. I made a couple of notes on yours. It's in there, too. Got anything new for me to read?"

Angel nodded. "On my desk. It's marked *Maggie*."

"What a fucking coincidence." Cane patted Maggie on the butt and climbed the Phi Psi steps.

Maggie watched him go. "You wrote about me? Should I be worried?"

"No, like Cane said. It's just a co-incidence."

"Uh huh. So, Cane writes, too?"

"Yep. He's pretty good, and his feedback to me is brutally honest."

"What a shock," Maggie said. She looked wistfully at him. "Well, goodbye, Angel. I'm sorry for Cassie. You are a pretty good guy."

Angel nodded. He was sorry, too, but more for himself than for Cassie. Cassie could definitely do better.

Cane re-appeared holding a sheaf of papers. "Wow," he said. "Anal on the first date."

Maggie looked at Angel who shook his head. "He's kidding," Angel said with a smile.

"You boys," Maggie said.

"Hey, you heading out?" Cane asked. He went around the car and climbed in.

"How about a ride back to my dorm?" He leaned out the window and said to Angel, "Do something later?"

"I'm going to SAE around midnight to steal food."

"I'm in," Cane said. "Let's go, woman."

Maggie looked at Angel and shook her head. "You better talk to Cassie," she said.

Angel smiled and waved. He watched the car drive away. He could see Maggie watching him in her rearview mirror all the way down the street.

He took the steps two at a time and went to his room. He flopped in his chair and opened *Our Mutual Friend*. Finally, some peace and quiet.

Or not.

He had only read for an hour or so when he heard a tap on his door. He opened it to see Jane standing there, a bag by her feet.

But irritation gave way to tenderness quickly when Jane held up a bandaged left wrist.

"I couldn't go home," she said simply. "They would have made a big deal out of it."

Angel sat her on the bed and unwrapped the bandage. The first thing he saw was a burn mark, but, underneath it, he could discern four even strokes of a blade.

"Oh, Jane," Angel said.

"I wouldn't have gone through with it," she said. "I was just practicing. The knife wasn't even sharp."

"How did it get burned?" Angel asked.

"I tried to cover the cuts."

Angel held her to him. "I'm so sorry Jane." He turned her face to his. "Tell me truly. Have you tried before?"

Her face shook, and she spoke so quietly he could barely hear her, "Yes. Twice. Angel, I couldn't go home. My mother always freaks and puts me back in therapy."

"Is that bad?"

"Yes, I feel worse after sessions with that man than before I went in."

"Maybe you could change doctors."

"He's my third one. They're all the same."

Angel sat contemplating her.

"Are you going to send me away?" she asked.

Angel smiled. "Why do you always think that? Have I ever sent you away?"

Jane managed a slight smile.

"And I never will. I promise. But I am going to make you do something difficult," he said.

"What's that?"

"I'm going to ask you to shut the fuck up while I work," he said.

Jane smiled. "I can do that. In fact, I'll leave you alone. I'm going to cook spaghetti, the Angel recipe."

"We don't have any food in the house," he said.

"Yes, we do. I brought groceries."

"Ooh. I like groceries," he smiled. "Bacon and eggs for breakfast?"

"And English muffins and orange juice and coffee."

Angel gave her a light kiss. "No hurting yourself allowed on my watch."

"I promise," she smiled. She stood up to go downstairs.

"Wait," he said and went to his dresser and fumbled through the top drawer. He came back with a white cream. He gently rubbed it on Jane's burned wrist and then re-wrapped her. "I use this for road rash," he said. "It's great."

"Road rash?"

"When you fall on a motorcycle and slide, it's exactly like a burn."

Jane smiled. "You ride a motorcycle? Of course, you ride a motorcycle." She hesitated and frowned. "You didn't even react to my wrist."

Angel took her arm and kissed her palm. "You didn't come here for a lecture or for pity."

Her eyes teared and she left, bobbing her cute butt for him as she went.

Angel sat and picked *Our Mutual Friend* back up.

Why him, oh Lord?

But, he shook his head and smiled. He knew why him.

Chapter Ten

Friday December 18, 1970
I Think She Said Polar Bear
Manhattan West: The Claremont Stables

ANGEL LOVED THE THUNDEROUS CLOMPING THE HORSES made when they left their stalls and descended the ramp to be harnessed and saddled. It was as if the world above exploded, and equine warriors emerged from the heavens to restore order to mankind.

He breathed in the smell of hay, urine, leather, and sweat with relish. It reminded him of Stephen Dedalus, and he laughed.

Cassie spoke with the manager, a shrunken crone, behind a glass window. They both looked at Angel and chuckled. Probably discussing his equestrian prowess. As usual, no money was exchanged. There never was with Cassie. Even at Tiffany's, which, according to Cassie, was markedly inferior to Cartier's, a smug man allowed Cassie to just point to things which were then magically boxed and wrapped without so much as a signature. Everything was done with a smarmy smile. Ah, to be rich and known by the elite.

Angel watched a class of teenage girls in tight britches working in the ring. He leaned against a post and marveled at how well the stable had weathered both the years and its smoggy location just west of Central Park.

Angel clambered aboard the horse brought to him, and a wizened man adjusted his stirrups for him. When he and Cassie rode out into the lightly falling snow, the horses ignored their commands and obeyed traffic lights and crossed streets on their own the three blocks it took to enter Central Park. There, they graciously allowed Angel and Cassie to assume control of them.

Cassie kicked her horse lightly, and they began a canter towards the northern part of the park. Soon, they were far off the horses' accustomed path, and the great beasts snorted with excitement. They slowed and trotted towards the Metropolitan Museum whose flags gaily proclaimed a Manet/Monet Exhibit. Angel grimaced as they trotted. As when dancing, he lacked the ability to coordinate the rhythm of his body and that of his mind. The result was discouraging both to the horse and to Angel's balls.

They rode though snow which would have been virgin had it not been for the occasional track made by a bounding dog and the footsteps of its master who had been trying to keep up. They rode up and down hills. Cassie took pity on Angel at one point and slowed her horse to a walk. He came up next to her, and they held hands while their horses bumped and nipped at each other.

This was more like it. Both the trip from Cassie's house to the airport and the flight had been chillier than this snowy ride. On the jet, Cassie buried herself in *Madame Bovary,* and every time he asked a question, she replied curtly in French. She knew her French was better than his, so it discouraged conversation.

But, riding through the park, it seemed as if the old Cassie had reappeared and the old Angel held her hand. He could feel the life pulsing in her even through her glove. He couldn't decide whether their easy intimacy was reassuring or worrisome. Perhaps it would be easier if they were cold and distant all weekend. Then, things would be resolved.

But this was confusing.

They turned south and rode past the zoo and all the way to the skating rink opposite The Plaza Hotel. They would eat dinner there, at Trader Vic's, the night before they flew home. It was a ritual.

They had so many rituals. Sigh.

They halted and watched the skaters glide across the ice. The horses chuffed plumes of smoke and stamped their feet. They knew they were about to turn back towards the stables where food and a curry comb awaited them.

"Are we going to the Met tomorrow?" Angel asked.

"I thought so," Cassie nodded. "Did you have something else you wanted to do?"

"No," he said. "Just MOMA." He patted his impatient horse's neck. "Do you like Manet or Monet better?"

Cassie looked at him ironically. "Why do your questions sound like quizzes, sometimes?"

Angel smiled. Caught again. Cassie was too damned smart.

"Okay," he began again, "I think I like Manet better."

Cassie eyed him. "Of course, you do," she said. "Monet's are mostly studies of water lilies or of Parliament. Manet's tell stories. They're more psychological."

Angel thought that over. "You know, it's not always easy being with a woman who is considerably smarter than I am."

"I wouldn't say 'considerably' smarter," she said, and they both laughed. "But I'll bet you a dollar I know which painting you were thinking of and why."

"Okay," he said. "I'll pay a dollar to hear your reading of my mind."

"You were watching that girl skate," she said and pointed. "The sexy girl in the purple pants. And that made you think of the nude women in Manet's *Dejeuner Sur L'Herbe*."

Angel laughed. He had to admit she was good. "You make me sound like I'm sex obsessed, but those aren't nudes in *Dejeuner*."

"You are sex obsessed. It's my favorite thing about you. Well, that and the equipment you possess to activate your obsession. That's pretty nice, too. And, it looks interested in the discussion."

It was true. Thor was springing to life.

"And, I know they aren't nudes," she said. "Nudes wouldn't interest you. I should have said they were naked. You like the women in the painting because it's their lunch break and they haven't bothered to put any clothing back on. It excites you to think that a model would just sit around eating lunch completely naked with a bunch of clothed men. You like that they are happy to display their bodies, that they are free spirits and would probably, in your little mind, be good in bed."

"You got all of that out of the fact that I like Manet better?" Angel laughed.

"Yes," she said. "There's a story there. It's psychological. Monet is pure aesthetic experimentation. How does shifting light affect perception?"

"I would kiss you right now, but I would fall off my horse," he said.

"Well, if you can catch me, you can kiss me at the stable," she said and took off on a rapid canter. Angel kicked his horse and followed her. She looked back and urged her horse into a full gallop. Angel shook his head but tried to keep up. They flew past amazed women pushing perambulators and slender men walking dogs. The horses were all in: they knew they were heading home.

They walked the few blocks to Cassie's apartment in the Hotel Delmonico. It was on Park and 59th, a fact that boggled Angel's mind. He had never gotten used to how uptown he felt when there. By the time they reached their room, the heat from the horses had worn off, and they were thoroughly chilled. Cassie beat him undressing and climbing in the shower. She was the one who had taught him to love scalding showers, and she climbed into the tub and under the water before it was fully warm. She squealed and laughed. Angel waited and stepped in when it was hot.

Angel grabbed the shower head and sprayed her in the face. She laughed and backed off, but it was cold out of the spray, so she moved back towards him. Angel grabbed her and held her in the burning water until she screamed. Then, he began to tickle her. Cassie flailed helplessly at him and doubled over in laughter. Angel relented and kissed her softly. Her laughter slowed, and she smiled at him. He kissed her again, and she melted against him.

Without makeup, her face was square and plain. Her hair was parted in the middle, and she looked faintly like a middle-aged Cherokee woman. He soaped her body with a tiny hotel soap. It smelled of lavender, and she oohed as he rubbed her. She had a nice back, and, though there wasn't enough distinction between her waist and hip, she had a nice ass. He rubbed it, and she looked over her shoulder at him to determine if he was initiating what she thought he was. He grinned at her and moved his hand between her cheeks. Cassie parted her legs and put her hands against the shower wall to support her.

He found her center and soaped gently. Then he inserted a pair of fingers in her.

"Well," he said, "At least I can still get you wet."

"Ha ha. Very funny."

"I mean, we are in a shower and all, but," he continued.

"I got it the first time," she said.

He took his hand away. "Oh, well, then."

Cassie squawked, "Put that hand back where it was right now, mister."

Angel ran a finger around her nether opening and pushed it in just a bit.

"No, the other place," she laughed. "Although that feels, good, too."

Angel kissed her neck and removed his hand. "I was just finishing anyway." And he stepped out of the shower.

"Angel, you get right back here," she laughed.

"Sorry, I'm clean enough."

"You are the meanest man I know," she said.

"I've heard that before," he said. "Don't forget to rinse your hair," he said and left to dress.

As they walked hand in hand to The Music Box Theatre, it felt like old times. The past months seemed little more than a bad residue, trying but failing to spoil their mood.

Inside, Cassie went to Will Call to retrieve their tickets. Angel meandered from poster to poster, marveling in the theatre's history.

Cassie joined him and took his arm. "Okay Mister 'I Know Everything,' tell me about the theater."

Angel smiled. She was cute when she was sweet. "It opened as a music venue, hence the name, Music Box. It was built for Irving Berlin's orchestra. The first play was a shitty one called *Cradle Snatchers*. You'll never guess who starred in it."

"Margaret Lunt Fontaine," she said.

He laughed. "Humphrey Bogart."

"That was my next guess."

"Uh, huh. Guess what premiered here? How about *Of Mice and Men*? And Pinter's *The Homecoming*. Pretty strong, huh?"

"You told me to read Pinter, but I haven't yet. I bought *The Birthday Party*. Is that good?"

"Killer," he said.

They found their seats and held hands contentedly until the house went dark. The lights came up on a room filled with every kind of toy or game imaginable. Cassie squirmed with delight when Anthony Quayle made his entrance, and *Sleuth* was underway. For the next ninety minutes, without an intermission to allow the audience to breathe, the antagonists played their psychological games. Cassie seemed, on several occasions, about to lean over and whisper a question to Angel, but she refrained each time. At one point, she leaned forward, as if to hear subtle sounds. Angel watched her and listened to the lines. This was the Cassie he had loved, the Cassie who knew to choose a play by Peter Shaffer's brother, the Cassie who knew Angel loved mind games and dialogue above all else.

Afterwards, they walked down the street to Sardi's. Their waiter practically sniffed with disdain at them.

They dawdled through dinner and talked of the play.

"How did you get to be an Anthony Quayle fan?" Angel asked.

"From *Lawrence of Arabia*," Cassie said. She stopped and put a hand on Angel's. "Don't look. Is that Henry Kissinger?"

"How am I supposed to know if I don't look?"

"Silly. Just be casual."

Angel smiled and turned slightly. "No, that's William Rogers," he whispered.

"Across from him."

"Yes," he smiled. "That's Kissinger."

"Do you think he was in the theater with us?"

"I don't know," Angel said. "Want me to ask him?" He made as if to get up. "Henry!"

"No," Cassie said and grabbed his arm. She slapped at his hand. "I can't go anywhere with you."

Afterwards, they walked up Fifth Avenue. It began to snow again, a fine powder which made the city smell new and clean. The street lights sparkled, and the Christmas decorations beckoned them from every store window.

Cassie stopped in front of Macy's, and they watched a woman arrange the backdrop for a group of mannequins wearing furs. She was stringing lights in a winter wonderland, and the mannequins clutched their furs tightly about them, as if fighting the cold.

"What kind of fur is that?" Cassie asked and pointed to a white coat.

Angel shrugged. "Ermine, maybe?" Cassie tapped the window until she got the woman's attention. She pointed and mouthed 'what kind of fur is that?' The woman looked confused but mouthed something back which Cassie couldn't interpret.

Cassie shook her head. The woman mouthed it again, more slowly, exaggerating each syllable.

Angel leaned towards Cassie. "I think she said Polar Bear."

Cassie slapped at him. The women pointed to Angel's cowboy boots and gave him a thumbs-up.

He smiled and mouthed, 'They're made from Irish babies.' The woman smiled and nodded.

"What was that all about?" Cassie laughed.

"I think she's a Swift fan," he said.

"What?"

"She's clearly read *A Modest Proposal,* and she likes my boots."

"She was being sarcastic," Cassie laughed and pulled him away. Angel waved to the woman who smiled and returned his wave.

They walked all the way to the southern tip of Central Park and spoke to the carriage horses who were stamping and loosing pure white smoke from their flared and outraged nostrils.

There were still plenty of skaters going like crazy around the frozen pond. Angel looked for purple tights, but she was gone. Pity. She had a fine ass and finer legs. The line from *Ulysses* about Bloom watching the neighbor's wife beat the carpet with her 'thwacking thighs' floated up from somewhere, and he smiled.

They walked past the entrance to The Plaza and said, 'good evening' to the doorman who nodded and tipped his cap.

The snow had picked up, and Angel made Cassie stand under a streetlight and look straight up into the falling powder. She held out her tongue trying to catch flakes.

"That's so cool," she said.

"I know," he said. "It looks like they're falling so much faster when you look up into them. It's as if a comet shower were coming straight at you, and the streetlights illuminate the water droplets from within."

As they walked back to the hotel, they were silent. Angel thought about Maggie, sixty or so miles away on Long Island. Or was she, too, in the city that night? Perhaps for a play or musical with a date. Some boy she had known in high school and thought little of but went out with from loneliness or boredom. She would know that Angel was in Manhattan with Cassie that night. She would know that he and Cassie would sleep together and make love.

A heavy weight lay on his chest. *Dukkha.* All is sorrow. The Buddhist concept had never seemed more real. He knew that what he was feeling must be compassion, but he knew, too, that he was the source of Maggie's discomfort. Could one truly feel compassion if he were the source of the sorrow? It was a knotty problem. He looked at Cassie, whose face had settled into her pug look, her cheeks squared, and her eyes looked brooding and malcontent. So, he was worrying about Maggie, and Cassie was worrying about Cassie, but he was the source of discontent for both. What a swell guy he was. He, who thought he was a protector of women. What rubbish.

But Cassie's mood lifted as soon as they were alone in her apartment. It was love-making time, and they both knew it. That was easy. They were good at that. They knew each other's bodies and tastes.

Cassie pulled him to her and kissed him, and, just like that, Maggie was gone, and he and Cassie were a couple.

"You know what you taste like?" he said.

"What?"

"*Boccone Dolce*," he said. "You taste like dark chocolate and meringue."

She kissed him again. "You are the sweet nothing," she said. "Go entertain yourself for a few minutes. I need to call my parents before they start to worry."

Angel caressed her face and meandered into the library, his favorite room in the apartment. It was one of those dark-wooded rooms lined by hard-backed books and smelling of old leather. Angel poured a Cognac into a giant snifter and opened the humidor. Cassie's father didn't smoke (he didn't have any vices at all, as far as Angel knew) but kept Cubanos for his guests. Well, Angel was a guest. He plucked the smallest cigar and lit it with a jetted lighter that resembled a small blowtorch. That was pretty cool.

He pulled *Les Miserables* from the shelf and opened it. It was in French. Of course, it was. Cassie sniffed at those who read translations, the poor benighted souls. Angel smiled. That was the only snobby part of her, and he heartily approved. He sat in a red leather chair and put his feet on the ottoman. He sipped the Cognac which burned its way down his throat, erasing the *Boccone Dolce* kiss Cassie had given him. He puffed the cigar and blew rings towards the chandelier which seemed to disseminate eddies of smoke which lazed their way towards the coffered ceiling. Trapped there, they swirled in a decadent manner. Very T.S. Eliot-ish.

He sipped the Cognac again to chase the acrid taste of the cigar and opened Hugo. He had only read for a few minutes when Cassie appeared in the doorway wearing a rose-colored peignoir, backlit by the hall light. Her hair was down and she had retouched her makeup. Angel had never seen her look lovelier.

She bent before the fireplace and lit the logs with a long taper. The room got smoky for a moment, but then the chimney began to draw and all that was left was the odor of oak.

She blew out the taper in a seductive manner *a la* Lauren Bacall. Then, she took the cigar and Cognac from him, taking a puff from the one and a sip from the other. She put the cigar in an ash tray and the snifter down beside it. She pulled the book from his lap and perused it. "Il vaut mieux en Francais, n'est-ce pas?"

Angel nodded and watched her with amusement. They hadn't seduced each other like this in years. It was a good move on Cassie's part. He hadn't been sure how to initiate sex after a two-month lapse, especially with his peccadilloes fresh in his mind.

She sat in his lap and kissed him.

"You don't mind that I taste like a cigar?" he asked.

"No," she purred. "I like it. I like the brandy, too."

"Cognac."

"I like the Cognac, too. You taste expensive and cultured."

Ha. He'd never been described that way by anyone but her.

"Well, you're about to see how cultured I am," he said, "Because, in a moment, you are going to resemble the women in a Manet paining."

"Whatever do you mean?" she cooed in his ear, flicking a tongue in and out as she spoke. "Am I about to be nude?"

"No, you're about to be naked."

She laughed and got off his lap. She pulled the peignoir over her head and stood before him.

He sat forward and ran a hand from her throat to the furred area between her legs, eliciting goosebumps as he lightly scraped a nipple and ran a finger down her belly. He rose, too, and pulled his shirt over his head. He pulled her face to his chest, and she sucked on a nipple. He entangled his fingers in her hair and pulled backwards roughly until her face was tilted to him. He wasn't going to play effete gentleman for her. He was going to play the beast.

He picked her up and carried her to the couch where he dumped her. He stood over her and peeled off his trousers, revealing his fully erect dick. He kicked off boots and pants and, grabbing her hair again, forced himself into her mouth. She held him in her hand and began to suck furiously. She withdrew and looked up at him. With her eyes still on his, she licked his shaft from his balls to the tip.

"I love to suck you," she said and pulled him into her mouth again. She took him as deep as she could and almost gagged. She released him and gasped for breath. "Fuck me," she said.

She lay on her back, and Angel spread her legs wide and knelt between them. He ran his hands over her wetness and inserted first two, then three fingers and began thrusting them ever deeper and ever harder. With the thumb of his other hand, he rolled her clitoris until she moaned and began to thrash. She clutched at the couch and arched her back. Angel let her come, and, then, when her paroxysm began to subside and her breathing threatened to return to normal levels, he entered her, hard. He pushed inwards until he reached full depth and all his weight pressed on her pubic bone. Cassie made a few inchoate sounds, and then Angel began to fuck her for real. When her respiration seemed as if it was reaching a peak again, he flipped her over and pulled her ass up in the air. He entered her from behind and pushed her face into a pillow. She turned sideways to breathe and clutched the pillow as if it would save her. But it didn't.

Angel pounded her without mercy until she came again. Then, he slowed and withdrew. When he felt her begin to relax, he rammed himself back in her and began his attack, anew.

Cassie was screaming her 'Oh Lords' but they didn't even register on Angel who rode her as if in a trance, trying to will his mind not to think of Maggie. He flattened her on the couch and finished, coming in a gush and lying on her and in her until his breathing normalized. Then, he climbed off her and sat on the floor, leaning back against the couch and pushing the coffee table away with his feet. Cassie, aside from her heaving chest, didn't move for what seemed an eternity. Then, she sprang and ran laughing and dripping to the bathroom, her hand trying to hold in the liquid pouring from her.

Angel rose and retrieved his cigar, which still burned, and his Cognac. He stood in front of the fire drinking and smoking.

Cassie returned a moment later with a moistened washcloth. She went to him and wiped him clean.

She stood back appreciatively and said, "You know who you look like standing there?"

"A lean Gerald Crich from *Women in Love*?"

She wacked him with the towel and picked up and put on her peignoir.

"Why do you always spoil my allusions?" she laughed.

"I'm sorry I changed scenarios on you so abruptly," he said. "You seemed to be going for Audrey Hepburn seducing Cary Grant. I didn't feel Cary Grant-ish."

Cassie laughed. "No," she said. "You know I love the *Beauty and the Beast* scenario just as much."

"Right," he said. "And you didn't have to change character much. It was all me. I was feeling a bit peckish after two months apart."

Cassie darted him a look which Angel thought he could read. It said, 'as if you've ever been two months without sex.' His face darkened.

"Give me some of that Cognac, and then I'm going to shower again," she said. She sipped and shook her head. "I don't know how you men drink that stuff. It burns."

"All good medicines are purgatorial," he said, "Including love-making. And we needed that."

"Yes, we did," she said smiling and left.

Angel sat and smoked. The fire seemed to be trying to tell him something with its strange greens and orange licks of flame, caused by whatever chemical the logs were sprinkled with, but Angel couldn't decipher its cryptic leaps and whorls. The cigar seemed as if it would burn all night, so he stubbed it out (or tried to) and finished the Cognac. He rose, sighed, and went to face Cassie. It was 'honey we need to talk' time.

Shit.

Cassie sat in the dressing room just outside the master bath brushing her hair and dabbing at her makeup.

"You just touched that back up," he smiled.

"Well, it did its job," she said. "You were certainly aroused." She contemplated him in the mirror and then put down her brush and wiped her hands and face with a Kleenex. She threw it away and turned to face him.

"Wow," she said, "I thought we might at least get through one day."

"No," he said. "We need to do this."

Cassie nodded and waited.

"Here?" he asked.

"Is there a proper setting for this kind of discussion? Maybe at dinner where we can act all civilized? As if we're not about to tear up our lives and throw them away like that last Kleenex I used and disposed of?"

Angel frowned. "I'll be in the library if you want to talk." And he left.

He poured another Cognac, but, after taking a sip, angrily hurled the snifter into the fire, where it exploded upwards, making a 'poof' sound. He grimaced. Pretty fucking theatrical.

He sat in the chair and waited.

He didn't wait long. Cassie entered quietly and sat on the couch.

Angel felt as if something in him was dying. "No," he said. "Come here."

Cassie went to him. He pulled her onto his lap, and she curled up against him.

"You start," she said. "I don't know what to say."

"I don't either," he said. He stroked her hair. "What's happened to us, Cassie?"

Cassie shrugged and shook her head. "I don't know. It seems like you've changed," she said.

"How?"

"I don't know. It began when you moved out of your dorm and into that fraternity."

"That's just geography. If you think the guys at Phi Psi have changed me, tell me how."

Cassie shrugged again. "Don't you have one of your famous Angel theories about what's wrong with us?"

"I do," he said. "But it will anger you."

"That's okay. I sit in my room at Smith night after night wanting to call you, but I don't because I feel as if the Angel I know is gone. And I get angry. I'm angry with you all the time."

"You just articulated my theory perfectly," he said. "There's an Angel in your head you're angry with, and then there's me. Your version of me is like your father's. He keeps thinking I'll wake up some day desirous of going into business and working for him. I won't, Cassie. I'm going to be a teacher, an English teacher, and then go to grad school to be a professor or a writer. You're just like him. You've had this notion in your head of who I could be or would be, and you just ignore the cowboy boots and the pot and the motorcycles and the paper mill and all the rest. I'll never be Cary Grant."

"I know all that."

"Yet that's why you're angry with me. You women fall in love with men and then want to change the very things you fell for."

"Not true," she said. "There's an aristocratic Angel. You're never happier than at a play or a museum or eating at an expensive restaurant."

"But I'm just as happy, if not happier, going a hundred on a bike, reading, or lying next to you after sex. I love working in the paper mill, too. All of it, the smell, the heat, even the crude men." He stopped. He wasn't conveying what he meant. "Cassie, what happened on our first date?"

She looked up at him. "I know. It was for a deb party, and you showed up on a motorcycle. My mom freaked and offered us a car. She said I wasn't going anywhere on that thing."

"What did you do?" he asked.

"I hopped on the bike behind you and said, 'Bye Mom,' and it was exciting, and I thought you were thrilling and wild. I know all that. I know I love that about you. I lived through all your stupid SDS communist pamphlet writing last year. I bailed you out of jail, remember?"

Angel ran a hand down her leg until he found a heart-shaped scar. "How did you get that?"

"We wrecked on that same stupid bike, and I burned my leg on the exhaust pipe."

"Right. Later that summer, we went to a beach party, and a girl asked you about it. Remember what you told her?"

Cassie sighed. "I told her my wild man tattooed me to mark me as his."

"There was a time when you didn't put up with me: you enjoyed me. What happened? See, I don't think I'm the only one who changed. I think you changed, too. Let me rephrase that. I think you always wanted me to grow up and be like your father, but you were enjoying the ride too much to complain. Now, not so much."

She shifted uncomfortably. He stroked her hair and buried his face in it.

"So, what do we do now?" she asked. "Do you still love me? Tell me the truth because I've wanted to ask you that for nearly a year but was afraid of the answer."

"I don't know," Angel said. "Do you still love me?"

"Yes."

Shit.

"Cassie, we're not making each other happy. Do you want to keep trying?"

"Yes. No. I don't know." She was silent. Then, "Angel, please don't lie to me. Have you been with other women?"

Shit.

"Yes." He felt trapped. He wanted to be truthful, but he didn't know where truth ended and wishful thinking began. "I met a girl a couple of months, ago. By accident. She came to see me and spent the night. But I sent her away and told her I couldn't see her any more, that I had to see where you and I stood."

"Let me get this straight. You have someone lined up in case we break up this weekend? You came with me to Manhattan and made love to me so we could have this discussion, and you could report back to some slut about her chances with you?"

Shit, that sounded rough but kind of accurate.

"Cassie, I don't see a path forward for us. We fly back to Jacksonville Sunday. The next morning, I go to the paper mill, and you fly with your family to The Homestead. We won't even see each other. Then, it's back to school where you avoid me."

"We invited you to go with us," she said.

"I have to work."

"No, you don't. That's just stubborn male pride. Your father has plenty of money."

"I have to work," he said. His voice was low and cold.

Cassie got up from his lap and went to the couch. She held out her hand, and he gave her his handkerchief.

"I know," she said in a small voice. Then, "I'm seeing someone, too, sort of."

Angel perked up. New data. This could be interesting.

"Anyone I know?" he asked. Cassie didn't answer right away. "Rod? The Harvard Law School guy?"

Cassie nodded.

Shit. Rod. Angel had been jealous of him in high school. Rod had been a junior at Harvard trying to date a sixteen-year-old Cassie. In a fit of jealousy, Angel had camped outside Cassie's house one night while she was out with Rod. He had watched her kiss Rod good night and had burned with anger for days. Fucking Rod.

"He came to Smith. It was that snowy weekend you wanted me to come up to Dartmouth. He just showed up. We didn't do anything. We made out, and he felt me up, but that was all."

Angel checked for signs of jealousy, but he couldn't feel any rumbling around. He would have liked to deck Rod, but the fact that Cassie might have another guy didn't seem to elicit much of a reaction. He tried to picture Cassie in Rod's arms. Nothing.

He looked at Cassie, who sat on her legs and dabbed at her eyes. She was a mute bundle of misery, and he felt for her pain. This was hard. They had so much history. They knew every inch of each other's body and what lurked in every crevice of each other's mind.

"Angel, I love you, and I don't want to break up, tonight," she said. "Maybe it's good we won't see each other over Christmas. Maybe we need a break. Maybe it's even okay if we see other people." She stopped and looked at him. She chuckled. "Do you remember a girl named Rose Bird?" she asked. "She lives on Ortega Forest Drive?"

Angel shook his head.

"Well, she remembers you. She called me to ask if you and I were still dating. She wanted to ask you to escort her to the Christmas Eve Ball."

"What did you tell her?"

"I told her we were still a couple but that it would be okay. She goes to boarding school in Switzerland and doesn't know anybody here. I told her you'd be a good escort. She's a sweet girl. You'd like her. She's your type, too."

Angel smiled. "What's my type?"

"Smart."

"And you said it was okay if I take her to the Ball?"

"It's at Timuquana. Even you couldn't get in much trouble at a formal dance."

Angel shook his head angrily. "I'm lost in this conversation. You don't want to break up, but you think it might be okay if we see other people, and you pimp me out to some nerdy friend of yours?"

"Angel, I do love you, and I hope this all goes away, and we'll be just like we used to be. But I don't want to come up to Dartmouth any more, and I can't see you driving to Smith on a regular basis."

Angel stared at her. She was a perfect bundle of mixed messages. But she had played the trump card. It was against every rule of sexual warfare to break up with a girl who said she still loved you. Especially after sex. But there was something about what she said and the way she said it that really pissed him off. He felt even more trapped.

"Sweetheart," Angel said, "please don't take this the wrong way, but I think I need some fucking air."

Angel grabbed his coat and closed the door behind him. It felt symbolic. *Doll's House* symbolic. He strode past the doorman and turned north up Park Avenue towards Central Park in a snow which fell with more determination than it had earlier in the evening.

Fuck. So, he was still in a relationship. Except it wasn't really a relationship. He didn't know what the fuck he wanted to do or to say to Cassie. He knew there were no talismanic words which would whisk them back a year or two and magically restore their amity, but this seemed like no man's land. He could see the barbed wire which lay in either direction he might turn, and he could smell the sulfur of distant gunfire, but he had no clue which direction would make either him or Cassie happier. The male in him had hoped for a clean split. The female in Cassie had hoped for a romantic reconciliation.

They were both idiots.

The cold and the snow and the gas lamps around Central Park were soothing. They reminded him of Dartmouth, but he found himself patting the carriage horses again and mumbling nonsense, so he turned homewards where he nodded to the doorman and got in the elevator.

He crept into the bedroom, stripped, and climbed into the bed with Cassie who lay facing the wall, pretending to be asleep.

Shit.

Chapter Eleven

Christmas Eve, 1970
Rose
Setting: Hudson Pulp and Paper
Palatka, Florida

WHEN ANGEL CLOCKED OUT, JACKIE, RANDALL'S GORGEOUS secretary, smiled at him. He scratched his arm and smiled uneasily back at her.

Jackie was something like ten years older than Angel, and he had never seen her pay any attention to the men who slouched past her daily with their tongues hanging out. To get a smile from Jackie was an anomaly. Angel wondered what it meant.

Jackie curbed Angel's foul mood for the moment, but, when he got in his car and waited in line for the spray which washed the black-flaked chemicals off everyone's cars each day, his discontent returned with a vengeance.

He had worked in isolation all week, most of it in the lime kiln, a hellish cylinder ten feet in diameter and twenty feet tall, kept at a constantly cozy one hundred twenty degrees to keep the lime mushy soft. It was a shit job and Randall, the asshole bigot that he was, almost always made old black men work there. The lime was used for several purposes, all corrosive and dangerous. It was in the water which simultaneously kept the de-barking machine cool and softened the bark of the fifty-foot pine trunks which came in on flat-bed trucks. A crane dropped one wobbling log at a time on a belt which ran it through the howling de-barker and then through the wood-chipper. The noise the machines made was infernal, the de-barker snarling like a stuck chainsaw, and the wood-chipper crunching like Polyphemus splintering Greek bones with his molars.

The lime softened the wood and readied it for slaughter, and it had the same effect on human flesh. Angel wore a white set of coveralls complete with helmet and mask to protect his skin from the burning lime, but he knew it did little good.

By midnight, he would burn all over, and his eyes would feel as if pins were being driven into them.

Randall had put him there to punish him for his three-day Manhattan tryst with Cassie.

Angel minded the lime and the heat less than he did the isolation, for it kept Cassie and Maggie always on his mind. Being in hell seemed an apt metaphor, not a cliché, as Angel tormented himself all day.

He was hurting Cassie, and, if he didn't figure out things quickly, he would soon be hurting Maggie, too. He had become an accidental shit. He knew he couldn't help that he no longer felt for Cassie what he once had, but he couldn't escape the feeling that he was still culpable for her suffering. What was wrong with him? Was he incapable of sustaining love?

He reached the car spray and rolled up his windows. The black flakes were still snowing on his car, even as he washed them away. He left the roadway into the mill and turned north on Highway 17. Every other car turned south, towards Palatka.

He ran along Rice Creek for three miles, inhaling its miasmal murk, the residue of all the nasty chemicals it took to make paper, and crossed the bridge near where it flowed into and poisoned the St. John's River. The bridge was free of its usual fog, and he flew over it fearlessly for once.

Twenty miles later, just before Green Cove Springs, he slowed. His radar tingled. Something bad lay ahead. He rounded a curve and saw long black skid marks leading to deep furrows cut in the muddy clay of the road's shoulder. He pulled over and raced to where the marks disappeared. There, he saw a car lying on its side in a marshy ditch with smoke beginning to billow from its engine. The acrid vapor burned his already stinging eyes and nose as he fought through the ankle-deep muck to reach the car. The driver's window was smashed, and he hit it with an elbow several times until it fell inward on the unconscious driver. He reached across her and turned the engine off. A smaller figure in the passenger seat was crumpled against the dashboard. He couldn't tell if it was a boy or a girl through all the smoke. He pulled his pocket knife, cut the seat belt, and dragged the driver through the mud and onto the bank. She was covered in blood and barely breathing. He went back to the car to retrieve the child, but the car rolled further and slid into the water. He tried to clamber through the driver's side, but two arms grabbed him and pulled him backwards. Angel thrashed, trying to get free of the man's grip, but voices began screaming 'get away from the car.' The cop pulled Angel to the grassy bank where he lay trying to suck in oxygen. Smoke tore his lungs, and he thought he might choke to death, but then the vomit came, burning its way through his gullet and throat. He threw up and coughed until he felt better and looked about him. The scene had become nightmarish. Blue and red flashing lights formed a psychedelic strobe sequence in the swirling smoke.

A medic leaned over the woman Angel had pulled from the car.

"She's gone," he said.

Angel stood over her and tried to discern her features through her bloody mask. Shit. She was young, perhaps even a teenager. Angel tried to tell the officers about the child in the passenger's seat, but they pushed him away.

The car shifted again, and whatever hope Angel might have had for the motionless child disappeared as it sank deeper into the marsh.

He went back to his car and sat, hoping the cold air would help his tortured lungs. A policeman tapped on his window, and he rolled it down.

"Did you see the accident happen?" he asked.

Angel shook his head. "I just saw skid marks and followed them to the car. I don't know what happened."

The officer handed him a clipboard and a pen. "Write down your contact information in case we need to get in touch." Angel did as he asked and handed it back to him.

Angel started his car and drove in a funk. When he got home, he peeked into the living room. His mother was absorbed in a fat book and didn't even know he was there. He smiled. Probably *War and Peace*. She had finished *Anna Karenina* a few days earlier. Maybe she was on a Tolstoy kick.

He took off his sodden jeans and work boots. He peeled his tee shirt off slowly because his entire upper body burned from the lime and, perhaps, from the burning car's hot smoke.

For once, he took a tepid shower. He scrubbed lime from every part of him as best he could and then did it again. When he was as clean as possible, he turned the water to cold and stood shivering under it for a long time. His body shook, and he felt as if he were weeping, though he knew that was unlikely.

He went to his room and stared at his tuxedo ironically. Was he really going to a debutante ball with a girl he didn't know? It seemed too ghastly and ridiculous to be true.

But he polished his boots, dressed, combed his hair back with his hands, and looked in the mirror. An alien Angel stared back at him. An Angel of whom Cassie would approve.

His mother looked up and smiled when he went downstairs.

"Is it Halloween?" she asked.

"Ha ha," he said.

"Eat the sandwich in the kitchen. I don't want you drinking and driving on an empty stomach."

Angel nodded and grabbed the sandwich and a Coke from the refrigerator. He bit into it. Peanut butter and jelly with real blueberries in it.

"Thanks mom," he said. "Enjoy Tolstoy. I'm taking dad's Porsche."

"It's not Tolstoy. It's *Dombey and Son*," she said. "Have fun. Be nice to that girl."

Angel smiled and left. He had finally gotten her to pick Dickens back up again. She was in for a treat.

Angel pushed the starter button, and the little car roared to life. He got out and pulled the top down. He would see what Rose Bird thought of a convertible on a chilly night. With debutante hair at that. He smiled cruelly and put the car into first and pulled away.

Rose Bird. She said on the phone that they knew each other. Cassie had said so, too, but her name rang no bells.

When, however, he turned onto Ortega Forest Drive and approached her house, Angel knew exactly who she was. Rose was the girl who lay on her dock during sultry Jacksonville summers while Angel and all his friends ogled her as they rode by in his boat. Rose of the large breasts and lonely look. Something about her, even at fourteen (or was it younger), had stirred his imagination. In his mind, he had named her Mercedes, Edmond Dantes' lost love in *The Count of Monte Cristo*.

Shit. Rose Bird. He had never known her name. He liked it. Rose was easily as evocative as Mercedes. He needed to name one of his characters Rose. The ambiguous symbolism would practically spill off the page.

He pulled into Rose's driveway and went to the door. A Mediterranean looking woman answered the door and let him in.

"Miss Rose will be right down," she said. "Would you follow me, please?"

She led Angel down a corridor and into a library much like Cassie's in New York.

She poured Angel a drink from a pitcher and handed it to him. Angel nodded, and she left.

When he sipped the drink, he almost choked. It was a glass of straight gin. He couldn't even smell Vermouth in it. It fit his dour mood, however, so he drank it while perusing the book collection. Someone was into history, particularly English history. There must have been fifty books on the Tudors and nearly as many on the Jacobeans. There was also a newer looking collection of books on Enlightenment scientists.

Angel poured another drink and sipped. At this rate, he would be drunk before they even left. He had never been much of a drinker, anyway, and the day had left him vulnerable. He longed to smoke a joint, but he knew he probably shouldn't.

He heard a quiet voice say, "Some are my father's, and some are mine. Guess which are which?"

Angel turned, and there stood perhaps the most beautiful girl he had ever seen. She was petite, only a few inches over five feet tall without her heels, but she had lush black hair, high cheekbones, and the same overly generous breasts and hips he and his friends had taken to bed with them in their pubescent fantasies. Yes, he remembered Rose Bird.

"Hi, Rose," he said. "I'm Angel."

"I know. I remember you. Take a guess about the books."

Angel looked at the shelves again. "I'd say the history belongs to your father, and the science is yours."

"Very good. How did you reach that conclusion?"

Angel smiled at being quizzed. Usually, he was the interrogator. "The history books haven't been touched in a long time. The science books look as if they've been pulled and put back recently. They're in no discernible order, and there are little markers sticking out of the tops of the pages. Plus, there's one on the side table. Someone's been reading particle physics recently."

Rose smiled. Oh, God, that was unfair. Her smile made her look even lovelier.

"You go to school in Switzerland?" he asked.

"I did. I'm at London University now."

"And you're majoring in physics."

She laughed. "Yes, Physics and Math. You're just showing off now. So, mister mind-reader, am I a mechanical or theoretical physicist?"

Angel scoured the shelves for a clue. Then he looked closely at Rose. "Theoretical, definitely."

"Ah, and does that meet your approval?"

"It does."

"How did you glean that from those books and your rather intense scrutiny of my physiognomy?"

Physiognomy. Good word. He needed to be careful with this one.

"Well, you're far too beautiful to be a mechanical physicist. They all have little worry lines about their eyes, and they wear glasses."

She laughed again. "Cassie warned me that you are too smooth by half. That was wonderful. You gave me a compliment but cut it with humor and wit to make it seem less obvious."

"Hmmm. Okay. But, I cheated." He pointed to the books on the table. "Two books on Bosonic String Theory. Hardly a force and momentum thing to be interested in. I'll bet you're only interested in the things too small to even imagine and the things too large to comprehend."

Rose took his arm. "Just leave the glass here. Sophia will get it. I think this might be the most interesting evening I've had in a long time."

"Wait," he said, finishing his drink and setting it down. "Was I right?"

"I don't give away all my mysteries in the first five minutes," she said and led him out to his car.

"Oh," she said, walking around the Porsche, "A 356 Super Cabriolet. Nice. Are we going with the top down?"

Shit. She even knew cars. Was he in over his head?

"Is that okay with you?"

"I wouldn't have it any other way," she said.

Angel held the door for her.

Please let her have a flaw. Several, preferably. What was Cassie thinking? Was this a test?

Angel tore through the Ortega Forest Drive curves. Rose's hair flew, but she neither complained about his speed nor made a move to protect her hairdo.

Rose smiled. Angel smiled, too, and went back to watching the road.

A mind-reading vixen. Where do all these women hide when you're looking for them? When you're in a relationship, they appear everywhere. Maybe not this fine, but Wanda fine. Shit.

Angel eschewed the valet parking at the door of Timuquana. He didn't want anyone else mucking with his dad's manual transmission. Besides, Rose had tightened up as they drew near.

He parked, instead, by the swimming pool. They sat for a moment in the car.

"You don't want to go to this Ball, do you?" Angel asked.

"No. But Cassie told me you could get me through anything."

Angel laughed. "Cassie spoke well of me?"

Rose looked at him. "She said you were the best man she had ever met, and that I could trust you implicitly."

Wow.

"Angel, is something wrong between you and Cassie. She didn't say anything, but I could feel it. I've known her for a long time."

Angel was silent. Finally, he looked at Rose.

"I don't discuss Cassie with anyone," he said. "I don't mean to be rude."

"Good," she said definitively.

"Everything you say or ask seems like a test," he said smiling.

"Look who's talking," she laughed. "Can we drive with the top down?" she mocked. "Pretty transparent. I thought you might show up on your motorcycle."

"It's broken," he said. "So, Cassie has told you a lot about me."

"Only good things."

"Such as?"

"Fishing for compliments? Well, she said you are intuitively brilliant. She said you're amazing in bed."

"She didn't really say that."

"Well, are you?"

"Intuitively brilliant? Definitely."

"And the other?"

"That is both private and moot."

"Moot because I won't get the chance to know for myself?" she laughed.

"Well, that and because it's a matter of perception. Cassie might truly find me wonderful. You, with your European background, might find me *jejune* or worse."

Rose blushed but said nothing.

"Are you ready to go in?" he asked.

"Can we sit here awhile? It's dark, and the night sky is gorgeous."

"You have to go to this thing at some point," he said. "Aren't you being presented?"

"Yes," she said.

"And look how much effort they've put into this shindig. The place has never looked better."

It was true. Timuquana was an old-fashioned country club, white with columns out front and massive windows, and someone had wrapped the columns with greenery and red ribbons. Candles lit every window, and, when the front door opened, light and mingled sounds of music and laughter permeated the fine night.

"I've got something to relax you," he said and produced a joint. He raised an eyebrow, but Rose said nothing, so he lit it and inhaled. He leaned back with his face to the sky and handed it to her. Rose inhaled and held the smoke. When she let it go, she didn't choke or cough.

"Ah," he said. "You've done this before."

"Never," she said. Both laughed.

"Do you really remember me, Rose? From a few years ago? You used to lie on your dock in a tiny yellow bikini."

"I remember you. You and a bunch of boys used to water ski behind my house."

"I thought you were the most beautiful girl I'd ever seen," Angel said.

"Oh, God," Rose said. "I was so embarrassed when anyone saw me."

"Why?" he laughed.

"You try being a twelve-year old girl with giant breasts, which came in, by the way, when I was ten or eleven," she said. "It's awful. You feel like, I don't know. It seems like everyone's staring at your chest all the time, even the adults. Even your teachers. Boys make remarks. Your friends couldn't get enough of my body, and I heard their comments. Sound travels well over water."

"I'm sorry. They were idiots. I promise I wasn't staring at your chest."

"No," she said. "That's why I remember you. You seemed to me a young Keats or someone like that. You had a visionary look. You looked at me, too, and we made eye contact."

Angel laughed. "I'm not immune. I did notice your chest," he said. "And I heartily approved. I still do, and that dress you're wearing isn't helping."

Rose blushed and laughed. "It's my mother's," she said. "I was too cheap and lazy to go dress-shopping."

Angel smoked and closed his eyes. "I love when it gets cool like this. That's one of the best things about my college."

"Dartmouth?"

Angel looked at her. "Is there anything about me you don't already know?"

Rose looked at him seriously. "Plenty. I think you're one of those people who thinks he is an open book but never reveals anything personal. I'll bet you would die before you would discuss your emotions."

"See," he said. "You get me perfectly." He took the joint from her and stubbed it out. "Party time," he said.

Rose put her hand on his. "Wait," she said. "I've been wanting to say this since we got here, but it sounds a little weird." She paused.

"Just say it," he said.

She blushed. "Do you feel as if we've known each other a long time?" she said. "Do you know who Ram Dass is?"

"Baba Ram Dass? Of course, I do. He's my favorite yogi."

"Well, I believe in the whole 'old souls' thing. I know how that sounds, but I do." She stopped again.

"I know what you mean. Yes, I felt like we had a connection the minute I saw you. Before that, really. When I was driving up to your house, I felt it."

"Good."

"But, don't discount the pot or the martinis I had before we got here. That'll accelerate all the mystical stuff in our heads."

Rose laughed. "That it will. I'm stoned. Maybe I'm too stoned to go inside."

"Nope. Not getting out of this," he said and held her door open for her. "I have the solution for that, too."

Angel took her hand and led her to the locked gate of the pool. He showed her how to squeeze between the gate and the posts holding it.

Rose shook her head and laughed. "I'll never get my hips through that opening."

"Turn sideways."

"Then I'll never get my chest or butt through. This isn't going to work. I'll tear up my mother's dress."

"Wow," he said. "You sure are whiny. I had you pegged for a badass. Oh, well. Guess I'll just go by myself," and he began to walk towards the pool.

"Okay," she laughed. "You win. *Merde.*" Rose tried to see which way she would fit more easily and ended up holding her breasts flat with her hands and sliding through sideways. She got stuck midway, and Angel took an arm and helped her.

"Oh, to be your hands a minutes ago," he said wistfully.

"I thought you weren't going to make me self-conscious about my chest," she laughed.

"Just making an innocent comment," he smiled. He took her hand and walked her around the pool and to the rail overlooking the St. John's.

"I love this view of downtown," he said. They gazed northwards towards the Jacksonville skyline and the bridges which delineated the curve of the river. Lights sparkled and reflected in the shimmering water.

Angel put an arm around her waist and pointed to the right. It was darker there, and the stars multiplied almost infinitely in the southern sky.

"See that red light?" he asked.

"Yes," she said.

"That's the Naval Air Station. When my friends and I weren't skiing and scoping out hot brunettes in yellow bikinis, we used to cut through a fence not far from here and race cars and motorcycles on an abandoned airstrip."

"No, you didn't," Rose laughed.

"Yep. That red light is about seven miles away. Everything between here and there is runway. I used to kick ass in drag races because my motorcycle was so quick off the line. I even beat TJ Rowden's Corvettes."

"Is that the bike which burned Cassie's leg?"

"Damn, girl, you know too much. No, that was a different bike."

He became quiet. Rose sensed his mood shifting and nestled against him to fight the chilly river air.

"I love that you didn't wear a coat," Angel said. "You've got to be freezing."

"It gets just a wee bit colder in Switzerland," she said. "And this would be a warm London night even in the summer."

Angel stared at the red light.

Rose tugged at Angel's sleeve. She could tell that his mind was elsewhere. "Hey," she said. "Where did you go just now?"

Angel didn't say anything for a long time. Then, he pointed south again. "Farther down the river, about twenty miles past that light, I saw a woman die today."

Rose sucked in her breath. She looked at him to see if he was kidding, and she put a hand on his chest.

"Her car veered off the road. I don't know why. She had a child in the passenger seat. Perhaps the child distracted her, or a raccoon or something else ran into the road. I don't know. But she slid off the road and into a ditch. I think she hit a stump or something, because the front of the car was mushed in, and the engine caught fire."

"Oh, my God. That's terrible. What did you do?"

"I tried to save her. I waded through swamp mud to get to her. I felt as if I was sinking, and I kept slipping, like in a bad dream, but I got her door open and pulled her out. The smoke from the engine was pretty fierce, and I could smell burning oil. I thought the car was going to go up in flames. It was pretty intense."

Rose gripped his arm.

"I carried her to the bank. She was covered in blood, and I think she must have already been dying by the time I got to her. I went back and tried to get the child, but the car was sinking. Then policemen dragged me away."

Rose touched his face. She could feel his pain.

"I tried to save them, but I couldn't. I was useless."

Rose pulled him to her and held him.

He gazed at her intently as if wondering who she was. Then, he slowly bent his face to hers and kissed her. It was a soft kiss, but a real one. He held her face in his and looked long at her.

"I'm sorry," he said. "I didn't mean to do that."

Rose raised her face to his. Her half-closed eyes said 'kiss me again.' Angel could see and smell her breath in the cold, clear air. It smelled as sweet as she had tasted.

And he pulled her to him and kissed her again. His arms encircled her tiny waist, and he could feel her breasts crushed against him. He automatically slid a hand down over the curve of her flaring hip but caught himself and put it back on her waist. He could feel himself getting hard. Shit. Down boy. She's not yours, and you already have enough trouble. But hot damn, girl.

"You taste good," he said smiling.

"You do, too," she said.

Angel pulled her to his chest and wrapped his arms around her. Rose sighed and clung to him.

Angel could feel the familiar heaviness coming over him, and Thor was still swelling, so he took her hand and walked her soundlessly up the steps towards the back of the club. He held a chair for her on the patio just outside a partially darkened room.

Angel took off his jacket and wrapped it around her shoulders. "I'll be right back," he said and disappeared inside. He returned a moment later followed by a tall, stooping black man.

"Rose," Angel said. "This is Train. Train, this is Rose."

Train and Rose shook hands.

"What are you doing with trash like this one, Rose?" Train asked.

"I had to come to this dance, and I didn't know anyone else," she said. "Beggars can't be choosers."

Train laughed. "What can I get for you two?"

"Coffees, please," Angel said. He looked at Rose who nodded. "Sugar and cream and…"

"I know," Train said. "A big ole pile of sugar, real cream, and some chocolate syrup to make sure he can't even tell there's any coffee in his mug. How do you take yours, Rose?"

"Black," she said.

"Uh huh," Train chuckled and walked away. "You in way over your head, Angel."

Angel smiled wryly and tapped his fingers on the table.

"You're gone again," Rose said.

"Sorry. I've been kind of a mess, lately."

Rose laughed and put her hand on his. "This is you as a mess? You barely have a pulse, Mr. Mellow."

Angel looked at her. "I'm sorry I kissed you. You didn't ask me to escort you so you could be kissed or groped."

Rose smiled sadly at him.

"Angel, don't you dare ruin that kiss with some Cassie guilt or anything else. That may have been the most romantic moment of my life. You told me your story about trying to save those people, and I felt your sadness. Then we kissed, and I felt your joy, your soul."

Angel smiled sheepishly. "It was a pretty nice kiss," he said.

"Pretty nice. Wow, you are so good for a girl's ego."

"Rose, I don't have to tell you anything about that kiss. You were there, too. You know how it felt."

"Now, if you'll just try the groping part, I can decide if I like you or not," she said.

"Ahem," Train said and put a tray down with a pitcher of coffee, sugar, cream, chocolate, and a pair of spoons. He handed a napkin to Rose and another to Angel. "Look at me, boy," he said to Angel. "You don't be groping that girl on my watch. It's not proper, and, besides, she's major league and you're single A. You deep in the minor leagues. You won't never even get a call-up to bat against that kind of quality. Don't make me get riled up."

"Thanks, Train," Rose smiled. She put a hand on his arm. "But I think I can handle this one."

"Begging your pardon, Rose, but lots of girls think they can handle this one." He eyed her severely. "But I guess you can take care of yourself. If he gets too frisky, you just call Train, okay?"

Rose nodded.

Angel beckoned to Train who leaned over. Angel handed him a fat joint and said, "Merry Christmas." Train smiled and walked away. He pointed to Angel and nodded his 'I got my eye on you' look.

"I like him," Rose said.

"I do, too," Angel said. "Train's kind of an artist. He's a master psychologist, and he's a good man."

Rose stared and shook her head as she watched Angel fix his coffee.

"Okay, Miss Smarty-pants," he said. "Taste this before you judge me." He held his cup for her to sip. Their eyes met and Angel felt the urge to kiss her sweep over him again. Rose's eyes widened. She could tell. Perhaps she felt it, too.

She sipped. "Oh, my God," she said. "That's really good."

"Right?"

Rose laughed and began to spoon sugar into her coffee. Angel poured a dollop of syrup, and she stirred. She sipped it and purred.

"You wanted to kiss me a moment ago, didn't you?" Rose smiled.

"Nope. Never crossed my mind."

Rose laughed. "All right. What should we talk about?"

"*Me parle de la Suisse*," he said.

Rose frowned. "*Non.*"

"*Pourqoui pas?*"

"*J'etais malheureux la plupart du temps.*"

"*Quel dommage*," Angel said.

They grew silent at that.

Rose bowed and nodded. She looked up brightly. "I spied on you one time."

He smiled. "When?"

"That summer of the yellow bikini. One day you and a friend anchored your boat in that little curve of woods next to my house."

"What did we do?" he asked.

"You shot a rifle at a big pile of driftwood in the bend of the river."

"I remember that. There was a nest of Water Moccasins."

"Did you kill them?"

Angel laughed. "I don't think so. It seemed as if we hit some, but they just slithered into the water. There was a roiling mass of angry snakes all around the boat."

"Right next to my dock?"

Angel nodded. "That's why we were shooting, to protect that lovely yellow bikini from harm."

Rose smiled and leaned back, sipping her coffee.

"I think you need to kiss me again," she said. "I've decided that you are a romantic devil."

"Not going to happen," he said with a smile.

"We'll see."

"If you won't tell me about Switzerland or why you were so *malheureux* there, tell me about your family. Why did they send you to Switzerland?"

"Ugh, that's an even worse topic. My father is a serial philanderer and, if you listen to my mother, either schizophrenic or manic depressive. I haven't seen or talked to him in nearly eight years. Mommy Dearest, on the other hand, is a standard issue drunken bitch who loves to ruin anything good which might come her way."

"Wow."

"Yeah, wow," she laughed. "You asked. God, I'm such a downer. Let me think of something more uplifting. Okay. I began taking piano lessons when I was four. I got to be quite good."

"Do you still play?"

She laughed and blushed. "No, I quit."

"Me, too."

"You, too, what?"

"I played hours a day until I was eighteen. I gave a big concert with another guy from Tallahassee. Huge crowd, the whole deal. I quit, cold, the next day."

"Why?"

"Just burned out. I can't explain it."

"That's exactly my story. I was at Miss Porter's School. That's how I know Cassie. We'd never met here. I went to Switzerland in tenth grade and played piano like a maniac. I think it was my whole social and sex life, or something. Then, boom. I just couldn't do it anymore."

Angel contemplated Rose. He was still hard and had given up trying to convince Thor to go back to sleep. Cassie had to have known he would react this way. Was she testing him? If so, he would pass, sort of. He wasn't going to do anything with Rose, but he sure would have loved to. Shit.

Angel took a long sip and set his cup down. "Would Milady dance with me? I have to warn you, I'm not very good."

"Milady would," she said and rose. She presented her hand to him, and he escorted her inside.

As they opened the door, the music and happy pandemonium hit them all at once. It was a Gatsby-esque world of sights and sounds. There were tipsy old people thrilled to be around the young folk, and there were fifty bright, shiny debutantes with their penguin-suited escorts. It seemed as if Rose and Angel were the only sober people there.

They wove through laughing couples on their way to the dance floor. The band was Question Mark and the Mysterians, and they had just finished playing *96 Tears*. The crowd was going wild. Girl after girl hugged Angel and whispered something in his ear as he and Rose passed.

A slow song began, and Angel put an arm around Rose's waist and offered her his other hand. She laughed at him and threw both arms around his neck. He sighed and encircled her birdlike waist. His hands rested on her hips. Rose kissed him on the neck and buried her head against his chest.

Then she looked up at him and raised her face to his ear. He bent to hear what she was saying.

"Do you know every girl here?" she said.

Angel smiled and shook his head.

"But you've dated several of them?"

Angel surveyed the dance floor. "Most of them," he said.

"And how many have you slept with?"

Angel laughed. "Most of them, including their mothers and fathers. Why are you so interested?"

She pressed against him. "Because it feels as if you'd like to sleep with me, too," she said.

"You're not making this easy," Angel said.

"Oh, am I making it hard?"

He slapped her on the butt. "You behave."

"I'm just teasing. I know you're still with Cassie and wouldn't dream of cheating on her. But a girl can tease a boy, can't she?" And she ran a hand across the front of his trousers.

Angel slapped her hand and pointed a finger at her. "You're a very bad girl," he said. "I'm going to get drinks for us. Is a daiquiri okay?"

Rose nodded. She blew a kiss at him as he made his way back through the throng of revelers.

As he stood in line at the bar, Angel took stock of his situation. Why did this keep happening to him? He watched Rose reply politely to an old couple who cornered her. Train was right. Rose was way out of his league. So was Cassie, but at least Cassie wasn't *Playboy* centerfold material. He got Rose's daiquiri and a Coke for himself and worked his way back towards her. She had disappeared, and Angel stopped and looked around for her. He saw her surrounded by a group of boys. She looked distinctly uncomfortable. Angel pushed through the crowd, elbowing a boy aside and handed her the daiquiri. He nodded at the boys and took her hand to lead her away.

"Goodbye Rose," a pimply faced boy with curly hair said. And to Angel, "I don't know you, but have fun playing with those knockers."

Angel turned back. Rose put a hand on Angel's shoulder. "Don't, Angel." But she was too late. Cassie and the lime kiln and the dead woman all coalesced in his head, and something snapped.

"What did you say to her?" he asked Pimples.

"Take a chill pill. I just said she has great melons. I mean, duh, look at her. Like you haven't been planning on milking those babies all night."

"Please, Angel," Rose said.

And Angel tried. He really did.

"Apologize to Rose," Angel said. "Right now. Get down on your fucking knees and thank her for allowing you to breathe the same fucking air as her. Do it now shit-for-brains."

"Fuck you," Pimples said. His friends edged closer to Angel, forming a semi-circle.

Angel eyed them and smiled. "I'm sorry, Rose," he said. He handed her his Coke and lunged for Pimples, grabbing him by the throat and shoving him backwards until he hit a wall, hard. Angel squeezed his throat and pulled his hair back until he faced the ceiling. Pimples put his hands to Angel's wrist, but Angel choked him until he began to gurgle and flail. One of his friends grabbed Angel's shoulder and tried to pull him away.

"Don't you ever disrespect Rose or any other fucking girl that way. Ever. Not in your whole fucking pathetic life. Do you understand me?" He shook Pimples like a dog with a rat in its jaws. Pimples' eyes bulged and snot ran from his nose. The boy behind Angel grabbed his shoulder and tried again to get him to let Pimples go. Angel released Pimples, who slid to his butt and put his hands to his throat. Angel turned to the boy with the hand on his shoulder and hit him in the stomach. Another boy stepped forward yelling "Hey" or something equally inane, and Angel hit him square in the face. He felt a pair of arms encircling him and tried to shrug them off. He turned to dislodge himself and raised a fist, but it was Train who held him.

"We going outside, Angel," Train said in his deep, soothing voice. "Going to get some fresh air with the lady."

Angel looked around. Rose was gone. Shit. The old people were talking to each other in hushed, shocked tones. Angel allowed Train to pull him through the front door and onto the lawn where Angel panted and tried to slow his mind down. Rose appeared from somewhere and put her arms around Angel. Mutely, the two followed Train across the street and into the caddy shack.

There, Train pulled the joint from his pocket and waved it in front of Angel, like a hypnotist with a watch. He tore a match from a matchbook and scratched it across the bottom. A flame shot up, and Angel smelled the sulfuric stench he lived in at the paper mill.

"Nobody's going to bother us in here," Train said. He inhaled deeply. "Mmm. Mighty fine." He passed it to Rose who inhaled while still watching Angel.

Angel took a hit of the joint and passed it back to Train. He removed his coat and pulled off his bowtie. "I'm okay," he said. He looked at Rose. "I'm so sorry, Rose. I just..." he trailed off and shrugged.

Rose put her arms around him and pulled his face down and kissed him. "My hero."

"What you hit those stupid boys for?" Train asked. "You don't remember what it feels like to be a boy virgin? It's humiliating."

"They said stuff about Rose's chest," Angel said.

"So?" Train said. "No offense, Rose, but you got a remarkable bosom, and that dress don't hide much at all."

Rose smiled. "No offense taken."

"See? She's cool. What's wrong with you, boy? How do you think I'd be, a black man at this lily-white club, if I took offense every time someone said something, especially something true? Look at that girl you with? Look at her? What you think those boner boys see when they look at her? They just a pile of hormones. Angel, you admit to me right now that you see exactly what those boys see?"

"Boner boys, huh?" Angel said, and everybody laughed. Angel looked at Rose. "You want the truth, Train? I think Rose is the most beautiful woman I've ever seen."

"And you almost killed that boner boy for seeing the same thing you and I see. No offense, Rose."

Rose shook her head. She wrapped her arm around Angel's. "Leave him alone, Train. I think he was being sweet."

"Sweet? That boy going to talk like Louis Armstrong for a month. Shit, sweet."

"Train," Angel said. "Smoke the joint and shut the fuck up. You've made your point. I may have over-reacted a tad."

Train shook his head and smoked the joint. He looked at the smoke rising from the reddened tip. "This is some good shit."

They all laughed again.

"Can we go home, Angel?" Rose asked.

"You most certainly cannot go home," Train said. "I done too many of these things. You have to march back in there and stand in that line they make when they introduce you. And you gotta smile."

"I can't do that, Train."

"Uh huh, yes you can. You just stand up there and smile and think to yourself, 'I'm with the craziest motherfucker on the planet. You don't like it, stuff it. Pardon my French."

"Do I have to?" Rose laughed.

"Yep. Now, come on. I'll take you back inside. I expect Angel needs to wait at his car. They're not used to his type of excitement in this club."

And Train led a still protesting Rose back inside for her debut.

Angel shook his head and finished the joint. He put his coat back on and stuffed his tie in a pocket. He wandered down the eighteenth fairway, dodging sprinklers and contemplating the stars.

He pondered his plight. He wasn't worried about tearing into Pimples. His father would get a nasty letter from the club threatening to terminate his membership, and his father would laugh and tear it up. His father didn't suffer fools too well. And, besides, at the paper mill or at Dartmouth, a fight to protect your woman would be expected, not frowned upon.

But he was worried about Cassie and Maggie. His instant attraction for Rose showed him just how susceptible he was to falling for women. He needed a long time-out, someplace without any women, so he could think things through. He walked behind the caddy shack and past the tennis courts. A car swooped by, its lights breaking his solitude. He waited for it to pass and crossed the road. He went to his car and sat. He turned on the radio and leaned the seat back. It had been a long day, and he could feel the lime burning his throat and his eyes.

Boom Boom Boom Boom by the Animals came on the Big Ape, the Mighty 690, and it lifted his spirits.

He saw a shadowy figure cutting across the lawn and wending her way around the trees. He could tell, even in silhouette, that it was Rose.

She quietly opened her door and sat beside him.

"That was quick," he said. "So, now you've officially made your debut?"

"No, I waited until Train wasn't watching and snuck out. I wanted to be with you."

Something stuck in Angel's throat. Shit.

She leaned across and kissed him softly.

He clicked the radio off, and they drove home in silence.

At her door, she put her hands on his chest and leaned against him. "You won't come inside, will you?" she asked.

Angel smiled and shook his head.

"Because of Cassie?" she asked.

Angel shook his head. "No. Because of you."

"Are you intimating that I am so charming and irresistible that you don't dare be alone with me?" she asked.

Angel laughed. "That is exactly what I'm intimating." He kissed her. "Goodbye, Rose Bird. It was a pleasure meeting you."

Rose smiled. "You are not stupid or naïve enough to think that this is over, are you?"

Angel smiled. No, he wasn't.

"I'm going to write you, Angel, and I want you to write back."

Angel began to demur, but Rose put a finger on his lips. "That wouldn't be cheating on Cassie," she said.

"All right," he said. His voice was hoarse.

"Good night, Angel, and I don't care what Train said. It was thrilling to watch you hurt that boy. I was serious out on the deck. This may have been the most romantic night of my life, and I thank you for that."

She stood on her tip-toes and held his face in her hands as she kissed him. She dropped her right hand and ran it across the front of his pants.

"I told you I'd make this hard for you," she said. She blushed at her boldness and disappeared inside.

Angel went to the Porsche and sat in silence, contemplating Rose's house. Was she watching him through a window? He blew a kiss towards the house, just in case she was. Merry Christmas, Rose.

He sighed and stared straight up into the heavens.

Thank you, oh Lord, for this amazing life, but why do you test me so?

He shook his head and pushed the starter button. He put the Porsche in gear and released the clutch.

He was pretty sure he could feel Rose's eyes on him as he drove off.

Thor made sure Angel knew that he was disappointed with the way the evening ended.

Fuck you, Thor. Go to sleep.

But he smiled as he drove away.

Chapter Twelve

Saturday January 9, 1971
Angel at the Clavier
The White Mountains, New Hampshire

ANGEL'S MIND FELT AS LABYRINTHINE AS THE ROUTE THE
pick-up truck had taken from Mt. Moosilauke to the foot of the trail. He gazed
around him but had no idea where Moosilauke was.

As he, Medlin, and the four newbies (two of whom who were obviously freshman and two older, tougher looking co-eds) bounced around in the bed of the truck,
Angel tried to make sense of his last talk with Cassie.

She had called just after he had gotten home from dropping off Rose.

"Merry Christmas, Angel," Cassie chirped. She always chirped when trying to
feign high spirits. Cassie was nervous calling him. The wonder of that simple fact
boggled the mind.

"Hi, Sweetheart," Angel said. "Merry Christmas. I was just thinking about you."

"I've been thinking about you non-stop for three months."

Angel laughed. "No, you've been pissed at me for three months. That's not the
same. I was thinking nice things about you. I was trying to imagine what you were
doing."

"What did you decide?"

"I decided you were asleep on your side, clutching a pillow the way you do when
I sneak out of bed to read or write. You had your face almost tucked into it and a
half-smile was playing on your lips."

"No, silly. I was chewing my fingernails, trying not to call you."

"Why would you resist calling me?" Angel asked. But he knew the answer.

"Didn't you go to Timuquana with Rose?" she asked.

He knew it. He smiled bitterly. This was a spy call, to see if he was out late, or, if he did answer, whether he sounded guilty.

"I did. I was irked that I had to be sociable tonight. I had a terrible day and really didn't want to go, but I'm glad I did."

"What did you think of Rose?"

Hmmm…Cassie sounded coy.

"I really liked her, but it's tough going from you to Rose."

"I know. She has breasts, and I don't."

"No," Angel laughed. "That's not what I meant, and you know it. I meant it's humbling going from one girl who is smarter than I am to another."

"Ah, yes, Angel's famous low self-esteem. How do you manage to survive with such a low watt brain?" she laughed.

"I love it when you mock me."

"And why is that?"

"That's when I know we're okay. We used to crack each other up. We haven't laughed much for a long time."

Bad move. He could almost feel her growing somber across the phone line.

"Did you get my Christmas present?" she asked.

"It's under the tree."

"Go get it," she said. "I want to know if you like it."

Angel set the phone down and went to the living room. He returned with the package. Its size and shape offered no clue as to what was in it. He shook it gently. It was light, and nothing jiggled.

"I'm back. Opening it now. Pretty paper," he said.

Under the paper was a white box with a Cartier stamp. He cut the scotch tape with a fingernail and opened it. Inside lay a porcelain figurine.

"Don Quixote?" he asked.

"Uh huh. It reminded me so much of you. I remember what you told me when I asked what the book was about, beneath the silly misadventures and all."

Angel smiled. Only Cassie would use the word 'misadventure.' "I said Don Quixote was trying to put beauty and truth back into a world which had lost both."

"That's you, Angel."

Angel was silent. That was the first nice thing Cassie had said to him in months, other than 'oh my God' during lovemaking or some other purely involuntary compliment. This was one she had planned.

"Angel, I know you think my father and I scoff at your plan to be a teacher, and maybe he does, but I don't. I know that you read your great books and want others to see their beauty and their power. I read them, too. I know how much they offer. I love your idealism, your Don Quixote side. It's part of why I love you. You do things that hurt me, or, at least, I imagine that you do. But I have faith in you. I have faith in us."

Angel was silent. In class, he had offered up the great comic novels of all time and had forgotten *Don Quixote*. His professor had to bring Cervantes up. Maybe he was smoking too much.

And her 'faith' line sounded dangerously evocative. Cassie didn't repeat words gratuitously.

"What do you imagine my doing that hurts you?" he asked quietly.

"Well, for instance, tonight. I pictured you doing things with Rose."

"Ha," he laughed. "You set me up on that date and then fantasized evil things. You are seriously warped. Why would you talk Rose into inviting me if you thought something might happen? Were you testing me? Pretty lame research plan if you were. Forget about my weaknesses. You can't have thought Rose would have sex with me. First, she knows you, and second, she just wouldn't."

"Actually," she laughed, "it was out of pique. I only suggested she ask you because I was so angry with you. I was thinking 'fine, go do whatever you want. I don't care.' And, while I trust Rose, I knew how much she would like you. She does, doesn't she?"

"I don't know."

"Liar," Cassie laughed. "Rose found you smart and sexy and romantic, didn't she?"

Something in Cassie's cavalier attitude about his supposed infidelity whispered to him that Cassie wasn't telling him something.

Shit.

Angel began to laugh, "Cassie, you called Rose, didn't you? You've already talked to her."

"Maybe," she said.

"Uh huh, what did she tell you? Did she tell you about the fight?"

"Fight? No. What fight?" she asked. "She just said that I'm lucky and that you're adorable."

"Adorable, huh?"

"Yes, and that she kissed you. She made sure to emphasize that she was at fault. She was unnecessarily adamant on that last point."

Angel smiled. So, Rose covered for him, but Cassie knew what Rose was doing. Women were so devious.

"Did you tell her 'stay away from my man' or something of that ilk?" Angel asked.

"No," Cassie laughed. "I told her 'God help you.' Kissing you is like entering Dante's *Inferno*. You can't go back. But tell me about this fight."

Angel sighed. "It was nothing. A group of boys insulted Rose. They made crude remarks about her chest. I stopped them."

"So, there wasn't really a fight?"

"Well, I stopped them abruptly."

"Abruptly," Cassie laughed. "Did you hit anyone?"

"Not really. Well, two guys, and I choked one guy pretty thoroughly. It wasn't much. Train got me out of there before I could do too much damage."

"I'll bet that went over beautifully at a deb party. You are too much. Are they still punishing you at the paper mill for going to Manhattan with me?"

"Yeah, I was in the lime kiln for three days. I can't breathe, my eyes burn, I itch all over, and I have pretty bad headaches, but it's not that bad."

Cassie was quiet. "I'm sorry, Angel. I wish I was there with you right now. I give good scratches. I'll bet a back scratch and a head rub would soothe your mind."

"That would be amazing," he murmured. "Is this a new tack? You're not going to tell me to stop working at the mill?"

"No, sweetheart," she said quietly. "I know it's important to you. I know working there makes you feel, I don't know…"

"Cleansed," he said.

Cleansed. That was what he was doing in the back of the pick-up truck in the middle of the White Mountains. He was going to clear trails for the Dartmouth Outing Club, something he hadn't done since his freshman year, and he was going to get away from Cassie and Maggie and Rose and Jane and Wanda and every tempting woman on the planet. He was going to let his mind clear in the cold air. Where better to do a monastic retreat than the remote cabin he would doubtless hike to? He and Cassie had stayed in several of the DOC cabins dotting the mountainside, and now he would work so that other lovers might do the same.

The trucked jolted to a stop, and Angel and the others climbed out. The temperature couldn't have been much above zero, and Angel was frozen. He stamped his boots on the packed surface, trying to force blood to his feet.

"Where are we?" a lost-looking freshman asked.

"Moosilauke is that way," Medlin pointed.

Angel looked. How did Medlin know that? His internal compass must be a shitload better than Angel's.

"What's Moosilauke?" a co-ed named Helen asked.

"It's that big lodge we left from," Medlin said.

"Duh," the girl said. "I know that. I mean what's its significance? Everyone speaks as if it's Valhalla."

"It is," Angel laughed. "All new students have to take a freshman trip, and they all finish at Moosilauke. The college president greets them and tells them a ritual series of ghost stories."

"We didn't have anything like that at Bryn Mawr," the other girl said.

"I thought you guys had all kinds of rituals," Medlin said.

"We do, just not anything like that. We don't own half a state the way Dartmouth does. There's a largeness about your rituals. The Homecoming bonfire, for example. I came up last year. It's hundreds of feet tall."

Angel smiled. The 'mythy mind.' Who said that? It was true, though. He felt often as if he were just following some arcane set of Dionysian rules designed for males.

The guy driving the truck opened the tool box and everyone grabbled an implement of destruction. Medlin was given a long, sharp pole. He had the most experience and would lead the expedition, stabbing the snow, trying to ascertain where the oft invisible path lay. Angel would follow with an ax, chopping asunder small trees which had fallen across the path and hacking away underbrush. The other four wielded snow shovels. They would do the arduous task of clearing the snow from the path.

A long, high cross between a shriek and a growl echoed dimly through the trees.

"What's that?" one of the freshmen asked.

"That's the big boys," Angel said. "They're on snowcats. They bad-ass around looking for potential avalanche drifts. Sometimes, they even initiate one to clear the side of a mountain. Those are the guys who know these mountains as intimately as you two freshman putzs know your dicks."

Everyone gazed in the direction of the growling, and then Medlin began excavation of the path, prodding the snow in front of him for rocks or tree trunks. The snow was almost waist high, so the going was slow.

It took them four hours to reach the cabin. The women were red-faced but glowed with health. The freshman boys were done in.

"I can't lift my arms," one groaned.

"Tough shit," Medlin said with a smile. "Now, you get to split all those logs." He pointed to a massive pile.

The freshman sat on the steps of the cabin. "I can't," he said. "I tell you, I'm dying."

Angel laughed. "He's kidding. You four get to walk back down and catch a ride back to Moosilauke. Medlin and I will chop all that shit and repair whatever needs repairing in the cabin. All so you little crapweasels can pay three bucks and bring your home-town honeys up here."

Helen stood up. "All right, then. Let's head back down."

"Can't we rest for a while?" the boy asked.

"Sure, if you want to help chop wood," Medlin said.

The boy hopped up. "No," he said. "I'm good." He and Helen began down the path, and the other two wearily followed.

Medlin and Angel had stripped to their shirts and gloves as they worked their way up the hillside, but now, chilling, Medlin put his coat back on. He reached in his pack and produced a flask. He took a swig and handed it to Angel. "Irish whiskey," he said.

Angel took it gratefully. It burned down his throat. "I'll start splitting these logs. You check the cabin. It looks pretty sound to me."

Medlin took the flask back and sipped. "You don't remember me, do you?"

"I know I should, but I don't."

"Dave Medlin. Freshman trip. You went to Boston with me for that Led Zeppelin concert."

"Shit. The one where the bikers and college kids got into it down below us."

"Yeah," Medlin said. "Beating each other with folding chairs and everything. That was great."

"Johnny Winter was playing the opening set."

"Yeah, and his brother Edgar was with him."

"You took me to a party in a barn," Angel said. "A chick tried to seduce me. I almost did her, but I kind of thought you liked her, so I backed off. I'd forgotten. She was hot. What was her name?"

"Kathleen."

"That's right. Kathleen. I remember those wild, green eyes. Shit. Did you ever date her?"

"I was dating her, then. We broke up last week. That's why I'm up here, with you, chopping crap."

"You were dating her then?" Angel smiled. "Guess it's a good thing I didn't do her."

"Yeah. You might have saved me three years of shit if you had. She was always doing stuff like that, driving me crazy on purpose."

"Sorry I didn't recognize you. You look a lot different," Angel said.

Medlin laughed. "Forty pounds and a full beard. That'll do it. My mother pretends she doesn't know who I am."

Medlin put the flask in his pocket, picked up his pack, and went inside.

Angel hefted the ax and set up a log to split. He hadn't done this in years. He hoped he was still good at it. His first chop was accurate but tentative. The ax buried into the log and stuck there, but the log didn't split. Angel swung again, smashing the log down on the stump. It split cleanly. Nice. He took his coat back off and breathed in the cold, clean air. Through the trees, he could see the tips of several mountains. He could tell from the sun that he faced east. It was good that he had a view. There would be a full moon that night, and it would rise majestically over a peak. Off to the left, he saw smoke drifting from a hillside. Someone must have made it to that cabin. He could smell smoke, so he knew Medlin had lit their fire. Good. Angel couldn't light a fire to save his life. Literally.

Angel's second pass at a log was perfect. He split it all the way through and tossed the halves on the beginning of a pile.

Medlin joined him.

"Found another ax inside," he said. "The cabin is fine. I lit a fire and saw the smoke hauling ass towards a crevice, so I patched it. Everything else seems fine."

"You might want to check the roof," Angel said. Medlin nodded and climbed from the railing onto the roof over the porch. From there, he crawled onto the main roof and walked it, kicking away piles of snow. He nodded to Angel that it was cool and climbed back down. He took off his jacket and began to split wood alongside Angel. He was better at it and worked considerably faster. Angel didn't take breaks, though, so, after an hour or so, their accumulated piles were pretty equal.

They worked in silence. The rhythmic thunk of the axes hitting wood was company enough. The syncopated cadence of the clonks was jazz-like and fed their meditative moods.

Angel smiled at the burning in his back and shoulders. He would hurt for a week after this. It felt unbelievably good.

The sun began to sink, and the chopping became dangerous. When neither man could raise the ax above his shoulders, Medlin signaled for them to quit.

The two looked at each other and smiled. The stack they had split was impressive.

"I'm glad I didn't bang your girl," Angel said.

"Me, too," Medlin said. "I would've killed you, and then I'd of had to chop all this by myself."

They began carrying armloads to the porch and stacking it so lovers would have firewood for the winter.

"What do you figure?" Angel asked. "Another couple of hours in the morning?"

"Shit," Medlin said. "We've probably got enough done for the whole winter, but a couple of hours tomorrow would make sure."

Angel nodded. He cleaned his ax with an oiled rag from the toolbox on the porch and put it away. Inside, he dragged a chair in front of the fire and flopped in it.

Medlin fished through his backpack and pulled out a tin with sandwiches in it.

"I've got a whole pizza," Angel said. "You can have half if you can figure out how to heat it up. It's kind of folded and mushed, but it should be tasty."

Medlin pulled an iron skillet off the wall and showed it to Angel. Angel nodded. That would probably do. He groaned when he got out of the chair to get the pizza. He unloaded books, a notebook, and a bottle of rum onto the table. The pizza was on the bottom, and it, indeed, was squished. But Medlin straightened it out. He picked cheese off the Reynolds Wrap and put it back on the pizza. He licked his fingers and held the skillet over the fire. When the cheese and tomato sauce began to bubble, he removed it and the two men ate.

"You were dating a girl back then," Medlin said. "A hometown honey."

"Cassie," Angel said, munching on pizza.

"Whatever happened to her?"

"We're having problems, but we're sort of together."

"That's too bad. If we'd done this before I broke up with Kathleen, we could have traded."

Angel laughed. He remembered Kathleen. That might've been fun.

"So, what's this problem's name?" Medlin asked.

Angel looked at him. "Problem?"

"If you and Cassie are fighting, you probably have another chick, or she has another guy," Medlin said.

Angel nodded and chewed. He didn't think Rob was a 'problem.' Mostly because he didn't even feel a flicker of jealousy when he thought of Cassie with Rob. But Maggie--that was different.

"Maggie," Angel said finally. "She goes to Colby."

"Maggie," Medlin repeated. "Margaret, maybe? I know a bunch of Mary Margarets. Is she Catholic?"

"I don't know," Angel said. "I really don't know much about her at all."

"It's not about knowing things about them, is it?" Medlin said. "It's about having them stuck in your head all the time. It's about thinking about them when you don't want to, like when you're studying or sleeping, or when you're with Cassie."

Angel looked at Medlin. When did Medlin become such a deep thinker? But he was exactly on point. Angel didn't try to think about Maggie rather than Cassie--he just did. Worse, when he thought about Cassie, it was always, 'what went wrong?' or 'should we break up?' And when he thought about Maggie, it was always 'I wish she were here with me buck naked.'

"Give me a sip of that rum," Medlin said. "I'm going to take a nap. I haven't slept in days."

"Kathleen?"

"That and a bunch of other shit."

Angel nodded. He didn't ask 'what other shit?' He didn't want to know. Knowing meant more talking, and the purpose of the weekend was to do some backbreaking work, get an essay started which had been mysteriously eluding him, and have time to reflect on Cassie and Maggie.

Medlin climbed onto a bunk and fell asleep quickly.

Angel pulled a joint from his pack and went outside. God, it was cold. The dark had come on almost immediately, and it seemed even more profound, here, in the wilderness.

The stars seemed closer to earth on the mountaintop, and he could see the glow of the incipient moonrise on the edge of the mountains.

He went back inside and got his coat and gloves so he could watch the show. He sat in a rocking chair for a moment but got back up and went inside for a blanket. He sat down again and wrapped up. He took off a glove and lit the joint. As soon as it lit, he put the glove back on. It had to be below zero and dropping fast. This was going to be a cold one.

Angel preferred moonrise to sunrise. For one thing, he had to stay up all night to scc a sunrise, which rendered him too exhausted to enjoy it. Besides, moonrise was subtler. It seemingly offered none of the color a sunrise did, but that wasn't true. There were slight tints of golds and browns and yellows as the moon peeked above the mountain's tip. Blues, too. It came up fat, red, and insolent. Moonrise over water was even better. As the moon cleared the horizon, it lay a white dotted path along the water's surface like stepping stones to fairy land. But, over a mountain, it just ballooned into importance. It was like watching his dick grow in the reflection of a woman's eyes. He had done that with Maggie, watching her eyes widen as he lengthened and fattened. She, who thought dicks were ugly. Ha. He had won that round.

This moon looked insouciant. It was a 'fuck you' moon, and Angel felt as if he deserved it. He sighed. When the moon was completely clear of the mountain, and Angel had finished the joint, he rose and went back inside to the fire.

He pulled his notes and tried to get a handle on the elusive essay. It was like the moon, a flirt which peeked over the mountain as if to tease him. He could feel and see part of his idea, but he couldn't hear it. Poetry essays, like the poetry itself, needed to speak loud and clear. He opened his dog-eared copy of Wallace Stevens and turned to *Peter Quince at the Clavier*. Angel had no problem with the first two movements of the poem. The poem opened with a simple image: Peter Quince sat at a piano playing for a woman he wished to seduce. He told her that, like his fingers on the keyboard of the piano made music, so did her beauty make music on his soul. As Maggie did for Angel. Or Rose. Oh, my God, Rose. No, don't think of Rose. Maggie provided plenty of confusion for one febrile male mind. Anyway, cool line the guy had. Any chick would dig it.

He stopped. Shit. Where was Cassie in that little mental journey?

The second part of the poem was simple, too, but the connection to the first image was hazy. In it, Susanna, wife of a Jewish elder, was bathing, as, apparently, was her wont, in a stream behind her house when a pair of 'red-eyed' elders jumped out and told her to have sex with them, or they would accuse her of adultery, and she would be stoned to death. Angel had done his homework. He knew the episode wasn't in a normal *Bible* but could only be found in a *Douay Bible*. It was the story of how young Daniel, the lion's den Daniel, became an elder, even though he was too young to be one. At Susanna's trial, Daniel smelled a rat and saved her life.

But the poem didn't include that last part, Susannah's trial and Daniel's triumph. It created a weird parallel between the pianist-seducer from the first part of the poem and the horny elders trying to bang poor Susanna. How did that work? How did elegant courtship become blackmail rape so suddenly?

But none of that baffled him so much as the last stanza, which began, 'Beauty is momentary in the mind- A fitful tracing of a portal; But in the flesh it is immortal.' Okay, Angel's brain: scan that.

For it turned every conception of beauty he had ever heard on its head. He knew his Plato and his Christianity: beauty is immortal in the idea; in the flesh it is mortal. Flip that shit upside down, Wallace Stevens.

Okay, slow down. Begin the syllogism at the beginning. So, for instance, that would mean that Maggie, instead of just being a real-live rendering of Angel's internal, immortal concept of beauty, was just the opposite. When Angel looked at Maggie, the ideal of beauty was born in him.

Okay, that was cool. Carry it out, Angel. So, then, men had no concept of beauty until they saw beautiful women. Ergo, without beautiful women, there would be no beauty in the world.

He liked where this was going. He took up his pen and began to write. Suddenly he could hear Stevens whispering in his ear that Angel was indeed picking up signals straight from the old Horse, the All-Horse according to Plato and Christianity.

Maggie was Angel's Susanna. 'Thus it is what I feel, here in this room, desiring you, Thinking of your blue-shadowed silk is music.' Holy shit. His mind was on fire.

Stevens had just explained Angel to Angel. Now, he understood why his women meant so much to him. They weren't just bodies to lie under him while he ejaculated, an accusation Cassie had once made and one that he had heard throughout junior high and high school when he flitted from one pussy to the next.

No, women taught him the music of the world, the beauty and the sensuality and the moral possibilities which surrounded him. They were his religion and the avatars of the gods of order and meaning.

Okay, Angel, extend that idea. That meant that it was the same with his reading. Stevens had just been a Susanna teaching him, too. Oh, dear Lord. Was this a Joyce moment? An epiphany? Angel always had this feeling when reading or writing, but he had seldom, if ever, felt it shake his whole body and soul.

He wrote for two intense hours and then put his pad and pen down emphatically.

That, he knew, was a killer essay. A fucking killer essay.

He pulled a roach from his pocket and went back outside to mock the moon.

Fuck you, he shouted soundlessly. I didn't need your light or your snide irony. I figured out Wallace Fucking Stevens on my own, and he showed me my life and my future. The poem and my pen are my oracles. My women are my truth-tellers. I just need to open up to them and listen.

He danced a little dance and smoked his joint. Life was magical.

He went back inside and flopped on the bunk above Medlin, who hadn't moved in hours.

The conversation with Cassie floated into his mind. Yes, she was definitely a Susanna, too, and he knew that some part of him still loved her. But Maggie was, too, and he could feel her gravitational pull even more strongly than that of Cassie.

In his blissful mood, he wasn't even afraid to contemplate Rose, the fairest of them all.

And, potentially, the most damaged of them all. Her family sounded like shit. And who could refuse to talk of going to school in Switzerland by saying that she was unhappy most of the time when she was there?

And who looked like that and still detested her body?

But Rose was across an ocean and, besides, as Train had said, she was way out of his league, so Angel was safe from her. That just left Maggie and Cassie. He was making a modicum of progress.

The shitty truth was that he wanted both women. But maybe that wasn't shitty? Maybe he and Cassie loved each other, but the relationship was toast. That felt like truth. Now he was talking smack to himself.

And his attraction to Maggie wasn't going to go away just because his scruples told it to.

Perhaps Cassie had been serious. Perhaps they should date other people.

But, did he want Cassie as a 'date?' Probably not. She was a girl you had a relationship with, not a date.

And Maggie wouldn't stay a 'date' for long, either. And she certainly wasn't right for 'the other-woman' role.

Angel didn't have a clue what he was going to do about his two crazy women. That was what he had gone to the mountaintop to do: to decide on a path, and, in that, he had failed.

But he was so happy he didn't care. He lay on his back and stared at the shadows of the fire dancing on the rafters. He hopped down and fed more wood to the blaze.

Life was bountiful and beautiful.

Shantih

   Shantih

      Shantih

Chapter Thirteen

Sunday January 10, 1971
Epistolary

RIDING BACK DOWN THE MOUNTAIN THE NEXT DAY, ANGEL and Medlin crammed into the cab of the ancient Ford pick-up. Angel felt like groaning each time they hit a bump. He and Medlin had chopped more wood that morning and then had hiked down the three-mile trail to meet the truck. The truck was late, so he and Medlin played golf with Angel's ax and a rock for more than an hour. Every muscle in Angel's body screamed, and he knew it would be decidedly worse the next day.

His head, though, felt clean and clear, like the air they sucked in as they hiked.

He had decided little, but he didn't care. He would let fate and the women themselves work things out for him. That was the beauty of being male. He had no ultimate responsibility for things happening at the moment. He just needed to be ready to be contrite when he screwed things up.

He laughed at how slowly he climbed the Phi Psi stairs. He heard music coming from his room and knew that Jane or some other creature must be there. He hoped it was Jane. Maggie or Cassie would be too much to deal with.

When he opened the door, Jane was sitting in his chair with her feet on his desk. She had an entire pile of his work on the floor by her side.

She shrieked and hopped up to run to him. He tried to protest but was too slow, and she leapt up on him with her arms around his neck and her legs about his waist. She kissed his neck over and over.

"I'm so glad you're home. I have news and a present for you. It's sort of a late Christmas present but not really."

God, she was bubbly. Was this really Jane?

"I'm sorry, do I know you?" he said.

She laughed and went to his desk. She turned and handed him a sealed envelope.

"Here," she said. "Read this when I'm gone, which will be in about five minutes. My ride is on its way. Don't let your head swell up too much while you read. It's sappy but sincere." She whirled and picked up the stack of pages on the floor. "And these are wonderful. I read the one about the two junior high girls sharing the boy. That was you, wasn't it? You painted the girls perfectly. I mean, I wasn't having sex in seventh grade, but, if I had, that's exactly what I would have thought and felt. They are so funny. And I read the essay on what's his name?" She sifted through the pile. "George Meredith and *The Egoist*. That must be a really hilarious book. Your essay is so witty and funny."

Angel laughed and sat on the bed. "Slow down, Jane. I'm so tired and sore, I don't think I can keep up with this new Jane. Where is sad Jane? She was easier to deal with."

She sat by him and said, "Turn around. Shoulder rub time."

He did as he was bade, and she dug her fingers into his back. He groaned at the pain.

"I had the best time. I was so disappointed you weren't here, but I hung out with Sand and Eddie and Groucho and Blake. I don't much like Blake's girlfriend. She's snobby. And I think Eddie likes me. But he was gentlemanly enough to take 'no' for an answer and didn't make me feel uncomfortable after that."

"Jane."

"Huh?"

"What part of slow down didn't you get?"

"You're funny," she said and rubbed his neck. "So, we all just hung around and partied. Sand and Eddie took me with them to Bone's Gate and stole a keg and some food. I was the lookout. That was scary but exciting, but that wasn't the best part of the weekend. Guess who showed up at Phi Psi looking for me?"

Angel shook his head. "I have no clue. President Nixon?"

"Nelson," she laughed.

"Nelson? Who's that?"

"Nelson," she said and swatted him on the head. "The boy who now has a crooked nose and who looked terrified to enter Phi Psi."

Angel turned. Nelson? What the fuck was he doing here? "Was he threatening legal action or something? That little prick. I'll let Eddie take his knife next time."

"No, silly, he came to apologize to *moi*. Isn't that a hoot? His fraternity brothers made him do it, and he looked like a sulky little boy the whole time, but he told me he was sorry for how he had treated me. I said, 'Me? What about the other girls in the photos? Just because they didn't have avenging angels, didn't they deserve apologies, too?' He looked completely freaked. That hadn't even occurred to him."

"What did you tell him? Did you accept his apology or tell him to fuck off?"

"Mostly fuck off. I told him, 'I don't even think about you or what you did any more. I'm a new woman now and infinitely above scumbags like you.' He looked relieved. He took that as accepting his apology. But then, you know what I told him as he was leaving?"

"What?"

"I said he better find those other girls and apologize, or my boyfriend and his crew would find him, and they wouldn't be as gentle the next time around. I hope you don't mind. That implied you were my boyfriend."

Angel smiled and lay back on the bed. Jane lay next to him with her head on his chest. "No," he said. "I am your friend. I always will be. And I'm proud of you. The Jane I met on the steps would have leapt back into Nelson's arms and been grateful."

"That Jane is gone," she said. "Cross my heart and hope to die. Oops, I guess I shouldn't say that."

Outside, a car honked. Jane sat up, but Angel grabbed her arm.

"Hey," he said. "Look at me. Tell me you won't hurt yourself again."

She smiled at him. "As I said, that Jane is gone."

The car honked again.

"Got to go," she said. "Read my letter. It's silly, but it's a good one, and I meant every word." She leaned over and kissed him. "Tell the guys 'bye' for me." And she was gone.

Shit.

Angel felt as if he had walked into a storm. Hurricane Jane. Who would have suspected she had that much joy in her?

He groaned and sat up. He went to his desk and picked up her letter. Beneath it was the rest of his mail. He sifted through it and stopped. His pulse quickened. There was a letter from Rose.

He put both letters back on the desk and pulled a roach and a book of matches from his pocket. He lit it and walked next door to Groucho's room and knocked.

Groucho stuck his head out of the door.

"Hey Groucho," Angel said. "Is it cheating to get letters from a girl while you're in a relationship with another girl?"

"You mean, is it cheating to exchange letters with one girl while you're in a relationship with a girl but sleeping with two other girls?"

Angel nodded. About what he thought. Shit.

"Good talking to you, Groucho."

"Sure thing. Want some hash?"

"Later."

And the door shut.

Angel grabbed a towel and went to shower the weekend off him. He thought about Groucho's summation of his messy life. It sounded bad, but Angel couldn't find enough guilt in him to feel any less joyous. It had been good to see Jane, and the letter from Rose had him standing at three quarters mast already. In fact, he was going for a trifecta. He was going to call Maggie.

He turned the shower off. He lit the roach again and wrapped the towel around him. He scrounged up some quarters from his dresser and went downstairs. He bought a Coke and a bag of peanut M&Ms and dialed Maggie's number.

"Hello?"

"Hey."

"Angel? Is that you?"

"It is." Her voice fell like rain on his tired body and soul. Oh, shit. He liked this woman.

"Are you still there?" she asked. "Say something. You're spooking me."

"I want to see you," he said.

"Oh, God, you scared me. I thought this was a 'go away' call. I'm dying to see you, too. I can come up this weekend." She paused. "Angel, tell me the truth. Are you going to hurt me?"

Angel hadn't considered that. It was a fair question, though.

"I don't know. I hope not," he said. "I was hoping that what I was going to do to you was more romantic, more sensual."

"Oh," she laughed. "That sounds nice. This weekend, then?"

"I can't wait," he said truthfully.

He went to his room. He was buzzed, but his exhaustion had left him. He sipped his Coke and ate a handful of M&Ms. Thus fortified, he pulled on a clean pair of jeans.

He sat at his desk to read his letters. He opened Jane's first.

Dear Angel,

I am sorry I missed you this weekend. Much has happened. First of all, I have been accepted into a pre-law program at Northeastern that is really hard to get into. So, yay.

But something much more entertaining happened just now. Nelson came to Phi Psi to apologize to me. Think of that. I think he was made to do it, but I just sat on your bed like a queen while he stood awkwardly in the middle of the room. Eddie was waiting outside your room in case Nelson got weird. You should have seen Nelson's face when he saw Eddie. It was priceless. Anyway, he said his piece, and I basically told him that he was garbage, and I didn't care enough to accept or turn down his feeble attempts and that he better find the other girls and apologize to them, too, or else.

That was the most fun I've had in a zillion years. And I owe it all to you guys at Phi Psi. Everyone has accepted me without questions. I have never been insulted or assaulted at your house. Oh, dear Lord, now I'm crying. You must think me the biggest crybaby you've ever known.

But, most of all, I wanted to tell you what a good guy you are. I know you don't think I'm all that pretty or interesting, but you treat me like a lady. God, that sounds so old-fashioned. I hope Women's Liberation forgives me.

I especially appreciated how you took me in at Thanksgiving. That was extraordinary. No speech on suicide. No watching me suspiciously. Just acceptance without judgement. Do you have any idea how rare that is?

Anyway, thanks for letting me use your room this weekend (even if you didn't know I was here. Ha ha). It was my birthday yesterday. I know you didn't know that, so I'm not fussing or anything. But I want to tell you what my birthday wish was: It was that I can repay your kindness someday. I don't know how that would ever be, but if the day comes, I will be excited to help you out, to show you what unconditional friendship feels like.

Your friend always,

Jane

Angel folded the letter and put it back in the envelope. He felt chastened and grateful to Jane. Her letter was so sweet, and the writing was pretty damn good. A prestigious pre-law program? He had underestimated Jane, and he would prove it to her the next time he saw her.

He sighed. He picked up Rose's letter and looked at it. Her handwriting matched her personality. He smelled it. It wasn't scented, but he swore he could smell and taste her just holding it. He smiled at himself and tore it open.

Dearest Angel,

My emotions have been all over the place since our night together. As you probably know, Cassie called soon after you dropped me off. I felt so bad for her. I can't tell you what we said to each other, but she is so afraid she has lost you.

I felt guilty because I thought I had just found you. That sounds terrible, but let me explain. I am not trying to seduce you away from Cassie. Far from it. And I trust that you will treat Cassie well.

But something happened between you and me, and it has made me feel happier and more confused than I have in a long time. When we were riding to the dance, you were watching me, and you smiled. I didn't see it. I felt it. Something tingled up and down my whole body. I was serious about Ram Dass. He said that feelings like I had meant the recognition of our meeting in another life, perhaps in several. He said we should treasure those moments because they teach us how to find ourselves.

That's what I meant about finding you.

Oh, this is confusing. Let me begin again. Ram Dass said that the best people make us feel good about ourselves. That's what you did for me. As you seemed to intuit, I have never felt particularly good about myself. I am too moody, and I have an almost infinite capacity for taking something good and ruining it for myself. I thank my mother for that ability. It is disquieting, to say the least.

Disquieting. That was good. But she gave him too much credit. He had no inkling that she had low self-esteem. How was that even possible?

But you gave me some kind of little jolt, like the one in Cat's Cradle when you recognize someone from your Karass. Anyway, suddenly I was laughing and feeling at ease. Then, oh my God, you took me to the river and pointed first to the city and then to the stars and then to the spot where you tried to rescue a woman. And then you kissed me. I almost turned into vapor. Do you not understand how storybook that is to anyone who has been a little girl?

And then I got to watch you tease and be teased by Train. It was so much fun to just joke with the two of you. Men have it so easy. Did you not know I was a nervous wreck going to that ball? And there I was with a pair of strange men feeling more at home than at my real home.

That's it. You make me feel as if I'm home.

And then you just plain cheated. You couldn't rescue the woman in the car, and it hurt you deeply that you couldn't, so you rescued me from those boys. In my little world, people don't actually fight. It just isn't done. But it seemed so natural to you and so alien to them. It was like watching two different forms of maleness.

You terrified me, and I was repelled by how ugly the violence was, but I choose your version of what a man should be. Primal, yes, primitive, yes, but noble and chivalric, like a modern Don Quixote, only much cooler.

Your mood darkened though, when you fought, and it never returned to the easy joking manner of before. That made me just want to hold you and kiss you and not let go. I don't think I've ever felt so protective of anyone before.

I wasn't exaggerating: you are the most romantic man I've ever met. And it wasn't your trying to be romantic or seductive; it was just your being you. You are like that all the time, aren't you? Instinctive? Protective?

I don't regret our kissing. I know that wasn't fair to Cassie, but it had to happen. Neither of us willed it. In fact, it is the universe which seems to want us to be friends.

So, you have to write me at London University, the Westminster campus. You don't want to anger the universe, do you?

Thank you again for a lovely (and tres interresant) evening.

Your ardent friend,

Rose

My goodness. That girl writes well. She is crazy as a loon, but a really, really sweet loon.

Angel sighed and folded the letter, but, almost immediately, he re-opened and re-read it.

Okay. He was hooked. Thank God, she was across an ocean. If she were anywhere near him, Angel knew he would be in some deep-dicking trouble.

Angel knew what he needed, to hear some Yardbirds. He fumbled through his collection and found the album he wanted. He put the needle on *For Your Love*.

He stood in the middle of his room, half-dancing and trying to decide what to do. It was still early, and, though he knew he should be keeling over from weariness, he was suddenly brimming with energy. He probably needed to jack off. He had just been hit with a triple dose of sweet-hot estrogen, and he felt like a million bucks. Plus, he'd been without since Manhattan. That was entirely too long. But, no, that wouldn't do. And which woman would he fantasize about anyway? He smiled. It would be Maggie. He could almost feel the sudden rise of her hip as she lay on her side and the smoothness of her long legs. He shook his head. Enough of that. He would write. That's what he would do. He pulled his notebook from his backpack and turned to a story he was working on. He began to read it and nodded. Yes, that's what he would do. He would write. This was going to be a productive night. He was still linguistically pumped from his Stevens paper the night before. He was getting chilly, so he pulled on a sweatshirt and some socks.

"You're going the wrong way," he heard a voice say. He turned, and there was Maggie. "You should probably be taking things off."

She went to him, and he hugged her for a long time. She looked up at him with those Molly Bloom 'please kiss me' eyes, and he obliged her.

"I was just thinking of you," he smiled. "I mean literally. Sexual fantasy stuff."

"Well, that fits nicely into my plans for the rest of the evening."

"What are you even doing here?" he asked. "You said next weekend."

"Oh? What night is this?"

"Sunday."

"Well, isn't that part of the weekend?" She peeled his sweatshirt off and pushed him to the bed. She knelt and pulled his socks off. She moved to his belt buckle, but looked up at him as she unclasped it.

"Is this all right?" she asked.

Angel held her face and kissed her.

"This is perfect."

She sighed and returned to her task. She pulled down his jeans and smiled. She looked up at him.

"No," she said. "This is perfect."

Angel leaned back on his bed and prayed, 'Lord save me from myself and from these wicked women.'

He gave a start as he felt her mouth on him.

'But not tonight, Lord, not tonight.'

Chapter Fourteen

Later That Night January 10, 1971
The Midnight Rambler

A RACKET FROM BELOW AWAKENED ANGEL. MAGGIE SMILED
at him from his desk chair.

"How long was I out?" he asked.

"Not long," she said. "Long enough for me to read this very interesting piece
about a girl suspiciously like me." She held up a manuscript.

"Yes, that's *The Book of Maggie*. That's actually a chapter from somewhere in
the middle."

"She sounds sad."

Angel smiled. "She hadn't met her lover, yet."

Maggie went to the bed and lay next to him. She rubbed his forehead. "You
mean this lover?" she asked.

Angel smiled. "That feels good."

"I've never seen you tired before," she whispered.

"I get tired," he smiled.

"But it's weakness to show it?" She laughed and poked him in the ribs. She went
back to his desk to pick up a notebook. "And, I found this in your backpack. Wallace
Stevens. Is this a new essay you're writing?"

Angel nodded. "Did you like it?"

"I like the 'Maggie?' next to the part about women teaching men beauty. Am I
beautiful to you, Angel?"

"Well, you have a ridiculously fine body and are wearing nothing but panties,
so I'm not biologically equipped at the moment to comment on aesthetics." He
pulled the covers back to reveal a tumescent eavesdropper who seemed extremely
interested in her presence.

"Dear me," Maggie laughed. "I thought I took care of that little devil."

"Little?" Angel protested. He went to her and dragged her laughing from the chair to his bed where he plopped her down. "Let's see if you can make it bigger, then."

He tugged her panties off, and she screamed with laughter.

"What's going on in here?" a voice said, and Groucho's head peeked in the door. "Oh, sorry. I thought someone was being killed. Carry on, then. Just thought you might want to know there's pizza downstairs." And he disappeared.

"Pizza?" Angel said. "I guess this wenching can wait," and he rose and picked up his jeans.

"Angel! You get that tiny thing right back here. I took care of you. Now, you can take care of me."

She lay back and spread her legs provocatively.

"Well," he said. "I guess food's food," and he took his jeans back off. "Let's see what's on the menu. Maybe a little breast," and he nipped lightly at a nipple. Maggie screamed and swatted him. "Or maybe some navel." He licked lightly around and then into her belly button.

"Getting closer," she said.

"Or maybe, some of this exotic fruit down here," and he ran a finger over her. "Whoever cooked this left it nice and moist," he said. And he ran his tongue over her clit and over the inside of her lips.

"I think you're there," she moaned. "Eat up, cowpoke. It's a long time until next weekend."

Angel kissed her clit. He looked up at her and smiled, and then eased first two, then three fingers in her and began to slide them in and out.

"Oh, dear Lord," she said and closed her eyes. Angel removed his fingers and ran his tongue from her clit down to her ass. He tickled her rear opening, and she squirmed. He moved back to her clit and began tonguing it in earnest. He put his hand back inside her and fucked her rhythmically, increasing his pace as her breathing and twitching increased. She grabbed his hair and pulled, hard, and she began to convulse and scream. Almost in a single motion, he mounted her and rammed his dick deep into her. She screamed and began to quiver again.

"We'll see about 'little,' Missy," he said, and he pounded her. Then he abruptly stopped and withdrew until he was just out of her. The tip of his dick pressed against her clit, which was almost beyond sensitive. She shuddered and ground her nails into his arm. "Angel?" she said. "Yes, sweetheart?" he replied, and then slowly slid himself back into her so she could feel every inch as it disappeared into her. He pulled back out again. "Little?" he asked. "No," she said. Her voice sounded as if she was in agony. And then he dropped his full weight on her and rammed her until he came, and she began to shake again.

He rolled off and lay on his back, panting and chuckling.

He stared wide-eyed at the ceiling. She reached sideways and whacked him across the chest.

"What's so funny?" she asked. But she began to laugh, too.

"I have clearly been without for too long," he said. "That felt abnormally pneumatic."

She rolled towards him. "Angel," she said looking into his eyes.

He stared back at her, "I know, Maggie, pizza." He sat up and reached for his jeans. Maggie pummeled him on the back.

"You are the most annoying man on the planet," she said, but her laughter gave her away.

Angel raised his eyebrows at her and left.

"Angel, you get back here," she shouted after him. But no Angel re-appeared, so she lay back and pulled the covers over her.

Damn.

She rose a moment later and dressed to chase after Angel. She found him in the Blue Room in front of a roaring fire eating pizza with the whole gang.

Cane saw her first and roared, "Maggie!" Maggie went to him, and he enfolded her in a bear hug.

"We were worried," Groucho said. "We kept hearing screaming from Angel's room."

"Yeah," Cane said. "Angel screams like a little bitch."

Maggie laughed. "I'm afraid that was me."

"How can you even tell when Angel's in you?" Cane asked.

"Well," Maggie said. "My rear was almost virgin."

Cane stopped mid-bite and stared at her. So, did Sand and Groucho.

"For real?" Cane asked.

"No," she laughed. "You guys are too easy."

Cane relaxed and took a bite.

"My rear hasn't been a virgin since eighth grade," she said nonchalantly.

"Something you and Angel have in common?" Cane said.

"Angel, you told them about my strap-on?" she said and bit into a slice of pizza.

"Anybody else confused?" Groucho asked.

"She's kidding, Groucho, and she wouldn't tell any of you scumbags anything about our romantic interludes, anyway, would you Mags?" Angel said.

"I'd tell Cane that I'm pretty sure you are larger than he is," Maggie said.

"Ouch," Cane said.

The front door burst open to reveal Eddie with two girls.

"Allie! Sharon!" Sand yelled. "Close the door. We just got this place warm."

Eddie spotted Angel and went to him and clapped him on the back. "This is the man I've been telling you about," Eddie told the two girls.

"Why am I the man?" Angel asked, sipping on his Coke and chewing the cold pizza.

"These two sweet, young things missed their ride back to Smith, and I told them you would be glad to take them home," Eddie said.

Angel eyed Eddie and the girls. Eddie was so transparent. He had told the girls that to get them to come back to Phi Psi. It was a ruse. Eddie liked to think of courtship in strategic terms.

"Not me," Angel said. "I've got Maggie here."

"Oh, no you don't," Maggie said. "I've got to get back. I have a test first thing in the morning. I just came here to get my batteries re-charged."

"So, that's what all the screaming was," Sand said. "He electrocuted her."

"Ha," Maggie laughed. "He certainly did. And on that note, I am out of here." She kissed Angel and whispered. "See you Friday."

Maggie grabbed another slice of pizza and stole Angel's Coke. "Nice to meet you, girls. Sweet talk him. Angel can't say 'no' to a woman. It's not in him." And she left, waving over her shoulder.

"Is that your girlfriend?" one of the girls asked. Sharon maybe?

"Never saw her before tonight," Angel said.

Half an hour later, Angel had agreed to drive to Smith. In a way, it was good. It would provide him with an opportunity to talk to Cassie face to face.

This thing needed doing, and he knew it.

"Keys, Groucho," Angel said and held out his hand.

"Why don't you take your car?" Groucho protested.

"It's an Austin Healey, Groucho. It doesn't have room for three people. Plus, it's buried under a couple of feet of snow."

"Oh," Groucho said and tossed Angel the keys to the Impala.

Angel went to his room, changed his shirt, put on his vest, and brushed his teeth. He splashed cold water on his face and ran his wet fingers through his hair. He toweled and looked in the mirror.

"Ready for this?" he asked himself.

"Not really," the mirror replied.

"Pussy," Angel said.

"Douchebag," the mirror told him. "You know you look like shit."

"Well, I chopped wood all weekend."

"Whaaaa. Cry me a fucking river."

He picked up a stapled manuscript from his desk, folded it, and put it in the pocket of his coat.

In the cloak room, he fished for coins to call Cassie to tell her that he was coming. Calling her would scare the shit out of her, and she would sit worrying until he got there, but that was fairer than just showing up. The phone in her hall rang and rang, but no one answered. Angel was irked. It was midnight. There was no way Smithies weren't in their dorm on a Sunday night, and there was no way every single one of them was asleep. His coins jangled and re-appeared in the return slot. He re-inserted them and dialed again. Same result.

Angel drove across the Delaware River Bridge and turned south on I-91. The girls chattered happily to him and to each other for a few minutes, but their tipsiness was wearing off, and their conversation finally subsided. Thank God. Soon, their heads were back, and they had their eyes closed.

The one in the back, Allison or Allie or something, Angel couldn't remember, was a real ditz. He couldn't believe she went to Smith. Most Smithies were intellectual, but this one was a giggler. Not one of Angel's favorite traits.

He studied the one sitting next to him. He was pretty sure her name was Sharon. She wasn't beautiful, but she wasn't far from it. She had her hair pulled back, revealing a good profile. She had an intelligent brow with eyelashes which arched in long, graceful parabolic curves. She had a lower voice than her silly friend, and she laughed. No giggling or whinnying, thank God. At Phi Psi, she had been coatless, and her sweater and jeans had revealed a nice body. She was busty for a slender girl and had promising hips. Her lips were thin but pulled back in an inviting smile. Angel decided he liked her.

"And what are you looking at, Angel? That's your name, right? Angel?" Sharon asked with her eyes still closed.

He just smiled. This one's dangerous.

"Is that your real name? Angel?" she asked.

"You mean my birth name?" Angel asked. "Sort of. My middle name is Angell with two l's. It's a family name. But I've been called Angel since I was twelve or thirteen."

"And who named you that?" she asked sleepily.

"Dee Dee Minton and Serena Wojokowski," he answered. He smiled at the memory.

"And they were, what? Girlfriends?" she asked.

"Lovers," he answered. "And each other's best friends. A truly advanced pair who liked to share."

"Seriously?" she asked. "Thirteen. You lost your virginity at thirteen?"

Angel made a wry face.

"And had a threesome?"

"No," he laughed. "It was just one at a time, but it was exhausting. Some days I would go to Dee Dee's house after school. She lived right across the street. Then, that same night, Serena would be babysitting, and I would go over and, well, you get the drift."

"My, you were a bad little boy. So, why did they call you Angel?" she asked.

"Well, I think it was meant to be ironic. I was Lucifer, their fallen angel," he said. "But later on, I think it stuck because I look so innocent."

"Ooh, I like fallen angels," she murmured and went silent.

The car was quiet for another thirty minutes. Angel tried to imagine the conversation he needed to have with Cassie but gave up. He didn't really know what he was going to do when he got there. He guessed that Cassie's attitude would determine how things went.

"So why does Angel drive two strange girls to Smith at midnight on a gloomy Sunday? You must have done this before. Eddie knew you would say 'yes,'" Sharon said.

"Why does Angel drive two strange girls to Smith?" he repeated. "Angel is asking himself that right now."

She opened her eyes and turned towards him. Even in the dark he could tell that she had killer eyes.

"No, really." she said.

"I get talked into things easily," he said. "And I love driving at night. And you are both pretty. Sorry. Truth." He paused and thought. "Plus, I have a girlfriend at Smith, and I kind of need to talk to her."

"What's her name?" she asked.

"Cassie," he said. "Cassandra, actually."

Sharon shook her head. She didn't know a Cassie or a Cassandra.

"What's so urgent that you need to see her in the middle of the night on a Sunday?" she asked.

"My God, you are nosy," he said.

"Yes, but I am pretty. You said so yourself. Am I prettier than Dee Dee or Serena?" she teased.

How the hell did she remember their names?

"Serena, yes. Dee Dee, maybe not. Dee Dee was pretty fucking cute," he answered.

Uh oh. They were definitely flirting.

"Cassie and I are…not…" he started and stopped. He didn't know where he was going with that statement. He didn't know what he and Cassie were. "Cassie and I used to be lovers," he said.

"Used to be?" she asked.

"Maybe still are, sort of," he mumbled.

"Sorry. I know what you mean. Who wants to break up with who?" she asked.

"Whom," he said.

"What?"

"Whom," he said. "Who wants to break up with whom?"

She laughed.

"Neither, really," he said. "I think we both want to stay together, but..."

He felt like shit talking about a break-up before Cassie even knew it was coming.

"So, who is Maggie?" she asked.

He turned to look at her. He met her eyes and shook his head. "I don't know."

"You don't know who Maggie is?" she laughed. "You seemed pretty familiar."

Angel smiled. "Maggie is a friend. I don't know yet how much more than that she will become."

"Hey," she smiled. "Chill. I'm not being judgmental. I can tell you're one of the good guys. I don't mean to bust your balls."

Angel smiled and drove. A deer appeared in the headlights on the side of the road. Angel gave him a wide berth.

"Enough about me," he said. "What's your story? Are you studying to be a trial lawyer?"

Sharon laughed.

"Well, I'm from Minnesota originally," she began.

"Ah," he said. "Hence the lack of an accent."

"My father moved the family to Long Island. My mother stayed in Minnesota. I don't know why. She could have drunk herself to death just as easily in Long Island," she said.

"Ah, no bitterness there," he said.

Sharon made a face at him.

"My little sister didn't take the move very well. She cried for months," she said. She became quiet for a while. "My father is a neurologist. He pretty much works all the time, but he's a good father. And we're fine now. We're all just glad to get away from my mother. I like Long Island, but I don't have many friends there. The girls are all, I don't know the word I'm searching for. They're kind of coarse and hard."

"Oh, and you're Miss Shrinking Violet who never asks blunt questions," he said.

She laughed. "Touche," she said.

"Boyfriend?" he asked.

"No," she said.

They grew quiet at the question and the answer.

"I'm sorry," he said. "I wasn't trying to hit on you or anything."

"Pity," she said.

They both laughed.

"I heard Dartmouth guys were all assholes," she said. "But you are kind of sweet, aren't you?"

He smiled at her. He didn't feel sweet. He was going to cut a girl's heart out and dance on it.

"Do you come up to Hanover very often?" he asked.

"No," she said. "This was just my second time. I tagged along with a friend. It was kind of a strange situation, and she wanted back-up."

"What was strange about it?" he asked.

"Well, she didn't know the guy at all," she said. "She'd met him once for about five minutes. It was a friend of a friend thing."

"Let me guess," he said. "He went to her dorm and told her that some friend of hers had told him to say 'hi' to her."

"Yes," she said. "How did you know that?"

Angel chuckled. "That's the *Freshman Book* ruse," he said. He couldn't believe he was using Eddie's word 'ruse.'

"Come again?" she asked.

"It's a game to pick up women. Okay, say you are sitting in your dorm and someone knocks on your door. You open it. A shy, confused boy is standing there. He asks if you are Sharon. You say 'yes.' He says that he ran into Susie X in Boston, an old acquaintance of yours. He told Susie X that he was coming to Smith, and she told him to say 'Hi' to you. So, he says 'Hi' and leaves. He has now established contact. He lets about two weeks go by and calls you. He hems and haws and says something to the effect that you probably don't remember him, but he knocked on your door to say, 'Hi from Susie,' and he hasn't been able to stop thinking about you. Would you be interested in going out with him some time? You are flattered. He seems so innocent and sweet. You say 'yes.' That's the *Freshman Book* ruse," he said.

"I don't get it. How does he know Susie? How does he know anything about me?" she asked.

"The boy looked you up in the *Smith Freshman Book*. Step One: He jots down your school, home town, and some of your activities. You are a dancer, for instance. Step Two: he looks in the *Radcliffe Book* for someone from your town, preferably from your school. Step Three: He shows up at your door, says he met whomever from Radcliffe. Bingo. Works almost every time. It doesn't even matter whether you know Susie X, or whether she went to your school. Just as long as she is from your town. That way, if you say you don't know Susie or don't like Susie, the guy can say, 'she said you are a wonderful dancer.' Boom. Connection with truth."

"And this works?" she asked.

"Yep," he said. "It's almost like being set up by someone you know."

She laughed. He laughed too. It was kind of funny. He had always thought it was just business, but it did sound funny when he described it to her.

"Could you do this to a friend of mine as a prank?" she asked.

"Ah. You are cruel. I like that," he said. "But not tonight. It doesn't work late at night. Too creepy."

And then they were in Northampton. The campus was dark. There were lamps everywhere, but the snow-laden sky let no light shine through from the moon.

He walked Sharon and her groggy friend back to their dorm. The friend went inside, but Sharon lingered. Angel almost felt like he was supposed to kiss her good night. He said as much to her. She smiled puckishly and raised her face slightly towards him. He laughed and told her good night. He turned to leave.

"Mr. Angel," she said.

He turned back.

"Good luck with Cassie. I hope things work out the way you want them to work out. And you can knock on my door any day with a message from Susie," she said.

He smiled and shook his head. She was a vixen. He decided that he had wasted his freshman and sophomore years being a communist. He wished he had known there were all these fine girls in the world.

He crossed the quad to Cassie's dorm. He tried the door, but it was locked. He stood and pondered the situation. Shit. Nothing was ever locked at Dartmouth.

He went around the side of the dorm and tossed snow at Cassie's window. Nothing. He tried again. Still nothing. This was getting annoying.

He walked to downtown Northampton to find a payphone. He inserted a quarter and dialed her dorm. The phone was in the hall, so everyone on the floor should have heard it. But, if anyone did, she didn't bother to leave her room to answer it. Stubbornly, he tried again. Nada. He had called from Dartmouth at midnight and no one had answered. It was 2:30, and there was still no answer. Were they all dead?

He was at a loss. He trekked back across campus and got in Groucho's car. It would be stupid to drive back to Dartmouth. He had come all this way to talk to Cassie. He tried to curl up in his car and sleep. He pulled his jacket over him like a blanket, but in ten minutes he was freezing.

He walked back downtown looking for an all-night diner but couldn't find one. The only place he found opened at 6:00. Finally, he walked back to Sharon's dorm. He tried the door, and it was unlocked. He peeked in. Two girls were sitting on the floor in the hall across from each other talking. One was crying. They looked questioningly at Angel.

"Sharon?" he asked.

The weepy one pointed to a door. He stepped over them, saying "Thank you."

He stopped at Sharon's door and went back to the girls. "He's not worth it."

Weepy looked startled but smiled.

As he tapped on Sharon's door, he heard the crying girl ask, "Who's that guy?"

Sharon answered quickly. She was surprised, but he noted gratefully that she seemed glad to see him.

"I didn't know where else to go," he said.

"No luck with Cassie?" she asked.

"I couldn't get in her dorm, and no one would answer the phone." He shrugged.

"You can stay here," she said.

He looked at her. There was no suspicion on her face.

"Do you want to talk?" she asked.

He shook his head. "Not really. Not about Cassie."

He looked awkwardly about him. There was only one bed. The whole room could have fit in a prison cell. "I don't want to interrupt anything," he said awkwardly.

"I was just reading, she said. She pointed to a copy of *The Dharma Bums*. Angel's eyes widened. Cool.

"Do you need to wash up?" she asked. Without waiting for an answer, she handed him a towel, her toothbrush, and a tube of Crest. He obediently went down the hall and climbed back across the girls. They saw the towel and toothbrush and made a sound like 'a woo woo.' Angel smiled at them.

When he got back to Sharon's room, she was already in the bed. She smiled and patted the bed beside her.

"You can sleep here," she said. "I don't bite."

"Good. I don't like biters," he said.

There was a small lamp by the bed. He sat on the bed with his back to her and took off everything but his underwear. He climbed under the covers and turned off the light.

He was too nervous to make small talk, and she seemed to feel the same way. The only way they both fit into the small bed was to spoon. She turned towards the wall and he lay behind her.

"Good night," she said.

"Good night," he said.

They lay rigidly for a few moments, and then Sharon inched her way back up against him.

Shit. It was a tight fit.

He curled against her and put an arm around her waist.

She made a happy little sound.

Angel tried to think about Cassie. Or Maggie. Damn. He hadn't thought about Maggie since she left Dartmouth. He wondered what that meant.

But there was no escaping his situation. Sleep seemed unlikely. He was in bed with a girl who was wearing nothing but a thin tee shirt and panties. He hoped she was wearing panties. His arm cradled her where the waist ended and the hip flared out. It was his favorite part of a woman's body. He could see the curve of her hip and how long her legs were. Thor began to growl.

"Angel," she said. "Do you think if you kissed me we could relax and fall asleep?"

"God, no," he said.

"Oh," she said. She sounded like a child who had been remonstrated.

"Shut up," he said and pulled her tighter to him. He hoped that if she felt more pressure from the rest of his body she wouldn't feel how hard he had gotten.

"Angel," she whispered.

"No," he whispered back.

He took his hand from her waist and caressed her hair. He told her to go to sleep.

Eventually, he could tell from her shallow breathing that she had.

But he was wide awake.

There was no way that this was going to work with Sharon in his arms and Cassie a few hundred yards away.

He contemplated Sharon. She was a trusting soul. She had opened up to him easily about her family, and she clearly had no sexual fears. She was sharing her bed with someone she didn't know at all, but she was no tramp. Once again, he was with a girl he liked a lot.

What was it with him?

Eventually, he couldn't help himself. He leaned over her and kissed the back of her neck. She made a small moaning sound and wriggled even closer. He didn't repeat the kiss, so she opened her eyes and turned her head back toward him.

Angel knew better, but he kissed her. His hands went under her shirt and caressed her breasts. They were as ample as he thought. He kissed her, again. She returned each kiss and looked at him questioningly.

"I can't stay here," he said.

"Why not?" she whispered.

"Because you are too damned cute, and I am too damned male," he said.

He kissed her gently and sat on the side of the bed. He looked at the clock. It was almost six o'clock. He put on his clothes and pulled on his boots.

"Why do you wear cowboy boots?" she asked.

"I don't know," he said. "I played cowboy a lot when I was a kid. I got my first real pair when I bought my first motorcycle. I was thirteen and thought I was a badass. Why? Do you hate them? Cassie does."

"No," she said. "They fit you. Where are you going to go?"

"There's a diner open downtown," he said.

"Good," she said. "I'm hungry."

Angel laughed. "You're not coming with me."

"I'll treat," she said sweetly.

He kissed her. "Oh, in that case." He slapped her fanny. "Get dressed woman."

He sat on the edge of the bed and pulled on his jeans and boots. Sharon ran her hand down his back. He stood and drew his shirt over his head.

"You coming?" he asked.

She gave him a doe-eyed look and sat him down on the bed. She walked to her dresser and pulled out a sweater and a pair of jeans. She turned towards him and slowly drew her shirt over her head. She walked slowly towards him. She took his hand and put it on a breast. He turned her around and spanked her again. She laughed and danced away from him.

When they left Sharon's room, the talking girls had disappeared. A gust of cold wind hit them the moment they opened the outer door. He put his arm around her for warmth.

The diner was empty. Angel had a pecan waffle and bacon with his coffee. Sharon ordered oatmeal and black coffee.

Angel remembered drinking coffee at Timuquana with Rose. Rose took her coffee black, too. Were all these girls manlier than he? He spooned six sugars into his coffee and poured cream on top.

They talked of her studies. She was, like Maggie, a Biology major. She had two huge labs due later that week. She spoke animatedly when she described her work.

Angel listened to her and smiled.

"What?" she asked, poking him. "What's so funny?"

"You're just ridiculously cute," he said. "I like people who are into their work."

"Hmmm," she said and sipped her coffee.

He told her of his writing. He told her about Wallace Stevens, his newfound love.

She smiled at him.

"What?" he asked.

"I just like people who are into their work," she said.

They smiled at each other.

The sun was rising, and, by the time they got back to campus, the east glowed red and raw. They watched the gas lamps poof off, one by one, as they walked back to her dorm.

Halfway there, he saw Cassie.

And Cassie saw them.

Angel thought his best defenses were honesty and innocence, so he took Sharon over to introduce her to Cassie.

Sharon, God love her, bailed him out.

"You must be Cassie. Hi, I'm Sharon," she said. "Angel was just talking about you, and all I could think was how I envied you. That boy is a saint. I had a date with his friend Fast Eddie last night which didn't go so well. Angel bailed me out and brought me home. He said it was a good excuse to see you."

Cassie wasn't buying it.

"I called and called your dorm," Angel said. "I even threw snowballs at your window. Where were you? I was freezing."

"I was probably sleeping," Cassie said.

"I showed Angel the Jameson diner," Sharon said. "The poor boy was a solid block of ice when I found him wandering around."

Sharon patted Angel on the cheek.

"Thanks for the ride, Angel," she said. She looked at Cassie again. "He really is an angel, isn't he? Well, I have to meet my lab partner in a few minutes. It was nice meeting you, Cassie. We'll have to get together sometime. You can tell me what's wrong with Angel's demented friends."

Sharon left. Angel watched her go. She was the angel, he thought. What a cutie.

"Who is she?" Cassie asked.

Angel blinked stupidly.

"Um, Sharon? I don't even know her. I met her last night and gave her a ride here," he said.

"Not Sharon," Cassie said. "The girl you drove down here to tell me about. Who is she?"

Angel looked at Cassie. She didn't seem angry or jealous. She just looked tired. Angel could relate. He was bone weary, but he knew he had to go through with this. No more chickening out.

"Can we go back to your room?" he asked.

Cassie smiled sadly at him and took his hand. They walked wordlessly back to her dorm.

Angel took his jacket off and lay it across the back of her desk chair. He looked mournfully about him. Cassie's room was so familiar. There were pictures of her family on her desk and even more pictures of the two of them.

He picked up one depicting him with Cassie. They were holding skis and glowing with the cold. Their noses were red and their smiles huge.

"That was at Woodstock, wasn't it?" he asked.

Cassie nodded.

"We sat at dinner the night before and watched the snow blowers spraying powder on the slopes and the snow cats snarling and smoothing the trails for us," he said. "It seemed a metaphor, everyone trying to make us happy, everyone trying to perfect the world we lived in and loved in."

Cassie took off her coat and sat on the edge of the bed. She looked patient and old. Angel's heart was riven.

How could this be happening? They had been so in love.

"Angel, who is she?"

Angel sat at Cassie's desk. He had so much he wanted to say, but words wouldn't come.

Finally, he said, "Maggie, Rose, Wanda, Jane. Take your pick."

"You want to break up with me so you can have a *seraglio*?" she asked. "That doesn't sound like the Angel I know. The Angel I loved craves intimacy."

Angel got up to sit by her.

"Stay over there," she said curtly. "You don't get to be all sweet and cuddly while you're doing this, and you smell like another woman. You smell like sex."

Angel sat again. He idly picked up the open book on her desk. *L'Etranger.* En Francais, of course. He put it back down.

"Perfect book for this discussion," he said.

"Why is that?" she asked.

"You know why," he said. "Because Merseult feels alien even to his own life. That's pretty much how this conversation feels."

"Like it's not real?" she asked. "Don't kid yourself, Angel. This is really happening, and you are doing it. Thanks for spoiling the book, though. I hadn't finished it. Kind of like our relationship? You finished before I did."

Angel eyed her curiously. Did she really believe what she was saying? Or was this a defense mechanism? Blame it all on him. She wasn't involved in their schism at all. No, it must be another woman.

He was surprised. That wasn't very Cassie. But if she wanted to play it that way, the least he could do was to help her make a dignified exit. He would be glad to be the bad guy if it helped her.

But inside, he knew it wouldn't really make her feel better. Cassie would still do her six days or six months of crying and recriminations, both at herself and at him.

"Just say it, Angel."

Angel moved to the bed next to her, and, this time, Cassie didn't demur.

"I don't have anything to say, Cassie. That's the problem. Somehow, we grew distant. I'm not leaving you for another woman. I know that would be easy for both of us to understand and process, but it's not true. We've been apart for months."

"No," she said. "You've been apart. You were always with me in my head. But I don't exist for you when I'm not physically with you. Unlike your precious characters. I'm sure you think about Molly Bloom more often than you think of me."

Tears formed in her eyes, and she angrily brushed at them. She gave him an ironic smile and held out her hand. He handed her a handkerchief, probably one she had bought him.

"Cass, we kind of grew up together, didn't we?" he said.

She looked at him.

"I taught you love-making, and you taught me to love," he said. "We were such babies."

He held her and kissed her forehead.

"You used to make me feel beautiful," she said. "And now you make me feel ugly."

Her body stiffened as she said those words, and he sighed and released her.

He stood. Love scenes in movies didn't end this way. He should have something tender to say, some exit line.

"Just go," she said. She didn't even look up at him.

He put on his coat and remembered the missive he had brought her. He placed it on her desk.

She looked at him curiously.

"Christmas present," he said. "It's a short story. It begins with a young girl standing at a bannister to tell a young man that her sister isn't ready for their date. But she and the young man's eyes meet. And that's how love begins."

Cassie lay on the bed facing away from him. She wept into his handkerchief and waved for him to leave.

Angel closed the door behind him and went down the hall and out into the cold.

He unlocked Groucho's car and climbed in. There was a ticket on the windshield. Perfect. Eddie could fucking pay it.

He let the car warm up for a few minutes so that the defroster would clear the windshield.

He searched for feelings but came up empty.

Cassie was probably right. She would lie on her bed crying for hours, and he would drive home trying to decide what to write for Stone's class.

Why was that? The charitable answer would be that he lived in the present moment, and most girls live too much in either the past or the future. Cassie was perfectly capable of replaying their conversation in her head for hours. Why did girls do that? Why would they torture themselves over things that had already happened or hadn't happened yet?

Angel slowed as he prepared to merge onto I-91. Two shivering girls were hitchhiking. They looked as if they were wearing nothing but coats and boots and couldn't have been more than fifteen. He pulled over and stopped.

"Where are you two going?" he asked.

"Norwich," the taller girl said.

"Hop in," he said.

The girls exchanged looks. The shorter one nodded at the tall girl who sighed and got in the front seat next to Angel. The other girl climbed in the back.

Angel turned on the radio and found a rock station playing The Kinks. He smiled.

The girls took their coats off and settled in for the two-hour ride. In the stuffy car, they smelled rank.

He looked in the rearview mirror at the girl in the back seat. She, like the girl next to him, was in standard issue hippy chick wear, a mini-skirt, boots, and a bra-less tank top. He usually loved the look, but today it repulsed him. Though the girl had fat cheeks, the rest of her was bony. Her nipples pointed though her top, but the rest of her lacked shape or definition. She wore too much make-up and smacked her gum. While he watched, she rolled her window down a crack and threw out her gum. She folded her coat like a pillow and leaned against it, closing her eyes.

The girl next to him was taller and shapelier. She had budding breasts and hips.

A few hours earlier, Sharon had been sitting there trading witticisms with him. It was like going from Oscar Wilde to the *Playboy Forum*.

He was dying to ask the girl next to him how old she was, but he knew it wouldn't sound hip.

"I'm Julia," she said. "What's your name?"

"Angel."

"No shit?"

"No shit."

"Huh," she said. She moved a hand to change his radio station, but Angel shook his head and she left it alone.

"Fourteen," she said.

"Excuse me?"

"I'm fourteen. That's what you were wondering, weren't you? Everyone asks." Angel smiled.

He was with a vulgar version of Dee Dee and Serena.

"Cracker's thirteen, but she has a birthday pretty soon."

"Cracker?" Angel asked. "Her name's Cracker?"

"Well, yours is Angel."

Fair enough. They lapsed into silence.

"You aren't going to ask what two girls is doing hitchhiking on a Monday morning? Even truck drivers want to know things like that."

Angel shook his head. Normally he would care, but he was beyond exhaustion and beyond feeling paternal.

"Okay," she said. "I can take a hint."

She slouched back and closed her eyes.

Shit. She wasn't even wearing panties. If the women he knew were the fruit of the sexual revolution, these girls were the rotten husks lying under the tree.

They rode the rest of the way in silence. Angel thought of Cassie briefly, but he couldn't even muster empathy for her. The two rancid teenyboppers had taken his bad mood and made it pestilent.

He thought about Sharon instead. It had felt good to lie against her. Why was she so trusting?

He looked at Julia. She was staring at him.

"Boy," she said. "You were lost in thought."

"Julia, right?"

She nodded.

"Don't you worry about getting picked up by bad men?"

"Nah. It happens. You just gotta try not to think about it."

"Have you ever had anyone try anything?" he asked.

She laughed. "Lots. Cracker and I have both been messed with, but it's not a big deal."

"Messed with? Like raped?"

"Yeah, I guess. Cracker's had it twice. I've just mostly had to blow guys. It's cool. Nobody's cut us or anything."

Shit. What kind of world was she living in? What kind of world was he living in? Was it any different for Sharon to accept a ride from him? She didn't know him. And she had let him, a stranger, into her bed?

Angel drove in silence the rest of the way. He turned off I-91 into Norwich and parked at Dan and Whit's as Julia instructed. Julia poked Cracker who woke up and looked around confused.

Cracker got out and said, "Thank you, mister."

Julia wrapped her gum in paper and put it in the ashtray. She reached for Angel's belt buckle.

"What are you doing?" he asked.

"Giving you a blow job," she said. "It's my turn. Cracker did the truck driver that took us to Northhampton."

"I don't want a blowjob."

"Jesus, mister. I'm not doing any kinky stuff with you, if that's what you think."

"Just get out of the car."

"Listen mister, please don't hurt me."

"I'm not going to hurt you," Angel said. "Please, just get out and go with Cracker. I don't want anything from you."

Julia looked dubious but got out of the car. She said something to Cracker who turned and gave Angel the finger. "Fuck you, mister," she shouted. Julia grabbed her arm and pulled her away.

Angel watched until they were gone. Cracker was clearly messed up, but Julia walked with that stiff-legged gait a woman makes when trying to make a dignified exit.

So, he had insulted those two by not sticking his dick down their throats?

Oh, brave new world that has such people in't…

He began to drive away but stopped quickly and got out. He bent over and tried to vomit. His stomach retched, but nothing came out.

A woman came out of Dan and Whit's.

"Are you all right, son?" she asked.

He looked at her helplessly. He had a vision of a teary Cassie in his head.

No, he most certainly was not all right.

Chapter Fifteen

ANGEL LAUGHED ALL THE WAY HOME FROM STONE'S CLASS.

At Phi Psi, he ducked into the cloakroom and bought M&Ms and a Coke. He met Sandman coming down the stairs.

"Guess who's auditing Stone's class this quarter?" Angel asked.

"James Joyce?"

"Close," Angel laughed. "Cara Whitley."

"Isn't she that chick who hated you all first quarter?"

"Yep. She stopped me on the way out of class and told me to prepare for battle."

"Why is she auditing?"

"She couldn't get in," Angel said. "She doesn't have one of the prerequisites, but, get this, she told me she's there because she likes fighting with me."

"Where's she from?"

"I don't remember. Vassar or Radcliffe, maybe."

"Yeah," Sand said. "I guess they don't get to argue much in classes there."

Groucho came down the stairs, reeking of hashish. "Mail for you, Angel. I threw it on your desk."

"Anything good?"

"Yep. Letters from your harem."

"Ha ha," Angel said dourly. He plodded up the steps, desiring little besides passing out on his bed. On Monday, he had gone to his classes and then sat up typing an Ezra Pound essay for what seemed like an eternity. Between his penchant for re-writing constantly and his sudden ineptitude at typing, it was an ordeal. Tuesday had been a blur, too. He had a four-hour physics lab, two classes, and had finally gotten to the ski slopes and made three runs before the ski patrol closed everything because of icy conditions.

He didn't know why he hadn't slept Tuesday night. He had probably been too tired to fall asleep. He had ended up reading all night.

He sighed. His curiosity got the better of him, and he went to his desk to check his mail. Groucho hadn't been kidding. There were letters from Rose and Cassie. Wow! This could be interesting or really, really shitty.

Cassie's letter could pose several distinctly different dangers. What if she wanted to un-break-up? Or what if it was a tirade? Neither would be pleasant. So, he chose to read Rose's missive first. He could hear her voice and smell her hair even before he tore the envelope open.

Dearest Angel,

Yep, he could definitely hear her voice. It managed to be both musical and serious simultaneously. How did she do that?

I waited forever to hear back from you, and, when I did, your letter was, to say the least, disappointing.

Angel smiled. It was true. He had written very carefully to Rose. He couldn't tell her anything about his Cassie woes. It would have been wrong. Plus, Rose knew Cassie which further complicated matters. He had wanted to write a flirty, sexy letter to match hers, but that, too, would have been wrong. As a result, his letter sounded like the response to a solicitation: short and artless.

As you read this, I have no idea what I am doing. You are five hours behind London time. So, let's say you read this mid-day. Perhaps I am at dinner or in the physics library. Or, perhaps I am back in my room lying on my bed wondering if you are reading my letter.

Time is such a ridiculously funny physics notion, isn't it? I wrote this perhaps two weeks ago (by the time you get it) and yet you read it as if I am saying it right now. Trippy, huh? So, your reading and my writing are like a severely disjointed conversation, with weeks between question and reply.

I wonder if you even remember me or think of me. We had one date for a few hours on a day you will remember more for the woman who died in the car crash than you will for meeting me. I hope I made an impression which will survive Cassie, the intervening few weeks, and whatever barbarities I know you are up to at Dartmouth.

Yes, Rose, you made an indelible impression. Sigh.

I hope you appreciate the effort I put into this light-hearted tone. I was going for a Jane Austen effect, like the one the silly girl in Northanger Abbey might write. I am, after all, in London.

But I really want to talk about more serious matters. You were intrigued that I am reading theoretical physics. At least, you pretended to be. Was that because you feel women are too silly and shallow to read such things? I think not. You seem to genuinely admire female intellect. And you wouldn't be in love with Cassie if brains weren't a turn-on to you.

Anyway, to my real subject: Bosonic String Theory. Exciting topic, huh? I have been reading a lot about string theory. Do you know anything about that? (Probably. You are like an Oscar Wilde character: 'ostentatiously knowledgeable') Well, I have several questions about it. First off, the theory requires twenty-seven dimensions. How in the world can I be expected to wrap my head around that? I have enough difficulty with time as a fourth dimension. Sigh. So, any thoughts or help would be appreciated. Second, why just Bosons? What about Fermions? I know, the Pauli Exclusion Principle and all that, but still?

The idea is so exciting though, isn't it? What if there is no such thing as a particle? What if all of matter is comprised of tiny strings vibrating on differing wavelengths? Wouldn't that solve the Einstein paradox which means that Special Relativity and Quantum theory don't work together?

It is a very exciting time to be alive.

Which brings me back to my Angel and part of the reason for this letter. A professor of mine mentioned an Austrian (?) physicist who was tutored by a young Irish writer named James Joyce. (Did you say that you do or don't believe in synchronicity? I can't remember.) Joyce taught the young man that language and physics are like music. If you sit at a keyboard and hit a group of keys randomly, the chances of making music are small. That is because only certain permissible sounds go together to make chords. That's exactly like Quantum Theory, in which only certain packets of particles can be emitted on certain wavelengths.

So, does modernist literature act upon Quantum principles or on Relativity principles? I'm sure you have an opinion on this matter. You have one on nearly everything else.

Angel stopped reading and rolled a joint. He was getting hard. This little vixen was prodding him so he would have to write her back. He tried to remember the last time he got a hard on while reading physics. He smiled and lit the joint. Yep, this chick was dangerously cute. He shook his head and picked the letter back up.

Heretofore, I've been avoiding the subject, but you probably know I was watching you from my bedroom window as you drove away. I saw you glance up and wave. What's a male witch called? A warlock? You're one of those, aren't you? Or are we just connected by some invisible skein of like-minded thought? Cassie said you are one. She asked if you kissed me, and I said yes. Do you know what she told me? She said I was doomed. Am I doomed, Angel? If you want me to be, I will be. Cassie also said she feared your relationship with her was moribund. I'll bet you love women who use words like 'moribund,' don't you? Cassie always was brilliant. If you two are still having problems, I am genuinely sorry. I would like to be your friend, and I don't want you to think I have designs on you. I don't; I promise. Yes, you are sexy in an odd, violent way, and yes, you are passably intelligent, but, let's face it: you aren't a very good dancer. I guess I neglected the kissing. I would have to say you do that very well.

Write me and tell me your thoughts on physics or literature or whatever you are pondering. And please tell me that I kiss well, too. I am a bit lonely over here and in need of compliments.

Oh, that's not completely true. I met a barrister at a party who has asked me out. His name is Arthur. I haven't decided how to respond. He is terribly dashing, but he's in his thirties. Do you have any advice on the matter?

Your ardent friend,

Rose

Angel munched on an M&M and contemplated the wild, exotic Rose. Yes, her tone was flighty and silly, but her text was profoundly intellectual. The whole thing was a remarkable document in flirting. More than ever, he was grateful an ocean was between them. He had the feeling he would be overmatched if she were nearby.

How could she be friendless and lonely? It made no sense. Perhaps the generalization that men eschewed smart women was true. He didn't know how that could be. They were such a turn-on for him. He was still hard just from reading her letter. But did women also choose not to befriend smart women? It was true that there had been packs of popular dimwits in his high school. The country club girls who had grown up together poolside at Timuquana or the Yacht Club. He had dated smart girls who were part of those cliques. Did they have to bimbo down to be accepted by the other girls whose vacuous laughs and empty eyes repulsed him so badly?

And Cassie's attitude towards Rose intrigued him. Was Cassie devious enough to know that her time with Angel was over? Could she have picked Rose as a sort of successor? Here, Rose, he's basically a good guy. Maybe you'll have more luck than I did. For a guy who thought he understood women, he grew more ignorant daily.

Hubris, thy name is douchebag…

He picked up Cassie's letter and stared at it. He was almost afraid to read it. It was lighter and thinner, so it was probably cursory. He hoped it didn't contain bile or bathos. Both were beneath Cassie.

How could he love someone and still not want to see her anymore? It was an evening of paradoxes.

He sighed and tore open the envelope.

Dear Angel,

The day we broke up, I wish I had known you were coming to see me. I did hear the phone ringing the night before and chose not to answer it. You know why? Because I was afraid it would be you and that you would want to have the very conversation we had.

I had heard that phone ring almost nightly and had never answered it for that same reason.

It is also why I stopped coming to Dartmouth. You thought it was because I despised your Phi Psi friends. It wasn't. I don't dislike them; I envy them. They see you every day.

My fancy is that if we lived together, we would still be a happy couple. It is true, though, that you tend to forget people you aren't with. Or, rather, you tend to focus intently on the people nearby. That is what makes you such a good lover, in case you have ever wondered. You are not the handsomest and certainly won't be the most successful (in worldly terms), but you are the most focused on the wellbeing and happiness of the one you are with. It hurts me to remember how happy I felt when I was with you.

In many ways, you are a dream lover. You meld the bad boy with the sophisticate. The story you wrote for me was truly beautiful, and it epitomized both your poetic nature and your sexual voracity. It drives me crazy. You can be such a romantic. The story, however, was written nostalgically, as if you wrote it after you knew we were finished as a couple. It was a lovely farewell present, but it was just that, a farewell present. (Because I know you value my opinion, I would add that your writing is, indeed, getting better. Please keep writing.)

All I really wanted to say was that I love you and know you still love me, and I wish you well. I was hurt and bitter when you were here. I wish I hadn't been. We both deserved a better parting. Our love, when intact, was wonderful. It nurtured both of us for so long.

I hope we can remain friends, and I hope there may come a day when we can sit down with each other and not feel anxious. For you, that would probably require about two days. For me, it will require much longer.

Your erstwhile lover and always your friend,

Cassie

Wow. Not what he expected. To have written that eloquently and graciously… he was dumbfounded. Grace under pressure. It was practically her family motto.

Unless, of course, she was devious and trying for the moral high-ground to make him feel shitty. Possible but highly unlikely. Or that she was setting up a reconciliation. More likely, but still improbable.

Cassie had been hurting for months. While he sat at Dartmouth, irritated with her, she sat at Smith jealous. That was unfair and cruel. Male and female psychology were not his fault, but he knew he should have factored them better into his actions and thoughts.

Angel decided he would take her letter at face value, even though it made him want to get in his car and go to her. And almost certainly to make love to her.

No, that wasn't true. Rose's letter gave him a boner. Cassie's gave him a lump in his throat. Different vibes altogether.

Arghhh. He didn't deserve either of these women, much less Maggie.

He pulled several fresh sheets of paper and his lucky pen. Cassie first.

Cassie,

Of course, we will always be friends. No one knows me as you do. Of course, I still love you. I couldn't say that at Smith. It would have undercut the surgical nature of my mission, but I'm glad you know it to be true.

I agree that I don't really miss people when they are not around. Nor do I feel jealousy. I don't know how to change how I feel or don't feel.

I do know that I cannot stand the fact that I hurt you. That will always haunt me.

What I do feel, and I feel it keenly, is failure. Our breaking up shows that I have failed at one of the most basic parts of life. I couldn't sustain a relationship, even though I still care for and value you. I am afraid that what that says about me is not flattering. I hope you don't feel the same way about me. I assure you that I beat myself up enough on my own without your thinking poorly of me, too.

You are wrong though about one thing: I need time to deal with all this. I will write something more personal and with more feeling when I am capable, but I, too, am emotionally spent and somewhat dazed. A thought like a drum beat infects everything I do: how could this have happened?

I am sorry for my part in all of this. I truly am.

Angel

He reread Cassie's letter and his response. His was pretty unsatisfactory, especially the ending, but he had no clue how to improve it.

He re-lit the roach and finished the now warm Coke. He paced, trying to decide what to do but gave up and stubbed out the roach. He lay on his bed and bounced a baseball off the wall for what seemed an eternity.

He wandered Phi Psi. Things were quiet but for the crowd in the tube room. Eddie was telling a Viet Nam story that Angel hadn't heard, but he wasn't in the mood so he bought another Coke and headed back to his room.

He reread Rose's letter, which cheered him up. She was so unspoiled and funny.

She should date him for a while. Then, she would be neither unspoiled nor funny.

Shit.

Perhaps he could write Rose a better letter than the one he had written Cassie.

Rose du Monde,

Your writing style displeases me. It smacks of a horrid cross between Gwendolyn and Cecily in The Importance of Being Earnest without having the virtues of either woman.

I'm kidding. I smiled and laughed throughout. You are very quick-witted and entertaining, and I could hear your voice as I read.

Worse for me, I could smell your hair and taste your lips.

You accuse me of being a warlock. I think perhaps you are a witch.

Do a witch and a warlock make a good match?

Sigh. Time to get serious. Cassie and I are no more. Relax. I am not trying to win you. I tire of women who possess brains and beauty and breasts and wit and grace and breasts and charm and sensuality and intellect and breasts. None of those things interest me, particularly large, shapely, pendant breasts which wink seductively at a man when the women possessing them wears a dress cut practically to her navel.

I am simply immune to such temptations. The erection I got while reading your letter and which has returned whilst I write is purely an anatomical anomaly and has nothing to do with you (or your breasts.)

Sorry, that began on a serious note about my loss of Cassie. I guess I'm deflecting. There isn't much to say. We loved each other. It was first love for both of us, and we screwed it up, somehow. I don't really know how. I wish I did.

Wrong wavelengths perhaps. Impermissible wavelengths. Yes, I have read about bosonic string theory and discussed it at length with my physics professor the same day I received your letter. I know: synchronicity. His name is Hincker. Do you know him? He studied with Edelman at Columbia. As in studied with him, not under him. Isn't Edelman the boson fermion king? Hincker said that, as you suggested, newer theories would be spun that would, indeed, fold fermions into the mix. (That was a spin, anti-spin joke of sorts.) Better still for my weak mind, they will reduce the necessary number of dimensions considerably. Perhaps of greater immediacy, though, is the work being done on Quarks. And, thereby hangs a tale: James Joyce (yes, he of the physics tutoring) had a drunken character in Finnegans Wake raise a quart of Guinness to toast a man named Finnegan who had just died. He mistakenly said, 'raise a quark for muster mark,' and, apparently, Zweig or Gell-Mann or somebody important thought it so funny he named a sub-particle (a sub-string?) after the drunken toast. I thought you would like that story. You might want to check it. I tell it from memory, and my mind is addled from grief, marijuana, sleeplessness, and the mysterious image of large, firm breasts.

I am sorry my last letter was a dud. I was in the middle of breaking up with Cassie, and I didn't want to talk about her with anyone. It seemed unmanly and wrong.

I really don't know what to say about my attacking that boy that night. I just go off when a woman is threatened. I know that implies that I think women can't defend themselves, but I don't believe that. I am simply programmed to attack. It happens before I can even think to stop myself. I'm so sorry I did that. I didn't mean to embarrass or alienate you. I would just in all honesty say that if the situation came up again I would probably react the same way.

I know. I have issues.

If you still want to continue our pen wars, please write me. I hope your barrister turns out to be the one you seek. You are a remarkable woman, and I wish you joy and love. Something tells me intuitively that you have no idea of your worth and have been hiding it from everyone around you for your whole life. You make yourself sound friendless and loveless. That is astonishing.

I, for one, am your true friend. I know. We have only spent a few hours together. But, like you, I sense that our connection pre-dated that romantic night and will continue.

So, please write. I will write back and try to entertain you.
Angel

Whew. That pretty much used up all the wit Angel had for the evening. But it was a much-needed escape from thinking about Cassie, and he appreciated Rose's having provided it.

Angel stripped and grabbed a towel. Maybe a shower would clear his head enough to get some work done before his radio hour. He certainly didn't want to try to nap. He knew that would result in nothing but dark reflection and tossing and turning.

But the shower, usually his best friend, didn't let him off the hook, and his mood continued to plummet.

He thought of calling Maggie, but even Thor had lost interest in women for the night. He contemplated calling Cassie and was sorely tempted, but he knew to let her grieve and heal.

He wrapped the towel around his middle and climbed to the empty pool room and out onto the balcony.

There, he shivered and watched the first flakes of a new storm flutter down like penitential feathers.

His eyes filled with tears, and he sought a message in the falling flakes, but they just drifted silently and ignored him.

He smiled. This was the ending of *The Dead*. He pictured the Smith and Colby campuses and imagined the snow falling there, slowly but steadily blanketing the earth in a forgetful, frozen world of white.

Cassie would be crossing campus, returning to her dorm. As she climbed to the second floor and left the stairwell, she would stolidly ignore the phone on the wall, knowing it wouldn't ring, and that, if it did, Angel wouldn't be on the other end begging forgiveness and reconciliation.

Maggie would be in her dorm, reading and waiting patiently for midnight, when Angel's radio show would begin.

He had a couple of hours to decide what he wanted to play and what he wanted to say on the air that night. What message did he have for the Dartmouth world? And what secret message would he have for Maggie which would set her heart racing and her loins afire?

He didn't know.

He went to his desk and gathered the notes he had made for the night's playlist. He picked up his pen and scratched out some songs and added others. This would be a melancholy night, a true blues night. There would be no boastful or triumphant Muddy Waters or Howling Wolf. Testosterone was off the table. He would let women, like Billy Holliday, sing the blues to rid themselves of their suffering.

Their voices, he hoped, would match the stillness of the falling snow and birth a sadder, wiser world, a world in which pain was redeemed by art, and one in which art soothed his lovers' suffering.

Oh, that the music might reach Cassie and offer her solace. But he knew that it wouldn't, and that she would go to bed alone that night, more alone than he would ever be.

Chapter Sixteen

WHY DID YOUR ANGEL PICK THIS LADY SINGS THE BLUES line-up? It goes out in honor of my former girlfriend, Cassie, the best person I have ever known. I want everyone to raise your mug or take a toke in honor of Cassie. And then drink or smoke again for the sorrows of all lovers who have tried but lost. It's all Dukkha, anyway. And, in a strange way, it's all beautiful in its sadness and loneliness.

Angel put the needle down on a classic version of *Summertime*.

This is Eleanora Fagan, again, better known to you musically illiterate clods as Billie Holiday. Backing that track up will be Gloomy Sunday.

The first strains of the melody began, and Angel clicked off his microphone and waved Billy and Gandalf into the booth.

"What's up guys?"

"Well, first, here's that ounce you ordered," Gandalf said.

Angel opened the bag and smelled it. Ah, nothing like really fresh pot. But he detected something else. He raised an eyebrow to Gandalf.

Gandalf smiled and nodded. "Good nose, Angel. There's a little bit of hash oil in it and a bunch of Sensimilla."

"Nice," Angel said. He pulled out his wallet and handed Gandalf a crisp hundred-dollar bill. He turned to Billy who was pulling records from the shelf and admiring them.

"How did that essay turn out?" Angel asked.

Billy smiled. "I got an A. Thanks so much for helping me. I really appreciate it."

"My pleasure."

"We have a question for you. Billy's got an issue and needs advice," Gandalf said.

"Okay, no problem," Angel nodded gravely. "Billy, my advice is to stop hanging around with Gandalf. He'll make an outlaw out of you."

Billy smiled. "That's probably true, but my problem is my parents."

"Oh," Angel said. "They're hassling you again?"

"No, they're being nice, but they're coming for a visit this weekend."

"And this a problem because?"

"Angel, they don't know. I haven't told them."

Shit. Angel was pretty sure he could tell his parents he was queer without causing a scene. His father wouldn't care, and his mother would barely look up from her book long enough to smile and nod. He'd met Billy's parents, though, and they were Georgia Baptist stock. He could see why Billy might be hesitant.

"So," Angel said. "You want advice on how to tell them?"

Gandalf smirked, and Billy shifted uncomfortably.

"We were thinking of a ruse," Gandalf said.

Oh, Lord. Gandalf had been hanging around Eddie too much.

Angel held a finger up. He put the needle of the turntable down on *Gloomy Sunday*.

He turned back to his friends.

"Is Maggie coming up this weekend?" Billy asked.

"She better," Angel said. "I'm kind of bursting at the seams."

"We need to borrow her," Gandalf said.

"I want Maggie to pretend she's my girlfriend and go to dinner with my parents," Billy said and blushed.

Angel smiled. That was hilarious. He was confident that Maggie would be sympathetic to Billy's plight and go along with the scheme, dumb though it was.

"Okay," Angel said. "I'll ask her."

"They're taking us to The Hanover Inn, so it will be nice," Billie said.

"Hanover Inn? If Jane shows up this weekend, can we come, too?"

Gandalf laughed. "This is getter better and better."

Billy smiled and shook his head. "I have a bad feeling about this. It was Gandalf's idea. That should have been a tip-off."

"So, we can join you?" Angel asked.

"I suppose so."

"And Billy," Angel said. "Maggie doesn't have to screw you or blow you in front of your parents, does she? Not that she'd probably mind. She thinks you're cute."

"You are so gross," Billy smiled.

Angel held a finger up again and turned his mike on. He waved for Billy and Gandalf to take a hike.

And now, an entire album side from Ma Rainey. Ma was born in 1886, so this will be raw. I hope you like it. The album is entitled Mother of the Blues. The first song is called Deep Moaning Blues. I'm dedicating this to Maggie. She will know why.

Billy and Gandalf waved and left quietly.

Angel waved back and pulled out papers to roll a joint from his brand-new stash.

He watched his friends walk down the hall, Billy with his Beatle mop of hair and the diminutive Gandalf, dressed, as usual, all in black and wearing a cape.

What a freaky time to live.

Angel leaned back and listened to Ma Rainey. But his mind was already at The Hanover Inn trying not to bust out laughing.

This was going to be epic.

Chapter Seventeen

MAGGIE LEANED OVER THE BATHROOM SINK AT PHI PSI AND put the finishing touches to her make-up. She saw Angel smirking at her in the mirror, and she had to laugh.

"How did I let you talk me into this?" she said.

"You'll have a blast," Angel said.

Eddie hurried in and, seeing Maggie there, said, "Sorry Mags, I really need to take a leak."

Maggie laughed. "Go right ahead."

Eddie hit the urinal in a hurry. He unzipped and said, "Ah," as his stream began. "Too much beer, too early," he said.

Maggie finished and turned around. "How do I look?"

"Like a walking hard-on," Eddie said.

Maggie laughed. "I was asking Angel, but thank you anyway."

"You know this ruse is totally insane, don't you?" Eddie asked.

"It will be fun," Maggie said.

"You're probably gonna have to screw Billy to make it seem realistic. Right there on the table in front of his 'rents. They've probably been suspecting he was queer for years."

Maggie laughed.

"Oh, almost forgot," Eddie said. "Jane's in your room, Angel. I told her Maggie was here this weekend, and Groucho's already offered her his room. But with Maggie gone to dinner, I guess she'll have some Angel time coming.

"Yes," Angel exclaimed. "That means I have a date, too."

Maggie pinched his ear. "You better have a good explanation for this. Who's

Jane? Is that the girl I caught you with in the fall?" She turned to Eddie. "I caught him dressing with a girl in his room."

"Shocking," Eddie said. "We all thought Angel was a virgin."

"That was Wanda," Angel said. "And she was here on business."

"So, who is Jane?"

"Angel's little sex pet," Eddie offered.

"Angel?" Maggie said.

"Jane's the girl we did battle for at *Boar's Head*. She shows up when she's feeling bad. Everybody takes care of her. Ed's trying to get me in trouble, but he's the one who will hang out with Jane all weekend."

"I'll let you two sort this out," Eddie said gleefully and left.

"Thanks, Ed," Angel shouted after him.

"Angel?"

"Maggie, Jane is just a friend. Come meet her. You'll see."

"Then why did you cry 'yes' when Eddie said she was here?"

Angel put his arms around her. "Because that means I get to go to dinner, too. I get to watch my Baby pretend to be Billy's girlfriend. It will be hilarious."

Angel took her hand and led her to his room. Jane sat at his desk reading.

"Jane," Angel said. "I'd like for you to meet someone."

Jane rose and smiled "Hi," she said. "You must be Cassie. I've heard so much about you."

Maggie punched Angel. "No, I'm Maggie."

"Sorry," Jane laughed.

"Cassie and I broke up."

"Oh, sorry," Jane said. "Or congratulations. I know there were problems."

"Thanks, both probably apply."

So, is this the Maggie you were writing about?" Jane said. She held up a sheaf of pages.

"It is, indeed," he smiled.

"I put my stuff in Groucho's room," Jane said. "He said he'd sleep in the bunk room. I hate to put him out."

"He sleeps in the bunk room every night," Angel said. He went to Jane and hugged her. "How would you like to be my girlfriend for the night?"

Jane looked at Maggie, who threw up her hands.

"Do you remember Billy Brewster?" he said. "He went skiing with us once."

Jane nodded.

"Well, Maggie will be Billy's girlfriend tonight."

Jane looked confused.

"Billy's parents are here," Maggie said.

"Oh," Jane said. "And they don't know?"

"No," Angel said. "And Billy doesn't want them to know. So, Maggie is going to dinner as his chick, and you and I are going, too."

"I could be Billy's chick," Jane offered.

"No," Angel said. "Maggie's perfect. She for real dated a guy who was pretending to be straight."

"I still do," Maggie said.

Angel gave her a look.

"So, Jane, you disappear and dress. Did you bring anything nice?"

"Not really," she said. "I'll do my best."

"Don't worry," Maggie said. "You won't have to do much to look better than Mister Jeans and Boots, here."

"Hey," Angel said. "I can dress up."

Jane laughed and left to get ready.

Maggie sat at Angel's desk and picked up the manuscript.

"So?" she said.

"I swear. Just a friend. Jane gets depressed and comes to Hanover. We cheer her up."

"Uh huh," Maggie said. "Have you ever slept with her?"

Angel paused. "Maybe."

Maggie laughed. "But you won't anymore because now you are wildly infatuated with me."

"Exactly," Angel said.

Maggie stood and went to him. She got on her toes and kissed him. "I haven't thanked you for Wednesday night."

Angel looked blank.

"You sent me a sweet message on your radio show. You don't remember?"

"Ah, you liked that, did you?"

"Yes, you silly man." She kissed him again and went back to reading. "Will I like this?" she asked, holding up his manuscript.

"It's just a little story about a girl named Maggie who blows a Yalie while he fantasizes about doing the same thing to another guy."

"You shit," she laughed and chased him across the room, beating him with the papers in her hand.

Promptly at seven, Billy knocked on Angel's door to pick up Maggie. Billy wore a blazer and khakis and looked handsome. Maggie wore a simple black dress which flashed some cleavage.

"You look beautiful," Billy said.

"Thank you, sir. It's nice to be with a gentleman for a change," Maggie said and took his arm. Jane and Angel watched them leave.

"Shit," Angel said. "We're underdressed." He pulled off his shirt and found a clean white, long-sleeved one and began to button it. "Check Maggie's bag," he told

Jane. "Maybe she has something you could wear. Jane opened Maggie's bag didn't see anything dressy.

"Okay," he said. "You look great anyway." He lit a joint and offered it to her.

She shook her head. "No, I get paranoid when I'm stoned around adults.

When they got to The Hanover Inn, the Brewsters rose from their table to greet them.

"Tom Brewster," Billy's father said. He shook Angel's hand and nodded at Jane. "I'm glad you could join us. Billy says you have practically saved his academic life on more than one occasion."

"Billy's a talented writer," Angel said. "He just doesn't know it yet."

"He's always put himself down," Billy's mother said.

"This is my girlfriend, Jane," Angel said.

Jane nodded to the parents and put her arm through Angel's.

Maggie scowled at Angel but turned sweetly to Billy's family. "This is the first time Billy and I have double-dated," she said. "Usually, he just keeps me to himself. Some visits, I hardly get to leave his room at all."

Susan, Billy's mother, jumped in. "These boys. One track minds." She sighed dramatically.

"I don't mind, do I, Bill-bill?" Maggie said and pecked Billy on the cheek.

Billy turned crimson.

Tom put down his menu. "Let's order," he said. "I'm starved, and Maggie says she has to get back to Colby tonight."

"Yes," she said. "I have to write a research paper. Billy's been helping me, but I have to finish on my own. I don't know what I'd do without him." She put her hand on his.

Susan clapped her hands.

"This is so sweet."

A waiter delivered drinks to the table. Tom drank a scotch, as did Billy. Maggie had something pink and girlie looking. Susan had ordered wine.

"I didn't know what you wanted, dear, so I just thought we could share a bottle," Susan told Jane.

"That's perfect, Jane said. "Don't let me drink too much or I'll be dancing on the table."

They laughed.

The waiter put a Coke in front of Angel.

Tom raised his glass. "Here's to young love." Everyone clinked and drank. Jane bussed Angel on the lips, and Maggie, eyeing them, did the same to a sputtering Billy.

Susan laughed delightedly. "This is wonderful. Billy usually keeps his girlfriends as far away from us as possible. It's as if he's ashamed of us."

"Slow down on the wine, Susan. You know how you get," Tom said.

"Pish," Susan said. "This is a happy event."

They were interrupted by a waiter who took their orders.

When he left, Tom turned to Maggie. "So, how did you two lovebirds meet, anyway? Billy tells us nothing."

Maggie put her hand on Billy's arm and rubbed it affectionately. "He hasn't told you?" she said to Billy. "It will sound barbaric," she warned.

"Okay by me," Tom said. He took a belt of scotch.

"Well," Maggie said. "I was at Colby, walking with some friends, when, out of nowhere, this giant jerk confronts a group of my friends and began to harass us. He even touched my chest. I was scared to death."

"No," Susan said.

"Yes," Maggie said. "And Billy, who is braver than he is bright sometimes, came rushing up and defended me. Sort of. He got hit in the face for his efforts, twice. His lip and nose were bleeding, but he got right back up and stared the man down."

"Oh, dear Lord," Susan said, staring at her son. "What an adventure. Tom, would you do that for me?"

"I might have back when we were dating," Tom said. "Now? I'd have to see how big the guy is." He laughed. Angel smiled.

"So, what happened, then?" Susan asked.

"I took him back to my room, and, well, things developed quickly." She blushed.

Susan let out a little yip. "Oh, my."

Angel almost choked on his Coke.

"Are we talking about the same William Brewster?" Tom asked.

"Hush, dear, it was romantic." She turned to Maggie.

Maggie turned to Jane with a mocking smile. "Jane, since we're baring our souls, tell us how you met Angel. I've never heard that story."

Jane smiled sweetly. Angel and Billy exchanged glances. Angel's look said 'you owe me.' Billy's said, 'sorry dude.'

"Before I met Angel, I was," she paused. She turned aside and her voice quavered. "I can't tell this."

"It's all right, dear," Susan said. "You can tell us. We're not judgmental people." She poured another glass of wine and sipped it.

Jane wiped at her eyes and looked about her, her face aglow.

Maggie smiled. Angel did, too. Who knew Jane was such a good actress?

"Okay," Jane said in a tremulous voice. "I used to be an adult entertainer."

"You mean, like a dancer?" Tom asked.

"No, worse," she said. "I was in movies. Adult ones."

"Oh, my," Susan said.

"Yes, it all began when I was thirteen. I thought I was in love with an older boy.

He was twenty, and he drove one of those Mustangs, the ones which don't look like Mustangs."

"Not a Shelby Cobra?" Tom asked.

"Yes, that's the one," Jane said. She sighed, her whole chest heaving. "By the time I was fifteen, he had me doing horrible things on camera. Last fall, I was shooting a film here in Hanover."

Tom shook his head and squirmed in his chair. Angel smiled. He knew what that meant. Tom had a boner.

"I was basically being held captive," Jane said. "I got free one Friday night, the very same Friday when Maggie met Billy." She turned to Maggie. "Isn't it funny to think that? While you were with Billy, three men were, well, you know?"

Susan looked aghast. Tom practically danced in his chair.

"Anyway," Jane said. "I got away and found my way to Phi Psi. That's Billy and Angel's fraternity. I was crying and all covered in," she paused and looked around apologetically, "fluids. I'm sorry. I know that's gross."

Susan looked sick. She raised her hand for another bottle of wine.

"Angel and his friends took me in. I told them my story, and they went to where I was being held and beat those men unconscious. Angel almost killed the man who was filming everything. He came back to Phi Psi, and that was the first time we made love. Angel was covered in blood, and I was covered with…sorry. I don't have a filter when I drink wine." She stopped, again. "I know it sounds awful, but it wasn't. Angel and Billy and their friends treated me like a lady. And it worked. I quit the film industry and started college. All because they saw past my, well, my past. It was so romantic, wasn't it, sweetheart?" She stroked Angel's face.

Susan and Tom just stared. Maggie eyed Angel grimly. Billy and Angel tried to suppress grins.

Jane sat still and demurely sipped her wine.

"Since then, Angel and I haven't been able to keep our hands off each other, have we? Just telling that makes me want to…well…never mind. Angel always tells me I don't know when to stop. Talking, that is," she added quickly. She giggled nervously. Tom smiled reassuringly at her.

At dinner's end, Maggie folded her napkin. "Well," she said. "I really must get back to Colby. Billy can entertain you two, and I'm sure Angel and Jane can't wait to be alone." Her voice dripped acid.

Susan had drunk herself into a stupor. Tom had been drooling over Jane ever since her story, mortifying Billy.

Angel nodded at Billy who looked questioningly back at him.

"Oh," Billy said. "Let me walk you to your car."

"Isn't he sweet?" Maggie asked. "It's snowing dear. You stay and play host."

Billy rose and pulled her chair out for her. Maggie stood. She took Billy's face in her hands and kissed him long and hard. "Sweet dreams, lover. I'll be thinking of you."

Billy just stared. Maggie shook hands with Tom and Susan and walked away, waving over her shoulder.

Angel watched her go. He smiled again. He was in for it when he got back to Phi Psi.

"I think I will have a drink," he said. "Waiter, bring me whatever Tom's having and refill everyone's glasses."

Jane smiled at Angel over her wine glass. She looked like an evil pixie.

After dinner, Angel and Jane walked slowly back to Phi Psi. Jane was excited and bubbly.

"That was a blast," she said. "I've never had so much fun in my life. Did you see that woman's face? And Tom leered at me non-stop." She twirled in the falling snow, looking like a skater at Rockefeller Center.

"I don't think Maggie enjoyed it as much as you did," Angel said.

"Oh, poop on poor Maggie. She told a story, too. Imagine Billy standing up to a bully. He would pee in his pants."

"I'm not sure," Angel said. "Billy's no wimp. And he's bigger than I am."

"Oh, but that story was so silly."

Angel nodded. It was, even when he starred in it.

Jane stopped them just past Moe's. She turned her face to the heavens and stared up into the snow. "Can we go skiing tomorrow? This is wonderful snow."

Angel laughed. "I don't know. I'll see. Remember, I'm with Maggie, assuming she didn't bolt for Colby. I may have some explaining to do tonight. Maggie knew your story was partly true. She may not have enjoyed its climax."

Jane blinked and then began to laugh. Angel laughed, too.

Jane leaned against Angel, and he put his arm around her.

"Angel, do me a favor, and I'll leave you and Maggie alone all weekend."

"Shoot."

"Kiss me." She stared up into his face. She glowed with a light Angel had never seen in her before. Where was his Jane? And who was this strange, happy thing clinging to his lapels and beaming at him.

Angel held her face with his hands and kissed her. Her lips were soft, not at all the thin, hard ones he had first kissed. He could taste the wine she had been drinking, and he could feel the life surging through her.

"I could stand here all night kissing you," she said.

"I could too," he confessed. He felt an admixture of guilt and confusion.

"I know," she said. "Maggie time." She took his hand and pulled him towards Phi Psi. She sounded merry when she said in a little girl's voice, "You're gonna be in trouble."

Angel was comforted that Maggie's car was still in the driveway. Jane joined the guys playing poker. As usual, Eddie was chirping non-stop while Sand quietly accreted money.

Angel searched his room and the bathroom. No Maggie. He looked up in the poolroom, but it was empty, a strange sight on a Friday night. He went back to his room. Maggie's dress was hanging up, and her bag still on the floor.

He rolled a joint and went back downstairs for a Coke. He checked the kitchen. No Maggie. Finally, he leaned in the card room.

"Eddie, seen Maggie anywhere?"

"She came through a few minutes ago," Eddie said. "Did you check the bar?"

"Good idea," Angel said.

"Bring us some beers?" Sand said.

"Sure thing." Angel went downstairs to the bar. Lester and Blake were throwing darts. Their dates sat on a bench chattering animatedly.

Angel poured twelve beers, put them in a Coke case, and delivered them as promised.

"Thanks, Angel," Eddie said.

"Did you really see Maggie heading downstairs, or did you want me to get you beers?"

"Just wanted beers," Sand said. "We haven't seen Maggie."

"We're going to a Sigma Nu party as soon as I clean these douches out," Eddie said. "Want us to come get you?"

Angel nodded. "You guys taking Jane?"

"You in, Jane?" Sand asked.

Jane clapped her hands. She was in.

Angel turned and went upstairs. He lit the joint and opened his Coke.

Well, shit.

Where would he go if he wanted to sulk and be alone? Had she taken a walk? Then, he smiled and nodded. He took a hit on the joint and climbed to the pool room again. He opened the window and climbed out on the roof. There sat Maggie with a blanket wrapped around her. Snow dotted her hair, and he could tell from the way she shook that she was crying.

He sat next to her and offered her the joint. Maggie shook her head.

Angel smoked and drank his Coke. It was a fine night. The snow was heavy enough that he couldn't see the sky, but the path the flakes made as they meandered through the glow of the streetlamps was gorgeous. It was as if each flake sucked in photons and lit up, like floating, white lightning bugs, suddenly showing themselves and then drifting back into the darkness. The great trees in Phi Psi's front yard were already covered with snow. Icing on a cake, Angel thought.

Finally, Maggie spoke.

"I saw you," she said.

Angel waited. He had no idea what that meant.

"In front of Moe's. I saw you."

Ah. She had seen Jane kiss him. He poked about for guilt or remorse. Nope. He couldn't find any.

"And?" he asked.

Maggie glared at him. "You kissed that girl. You've fucked that girl. You fucked her the night you met me. The very same night."

Angel smoked the joint and sipped his Coke. Sitting in the snow, it was staying cold nicely.

"No," he said evenly. "The night I met you I waited all night for you to show up and fantasized about you when I went to bed. But, you didn't come, and Jane appeared. She wasn't kidding in a sense. She was covered in fluids, her own tears and snot. She was a mess. We did go the next night and punish the guys who made her feel like a piece of shit. I did beat up a guy who photographed her doing embarrassing things. And, yes, I had sex with her that night. I don't apologize for any of that. If I felt guilty towards anyone, it would be to Cassie, not to you. Cassie, with whom I broke up, partly so I could be free to court you."

Angel handed Maggie his handkerchief. She wiped her face and blew her nose.

"You make it sound as if there's nothing between you and Jane," Maggie sniffed.

"No, I don't," Angel said. "Look at me, Maggie." He held her face up. "I will never deceive you. I'm Jane's friend. You want more fodder for your irritation? She came here and stayed over Thanksgiving after I sent you away. She was depressed and nearly suicidal. She didn't want to see her parents with fresh scars on her wrist, so she came here. And, yes, I kissed her just now. Her exact words were, 'if you kiss me I'll leave you and Maggie alone all weekend.' But I probably would have kissed her anyway. I like kissing her. I'm sure I'll kiss her again, sometime. Clean up and come inside before you freeze. I'll be in my room."

Angel got up and went back inside. He took off his good shirt and vest and hung them up. He pulled on a tee-shirt and sat at his desk which was a fucking mess. Too many girls reading his shit. He sensed Maggie behind him and turned to her. She folded the blanket and lay it on the bed. She blew her nose again and sat next to the blanket.

"Do you want me to go?" she asked.

Angel shook his head.

"Why were you so mean outside?" she asked.

"I wasn't mean. I was honest."

"I thought you were going to hold me and tell me that it was a goodbye kiss or something, anything to make me feel better. You were just cold."

Angel went to her and sat. He took her hand. It felt frozen, and he rubbed it to warm it up.

"Maggie, I don't know what to say to you. Jane comes here a lot. She's not my girl. She's a friend, and she depends on me. She's not like you, Maggie. Sometimes, she's barely hanging on by a thread. You're Maggie. You're smart and sexy and sane. She needs me. You don't."

Maggie sat silent. She got up. "I think I'm going back to Colby."

"Okay."

"You're not even going to try to talk me out of it?"

"No," he said. "Understand me, Maggie. You know exactly how I feel about you. When we kiss, when we hold each other, when we make love, you know I care. How do I feel when Jane shows up? This shocks me to say it, but I'm happy. How do I feel when you show up? My blood races and my dick hardens. There's no comparison. But I've only been out of a long, serious relationship for a couple of weeks and still feel like a total shit. Cassie may still be crying herself to sleep for all I know. I don't feel guilty about Jane, and I'm sure as shit not jumping into another heavy relationship right now, especially if it involves arguing and emotional games."

"Games?"

"Yes, games. Like playing jealous girlfriend. I haven't done anything wrong or anything I regret. If you don't want to be here or don't trust me, there's the door. I don't plan to spend my weekend fighting or defending myself."

"Fine," she said and flounced off the bed. She knelt and began cramming toiletries and clothes back into her bag. She took the dress from its hanger and shoved it in, too. She looked around the room to see if she had missed anything. She went through the door and slammed it on the way out.

"Bye, Maggie," Angel said to himself. He lit his joint again and finished his Coke.

He made a face. Shit. He didn't feel a goddamn thing except pissed at Maggie. He balled up his fist and slammed it down on his desk. Fuck.

Well, it looked as if he was going to Sigma Nu with the gang after all. Cane would be there. That might be good for a few laughs.

Blake yelled up to Angel that he had a phone call. Angel stubbed out his joint and pocketed a handful of quarters from his dresser. He needed another Coke and some M&Ms.

He wondered who was calling. Cassie? His folks?

But it was just Billy, thanking him for providing cover with his parents.

"You're going to have to tell them," Angel said. "You know you are."

"I know," he said. "But when I do, it will set off a chain reaction. I'm not ready for that."

"Sorry buddy," Angel said. "Hey, it looks like the Phi Psi gang is raiding Sigma Nu. Want to come along? Good times. Maybe even a fight."

"Thanks, but no thanks. Hank is supposed to come over soon. He's pissed I won't introduce him to my parents. He says he isn't, but he is."

"Good luck," Angel said. "Maggie just stormed out of here. I guess we're not real popular tonight. Are you hanging with your parents all day tomorrow?"

"Yeah, what were you thinking?"

"Skiing."

"Rats. Can't do it."

And they hung up. Angel bought a new pack of M&Ms and a Coke. When he turned, Maggie was standing there holding her bag and looking forlorn.

He put the candy and the Coke down and held her. She sobbed against his chest.

"Can we talk?" she asked.

"Of course," he said. He pocketed the M&Ms, grabbed the Coke, and led her upstairs to his room.

Maggie sat on the bed, again. She looked defeated. Angel sat next to her and waited.

She shrugged her shoulders. "I don't know what to say." She looked at him. She shuddered, and Angel wrapped his arms around her.

"Tell you what," Angel said. "Let's not talk. Why don't you let me make you feel better? Okay?"

Maggie nodded mutely.

Angel stood her up and handed her a towel. "Shower time. But first, smoke some of this." He lit the roach and handed it to her. Maggie took it and puffed desultorily. "Now, take off your clothes."

Maggie took another hit and handed the roach back to Angel who stubbed it out. She grudgingly held her arms out. Angel smiled and pulled her sweater over her head. He unhooked and removed her bra. Bending slightly, he kissed her left nipple. Maggie shivered, and Angel saw goosebumps on her arms. He unbuttoned her jeans and pulled them down to her knees. He did the same with her panties and pushed her back on the bed. She raised her legs and he pulled off her boots and pants. He handed her a towel and began to strip himself.

Maggie stopped him. She stood and wordlessly pulled off his shirt and jeans. He grabbed a towel from a freshly washed pile, and the two of them walked down the hall to the shower.

Maggie made Angel stand in the hot water, and she soaped his back, stopping at each scar to trace it with her fingers. While he rinsed, she kissed his back and put her arms around him. She leaned against his back and murmured, "I'm sorry, Angel. I'm not trying to rush you."

Angel turned her to him and pulled her under the water.

Angel tilted her face to him and kissed her. "Don't be mad at me," he said and kissed her again. "Mags, I don't know where this relationship is headed, but you need to decide if you like me."

"You know I do," she said, but he put a finger to her lips.

"No," he said. "You need to like me as I am, not as some dream version you might have of my potential. The real me. Scars and all."

Maggie nodded. "You said something earlier about courting me."

Angel smiled. "I did."

"Then, I think I would like it very much if you would court me. It sounds sweet."

Angel smiled and held her.

They stood long, thus, with the hot water baptizing them and the steam filling the room. Angel had no idea what Maggie was thinking. Was she still angry? Her body was still and pliant, so he kissed her neck and squeezed her. She lay against his chest, and he could tell that tears were mingling with shower drops.

He whispered in her ears the ending to *Peter Quince at the Clavier*. She seemed to be listening because her sobbing ceased, and her body relaxed even more.

"Billy says 'thank you,' for helping with his parents," Angel whispered.

"That made me sad."

"I wondered about that," he said.

"I still haven't told Jeffrey that we're no longer a couple," she said. "I mean, I did, but not as thoroughly as you told Cassie. I kind of wimped out."

"I guessed as much."

"I tried twice over Christmas break. The problem was that it felt like I was breaking up with him because he's queer."

"You were," Angel smiled.

"I know, but it would have meant accusing him of lying to me and all sorts of things I didn't want to get into. I feel so protective of him. Besides, he was more normal over Christmas. Maybe he's not even queer. I don't know. I just know I want to be with you."

"More normal," Angel said. "Did you have sex with him? Is that what 'more normal' means?"

Maggie was quiet.

"It's okay, Mags," Angel said. "I don't care if you did or didn't."

"What does that mean?"

"We aren't even a couple yet," he said. "And I slept with Cassie in Manhattan."

"I thought we were a couple," she said. "Let me get this straight: if I have sex with another man, it won't bother you?" Her voice had turned peevish again.

"Mags, we've only seen each other a few times. It's a nascent relationship. But even if we were an old, committed couple, I wouldn't get jealous. I don't do jealous."

"What does that even mean? You 'don't do' jealous?"

"I trained myself not to. When I began dating Cassie, she was kind of seeing another guy, and I used to get so jealous I couldn't sleep or think. I made a decision never to do that to myself again. When you're not with me, I don't care what you do. Cassie is seeing that same guy again, and I didn't feel anything, not even a flicker."

Maggie sat silent. She was clearly trying to process that.

"Tell me our relationship isn't just 'I like to fuck Maggie,' because I feel more for you than that."

"No, Maggie. It's not." He pulled her to him and smiled, "Although I do like to fuck you."

Maggie stared for a moment but relented. She kissed his chest and sighed. "You're so bad."

This relationship stuff was hard.

And, thankfully, so was he.

Perhaps Thor could bring about a more festive atmosphere.

"Maggie," he said. "I think we need to continue this conversation in my room."

Maggie looked up at him questioningly. He nodded down, and she looked and saw what he meant.

"Oh," she said. "I think you're right."

He turned off the shower and handed her a towel. She dried and wrapped herself. He toweled, too, and she took his towel from him and wrapped her hair.

Angel led her to his bed and made love to her.

Thor did fine, but Angel's head was elsewhere.

Shit.

Life seemed upside down. Jane was the happy one, and Maggie was being a bummer.

Suddenly, Cassie was looking good again.

Chapter Eighteen

Saturday January 30, 1971
Palaeopitus

ANGEL SLID OFF THE CHAIRLIFT AND COASTED AROUND
the bend to the top of the run. He waited there for Maggie who had missed the chair
and was behind him. He took a deep breath and looked out over the mountains
and then down the steep slope they were about to tackle. It was early afternoon, but
the moguls were already beginning to cast shadows. He could see a storm brewing
far to the north, perhaps almost in Canada. From Angel's perch, it looked as if the
world ended just past the White Mountain Range. He was reminded of a German
modernist painting, but he couldn't think which one.

Maggie skied up to him.

"This has to be our last run," he said.

"How come?"

Angel pointed. "See the shadow on the bottom of that mogul?"

Maggie nodded.

"Shadows hide the ice. You think you're fine until you hit a patch of that shit
and wind up with six broken ribs and a breathing tube in your side so your lung
can re-inflate. Not cool."

Maggie laughed. "That sounded autobiographical."

"It was. Freshman year. We used to ski until dark. I only do that now when
there's a ton of snow. Most of the shit on this mountain is man-made. Last night's
snow has pretty much been skied off. The base is granular and freezes faster than
the powder."

Maggie leaned over and kissed him. "You're going to make a great teacher. You
lecture all the time."

"I do, don't I?" Angel grinned. "Sorry."

"I think it's cute," Maggie said and took off.

Angel pushed on his poles and followed her. So, she wanted a race to the lodge. Let's do this, sister.

Angel followed Maggie's path, and every time they came off or around a mogul, he tried to pass her. Maggie veered into his path each time, flashing a wicked smile.

So, Angel went for it. They were skiing the double diamond face of the mountain, and the final third was a sheer drop used by the ski team for Slalom and Giant Slalom races. Angel picked a spot and headed straight down the face.

And he almost made it. His feet and ankles were too tired, though, and he couldn't get his edges to catch when he tried to slow near the bottom. He flew over a mogul he had meant to ski around and lost his tips on the way down. He face-planted spectacularly not a hundred yards from the lodge, and Maggie cruised past him laughing.

Angel lay in the snow for a moment, trying to decide what, if anything was broken. Maggie took off her skis and climbed back to where he lay.

"Are you all right?" she asked.

He looked up at her, and her grin widened.

"I think I broke my dick," he said.

"Oh," Maggie said. "So, I need another date for tonight? Shouldn't be hard. Three thousand horny guys and only a quarter of them with dates. Sorry, sweetheart, but the math's on my side."

Angel pushed himself up into a sitting position. His back hurt, but that was about all.

"Good race," Maggie said with a straight face.

She helped Angel to his feet, and he hobbled down the hill carrying a ski. The other was somewhere at the bottom.

When they got back to Phi Psi, Eddie and Sand and the rest of the gang were already there. Jane saw Angel and Maggie and practically ran to them. Angel thought for a second that she was going to leap into his arms, but she skidded to a halt.

"Angel, there's a message for you. Some guy named JB said you have to meet him at Dean Hall's office at four."

"What time is it?" Angel asked.

"After four," Jane laughed.

"Shit. Okay." He put his skis in the cloak room and kissed Maggie. "Don't leave. I may be expelled and in need of comfort."

"I'm not going anywhere," Maggie cooed and kissed him.

"Oh, yes you are," Jane said. "Go clean up. We're going shopping. I have Christmas money I'm dying to spend, and, besides, I think we probably need to talk."

Maggie looked archly at Angel. "Yes, that should prove interesting."

Angel looked at the two women. Great. There was no way that could be good.

He sighed and left. He hiked up to campus. He saw JB coming towards him, so he stopped and waited.

"Where you been, man?" JB asked.

"Skiing."

"Oh, well, we're late, and Dean Hall is pissed."

"I don't even know who he is? What is he dean of?"

JB looked at Angel and laughed. "That's funny. That really is."

Angel grimaced. He didn't feel funny. Why was he always sore when Maggie was around? The girl was a menace.

"You still dating Cassie?" JB asked.

"Nope. Just ended that. I've got a new girl named Maggie. We'll have to get together some time."

JB laughed. "I'm not sure Marlene would approve."

Angel looked at JB. Surely, he wasn't still dating tiger woman.

"Yes, I'm with Marlene," JB laughed. "You should see the expression on your face."

"Is she still pissed about freshman year?" Angel asked. Angel had walked in on JB and Marlene while they were in the act. Marlene took one of JB's African spears off the wall and chased Angel down the hall. Angel thought it was pretty fucking funny. Marlene hadn't seen it that way.

"No," JB said. "She just doesn't like you.""

Fair enough.

"Did you box last fall?" JB asked.

"Yep, made it to the semis. Why?"

"'Cause we've got a new brother about your size gonna kick your scrawny white ass next year. He boxed in Ghana. He was some kind of champion in their version of Golden Gloves."

"Uh huh," Angel said. "We'll see. Probably a big chickenshit like you. I can't believe you're still dating Marlene. Are you so afraid of her that you can't break up? Is that it?"

JB laughed. "I just know when I got it good."

"So, where were you fall quarter, anyway?" Angel asked. "Somewhere in Africa? I went by the AA house, but they wouldn't even talk to me."

"Uganda."

"Uganda? As in Idi Amin's Uganda? That guy's a trip."

"He's cool. He loves westerners. You know he fought for England."

"Yeah, he loves to chow down on westerners. Did you share any delectable villagers with him?"

He punched Angel in the arm. "You're so fucking hilarious. Now I remember why Marlene hates your guts."

Angel understood what was funny about the dean as soon as they opened the door.

Dean Hall wasn't a 'he' at all. She was a woman, a very angry looking black woman.

"You're late," she said.

Angel stared at her.

"Sit," she said and pointed to a chair. Angel sat. Who was this bitch and what kind of trouble was he in? From her expression, it was serious. He tried to think what he had done. God, he prayed Jane or Wanda weren't underage or something.

Her next words left him confused, though.

"You have a *Palaeopitus* meeting coming up this week," she began.

Angel nodded.

"JB and I need for you to help us," she said.

Angel stared at her.

The dean turned to JB askance. "This boy's not mute, is he?"

"What did I do?" Angel asked.

"Pardon?" she asked.

"What am I in trouble for? Because if it was for that Boar's Head thing, they had it coming."

It was Dean Hall's turn to stare. She turned to JB. "Didn't you tell him?"

JB shook his head. "I thought I'd let you do that."

She looked exasperated. "No, you're not in any trouble that I know of, and I'm not a dean of discipline anyway." She shook her head as if to say 'men.' "You're here because you are, and I say this fully cognizant of the irony, a student leader." She shook her head again. "You are aware that there isn't a single black brother on *Palaeopitus*?" Angel nodded. "Well, JB says you are probably the *Palaeopitus* member most sensitive to The Afro-American Society and their issues. We need someone on the inside of student government."

Angel shook his head. He wasn't all that 'sensitive' to the problems of The Afro-American Society. They had kicked him out rudely when JB had taken him to a party they were having, and, from their recent pronouncements, seemed to be heading towards Black Panther status rapidly. Angel had gotten enough Chairman Mao crap his first two years as an SDS member, and the Panthers were worse.

"Actually, they don't like me much over there," Angel said.

Dean Hall looked at JB.

"That's not true," JB said. "Lots of us listen to his show every Wednesday."

Dean Hall tried again. "You have a blues hour, right?" Angel nodded. "JB says you play almost exclusively black artists." Angel nodded. "For heaven's sake, don't you speak?"

"Yes, I play black artists. Is that illegal or something?"

"Son, you are trying my last nerve." She turned to JB. "Are you sure this is the boy we want in our corner?"

Angel was tired, his back hurt, and his mood was souring rapidly. It kind of felt good. He couldn't remember the last time he even had a mood.

"Since my presence seems to bore or annoy you," she said, "I'll get right to it. JB says you delight in being a pain in the ass both at *Palaeopitus* meetings and on the air. I, we, need for you to be our pain in the ass."

Angel was totally lost. If he wasn't in trouble, why did she seem so angry with him?

"Have I personally offended you, somehow? I don't have a clue what you're talking about, and I'm not a big fan of your tone of voice," Angel said.

"Whoa, shit," JB said and ducked.

Dean Smith rose. She was a tall, fucking woman and looked like the serious end of a shotgun about to go off.

Angel wasn't buying it, though, and stood, too.

"If I'm not in trouble, I'm out of here. I don't have a clue what you're dean of, but I don't like games, and I don't like being glared at for nothing. I don't know when JB turned into such a pussy, but you don't scare me, and you don't impress me."

"Sit back down."

"I don't think so."

It was quiet for a few seconds. The air had the same electric quality it had before a boxing match.

The dean smiled slightly. She turned to JB. "No wonder Marlene can't stand this boy."

"Let's start over," she said. She gestured to his chair. Angel stared at JB and then at her. He slumped into the chair. She sat, too and motioned to JB.

"Angel, Dean Hall and I are trying to get the administration to listen to a set of demands we have," JB said.

"It's not politically wise to use the word 'demands' after last year's events," Angel said.

Dean Hall shook her head and laughed.

JB looked confused, but he smiled slightly, too. "Okay, requests, then," he said. "We want two things: more black professors and more female professors."

"Imagine being a black man or woman," Dean Hall said, "and every class you attended was taught by an old, white man. Every truth you learn comes from a white man. Every test or essay you write is graded by a white man. And you always suspected that they thought you somehow inferior. How would you feel?"

Angel smiled. "I'm not the best person to answer that. I consider most professors, most deans, too, to be my natural enemies. But I understand what you mean. I've been to classes at Smith and Holyoke, and they're completely different. I prefer our classes and our professors, but I learned a lot from the women. Different vibe. Different opinions. I'm sure black professors would be different, too."

"Exactly," she said.

"But you're a dean. Why do you need me to help?"

She leaned forward. "My job is minority enhancement. Of course, I'm asking the white power structure for more women and blacks. But they expect it from me. What if the student government also pressed them on the issue? And what if the college's most popular radio show did the same?"

Angel ignored the flattery. It was bullshit, and he knew it. The seven till nine slots had the ratings.

"So, I go to *Palaeopitus* and argue for this, and I go on the air and preach? That's what you want me to do."

"Yes," she said. "We have a written statement we want *Palaeopitus* to give to the Board of Trustees." JB handed a piece of paper to Angel.

Angel looked it over and handed it back.

"No dice," he said.

"You won't help us?" JB asked. "Seriously? This is important, man. I thought we were friends."

Angel smiled slightly and rubbed his temples. He needed a nap. "Oh, I'll do it. I just won't use your words. I'll say what I want to say."

Dean Hall stared and chuckled. "What if we don't like your words?"

"Then you get somebody else to be your little whitebread messenger boy," Angel said.

"Marlene is right. This boy is a pain in the ass."

"Well, if anyone would recognize a pain in the ass, it would be Marlene. All she has to do is look in a mirror. I told JB all freshman year to dump her. How do you know her?" Angel asked.

JB groaned and shook his head. He leaned back and grinned at the dean.

Dean Hall smiled, too. "You're asking me how I know my own daughter?"

Shit…

Chapter Nineteen

Wednesday February 3, 1971
WDCR

ANGEL DANCED IN THE CRAMPED STUDIO AND SANG ALONG. He plopped in his chair and flicked on his mike just as the song was ending. He lifted the needle and slid another on as he spoke.

And that was the badass, don't mess with me, Koko Taylor here on WDCR, the only cool station for miles and miles around. Koko was singing Voodoo Woman, and I live surrounded by voodoo women, so I can identify.

So, why have I chosen this mean snowy night to once again feature the great women of the blues? I'm glad you asked. The impetus came from a swift kick in the ass by our newest administrator, Dean Hall. Now, when I say 'dean,' what image appears? A middle-aged white man? Perhaps balding and working on a paunch?

That sure as shit isn't Dean Hall. For starters, Dean Hall is a woman, a woman who would make Koko Taylor tremble. We're talking industrial strength attitude. And here comes the best part, she is a black woman.

Why did she kick your poor Angel in the ass, you ask? That's easy. In case you hadn't noticed, we have a thriving community of African American men and a burgeoning population of women.

But almost every class is still taught by a white male. Think about that. We had the foresight and wisdom to recruit African American students and to admit women.

Then, we send them to classes taught by white men.

What is the subliminal message? Knowledge comes from white men. Your grades, the keys to your future, come from white men. White men will interpret the world for you. Truth can only be dispensed by white men. Quake in your chairs you silly women and blacks. Learn the great white truths of history.

Now, I've got nothing against white men. I'm one of them, and, collectively, we've invented and written and painted a whole bunch of fine stuff. But, because of my abiding interest in the fairer sex, I've been to Smith and Mt. Holyoke on several occasions, and I've been in many a class manned by women. (Catch that pun?)

Guess what? Women can teach. I know. Crazy talk, huh? Well, they can. And their classes offer a stark contrast to ours. Smith classes, for instance, tend to be civilized. People have discussions. People ask questions and listen politely while others speak. I know what you're thinking. Pussy stuff. But you'd be amazed how much you can learn without yelling or arguing.

Because, that's what most of my classes are, arguments. Or, they're competitions during which we practically shout each other down.

Don't misconstrue what I'm saying. I love our faculty, and I love the rough and tumble of our classes.

But, there are other ways to think and other ways to learn.

So, day before yesterday, I submitted a resolution at a Palaeopitus meeting to be presented to the Board of Trustees as a statement representing our entire student body. It asks the Board to instruct the college to begin an international search for highly intellectual female and African American professors. It passed Palaeopitus without a dissenting vote.

We are Vox Clamantis in Deserto, the voice crying in the wilderness. That cry must be against darkness and ignorance. Sometimes, it must also be against what is easy and familiar.

I'm not suggesting a quota system. Neither is Dean Hall. I want Dartmouth to be a leader of the new world which is forming, a world which has disdained segregation and second class citizen-ship for women. We need to find the best and brightest professors and bring them to Hanover, regardless of race or sex.

We need to be that voice fighting against the old order. We need to be the ones inventing the new order.

But, I need to know if you are behind our efforts. After all, we at Palaeopitus are supposed to be your student government. You voted for co-education. You have black friends. Let me hear from you. As always, send letters or notes to WDCR, and address them to me, your Angel.

And a word of advice: stay away from Dean Hall. She's intense.

Hi Marlene. That last was for you. Love and kisses. Does everyone out there know Marlene Hall? She's had a thing for me for three years. I'm sorry, Marlene. I'm not available. I belong to Maggie the Cat. Mags, I know you're listening and that's your shout out. You are a delectable piece of work, Maggie the Cat, and I plan to do unspeakable things with you this weekend.

Well, my time is up, and I need to leave before I break more FCC rules and Marlene has time to get to the station to bust my balls.

Hola y'all. Happy Wednesday.

This is your Angel, signing off with a tune from Ma Rainey called Prove it on Me Blues.

Mags, this one is for you.

Angel lowered the needle and flicked off his mike. He lit a roach and took a deep hit.

He did love to preach.

Chapter Twenty

March 12-21, 1971
Spring Break

ANGEL SAT DOODLING AT HIS DESK. HIS SPRING BREAK plans had been shot to shit. He was supposed to drive home and work in the paper mill for nine days which would have meant a ton of money. But his Austin Healey wouldn't start. It had been buried under snow all winter, and the battery, among other things, had died. A dour service station guy had driven up, opened the hood, and shaken his head.

"At least a couple hundred bucks, just from what I can see," he said.

His grumpy visage and shake of the head reminded Angel of Moe.

Well, shit. Who has two hundred bucks plus gas and tolls? He smiled. Every girl he dated, with the possible exception of Jane. That's who. He wondered if Wanda had money, too.

He drummed his fingers on his desk and opened his notebook. He had been thinking of Wanda a lot, lately, a sad commentary on his supposed love affair with Maggie.

The thing was, Wanda was just a funny, sexy chick he had spoken with twice. She was all upside and subject to his fantasies without reality intruding. Maggie was a real chick with real attractions but real drawbacks.

He began to doodle a plan for the week:

Friday through Sunday: Maggie

Itinerary: Read As I Lay Dying and The Sound and the Fury. Food and sex (not prioritized)

He wrote that last in case Maggie saw his list.

He sighed. Maggie's potential was vast. She was smart and picked up things immediately. He loved that about her. She was no Cassie in the brains department, but, then, who was? He certainly wasn't.

And his favorite moments with Maggie were those when she slept and he wrote late at night. The room was bathed in the light of his small desk lamp, and Maggie always slept on her side facing him. She cast off her sheets as soon as she fell asleep, content to warm herself with his body. When he snuck out of bed, she made a cute sound and turned towards his desk, like a flower seeking the sun. Some nights, when the writing was slow, he would watch her for an hour. She slept with a half-smile on her face and looked so young with her hands clasped under her chin as if she was praying. The sheets would partially cover her mid-section, but her breasts would peep out and watch him. And her hip rose amazingly and then tapered into her long, long legs. She was a painting come to life, just for him.

She wasn't half bad when awake, either, though Angel clearly preferred sleeping women to ones who disturbed his equanimity by speaking to him or doing other equally annoying things.

She was so quick with a riposte. She wasn't a Cane and couldn't defend herself when Angel ripped into her, but she was quicker than any of the rest of his friends. Quicker by a mile than Cassie.

And she would be at Phi Psi any minute. How delightful.

He went back to his itinerary. It looked very Jay Gatz and made him smile. He should make lists more often. They were kind of fun.

Monday: Go to the farmer's market for Moe. Read Light in August.

Tuesday: Go to the Budweiser Distribution Center for Moe and read Go Down, Moses.

Wednesday: Clean out Moe's storage shed. Begin Absalom, Absalom. Work on Maggie story.

Thursday: Deliver stuff for Moe. Finish Absalom, Absalom. Sit up all night staggered by Absalom and the week of Faulkner. See Gandalf to pick up acid. Sit in bed and weep for Quentin Compson and shake from the enormity of Thomas Sutpen's butchering.

It would be sad to listen to Quentin narrate when he knew that Quentin would drown himself only days after he and Shreve finished their story-telling at Harvard that fateful spring.

Friday Acid trip with Groucho and the guys.

That last was iffy. He didn't know who would be around to trip with. The Moe's stuff pained him. He was only working half a day each day, and he didn't want to think about how much money he was losing by not working at the paper mill. Oh, well, it was only tuition, books, and that sort of thing. Shit.

Saturday and Sunday: To Be Announced.

He smiled and put down his pen.

He lit a joint and sipped his Coke. Time to shower and get ready for Maggie. He had a surprise for her. Clean sheets. She would dig that.

He put the joint out between his fingers and finished the Coke.

He stood under the pelting beads of scalding water in the shower and felt the winter quarter dissipate. He had made straight A's again. It was amazing how much better a student one became when he stopped trying to be a Communist agitator. Nixon and Kent State had done a whole generation a favor by burning out their revolutionary ardor.

He had to admit that it had been fun writing pamphlets and speeches. And his vanity had been stroked by being constantly quoted in *Time Magazine.*

He stayed under the water until his fingers began to wrinkle, then got out. He looked in the mirror and saw a bright red reflection grinning back at him.

Maggie time. She was going to Long Island for Spring Break but had told her parents some preposterous story about why she couldn't leave until Sunday. He was going to repay her by courting her, as he had promised.

He buttoned a clean, white shirt and rolled up the sleeves. He put his favorite vest on and combed his hair back with his fingers. Glancing in the broken mirror on his dresser, he decided he didn't need to shave. He looked rock and roll-ish. He removed his belt, fished through his dresser for the one with the giant Harley buckle, and threaded it through his pants loops. Clean socks, a quick wipe at his boots, and he was ready for Miss Maggie.

He rolled a huge joint and climbed through the poolroom window to the roof to watch for her. He sat in an ancient wooden chair and smoked while perusing a yellowed copy of *Howl*. In a way, the Beats were as responsible for his attitude and philosophy as the hippies were. Maybe more. But he still couldn't, for the life of him, understand why *Howl* was supposed to be great. It was vivid. He would give it that. The images leapt off the page like vomit from the mouth of a demon child, but it was so…what?

He read for a few moments and then tried to answer himself.

It was derivative. That's what his problem was. Most Beat poetry was shitty because it was shit. It was the product of a bunch of stoners writing spontaneous lines like 'God is love' and thinking that they had discovered something. Kerouac for example. Sure, *On the Road* was important, but more as a sociological document than as art. The writing was awful. And *The Dharma Bums* was even worse. Cheap Buddhist thought masquerading as a novel. Cool but crappy.

But *Howl* cheated. It was a shit version of Whitman's *Song of Myself.* And it should have been titled *Peeing and Shitting on Myself While Using Heroin and Fucking Young Boys.* To use an expression of Cane's: it sucked more than a heroin hooker doing five dollar blowjobs outside a movie theater on a Friday night.

A car drove down the lane past Moe's and turned into the Phi Psi driveway.

Maggie.

Angel stood and waved when she got out of the car. Maggie waved back gaily. She wore a killer dress and a scarf inscribed with a Gaelic design. She looked like a million bucks. No one came to Phi Psi dressed like that. No one.

Well, maybe Cassie on occasion.

He went to the stairwell to greet her, and, when he saw that she carried a suitcase, descended to carry it. Let the courting begin.

But it began silently. At least on his part. Maggie chattered about how much grief her mother had given her for staying the weekend and how she couldn't tell her mother she was staying at Dartmouth because her mother would have said, 'Oh, a boy! And when will we meet this young man of yours?' Which would have been followed by 'Does your current boyfriend know about this new young man?'

Angel, however, was mute. He was struck by Maggie's beauty and the life which oozed out of every pore. She was excited and animated, and both brought out her exquisite eyes and mouth. Her hair was down, making her look older than the pony-tailed Maggie, and it shone in profusion. Angel was mesmerized.

Maggie laughed. "Are you not speaking to me for some reason? Is it because I'm babbling on like a maniac?"

"No," he said somberly. "I get this way in the presence of beauty, especially when it strikes me as profound. Like when I'm going to see a famous painting, and it's better than I expected."

Maggie laughed, thinking Angel was being facetious or delivering a line, but she sobered when she saw his eyes. She became quiet and shy.

Angel put her bag down by his desk and went to her. He took her face in his hands. "May I kiss you?" he asked.

Maggie looked as if she were going to say something like 'of course. Why would you ask permission for something like that?' But her tone dropped an octave from her previous silly stream of words. "I'd like that," she said.

It felt like a first kiss, and both seemed chastened and subdued afterwards.

"Whew," Maggie said.

She knew it was an affirmation kiss, the kind of kiss which says, 'I care for you. This moment is important to me.' And, though Angel had no clue what had come over him or what the kiss meant, he knew it wasn't an ordinary 'hello' kiss, nor even an 'I'm so glad to see you' kiss. No, it touched upon sacramental, and both were caught by surprise.

"Do that again," Maggie said, so Angel sat on the edge of the bed, gently pulled her down next to him, and kissed her sweetly and long. Maggie looked anxiously into his eyes afterwards, as if distrustful of her joy, then sighed and leaned against his chest. Angel could not remember a moment so tender. Perhaps he had never had one. It was an epiphany. Was this budding love? How strange. How had it crept so suddenly and surreptitiously past his conscious mind? And was this what Maggie longed for from him? What all girls longed for? This overwhelming urge to hold and merge with another? God, he sounded like D.H. Lawrence.

Angel lay down, and Maggie took her scarf off and lay next to him. She snuggled against his chest and sighed.

"What were you doing when I drove up that made you so romantic?" she asked.

Angel smiled. "Pondering how bad Beat writing is."

He could feel her smile against his chest and knew that she was thinking how strange men were.

"Sweetheart," he said, "Since you're so dressed up, can we go out for dinner? Maybe to The Woodstock Inn?"

"That would be nice," she said. "Whose girlfriend am I pretending to be this time? Billy's? Or some other desperate friend of yours?"

Angel leaned on an elbow and looked down at her smiling face. He brushed a lock of hair from her forehead and brushed her lips with his. "Maybe you could go as my girlfriend this time," he said.

"I could do that," she said.

They chatted for an hour and then rose to go to dinner. They drove Maggie's Firebird with the windows down. The sun had set while they lay there, and the night had just the right chill.

They were quiet on the drive to Woodstock. The moon rose and glanced off the rocks and turbid water of the stream which the road shadowed, sending little beams of light towards them like alien fireflies.

They crossed the covered bridge and turned into the Inn.

"I've never been here before," Maggie said. "It's beautiful."

"My favorite part is in the lobby. Wait until you see it."

They entered hand in hand, smiling at a couple who were leaving.

Maggie stopped still. At the back of the lobby was a fireplace, a great, gargantuan fireplace.

"The logs must be six feet long," she said. She put her arms around him and cleaved to his chest. Angel kissed her hair, and she squirmed happily.

They were taken to a table next to a window which overlooked Suicide Six, the Woodstock skiway. The sheer face of the nearest run was lit by huge spotlights, and they watched angry, buzzing Snowcats crisscross the slope in seemingly random patterns. Huge hoses blew newly created snow hundreds of feet in the air, and the cats, dragging things which looked like chunks of chain link fence, smoothed the clumps wrought by the huge nozzles. All the Snowcats had a pair of bright lights, and their movement played geometric counterpoint to the spotlights and the fledgling moon, creating a jazz pattern of lights.

"Can you hear the Snowcats?" Maggie asked. "I think I can."

"I can feel them through my chest," Angel said. "Sit still and see if you can, too."

Maggie sat and then giggled delightedly. "I can. That's so cool."

They ordered a bottle of wine from a rustic looking lass who only glanced at Angel's driver's license.

"You're not twenty-one," Maggie said.

"I will be when we make love tonight. That is, if Maggie the Cat wants to make love. I didn't mean to presume."

"First of all, Maggie the Cat does want to, and secondly, what do you mean about being twenty-one?"

"My birthday begins at midnight. It began ten minutes ago in London."

Maggie squealed and bemused diners turned to smile at the happy couple. "This is a birthday dinner? I'm here for your birthday?"

Angel got out of his chair across from her and moved to the one nearest her. He reached out and held her hand.

"You wanted to be courted. I'm courting. I have been told that when I'm not saying 'fuck' and 'shit' I can be very romantic," he said. "I wanted you to be with me tonight. Just you and nobody else."

"No Cassie? No Jane?"

"Just Maggie. My sweet, lovely Maggie."

The girl brought their wine and tried unsuccessfully to manage the cork. Angel took the bottle from her and rethreaded the corkscrew and opened the bottle.

"Thanks," the girl said.

Angel smiled and sipped his wine. "It's fine," he said, and the girl poured a glass for Maggie and filled Angel's. "You're not from here, are you?" Angel asked the girl.

"No, sir," she blushed. "I'm from Montreal."

"*Merci pour le vin*," Angel said.

"*De rien*," the girl smiled and left.

Maggie picked up Angel's hand and kissed it. "You're just showing off, now," she said.

"*Moi?*"

"Yes, you," she smiled.

They drank and watched the Snowcats work in an easy silence. The girl came back and Angel ordered dinner in French.

Maggie watched in amusement at the girl's blushing and nodding at each word Angel said. She smiled at Maggie and left.

"What did you order?" she asked.

"Snails," he said.

"No, really?"

He laughed. "*Vraiment. Escargot.* And cheese and pan-seared trout. Is that okay?"

She eyed him distrustfully. The cheese and trout sounded good. "I had snails once and didn't like them."

"Oh, you'll like these. They'll come in a scalding hot garlic butter sauce. And they'll be delicious with this wine."

"Hmm." Maggie shook her head. She leaned forward for a kiss. Angel brushed her lips. "Where is my Angel?" she murmured. "What have you done with him? Never mind. I don't want to know. I like this sophisticated, young man better."

"Oh, you do, do you? Well, don't blink, because the barbarian Angel will be back by the time I'm on you and in you."

"Oh, my gross barbarian. *Je m'excuse.* I was wrong. I like my bad Angel better, the one who gets hit in the face so he can meet me."

After dinner, Angel ordered coffees with Kahlua and bought a cigar from the cigarette girl who circulated among the tables.

A thin, balding man had begun to play the white grand piano in the corner. Angel sent Maggie to tip the man five dollars, and he met her on her way back to the table.

"May I have this dance?"

"Angel, there isn't a dance floor. No one's dancing."

"This is our dance floor," Angel said, gesturing broadly to the small space they stood in. He held out his arms, and Maggie went to him.

"You can't dance to Shubert," she said smiling up at him.

"I can't dance very well to anything," Angel said. "But it warms the cockles of my heart that you recognize Shubert." He puffed on his cigar and twirled her with his other arm around her waist. Maggie laughed and held on.

When the song finished, the other diners clapped. Maggie blushed and curtsied. Then, she half-dragged him back to their coffees.

At Phi Psi, they wrapped in a blanket and sat on the roof outside the poolroom and watched the stars thicken until the whole Milky Way unveiled herself to them.

"Okay, Mr. I Know Everything, can you point out stars and constellations?"

Angel toked on a joint and handed it to her. He nodded pleasantly.

"Well?" she prodded, laughing.

"Nope."

"Why not?" she asked.

"Don't feel like it."

Maggie punched him in the arm.

"Show off time's over," he said. "We're on to the next stage of courtship."

"Oh," she said. "And pray tell, what is that?"

"I ask sensitive questions about your family and shit like that."

"Really?"

"Really," he said. "I don't know anything about you."

Maggie stared and shook her head. "I'll give you the short version," she said. "My father used to own a CPA firm. He sold it for a bunch of money, and now he consults for fabulous sums and plays a lot of tennis. He and my mother go to the yacht club three nights a week and come home slightly drunk. They used to fight a lot when I was little, but they're nice to each other now. I have a sister who is fifteen. Now, can we go to your room and fuck?"

Angel looked thoughtfully at the glowing tip of the joint and took another hit.

"Not tonight," he said.

"Why not?" she asked, laughing.

"I'm not that easy," he said. "I don't put out on the first date."

Maggie punched him in the arm again. And then again.

"Okay," she said. "Courtship's over. I want Thor back and the human vessel who accompanies him. Inside Mister. Now. It's past midnight. It's your birthday. And you're going to ravish me until I have about ten orgasms."

Angel pinched the joint out with his fingers and sipped his Coke. He surveyed the Milky Way as if she might instruct him in the ways of romance, but, other than twinkling, she said little of importance. He guessed he'd have to wing it.

He stood and held his hand out for her. Maggie took his hand and rose.

"Ten orgasms?" he asked.

"At least," she said.

Angel looked down at Thor. Hmm. Maybe, now that he was older...

"Let's give it a shot," he said, and he took her to his room. They didn't make it to ten, but it wasn't for lack of trying.

Saturday

When Angel awoke, Maggie was gone. The bed smelled like the two of them which made Angel happy.

He was also pleased that he had an entire day off. Two, really. He didn't work for Moe until Monday.

He pulled on a pair of jeans and went to pee.

The bathroom door opened, and a voice said, "There you are." Angel turned to see Groucho. "Be right back," Groucho said and disappeared. Angel shook himself and carefully zipped his zipper. Groucho re-appeared almost immediately with a long tin-foil thing which looked like a hot dog.

"Happy Birthday," Groucho said. Angel unwrapped the foil to find a huge joint. "It's laced with hashish," he said. "And I mean laced. Be careful. That should be about ten smokes."

Angel smelled it. God, he couldn't even smell pot, the hash was so pungent. There must have been fifty bucks of hash in the thing.

"Thanks, Groucho," he said. "But I didn't get you anything for your birthday."

"I know," Groucho said brightly and disappeared. Angel laughed and left the bathroom, but Groucho had vanished.

Angel deposited the joint in his room and descended the stairs. He smelled bacon and knew it was for him. In the kitchen, he found Groucho with Maggie. Cane was sitting astride a chair and everyone was laughing.

Angel entered and the laughing went up a notch.

"Cane was just telling me the story about the night he accidentally beat you up at Sigma Nu," Maggie said.

"Accidentally? He rammed me into a post and knocked me out."

"I carried you all the way to Dick's House so they could fix you up," Cane said.

"Yeah," Angel said. "And you literally dumped me on the admitting desk, said, 'fix him,' and left."

"Hey, you interrupted me. I was dealing that chick," Cane said.

"You were hurting her to piss off her date," Angel said. "You weren't dealing her."

"I just tried to untie the bow in her hair," Cane said.

"Which was tied in a knot. You almost lifted her off the ground."

"Yeah," Cane said. "And her date just sat there, doing nothing, with this queasy grin on his stupid fucking face."

"Okay, stop," Maggie said laughing. "Let me process this. Angel, you tried to save a girl, and Cane hurt you. Is that right?"

The two men looked at each other and shrugged. "I guess," Angel said.

"So, what you did at Colby for me you do in real life?" she asked Angel. "And Cane, you hurt him in real life?"

"I guess," Cane said.

"You two are morons," she said.

"I guess," Groucho said, and everyone cracked up.

After breakfast, Maggie and Angel went to his room. They sat on his bed, and she kissed him. "What would you like to do today more than anything else in the world?"

Angel thought. "I'd like to stay up here and read."

"That's it?"

"For a while. I just want it to be as if we live together and don't have to do anything special."

"I can do that. You stay and read. I'm going shopping for a birthday present."

"Where?" he asked.

"Not telling you," she said. She kissed him on the nose and pranced out.

Shit. She was cute when she was happy. Maybe all girls were. Maybe the *Wife of Bath's Tale* told the truth: love a girl, and she turns beautiful.

That didn't explain what had happened with Cassie, though. Angel pulled on a shirt and picked up *As I Lay Dying*. He flopped in his desk chair and put his feet up. Soon, he was under the Bundren spell and happy as a clam.

When he finished, he went to the roof to meditate on the final image--Darl's schizophrenic vision. He leafed back through the pages until he found Darl's meditation on going to sleep and not being.

In a strange room you must empty yourself for sleep. And before you are emptied for sleep, what are you...I don't know what I am. I don't know if I am or not. Jewel knows that he is, because he does not know that he does not know whether he is or not.

Faulkner was riffing on Hamlet, of course. *To be or not to be*: the existential question of all time. Being or non-being, Sartre style. But at least Darl knows that he does not know whether he is or not. Hamlet thinks being is a decision which can be made. Sorry, H, it ain't that simple. Darl may be insane, but at least he isn't crazy. He knows he can't will himself into being. Huh.

Pretty fucking interesting start to Faulkner week.

He leaned back in his chair and put his face up to the sun. Maggie had been gone for hours. Maybe she got lost. Maybe she ran away. He smiled and soaked in the sun until his face felt about twenty degrees warmer than the air.

Snow still lay under trees and in corners of buildings which got no light, but spring was decidedly on the way. It couldn't have been more than fifty out, but the rays were hot. Were it not for the steady breeze, he could have sun-bathed. And if he drifted off, then, according to Darl, he would 'not be'. He smiled again. Life was good.

He heard a car door slam and laughter. He stood and looked down to see Groucho carrying a large box and Maggie bent over getting something from the back seat.

"Nice ass," he called.

"Thanks," Groucho shouted back.

Maggie looked up but was blinded by the sun, so she just waved in his general direction.

He went back inside and met Maggie entering his room.

"You stay there," she said and disappeared inside.

Angel waited for a few moments, but his curiosity was piqued. "Hurry up," he said in his best through-the-door voice.

"Oh, oh, oh, Groucho," Maggie moaned loudly.

"Very funny," Angel said.

Maggie peeked out. "Do you have somewhere you could go for an hour?"

Angel smiled. Devious woman. What was she up to?

"Hand me *The Sound and the Fury*. It should be on my desk. I'll go to the library. I need to give Mrs. Sellers a list of books, anyway."

Maggie disappeared and shouted, "Where is it? Never mind. Got it," and reappeared. She handed him the book and put her face up for a kiss. Angel kissed her and whispered, "Groucho better not be smiling later."

"I thought you didn't get jealous."

"Good point," he said. "Go for it Groucho," he shouted.

"Righto," Groucho shouted back.

Angel pushed Maggie's face back into his room and closed the door.

The walk across campus felt good, but he really should have worn a jacket. Every time he walked under a tree the temperature seemed to drop twenty degrees, and the wind wasn't helping, either. He crossed the middle of The Green to avoid shadows and went into Sanborn. Mrs. Sellers wasn't there, so he left her a long, humorous note with his book requests for Monday. He sat in his chair and opened *The Sound and the Fury*. He took a deep breath and began to listen to Benjy. He made a mental note to look up the date of the first section. April 5th. It had to have been sometime near Easter, maybe even Good Friday?

Nearly two hours later, he put the book down. He looked out the window. It was black outside. Good. That matched his mood. He felt as close to despair as he ever remembered being. He watched the gaslights around campus come slowly on, as if beckoned by the gloom of the evening.

Good God. Why did he, Angel, even bother writing when there were men like Faulkner walking the earth to do it for him and for all the other benighted souls careening between cruelty and idiocy? Angel knew why Faulkner had stolen Macbeth's lament that life 'is a tale told by an idiot, full of sound and fury, signifying nothing.' Angel had always thought that the darkest of visions. At least until he heard Benjy babble, not even knowing whether he was in the past or the present. Angel wondered what Benjy would make of the gaslights coming on. Just another daily miracle, like grass growing or the sun coming up?

Shit. Maggie. What time was it?

He walked out into the cold and shivered his way home. He bounded up the stairs and knocked on his door.

Maggie peeked out again and smiled. "I just finished. Close your eyes," she said and took his hand. She led him to the middle of the room. He could tell he was facing his desk.

"Open them."

The first thing Angel saw was the huge IBM Selectric typewriter sitting where his old one had been.

The second thing was that all his papers had disappeared. The desktop was bare, save for the typewriter.

"Um, Mags," he said.

She laughed and opened his desk drawer. There, neatly filed and separated by orange and blue binders, was his work.

Maggie pulled three boxes from under his desk.

"The folders hold all your schoolwork. That box holds fiction, that one poetry, and that one I marked miscellaneous. It holds a bunch of things I didn't want to go through. It's mostly letters, but there are a number of what look like philosophical rambles."

Angel couldn't speak. His order was gone, and hers had taken its place. How would he ever find anything again? He knew she meant well, but shit.

He touched the typewriter. "Maggie, I can't take this. It's amazing, but it's too expensive."

Maggie laughed and wrapped her arms around him from behind. "It was free," she said, "And even if it wasn't, how much do you think that Don Quixote porcelain figure from Cassie cost?"

"I have no idea."

"More than the typewriter. It's from Cartier. But my father paid for everything, or, more accurately, Bessie paid for it."

"Bessie?" he asked.

Maggie laughed again. "I charge my school supplies, and Bessie, my father's CPA and just about everything else, pays my bills without asking any questions."

"She won't think it's odd you bought a five hundred-dollar typewriter?"

"No. I already have one. If she asks, I'll just say mine broke. Besides, Bessie writes everything off as office equipment. So, it really is sort of free."

Angel sat at his desk and put a piece of paper in it. He turned it on and typed 'my sweetheart is nuts.' He liked the hum it made. Mesmerizing.

Maggie showed him how to erase mistakes with a piece of white, chalky paper she put between the paper and the keys. She typed over his sentence, 'my sweetheart is sexy.'

"Holy shit," he said. "That's cool."

"Uh, huh," she said. "No more re-typing the whole page when you make a mistake."

"Geniuses don't make mistakes," Angel smiled. "Their errors are volitional and are the portals of discovery."

"Okay, who said that?"

"Stephen Dedalus in *Portrait*." He ran his hands over the machine and pulled a file from the drawer. He looked up at her. "Thanks so much. How am I supposed to repay this?"

Maggie bent and wrapped her arms around his neck and kissed his cheek. "Are you kidding? You do so much for me."

Angel rose and took her hand. He led her to his bed and lay down. He pulled her next to him, and she curled in his arms with her head on his chest. He kissed her forehead.

Maggie looked up at him and murmured, "Was it okay that I re-arranged all your work? I know it's all personal. I would feel weird if you re-arranged my closet or something."

Angel poked her nose and smiled. "I was taken aback for a moment, but now I just feel flattered."

"Flattered?"

"The whole thing, the typewriter, the folders, your separating everything, seems so, I don't know, maternal."

"Maternal?" she laughed.

"Wrong word, maybe, but you were taking care of me. To me, that's what a relationship is, not a string of words or promises, just the little things we do for each other because we care and want to take care of each other."

Maggie lay still contemplating what he had said. "Is that why it's such a big deal to say 'I love you?' I know men hate to say it."

Angel traced a pattern on the wall with the hand that wasn't holding her. "Maybe." He was silent. He thought of Kesey in the Menlo Park VA Hospital, being paid to take LSD and the man who had drawn a Buddha on the wall next to his bed. Angel traced a Buddha and thought about the word 'love.' "That's not what bothers me," he said, finally. "It's that the word is so imprecise. 'I love to read. I used to love Cassie. Christians love God.'" He sat up and leaned against the wall. Maggie shifted until her head was lying in his lap. He took Groucho's joint from his shirt pocket and lit it.

"Do you remember the first time you went on a date with a boy who was your friend?" he asked.

Maggie looked up at him and nodded. "Todd Kovensky," she said.

"One minute, you're friends. But then, he picks you up, and he holds the car door for you. You slide nervously into the seat. Perhaps you fasten a seatbelt. He gets in and fumbles with the key. He gives you a smile and starts the car. Do you remember what you felt?"

Maggie took the joint from him. "Yes, as if our whole relationship was changed forever. What am I smoking? It tastes funny."

"Something Groucho gave me. Go easy. Two hits maximum. But, back to your date. You realized you would never be friends again, at least not like before. You hadn't even kissed, let alone made love, but everything was different."

Maggie drew on the joint and held it up for him to take back. She exhaled. "And that's what happens when people say 'I love you?'" she asked.

Angel nodded slightly. "I think guys are afraid it will destroy everything they have with a girl. Whisk it all away. They're afraid to lose what they have for some indefinite future."

"Hmm," Maggie said. "So, they are afraid, but not of commitment like we think they are? They're afraid of losing the girl?"

"Exactly," he said "But they're screwed because they feel as if they have to say it anyway or lose the girl. That's if the relationship has reached a certain momentum, and forward is the only possible way to go."

Maggie looked up at him. "So, you've said it to girls when you didn't really mean it? That's horrible."

He laughed. "No, I meant it when I said it. I was just wrong. I didn't love them. I didn't know what love was before Cassie. Have you ever told a boy you loved him?"

"Just Jeffrey. But it's like you said. I was wrong. At least I hope so." She put a hand on his face. "I feel more for you than I ever did for Jeffrey."

"Will you see him when you go home?"

"Yes. I promise I'm going to break up with him. I know. I said that over Christmas, but I just couldn't. It would have hurt him."

Angel smiled. "You might be surprised. It might be a relief."

"Sweetheart," she said, "can't you come to Long Island? Even for a couple of days?"

He shook his head and pinched out the joint. "No. I'm working for Moe all week. Plus, my car won't run. I need to work to pay to get the car fixed, but then I won't have money to go anywhere in it. Catch 22."

She smiled. "Is everything literary to you?"

"Pretty much. Except you," he said and ran a hand up her leg.

Maggie shivered and laughed. "Don't start unless you mean it."

Angel bent and kissed her lightly. "Later."

"Promises, promises," she murmured. She lay silent for so long, Angel thought she had drifted off. He traced his imaginary Buddha on the wall and wondered what she was thinking.

Maggie spoke without opening her eyes. "What would you be doing right now if you had gone home?"

"Working at the paper mill," he said.

"It's dinner time," she said. "Wouldn't you be going home or preparing for a night out with your friends or something?"

"No," he said. "That's what you would be doing if you were home, but I would be a quarter of the way through my second shift of the day. My back would be killing me, and I would have sweated off ten pounds of water."

"Wow. What specifically would you be doing? Paint me a picture, Mister Writer-man."

"Okay," he said. "Well, if I had my druthers, I'd be working on the loading dock."

"What?"

"The loading dock. Box cars would be lined up for us to load with bundles of sacks. It's intense. The cars hold a quarter of a million pounds each, and we work in two-man shifts. A tow motor, that's what they call a fork-lift truck, brings us a pallet loaded with bundles of sacks." He gestured with his hands to show how big the bundles were. "We've just cut the seal on the box car and opened it up. It's been sitting there, empty, waiting for us. The sun has been baking it all day, and when we slide the door open, the heat is shocking, like when you open an oven to check on a turkey or something. Whoosh, out comes this wave of heat. It's almost visible. In the summer, it might be a hundred forty degrees in there. It's spring and about eighty outside, so the cars now are probably a little over a hundred."

"It's eighty in Jacksonville right now?"

"Yep."

"Must be nice."

"It is. You need to come home with me sometime. Anyway, the tow motor drives partway into the box car, and my partner and I carry the bundles and begin to stack them. At first, we have to walk forty feet with each bundle. We stack them as high as we can reach. Then I stand on the ones we've already stacked, and my partner hands up bundles and I start another stack on top of the stack."

"How much does each bundle weigh?"

"Sixty-four pounds."

"Oh, my God."

"I know. You wouldn't believe what kind of shape I'm in after a week on the dock. So, we keep stacking, moving towards the middle of the car as we work. Each row we stack means we don't have to carry the bundles as far for the next row. When we get to the middle, we start on the other end of the car."

"And how long does it take to fill a car?"

"Most of a shift. It's probably faster now that it's cooler. Christmas is perfect. It's cold, so you can work really fast."

"You work Christmas, too?"

"Of course," he laughed. "I have winter and spring tuition to pay."

"But, not really."

"Yes, really. You mean my dad could pay it? What kind of man lets his dad pay his way?"

"Jeffrey does. I do."

"Well, that's different."

"Because he's queer? Because I'm a girl?"

"No, because you guys grew up that way. I'm not trying to sound virtuous. It's selfish, really. My dad would be fine with paying for me, but I feel better this way."

"Hmm," she said. "And I benefit when you feel manly?"

"You most certainly do."

She was silent for a long time. "Is that a male, female thing?"

"I don't think so. Cassie was stubbornly independent. That sounds funny for a rich girl, but she was. Maybe more males are that way, though. I don't know."

Angel sat still for a long time, stroking her hair.

"Mags, pretend that we're sitting on the roof looking up Moe's alley."

"Okay," she smiled. She had no idea where he was going with this.

"There's this family walking up the alley, going to the pizza shop. A mom, a dad, a boy, and a girl. The little girl is holding onto her dad's hand with both of hers, and hopping up and down with excitement. Can you picture this?"

"Yes." She looked up at him still smiling. He was so cute when he pontificated.

"The little boy is climbing on those planters in front of the pizza shop, and his mother is fussing at him to get down."

Maggie laughed. "Okay. I get it. The little boy wants to climb on things and the little girl wants attention from a parent. But isn't the little boy begging for attention from the mother, too?"

"No. I know that's what the mother thinks he's doing, but he's not. He's just climbing, not acting out to get attention. He's being completely spontaneous. See the planter. Climb on the planter. Your Jeffrey was that little girl. He grew up seeking approval and attention. He never climbed on the planter or up the tree. He never wrestled with the other little boys. His father tried to roughhouse with him, but Jeffrey hated it. He played piano, instead, and his mother dressed him up for recitals, maybe even for school. He played tennis, not football."

"Wait, are you saying all artistic boys are queer?"

"No," he laughed. "I write, and I played piano, too."

"You play piano?"

"Played, past tense. I don't remember much. I could probably sit down and play you some Bach and maybe *The Sabre Dance*, but that's about all."

"*The Sabre Dance?*"

"You know, by Khachaturian." Angel tried to half hum and half sing it but failed miserably, and they both laughed.

"How do you know all that about Jeffrey? Did I tell you all that?"

"No," he admitted. "I made it up."

She eyed him skeptically. "Okay, smartie, then what was I like?"

Angel smiled. "You were the little boy. You were a complete tomboy when you were little. You would come inside for dinner, and your mother would ask, 'where did you get that scratch?' But you wouldn't have any idea where you got it."

Maggie sat up. "You've been talking to Delilah, haven't you?"

"Who's Delilah?"

"My little sister. You talked to her, and she told you about Jeffrey and about me."

Angel laughed. "No, I swear. I didn't talk to anyone."

"Then how did you know all that?"

"I'm not even finished," he said. "Want to hear the rest? It gets better."

Maggie sat up and stared at him suspiciously.

Angel continued, "When you hit puberty, pretty early, I'd say, maybe sixth grade, you changed completely. You started hanging around your country club pool and worrying about everything. Your complexion was awful. Your chest was too flat. You hated your hair. You turned into the little girl holding daddy's hand. In seventh grade, you had a crush on a teacher. He was animated and beautiful. No one else thought he was cute, but you did. You always made straight A's, but you started to work even harder."

"Stop. Mr. Eisenhower, and it was eighth grade. Angel you're scaring me. Seriously, how do you know all of this?"

"I don't know. I just do. People are like rockets. Their lives have trajectories. It you see one going up, you can imagine backwards to the launch and see its path. To me, it's obvious."

"Can you do more?"

"Sure, you started dating in tenth grade, but you were totally freaked out by sex. You thought it was gross. Your chest finally turned into the masterpiece it is now."

Maggie giggled.

"You made out with boys but didn't really like it. The boys were all tongue. It was like they were licking the inside of your mouth."

"I like it when you lick me."

"Yes, and I'll do it later if you'll shut up. I'm on a roll. Have I misstated anything yet?"

Maggie shook her head.

"You liked a boy in eleventh grade and let him feel you up. You saw him for a long time, but one night he tried to finger you, and you kind of freaked out. You didn't make a scene or anything, but it scared you. You knew boys were going to demand more. After that, you and that boy drifted apart. He started dating a close friend of yours who probably gave him more than you would."

"Lots more."

"Uh huh. You didn't think that was fair and you thought she was trashy. Then you met Jeffrey."

"That summer, actually, and I already knew him."

"That summer you started dating Jeffrey. You dated him during your senior year, too, but you broke up several times. Each time, you would cry and think the world had ended, but something told you there was something wrong with Jeffrey. Do I have to call him Jeffrey? Can I say Jeff or something? Jeffrey. It sounds pretentious. Not that he's pretentious. He's not. I kid about Yalies, but he's probably really a good guy."

"He is."

"Anyway Jeff, no Jay, that feels better. Jay would woo you back each time you broke up. You liked that he was sensitive. All the other boys were gross. There you were, with a high IQ and the sexual IQ of an eighth grader. When you got to Colby, no, that's not right. Your senior year, especially the summer after, everyone you knew was losing her virginity. Jay was considerate, though, and told you he could wait until you were ready. During one of your off periods with Jay, you dated a boy who was in college. Maybe that summer after high school. You liked the way it felt when he touched your chest, and you let him finger you. You had what you thought was an orgasm. You had tried to masturbate before that, and it felt pleasant, but it didn't rock your world. After that boy, we'll call him Mick, you learned how to pleasure yourself better. You started back up with Jay, and that's when you gave your first blowjob. You thought that was gross, too, but you thought you were a badass for doing it. It felt wicked, so you liked that part of it. You began giving Jay a blowjob every time you were together. Friends whispered rumors about Jay's sexuality to you. It wasn't the first time you had heard them, but it was the first time you took them seriously." He stopped abruptly.

"Go on."

"Then you met me. I'm missing the part where you first got laid. Mick?"

"Yes, and then Jeffrey, too. And you're way off about a lot of that."

"Such as?"

"I had sex with David, that's Mick, three times my senior year, and I gave him a blowjob. Do we have to use that word? I hate it."

"If I don't have to say Jeffrey, you don't have to say blowjob. Hummer? You sucked him off?"

"Okay, maybe blowjob is the best, but, seriously, how do you know all that stuff?"

"So, I was pretty accurate?"

"No," she laughed. "You were extremely accurate."

They grew quiet.

"You know my whole life, and I don't know anything about you," she said. "What were you like when you were little?"

"Don't remember."

She punched him in the arm. He pinned her arms to her side and rolled on top of her.

"Want to play rough?" he said. "I'll rough you," and he bit her ear and blew farting noises into her neck while she laughed and tried to escape. When he tired of torturing her, he rolled off and pulled her to him. She punched him again, but lightly this time and kissed his chest.

"You know me," Angel said. "I'm not a rocket. I've always been the same. Besides, everything I've done since about seventh grade is in one of those cool folders you stuffed for me."

"You don't like my folders," she said.

"I do, but I like you better than I like them, and I appreciate the idea even more than the doing. Cassie wasn't whole-heartedly behind my doing the writer thing," he said. "That's not fair. She was. Her father wasn't. But she thought it was a phase."

"I don't need to read your writing to know you. You're a sweet man who pretends to be tough."

Angel smiled. "So, I'm faking the tough part."

"No," she said. "It's real, but you're not like Fast Eddie or Cane. Your core is sweet and gentle. You are a protector." She chuckled.

"What's funny?"

"I just realized that you are kinder and more loving than Jeffrey."

"As she stabs him in the heart."

"Why do you do all the stupid stuff, the dangerous stuff? Are you trying to prove to yourself that you don't fear anything?"

Angel thought. "I don't know about all men, but my father told me to seek out and befriend my fears. He said fear offers the greatest challenge but the greatest reward at the same time."

"What does that mean?"

"Well, for example, I have been afraid of heights my whole life. When I was a kid, I remember seeing a high dive for the first time and being petrified. I was too young to jump off it, but, one time, the lifeguard was yelling at some kids, so I climbed up and stood there. The lifeguard saw me and started giving me shit, so I closed my eyes and jumped as far out as I could." Angel began to laugh. "I belly-flopped so hard. My stomach was red for two days. Once I was old enough, I jumped off it every day for weeks. Like I was mocking my terror. Kind of 'take that, fear.' I still do. I ski for the same reason. I ride motorcycles at a hundred miles an hour in the rain without a helmet. Anything, everything to say, 'fuck you fear.'"

"You let Cane hit you in the face, to prove what? That you don't mind pain?"

"And that I can stand there without flinching. Flinching would ruin the whole effect."

"And you walk into fraternities to beat up their brothers who have offended the Janes of the world."

"And steal kegs for the same reason. Danger is a kick."

"And Jeffrey would disagree."

"Jeffrey would probably disagree," Angel nodded.

"Would you risk getting hurt for me?" Maggie asked.

"I don't know, would I?"

"Yes, you would. I was teasing. But girls don't think like that, do they?"

"Yes, they do."

"I don't do any of those things, at least not for your reasons."

"Not true. Women love to do dangerous things. Not necessarily physical things, though you used to when you were little if you were a tomboy. But women do dangerous things all the time."

Maggie shook her head. "Like what?"

"Like giving their hearts away. Women are emotional thrill-seekers."

Maggie thought about that for a moment. "That's true. It's terrifying to love a man. It would be awful to fall for you, which is what I think I'm doing."

Angel smiled. "Why would it be so awful to fall for me?"

"Because you will hurt me."

Angel had no reply.

"Oh, God," she said. "You will, won't you?"

Angel leaned over her and kissed her.

"Did that hurt?" he said and kissed her again.

"No."

He pulled up her blouse and kissed her stomach. "How about that?"

"No."

He unbuttoned her blouse. She sat up so he could remove it. She unhooked her bra and took it off. He got up and went to the foot of the bed. Maggie unzipped her skirt, and Angel helped her shimmy out of it. She shivered while Angel contemplated her.

"You really are the most beautiful woman I've ever seen," he said.

She hooked her fingers in her panties and arched her back to slide them down. Angel pulled them over her feet and tossed them aside.

"Spread your legs for me."

She did.

He crawled up the bed into the V she made and kissed her thighs. Maggie shivered again.

"Are you courting me again?" she asked.

"No, this is barbarian Angel. Do you know where the word *cunnilingus* comes from?"

"From Latin."

"Uh huh," he said. "The *lingus* part means tongue, and the *cunni* part means cunt. So, guess what I'm going to do?"

"Oh, my, please proceed, my learned barbarian."

Angel lowered his face to her and touched her so lightly with his tongue that she thought she might have imagined it. She started, as from an electric shock, and arched her hips to meet his tongue. With his fingers, he separated her lips and kissed her clit. He tongued her opening and pushed his tongue into her. He licked upwards and circled her clit. Maggie trembled as he flicked his tongue across her.

"You taste amazing," he said. When he looked up at her, she had tears in her eyes.

"What?"

"Nothing," she said. "Don't stop. I'll tell you later."

Angel went back to work.

He ran his tongue around her clit again and licked all the way down to her ass. He lightly touched her there with his tongue and traced with a finger where his tongue had been. He slowly pushed at the opening with his middle finger. Maggie moaned and pulled her knees up to give him better access. Angel smiled and slowly inserted his finger into her. Her ass was tight but felt so amazingly smooth. He put his thumb into her pussy and fucked both openings at once. Maggie began to shake and repeat 'Angel' over and over, again. Angel put his face to her again and licked furiously while his fingers accelerated in and out of her. Maggie infinitesimally met his hand with thrusts of her own until Angel could feel her thighs shaking and her whole body began to seize up. All her muscles tightened, and she said something like 'Gah' which he couldn't interpret. Then, she seemed to explode in motion and sound, and he was inundated in her juices which he lapped gratefully. The tremor slowed for a second and then began again, this time even more intensely, and Maggie screamed at the top of her voice in some vague sybaritic language taught to her by ancestors long dead and forgotten except on some cellular level.

When she slowed, he slowed, and he removed first his tongue and then his fingers. He patted her pussy for its good work and leaned on an elbow to observe her.

Tears still flowed, and, as he watched her, they turned into sobbing.

He moved next to her and cradled her head against his chest and shushed her.

"It's okay," he whispered. "My little libertine. My lovely, lovely libertine."

When her crying ceased and her chest stopped heaving, he kissed away her tears, and she finally looked up at him.

"I'm sorry," she said.

Angel was perplexed, so he just let her be. She would tell him what was going on in her head when she was ready.

So, he contented himself with kissing her forehead and holding her tight.

"I don't know what came over me," she said finally.

"Did I upset you?" he asked.

"Oh, dear Lord, no," she said. "You were perfect. You were too good. I don't know. Can you cry from excess of feeling?"

"I don't know," he said.

"Of course. You've probably never cried in your life."

Angel smiled. He had teared up when reading Benjy, and he knew he would tear up again when he read Quentin's section.

"I know what you mean about excess of emotion," he said. "I feel it when I read. Sorrow and joy are too closely intertwined."

Maggie was silent. Then she smiled slightly. "Remember that Yeats poem you read to me?"

"Which one?"

"He was sitting with his lover and a friend of hers."

"Ah, yes." He knew where her head was now. "We grew quiet at the name of love," he said.

"Yes. You and I were talking about love, and I asked if you would hurt me. You grew quiet. You changed the subject and began to make love to me."

"Sorry. I didn't intend that."

"No. That's not what I mean. You did what you said about male love. Instead of saying the word or making some vain promise never to hurt me, you acted out how you feel about me. You loved me with your tongue and hands and, oh God, no one has ever done that to me before, not like that, not with that much feeling."

"So, you liked that?"

Maggie sniffed and wiped her eyes. "I'd punch you again if you weren't holding me so tight. It's not just how you made me feel physically, although that was the most intense feeling I've ever had. It felt like, I don't know what."

"Like you were California and your tectonic plates were shifting?"

"You're being funny, but I'm serious. You make my body feel like its undergoing a religious ecstasy or something." She chuckled. "Okay, I need another line from a poem. It's from when you tutored me. What did Whitman say about the human body?"

Angel smiled. "That it's holy and clean and pure."

"That's how I felt. I feel dirty with Jeffrey. Sex has always been exciting because it's sinful and forbidden. Girls are taught that."

"William F. Buckley said that society was destroying sex by taking the sin out of it."

"Well, they're wrong to do that."

"So, you were crying because you were happy?"

"Yes, but no, too. The more my body and soul gave way to you, my mind screamed louder that you will take all this away, someday, like you did with Cassie."

"Maggie, may I ask a serious question?"

She looked at him and smiled her 'what are you up to this time' smile. "Of course."

"Why do women worry about things that have already happened and can't be changed and things which haven't happened yet and may not ever happen? The past is over. You can learn from it, but there's no point stressing out about it. And the future you fear may never eventuate. Why would you worry that I will hurt you? You can't seize the present moment if you are living in the future. And why is the future always negative? Maybe it will be brilliant. And why focus on the bad things in the past? Who cares what so and so said or did? Remember the good stuff and anticipate even better stuff. Sanity that way lies."

"My little Buddhist pedant," Maggie said.

"Little? Always with the little. Does this look little to you?" And he rolled away so she could see the bulge in his jeans.

"Yes," she said. "It's not even worth my time."

"Oh, well then," he said. "I guess we're done for the moment."

"Maybe if I kiss it, it will get bigger," Maggie suggested helpfully.

"I doubt it, but it's worth a try. But you hate blowjobs. You said so."

"Who cares what so and so said or did?"

Angel laughed and unbuckled his belt.

"Let me help you with that," Maggie said.

And she did.

Sunday

Maggie left early Sunday while Angel was asleep. She typed him a note on his new typewriter thanking him for a joyous time and snuck out, leaving a plate of scrambled eggs and bacon on his desk. A note said, 'Warm me up and eat me. Ha ha.'

Angel smiled and took a bite of bacon. No coffee? Lazy wench.

He showered and went to the roof to check out the day. The sun was directly overhead and hot, melting the snow and causing little streams of water. He could hear rivulets making miniature river sounds below him in the dingle. Soon, the patches under the trees and behind the rocks would be bare, and, soon after that, green would envelop everything. Then, it would almost be time to go home for summer. Union Village dam would have a cascade of frigid water pouring off the mountains and over the twin falls which fed the swimming hole favored by Dartmouth men for two hundred years. Soon, it would be warm enough to swim there.

He returned to his room and pulled on jeans and a tee shirt. He went downstairs to check the message board and to buy a Coke. He ran up the steps to get his blood circulating and ate his eggs and bacon cold.

He opened *The Sound and the Fury* and settled in for a tragic afternoon. Two

Cokes and a pack of peanut M&Ms later, he put down the book. He was glad no one was around because he didn't want his mood broken by triviality.

When he had finished the Quentin section, he had read straight through Jason without pause. He couldn't let Quentin's death and his conversations with his father linger and take over his head. They were too much. Thank God Jason was a pompous ass and his section was comic. After Benjy and Quentin, Angel couldn't have stood much more.

The most apocryphal line in the novel was delivered by Quentin's father after Quentin tried to convince him that he and Caddy had committed incest and would suffer in hell together. His father didn't believe it and said, "You are contemplating an apotheosis in which a temporary state of mind will become symmetrical above the flesh and aware both of itself and the flesh it will not quite discard." Now, that was some fine shit.

But the line which kept hammering at Angel's head was the one in which Quentin summed up his family's demise in a phrase. The Compsons had sold Benjy's pasture, and his older sister Caddy had married a man she didn't love for money. Why? "For a fine sound."

The 'fine sound' was the word Harvard, to be bandied about proudly at church and at dinner parties. 'Yes, my son goes to Harvard.' Quentin's father had paid for Harvard with money earned by selling off their patronymic lands and by whoring Quentin's beloved sister.

Oh, Caddy.

No wonder Quentin couldn't bear being at Harvard. No wonder he put the weights in his pocket and pulled a Virginia Woolf into The Charles River.

A medallion the size of a basketball honored the spot on the bridge where Quentin had stood and jumped.

For a fictional character.

Cassie was right. Angel reacted more to fictional characters than he did to real people. Why was that?

Faulkner was such a shit. He fucked with your mind worse than Shakespeare did. After Quentin and the comic Jason section, the reader felt copasetic attending Easter services with Dilsey and her black congregation. The novel would have been bearable had it ended in church, but it didn't. It put Benjy in a carriage and sent him to the churchyard where his father and his brother Quentin were buried and left the reader with the image of Benjy wailing his confusion after being taken the wrong way around the Oxford circle.

Benjy was pacified for the moment by chewing on jimson weed. But there wasn't any jimson weed for the reader.

Angel's eyes filled with tears, and he lay on his bed bouncing a baseball off the wall until his grief lessened and his anger subsided.

It had long been as dark outdoors as it was in Angel's soul, and he crept out of his room, hoping no one would be around.

No such luck. He heard voices from the kitchen and Groucho's merry laugh, and he went, resignedly, to investigate.

"Where have you been?" Groucho asked.

"Reading."

"I saw Maggie leave this morning. She looked to be in a blithe mood," Blake said. "I take it things are going well between the two of you?"

Angel opened the pizza box on the table and snagged a piece.

He nodded to Blake and chewed.

Blake eyed him. "What have you been reading?"

"Faulkner."

"Ah," Blake said.

Angel went back to his room and pocketed *Light in August*, partly because he was on a reading roll and partly to rinse Benjy and Quentin from his palate.

He put on a coat and descended the stairs. This time there was a message folded and pinned to the board with his name on it.

He opened it. Maggie was home on Long Island safe and sound and sent her phone number and address. 'Just in case you change your mind.'

Angel smiled. He was beginning to like that chick. She put up with his bullshit, and that was saying a lot. She was fighting to hold on to herself and not give in to his ways, a battle she would lose. Did he want her to lose? Did he want the responsibility of another lover he would surely disappoint? Even after the pizza and Coke, he could taste her as he read her words. That must be a good sign.

He crossed campus to Sanborn and plopped in his chair. He stared at The Green for a long time, though no one was there, and nothing was transpiring.

He sighed and opened *Light in August* and read until after midnight.

Joe Christmas fascinated Angel, but the book left his soul unsmirched. He looked back through and re-read the part in which Joe ate breakfast by the stream and then climbed Joanna's stairs to cut her throat.

There was a poem there. Maybe if Angel painted Joe he would discover what Joe was thinking. He owed Eberhart a new poem, anyway.

He trudged back to Phi Psi and, finally, met a few partiers headed for Fraternity Row for late night orgiastic excess. He nodded to a guy he knew and continued home.

In his room again, he sat at his new typewriter and began to write.

Okay. Time to figure out Joe Christmas.

He typed a stanza and then went back and made corrections the way Maggie had showed him.

What was Joe thinking while he was at the creek, shaving and reading that short story? Was he imagining cutting Joanna's throat? Angel began thus:

Joanna lay inside, he knew,
Up high, waiting for a death.
He'd mount the sighing steps once,
Younger as he rose.
She'd twist and offer up her throat,
Past white, past soft, past passion, now.
A razor is a wondrous thing—
It knows just what to do.
Sliding, sibilant, a thousand moans
Caress its edge—
I love you, love you now my love—
A steaming union thus is drawn.

He looked it over. Not great but not horrible for a first pass. That was why Joe had been okay with Joanna's using him for her sordid sex games. Though revulsed, he had gone along with all her degradations, her rape fantasies, and all the other masochistic scenarios which had been trapped in her for nearly forty virgin years. Joe could tolerate an aging, frustrated spinster. But then she had begun praying over him. Angel sat back and spread his arms. Shit. That was it. Joanna had hit menopause. She had gone from lover to mother, a fact which repelled Joe even more than the slut spinster had. So, that fateful morning, she waited for Joe with an old pistol of her father's while he ascended the steps with a freshly sharpened and cleaned straight razor. It was a duet, not a murder.

Angel sighed.

He found his watch. It was nearly dawn. He nodded his satisfaction with himself. It was amazing how much work got done when he was womanless.

But, no time to rest. He had to go to the Farmer's Market in Vermont for Moe. He searched for his list. Shit. Where had Maggie put it? But it was right there in the flat desk drawer, and he put his coat back on and took Groucho's car to Norwich. It was cold as hell, and much of the previous day's melt had turned to patches of ice. He parked at Dan and Whit's and walked back to the market where he gathered together and signed for several bushels of corn and tomatoes and potatoes. They had all been shipped in from southern farms or from ones in Iowa. The local produce would begin soon, though. A miniature woman helped him carry the baskets to his car. She had no teeth but otherwise looked like a Halloween caricature of a sweet witch. He started the car and sat still. Shit. He had forgotten apples. They were Moe's biggest seller. He went back and got several bushels of apples. The same little granny walked with him. This time she spoke.

"What's it like working for Moe? He's a cranky one, isn't he?"

"He is," Angel smiled.

The woman flashed him a huge, toothless smile and vanished, a spirit from another world.

Angel drove back to Hanover and unloaded his prizes into Moe's storage shed. He took over the cash register for a couple of hours while Moe went somewhere trying to collect a debt, and, by noon, he was told to go home.

He crashed on his bed for a couple of hours but woke to hear *Go Down, Moses* beckoning him.

Angel was shocked. *Go Down, Moses* was one of those 'holy shit' epiphany moments. He wasn't sure it wasn't the best thing he'd ever read. Less than a page into the first story, *Was*, Angel knew he was reading something new and different. *Was* unfolded like a *commedia dell'arte* farce. The card game was unimaginably funny and wise. The ruse by which Miss Sephonsiba trapped poor Uncle Buck into marriage was hysterical. Angel gleaned that, somehow, Isaac was the link between the stories, Uncle Isaac, who would father no children.

But, oh dear Lord, farce turned to pathos so fast in *Pantaloon in Black*. Then, *The Old People* and the mythic deer made of light which Isaac, just ten years old, was taken to see, transported Angel to a mystical place, and *The Bear* just flat ripped him apart. The death of Sam Two Fathers and the revelations of the journals rendered Angel null. He shook as he read them, just as Isaac had as he read them in the aged ledgers.

Angel went through the ledgers three times to make sure he understood. Yes, he did. The eldest McCaslin, the patriarch, had impregnated his slave, Eunice, and then impregnated her baby, his own daughter, leading to Eunice's drowning herself. Tomy's Turl, the freed slave in *Was*, was a misspelling of Thomasina's Terrel. Thomasina was simultaneously McCaslin's daughter and granddaughter, so Turl had more McCaslin blood than even Isaac himself did.

When Isaac as an old man stepped on the great rattlesnake while visiting Sam Two-Father's grave in the Big Woods, the snake raised its head, and Isaac hailed it in the Indian tongue as 'Grandfather.'

Holy shit. Holy fucking shit.

It was nine o'clock, and Angel felt as if he was strangling.

He showered and took a couple of tokes from Groucho's joint. Wrapped in a towel, he gathered up quarters and went downstairs and called Maggie.

"Hello."

"Mags?"

"Angel, oh thank God. I thought you'd never call. I called Phi Psi, but the phone just rings."

There was a silence. A happy silence.

"What have you been doing?" she said.

"Reading, mostly. I worked for Moe and wrote some poetry, but I've probably read twenty or more hours."

"Faulkner?"

"Uh, huh."

"What's this for? A class?"

"Sort of. I have an American Modernism class this spring. We'll read *The Sound and the Fury* and maybe *The Bear*. I wanted to wrap my mind around Faulkner. It didn't work. Faulkner crushed my mind into a little ball and then stomped on it. He's amazing.

"Wait, you have read, how many, five novels because you have to read one for class?"

"Uh, huh."

"Why?"

Angel paused. He didn't know. It's just how he had always worked. "Do you know Nabokov?"

"He wrote *Lolita*."

"Right. Nabokov said that reading a book is like meeting a person. The first time through, you just get introduced. Real reading consists of re-reading. Well, my method is a version of that. I feel like you can't understand a book until you've read a lot of other works by the same author."

"Angel, hush. I don't want to talk about books. I love your passion for your work, but I want to tell you something."

"Okay."

"Jeffrey came over last night."

"Okay." Angel didn't like where this was going.

"I tried all night to break up with him, but I just couldn't. I promise I will, but it's hard. I don't know how to do this. I cried for hours after I saw him. I wanted to talk to you so bad."

Angel laughed. "You scared me. I thought you were going to tell me you didn't want to see me anymore or something. I'm sorry you're having trouble. I know how hard it is. It took me months to break with Cassie. I was only able to do it when I did because it happened spontaneously."

"So, you're not mad?"

"No, not at all. I didn't ask you to break up with him, anyway."

There was a silence.

"What are you saying, Angel? You don't mind if I'm seeing Jeffrey and you?"

Angel hadn't thought it through that far. He shrugged. "Not really. I'm happy when I'm with you. That's all I care about."

"Oh." Her voice was cold.

"Maggie."

"No," she said. "I understand. To you, we're not a couple."

Angel laughed. "You are twisting this. But, okay, I want to proceed slowly. I just finished with a long relationship. If you and I are to be a real couple, I don't want it to be a rebound kind of thing."

"So, I'm just a rebound?"

Angel sighed. For a writer, he sure hated words sometimes. They were like little traps.

"No, that's not what I said. We've gone over this before. You were with me last weekend. Did I have feelings for you? Were they real?"

"I thought so."

"Then why can't that be enough for right now?"

She was silent.

"Mags, I like you. I enjoy being with you. I fantasize about you. Please let us grow organically. Don't try to force things. You'll mess them up. Like this conversation. I called wanting to hear your voice."

"And now?"

"Now, I want to hang up and go smoke a joint."

"Well, why don't you do that, then?"

Shit. This was getting them nowhere.

"Mags, a truce. Okay?"

Silence.

"Please, Mags."

When she spoke again, he could tell she was crying.

"Okay," she said.

"I'm going to hang up now," he said. "And I want for you to think something nice about me. Okay."

"Okay."

"Goodnight, sweetheart. I can't wait to see you again. Why don't you come to Phi Psi this weekend?"

"I can't. My mother has a bunch of plans for us on Saturday. She's throwing a big party."

"Okay. Next weekend then?"

She sniffed and laughed. "Okay. Next weekend."

After they hung up, Angel stared at the phone for a long time. Shit. He wouldn't call her again any time soon. Things went sideways too fast when he couldn't hold her or touch her.

Blake and Groucho saw him standing there.

"Going to Sigma Nu. Wanna come?"

"Sure," Angel said, and off they went.

Tuesday and Wednesday passed in a blur. Angel and Moe drove Tuesday morning to the Budweiser Brewery for a tour and a series of sales pitches, all of which were enjoyable but completely unnecessary because Moe was already the biggest single distributor of Bud kegs in New Hampshire, and Angel's brethren at Phi Psi would have de-balled him if he had ordered an inferior keg.

Angel re-read *The Bear* and started *Absalom, Absalom,* but first he pulled his Bible and looked up the Absalom story. Initially, he didn't understand its connection to Faulkner, but by the time he got to the part where Henry and Charles Bon stood outside the Sutpen gate and Henry slew Bon, he could feel Faulkner's dark magic at work. Brother killing brother to avenge a sister's not yet lost honor. Her never to be lost honor once Bon was dead, and her early entombment in Sutpen's unfinished mansion, full of dust and cobwebs and visited too often by straggling Union soldiers who had stayed behind after the great war to ravage and plunder and by early versions of the Klan, riding from house to house to protect the unmanned women and children from the marauding northern bastards.

Of course, he had to extend King David's family to include Amnon, David's oldest child, who dishonored Tamar, David's youngest daughter and to Amnon's slaughter by his own brothers, led by Absalom, he of the long golden tresses who was thrown in battle from his chariot and hung by the same long golden tresses.

Shit. And Maggie wanted to bandy terms of affection with Angel. How trivial Faulkner made her seem.

Yet, to Maggie, he, Angel, played a role as portentous as any in Faulkner's world. His words reverberated in her female ear louder than they were meant. And they had doubtless been picked over and twisted and worried about the past two nights.

She deserved better from him. Moe had told him he didn't need him anymore that week. Sigh. Angel knew he should drive to Long Island to reassure Maggie. In the flesh, he would seem substantial to her, not a voice on the phone confirming her fears and neuroses.

But first, he had to finish *Absalom*, and he was almost afraid to do so.

By nightfall, he had finished, and he had been right. The final chapters tore something Angel wasn't sure would ever mend. How could he ever look at the world again without seeing Sutpens everywhere forcing women to their wills and entire families rent by avarice and pride? Male pride. For Angel knew he had been indicted, too.

And Sutpen, a latter day McCaslin, had seduced or raped Milly, the grand-daughter of Wash Jones, a squatter living on Sutpen's land in an old cabin. Angel frantically looked through *Go Down, Moses* and *Absalom*. Yes, Wash's cabin, where he hacked Sutpen to pieces and whose ancient wooden floor was baptized in Sutpen's blood, was the great hunting lodge from *Go Down Moses*, the cabin in which the now dead civic giants of Oxford, Mississippi had gathered to drink, tell tall tales, and hunt old Ben, the monolithic bear.

Angel didn't even want to attempt to deal with the fact that the narrator for most of the Sutpen story was Quentin, sitting in his room at Harvard with his roommate,

Shreve, piecing together the narrative by saying, 'And Henry must have said,' and 'And Sutpen must have said.' The story wasn't told, it was derived from clues and guesses. How could it have so much power, so much finality, if it might not even be accurate? And the idea of a fictional character narrating the life of another fictional character and then walking out onto a bridge and leaping into the cold, dark Charles because Sutpen's world of incest and lost hope mirrored his own too closely? Oh, God, it was too much.

Angel lay on his bed and stared at the ceiling. He was spent. He could trace all of Faulkner's connections, but the synaptic way they formed a unified myth was beyond him.

He fell asleep depressed and ennobled.

Thursday

Up early. Shit. A man's gotta do what a man's gotta do.

Angel borrowed Groucho's car and headed down I-91 towards Maggie.

It was another gorgeous New England day with its high, blue sky, slightly higher and slightly darker than the Florida skies he was used to.

As he passed Northampton, he thought of Cassie. Smith was still in session. Their Break coincided with Easter while Dartmouth's coincided with Angel's birthday. How considerate.

Sharon was somewhere there, too, wandering the campus or reading in her room.

Nope. Focus on Maggie.

But seeing Sharon would be sweet. He didn't know her well, but she seemed…

Nope. Focus on Maggie.

I'm trying, you douche.

Angel thought of Wallace Stevens as he passed New Haven. How could a poet with a voice as sweet his be an insurance executive?

But passing New Haven brought Yale to his mind and, thus, Jeffrey, Maggie's current and possibly soon to be ex. He didn't expect it to happen, but he hoped to meet Jeffrey while visiting Maggie. He needed to see for himself whether Maggie was nuts. Meeting an ex was good for that. Not that they were infallible. He knew plenty of guys with great girlfriends who were complete assholes. Often neurotic assholes. Sometimes, destructive, threatening assholes.

Angel pulled off to get gas and call Maggie. He didn't even know whether she would be home or not. He was just about to hang up when a girl's voice answered.

"Maggie?"

"No, this is Delilah."

Delilah? Who the hell was that? Ah, Maggie's sister? "Is Maggie home?"

There was a pause and then, "Is this Angel?"

Angel smiled. His reputation preceded him. He hoped that was a good thing.

"Yes."

"Hi! I'm Margaret's sister. Oh, my God. She talks about you all the time."

"Is she there? I was driving down to see her."

"She's not right now. She's playing tennis with a friend. But they're coming home, soon. When will you get here?"

Angel looked at his watch. Hmmm. Allowing for horrible New York traffic. "Maybe around seven."

"Perfect. I'll tell her. She'll be so excited to see you."

Delilah sounded like a younger Maggie. She also sounded like a little devil. This would be fun. This would show Maggie that he cared for her.

Angel got back onto the interstate, and, when he merged onto I-95 south, traffic began to get worse. By the time he skirted Manhattan on the Harlem, it was total shit. When he finally hit Long Island, he was shocked to see a sign for Bridgewater, Maggie's hometown, telling him he had almost another two hours. He had no idea Long Island was so, well, long. When he got to the little town center, he stopped at a bar and got a Coke and directions. The bartender who painstakingly wrote down each turn and landmark for Angel's journey looked like a caricature of a Maine lobsterman, white beard, cap, and all. All he needed was a pipe to adorn a billboard advertising clam chowder or something. He spoke in a craggy, throat damaging growl which evinced experience and hard-earned wisdom. Angel liked him immediately.

"Name's Nick," he said. "If you get lost, come back by and have a beer to think it over. If it's a woman you're seeking, tread lightly. These women are rich and don't think a lot of us working folk." And he honest to God winked at Angel.

Angel smiled and nodded. He thought about leaving a joint with the man but decided that might label him a hippie. He was probably better off as 'us working folk.'

Despite Nick's byzantine directions, Maggie's house was only a few minutes from downtown.

Angel paused before turning into the driveway. What had he gotten himself into? This looked like another Cassie situation. Maggie's house was gigantic. It was covered with gray shingles and sat raised at least twenty feet above the rest of the property. Shit. They built their own hill. He wondered if it had a name. Mount Margaret, maybe.

But he had driven seven hours to assuage Maggie's tender feelings, so there was no chickening out now.

Angel parked under a windblown tree and rang the doorbell. After a minute, he heard the scampering of feet, and a merry voice shouted, "I'll get it."

The door opened, and Angel was confronted by a mini-Maggie with wild curls and a wilder set of eyes. He would have thought her a demon child but for her budding breasts. She couldn't have been much more than five feet tall.

"You're Angel, aren't you?"

"I am. Are you Delilah?"

The girl stood wide-eyed gazing up at Angel. She reached a tentative hand up and touched the scar on his right cheek.

They stood that way for a moment.

"Is Maggie home?"

Delilah's eyes lit with a malevolent glee.

"Yes, she is. Come in. I'm glad to meet you. Margaret really does talk about you all the time."

"Good stuff, I hope," Angel said.

Delilah just chuckled.

"Margaret is up in her room. And, don't call her Maggie around my parents. They can't stand that. And Mags is even worse."

They stood smiling at each other for another moment.

"Are you going to call her?" Angel asked.

"No. You can go on up. It's not really a bedroom. It's more like a wing of the house. She entertains up there all the time." She paused and added, "She has a friend up there, now, so you're cool."

Angel went to the staircase and pointed. Delilah nodded. "Down the hall on the left," she said. "She's got that whole wing to herself."

Angel ran his hand over the bannister as he ascended. This reminded him too much of Cassie's world. He walked down the long hall towards the back of the house and stopped at what had to be Maggie's door. It was closed. He listened but couldn't hear any voices, so he knocked lightly. There was no answer. He knocked again and cracked the door. He peeked in. He heard laughter and music from somewhere inside and opened the door and said "Hello. Anyone?"

He found himself in what in most houses would be a large den which led to a pair of French doors open to Maggie's balcony. He could see the Sound from where he stood, and the wind freshened the curtains and the air.

The music came from his left, so he entered the room tentatively and walked towards the sounds. He heard Maggie laugh delightedly, as if being tickled or teased, and he smiled.

He strode to the opening into her bedroom proper and froze. Maggie lay on her bed, kissing a boy. She broke away to laugh, again, but he pushed her flat on her back and leaned over her. He kissed her long and hard, and she put her arms around his neck.

Angel stood, paralyzed. He had no clue what he should do. Making his presence known would embarrass the shit out of Maggie and the boy, presumably Jeffrey, her Yalie boyfriend.

The boy unbuttoned Maggie's blouse and fumbled with her bra snap. Maggie broke away from his kiss, laughing merrily, and unsnapped it for him. He pushed it up and crushed her left breast with his hand. Maggie made a slight moan and pulled his face back to hers.

Angel tried to make himself leave, but he couldn't, so he stood, stupidly looking on.

Maggie broke the kiss and raised up. She flicked her pony tail over her shoulder and gestured for him to lie down. The boy grinned and lay with his arms behind his head while Maggie, Angel's sweet Maggie, unbuckled his belt, unzipped his fly, and tugged his slacks down. Jeffrey, or whoever it was, was semi-erect, and Angel watched transfixed as Maggie stroked him, leaned over, and put him in her mouth. A little spasm ran through the boy's midsection.

This was all wrong. Didn't Maggie know he was coming to see her? Or hadn't Delilah, the little minx, warned her. And the music for her dalliance was James Taylor--fucking James Taylor.

Again, Angel tried to make himself leave, but he hadn't ever seen live sex before, and he felt a stirring in his pants.

Shit. This was all wrong. His girl, James Taylor, his mild excitement, all of it.

Maggie took the boy out of her mouth and kissed her way up the underside of his cock, smiling at him the whole time. The guy looked delighted, as well he fucking should. Angel would have been, too.

Angel finally broke free of his spell and tip-toed towards the door, but when he closed it, the door creaked, and he heard a sudden yelp from Maggie, "Delilah? Is someone out there?" And when he closed the door, it made a decided click. The last thing he heard as hurried down the hall was Maggie shouting, "Delilah, you little pervert. I'm going to kill you."

Angel raced down the stairs and called, "Delilah."

"In the kitchen."

He followed the sound of her voice and found her spreading jelly on a piece of bread.

"You truly are a little demon," he said.

Delilah smiled happily at him. "I'm not that little. Did you find Maggie?"

"You know I did."

"And did you meet her friend?"

"No, they were engaged."

Delilah looked mystified for a second and then said, "Oh, sorry. I didn't think of that."

She put the two pieces of bread together and lay the sandwich on a plate and cut it in two.

"Well," she said. "Truth will out. Though it hath no tongue, it will speak with most miraculous organ."

Angel chuckled. "That's from two completely different plays, and you mangled the wording. Shakespeare would not be pleased. And I saw the organ, which was impressive, but I wouldn't call it miraculous."

Delilah blinked and then both laughed together.

"How old are you?" Angel asked.

"Fifteen. Do you mean they were doing it? He had his thing out and everything?"

"Well, it wasn't out, the last I saw of it."

Delilah made a face. "Gross," she said, and they both laughed again.

"Well, that was interesting, but I think I'm heading back to Dartmouth. Tell Maggie, I said 'hi.' Or, if she didn't know I was coming and blames you for spying, don't tell her I was even here."

"Want a peanut butter and jelly sandwich. You must be hungry. It's good. I use Smucker's blueberry jelly."

Delilah handed the plate to Angel and went to the refrigerator for a Coke. "See, I know all about you."

Angel bit into the sandwich. It was good. He took a sip of the Coke.

Then, they heard a sound like an elephant down the stairs and Maggie bellowing, "Delilah."

Delilah smiled. "In the kitchen."

Maggie stormed in shouting, "You little bitch. What have I..." but she stopped short when she saw Angel sitting there. She looked as if someone had punched her in the stomach.

"Angel," she said breathlessly. "What are you doing here?"

"Eating a sandwich," he said. "I'd offer you some, but I'm pretty sure you're full."

Delilah gasped. "That's what they were doing? Gross me out."

Maggie turned such a dark shade of red that Angel thought that something might have burst in her. She sputtered something intelligible.

Angel went to Maggie and dabbed at the side of her mouth with his napkin. "You missed a spot," he said.

She swatted at his hand angrily. "Did you, were you upstairs just now? Did you see? Oh, shit."

"Yes," he said. "Oh, shit."

Maggie burst into tears.

Angel wrapped his arms around her. "It's okay," he said soothingly. "I would kiss you, but I'd rather you brushed your teeth first."

Maggie recoiled and stared at him. This time she lashed out at his face, but he caught her hand.

Delilah tried but couldn't suppress a laugh.

Maggie turned to her. "This is your fault, you little shit. You'll pay for this."

And she stormed past Jeffrey who had appeared. He reached for her, but she pushed him away and fled up the stairs.

Delilah and Angel burst into laughter. Angel sat back down and took a bite from his sandwich.

"That was so mean," Delilah said.

"What's wrong with you?" Jeffrey said.

"With me? Nothing," Angel said. "I was just leaving. I didn't mean to interrupt your little tryst. You should go after Maggie, excuse me, Margaret. She seemed upset."

"I ought to kick your ass," the boy said.

Angel's voice dropped almost to a whisper, "I don't think that's a good idea."

"Yeah, I know about you. You're Angel, the tough guy Margaret's been seeing. Or slumming with, I should probably say. You don't scare me. I heard about you from a Dartmouth friend. You hit him in the face while he wasn't even looking and broke his nose. You're a cheap shot artist."

Angel stood. He wiped his mouth and took a sip of Coke. "Listen to me Jeffrey. You are Jeffrey, right? Maggie's not blowing men randomly, is she?"

Jeffrey nodded.

"Well, Jeffrey, look at my face. It's not as pretty as yours, is it?" He moved towards Jeffrey who instinctively backed off a step. "A friend told me a long time ago that, all other things being equal, the man who fears being hurt the least usually wins a fight. Well, Jeffrey, I don't mind being hurt, and I suspect that you don't want that pretty face of yours messed up. Did your friend's nose look normal after I finished with him? Did his plastic surgeon make him pretty again? I doubt he will ever look the same."

Jeffrey looked unsure, but he didn't move.

"I would enjoy beating the shit out of you, Jeffrey. I really would. It would be epic, but the sad truth is that we don't have any reason for enmity, do we? Margaret has some explaining to do to you, but, more importantly, she needs a big, strong man to go upstairs and tell her things will be all right. And I'm not going to do it. I'm going to get into my car and drive back home, away from all this sanctimonious rich chick shit. So, why don't you trot back upstairs like a good little rich boy and comfort her. She may even blow you again for your kindness. You like blowjobs, don't you?"

Jeffrey stood indecisively.

"Better do as he says," Delilah chirped. She was trying hard not to laugh again.

"You'll pay for this, you little bitch," Jeffrey said, pointing a finger at her.

Angel grabbed Jeffrey's finger and bent it backwards until it cracked and Jeffrey yelped.

"Don't ever threaten Delilah again. If I hear that you've even spoken unkindly to her, I'll drive down to Yale, rip your dick off, and stuff it down your throat. Do you hear me?"

Jeffrey backed off, holding his finger and staring at Angel as if he were the devil. He took a look at the stairs, but he chose the front door instead and left.

Delilah looked at Angel with wide eyes. "That was so badass," she said.

Angel sat and bit into the sandwich. "Got any chips?" he asked.

"We sure do," Delilah said. "Charles Chips, best in the world." She stood on tip-toes and pulled the familiar yellow can off the top of the refrigerator.

Angel ate and contemplated going to Maggie's rescue. He wished he hadn't made the gross jokes, but they were just sitting there for him to verbalize. He sighed.

"I think Maggie's pissed at me. What do you think?"

"Honestly?"

"Honestly."

"I think she's totally crazy about you. She makes you sound like a cross between Einstein and Casanova. And she's told me about a thousand times about all the scars you have from your misadventures."

Misadventures. That was good. He looked again at Delilah. She was diminutive, but she wasn't as young as he had first thought. "What are you in? Tenth grade?"

"Uh huh. And what are you? A junior?"

"That's right. How do you know multiple Shakespearean plays and use medieval words like misadventure?"

"We're rich. I go to a good school. I can do math, too. I know that when you're twenty-seven, I'll be twenty-one, old enough to date you."

"Oh, you will, will you?"

"So, you better get ready, because I'm not a pushover like Maggie, Margaret, now you've got me saying it, too."

Angel smiled. This was the age of the kids he was going to be teaching. He didn't know if that sounded exciting or daunting. Probably both.

"Well, goodbye, little evil. I hope to see you again. Keep reading Shakespeare."

"I will, and Faulkner, too. Margaret told me he's your favorite."

Angel smiled and finished his Coke. He put his plate in the sink and folded his napkin.

Delilah went to him and hugged him.

"It was really nice meeting you," she said. "Your merits weren't overstated."

Angel kissed her on the forehead and left. He sat in the car and rolled down the windows. The wind from Long Island Sound whipped through the car. He wondered if it was always this blustery. And this cold. He leaned over to get out of the wind and lit a joint. He turned on the car so he would have music and sat, musing.

He knew he should go back in and apologize for embarrassing Maggie. She hadn't done anything wrong. He had sex with Cassie while he was trying to break up with her. He had sex with Jane while Maggie wasn't around. In fact, he was in no position to criticize anyone's libidinal pursuits. And Jeffrey really was a good-looking guy. If he swung that way, he would be all over Jeffrey.

And, from what he had seen, Maggie was at least half wrong about Jeffrey's tastes. He certainly seemed into kissing Maggie and fondling her breasts.

God, that was strangely arousing. Angel had never seen real people having sex before. He had seen *Deepthroat*, but that was a movie. And it certainly wasn't with someone Angel knew and cared for. He pondered that. Did he have some voyeur in him? Probably. Maybe all men did.

But he didn't go back inside to comfort Maggie. First of all, it would have led to an hour-long discussion of their relationship and all that pointless bullshit. When, in the history of mankind, had a relationship ever been improved by talking about it? Never, probably.

He put the joint out. He needed a coffee for the road. Maybe, more than one. He went around the circular driveway and made his way back downtown. His nautical friend Nick at the saloon would brew him some coffee. It would be a long drive home.

Three hours later, Angel was off the island and around Manhattan. I-95 North beckoned like an old friend. He pulled off in Greenwich and got gas. He got change from the attendant who told him he was a pint low on oil.

"Sure. Put one in," Angel said. "Payphone?"

The attendant pointed around the side of the station, and Angel walked in that direction, trying to decide what he wanted to say. He had no idea. He would wing it, he guessed.

He used the men's room to buy his febrile brain some time to formulate a plan, but nothing came to him.

He sighed and dialed Maggie's number. He dropped in coins as instructed and waited. When it rang, Maggie picked up immediately.

Shit. She had been sitting by the phone waiting for him to call. He should have called sooner. Inconsiderate asshole.

"Hey," he said.

"Oh, Angel, I'm so sorry. I've never been so embarrassed. I was trying to break up with Jeffrey. I swear. That's why I invited him over."

"No, I'm sorry. I made rude jokes at your expense. That was inexcusable."

"Rude jokes? Angel, I was doing things with Jeffrey, and you saw me. I don't care about your jokes. I know you were hurt and just striking out in your stupid Phi Psi manner."

"No, that's charitable of you, but I wasn't angry or hurt. I was just mean. And I should have gotten out of the room the second I realized you were with someone. I can't explain why I stood there. I just sort of froze. Like it wasn't really happening."

"Of course, you were hurt. I'm so sorry. I know you probably never want to see me again, and I understand, but please don't hate me."

"Hate you? I'm not even mad at you, and, of course, I want to see you again."

Maggie was silent. Angel sensed he had said something dreadfully wrong. He began to play back the conversation in his head, but Maggie saved him the trouble.

Her voice was cold. "I forgot. You don't get jealous. You don't have feelings. You don't give a flying fig what I do or don't do. For a moment, I forgot how little I mean to you."

Angel couldn't help himself, and he laughed. "Maggie, don't you think you're over-reacting just a tad." The minute he heard the words leave his mouth and enter the telephone speaker, he knew he was fucked.

"Over-reacting? You think I'm over-reacting? To you, this is no big deal. Let Maggie kiss whomever she wants."

"You mean blow whomever?"

"Yes, I was blowing Jeffrey. I didn't want to and I didn't like it, but that's what I was doing."

"Mags, don't tell me you weren't enjoying yourself. Remember, I was there and saw you. I believe the part about trying to break up with Jeffrey, but you were turned on. I get it. Jeffrey's a fine-looking guy. And I remember things I did while I was trying to break up with Cassie, but don't make this a bigger deal than it is. It's kind of funny if you think of it the right way."

"Funny? Everything's a big joke to you, isn't it? Jeffrey was right. You're an asshole. I can't believe I fell for the radio voice and the getting hit by Cane and all that bullshit." And she burst into tears.

Shit.

Angel tried again. "Mags, I'm sorry I walked in on you. I'm sorry I embarrassed you. I'm sorry I don't feel the right things. Truly. Please just try to relax. And don't yell at your sister. She didn't know what I would walk in on. She was as surprised as I was. I'm hanging up now, but I'll call if you want when I get back to Dartmouth. Just try to calm down. Okay?"

"Calm down? My boyfriend, I was going to say my lover, but I'm forbidden to mention the word, doesn't care what I do or don't do, and it's no big deal. You have no heart, Angel. Normal people feel things."

"Like this is all my fault? I drove seven hours because you begged me to come meet your friends and parents, and I walk in on you with Jeffrey's dick down your throat, and my response, or lack thereof, is the problem. I have feelings. You want to know what I'm feeling right now? I'm pissed I wasted an entire day on you."

And he hung up.

He didn't like putting the guilt back on Maggie's side of the fence, but it seemed tactically preferable to having her dwell on his shortcomings.

See. This was why guys hated discussing feelings. Nothing good ever came of it.

But he felt better as he drove north. He tried to figure out why. For one thing, this bullshit freed him from having to declare his undying love to Maggie for a long, long time. That was a relief. Then, too, it assuaged whatever guilt he harbored over his relationship with Jane.

It was good that Maggie wasn't perfect. It was good that she could desire someone other than Angel.

Shit. He hadn't realized how the whole Cassie thing had spooked him about commitment.

On a more carnal level, seeing her with Jeffrey was surprisingly aphrodisiacal. If Angel had ever treated Maggie with kid gloves, sexually, he was done with that. He was going to go full Thor on her from now own. He had tricks up his sleeve, or in his trousers, at least. Maggie would now get the benefit of his lifetime of exploration. Maggie would reap the rewards of her own treacherous cupidity.

Angel lit the joint he had started in Maggie's driveway and took the lid off the second cup of coffee he had bought. He turned the dial until a British Invasion channel appeared and The Kinks sang to soothe his savage breast.

He drove with his knees while he smoked and sipped coffee. Then, he ground out the joint and changed into the right lane. New Haven was just ahead. Perhaps he could find Jeffrey's room. There, he could pull a Cane and pee on Jeffrey's record collection or something. But he didn't get off the highway. He would never have found Jeffrey's room. And, if he had, it would have been locked. Besides, he had told Jeffrey the truth. He had no animus towards Jeffrey. Peace, brother. So, they had shared a chick? If anything, he, Angel, was the interloper.

When he approached Northampton, though, he couldn't resist pulling off and driving to the Smith campus. He got out, stretched his legs, and, leaning on the front fender of the car, contemplated Sharon's dorm. The room he thought was hers was lit up. It wasn't much past midnight, and she didn't strike him as an early bird, so he could probably walk right in and knock on her door. It was Thursday. The odds of walking in on two women *in flagrante delicto* on the same night were infinitesimal.

But what of the ethics of the situation? That was trickier.

He decided on the 'fuck it' principle and went to her dorm. The outer door was unlocked, so he walked in and knocked lightly on her door. Déjà vu. Sharon opened the door and stared blankly at Angel for a moment with a 'what the fuck' expression, and then broke into a big smile and threw her arms around him and hugged him until he almost choked.

"Two months! It took you two months to come back and see me!" she said and beat him on the chest. She hugged him again and dragged him inside. "God, Angel. I can't believe it. And I look like crap."

Sharon was right. Her hair was twisted on top of her head and looked as if it hadn't been washed in days. She wore striped pajama bottoms and an Oxford tee shirt. But, even with her hair in disarray and without makeup, Sharon still had it. Angel was smitten.

"I had forgotten how beautiful you are," he said quietly.

Sharon laughed. "Flattery will get you everywhere," she said. "But sit. Tell me what brings a road warrior to my door this lovely eve."

Angel looked for somewhere to sit, but the place was a mess. Books and notebooks seemed to have sprouted and grown wild. Sharon laughed again and cleared a space on the bed, and the two sat, quiet and happy to see each other.

"Why does this place look as if a library exploded?" Angel asked.

Sharon laughed and looked about her. "Midterms," she said. "I have three papers due and a lab report I haven't even started."

"Oh. I'm sorry I dropped in. I can leave. I was on my way back to Dartmouth anyway."

"No. You're not going anywhere. You're going to sit here and tell me what happened with Cassie the last time I saw you and everything else you can think of. My boyfriend says I talk about you more than I talk about him."

"You have a boyfriend? Did you have one when I was here before?"

Sharon blushed and ducked her head. "Maybe."

Angel laughed. "You little minx. And I've been laboring under the delusion that you were trying to seduce me that night."

Sharon laughed, too. "I was. I know. I'm a horrible tramp. But you were so sweet and cute. And you were so confused. You were adorable."

"Hmmm. Way to make a guy feel manly. Adorable, huh?" Angel pointed to her pajama bottoms. "And did you have those when I was here?"

"Yes."

"And it was about ten degrees, yet you chose to sleep in little, tiny panties?"

"Maybe I was just testing you. You seemed so chivalric."

"Chivalric sounds better than adorable."

"But I'm not trying anything tonight. My little friend is visiting me, and I have horrible cramps."

"I'm not feeling very sexy tonight either," Angel said.

"Wow. I didn't know that was possible." She put her hand on his arm. "Want anything to drink? I have some Vodka."

"No. I'm just going to sulk. I have a joint in my car. Or would that mess up your studying?"

"I'm officially done for the night," she laughed. "The rest of my night will be spent plumbing the depths of your self-pity."

Angel smiled. "You are unfairly cute. May I at least kiss you?"

"You may, indeed, but then you have to tell me what's bothering you."

Angel put his hand to her cheek and looked closely at her. Her eyes were brown and would have been unremarkable but for the light they seemingly emitted. They had little, green flecks in them which shone when she smiled. He leaned towards her, but she met him more than half way and they kissed greedily.

Angel withdrew and widened his eyes comically.

"Gracious," Sharon said. "That was something. I guess it's been a long time between our kisses."

Angel kissed her again, lightly this time, and sighed. Sharon was definitely an 'if only.'

"I'll tell you why my mind is askew if you'll take off those pajama bottoms," he said.

"I thought the deal was for a kiss?"

"Shit happens. Deals change. Look at Russian treaties."

Sharon stood and slid her pants to her feet and kicked them off.

"Now I remember you," Angel said. He patted the bed beside him and slid back until he was leaning against the wall. "You have the best legs on the planet."

"Flatterer. You're still not getting any tonight. Now, talk, mister. What's up with you?"

"Okay. First of all, Cassie and I broke up right after I left you. Like, completely, no going back, split up."

"Wow. I wondered about that. I've seen Cassie around campus, but I don't think she wants to talk to me."

"But that's not what's up today," Angel said.

"Whoa. Hold up. You broke up with Cassie right after you left me?"

"That's right."

"And you didn't come back and make mad, passionate love to me?"

"Oops. I didn't know I was supposed to."

"And you never called me, not even after I was charming and seductive and supportive?"

Angel thought that over.

"I thought discretion was in order," he said finally.

Sharon burst out laughing.

"No," he said. "Really. There was another girl in the picture, and you would have undone me."

"Ignoring the intriguing 'I would have undone you,' which, by the way, is one of the oddest compliments I have ever gotten, tell me about this other girl. You were cheating on Cassie?"

Angel tried to think how to explain Maggie. He didn't mind the implication that he was a shit, but he didn't want her tarred in his iniquities.

"That would be Maggie. I had met Maggie while I was trying to break up with Cassie. Maggie didn't cause anything. And I told Maggie I couldn't get into a relationship with her until I was officially single. She didn't like that."

"No, of course not. That's what every married man tells every mistress at some point."

"I don't think it was like that. I felt drawn to Maggie, and I didn't want it to be a rebound thing, so I told her to go away until I dealt with Cassie."

"Dealt with?"

"Poor choice of words. Simple version: yes, I was drawn to Maggie, but I was obligated to Cassie and wanted to end that honorably before beginning anything with anyone else."

"Which is why you had the temerity to reject me that night."

"Yes. But there's more to it than that. I'm not sure why I'm telling you all this, but I have fewer scruples sleeping with women I'm not attracted to than with ones I would almost certainly fall for. You're in the latter camp, and, yes, that is definitely a compliment. You're like a big planet, and I'm just a comet. Your gravitational force would have sucked me in, and I would have crashed and burned."

"I'm a planet, huh?"

"Metaphorically."

"I got that part. So, back to Maggie, and thanks for that rather weird compliment. I felt the same towards you. Only I thought you were a dangerous man, an addictive man, and I had a sort-of boyfriend. Actually, he's still only a sort-of boyfriend. I think I like you a lot better than him. But, Maggie?"

"Maggie. After I broke with Cassie, I began seeing Maggie, and it was good for the most part. Today, I decided spontaneously to drive to Long Island to visit her and meet the family. Bad call."

"Why? I would think it sweet if you drove that far to surprise me."

"It was a bad call precisely because I surprised her. Surprised them, I should say."

"Them? Ah. I think I see. Maggie has a Cassie of her own?"

"If I follow your analogy, yes. She has a boyfriend she's supposed to be breaking up with, but, apparently, she's been less than successful."

"How less than successful has she been?"

"I walked in on them," he said.

"Oh, my God. And they were…?"

"Exactly."

Sharon began to laugh. She put her hand to her mouth, but the chuckles just kept bubbling out. "I'm sorry," she said, "but picturing you standing there. It's kind of funny."

"That was my response. Maggie didn't appreciate my levity."

Sharon laughed harder and leaned against him. Angel put his arm around her.

"You weren't jealous? You didn't beat up the other guy? I can't picture you just accepting it."

"Why? He hadn't done anything wrong. And she was doing with him exactly what I had done while trying to break up with Cassie. No, I thought it was good for a few laughs. Guess I was wrong. Apparently, I'm an insensitive asshole." He began to chuckle, too, then stroked Sharon's head. "You and I could be good, together, couldn't we?"

"Another time, another place," she said.

Angel nodded.

As he had before, Angel showered, but not before going to Groucho's car for a joint and his bag. They smoked, and then he stood under the hot water for a long while, trying to eradicate the day from his memory banks.

While he put on fresh clothes, Sharon dressed, and they walked hand in hand to the same diner they had eaten at before. The owner was trying to close, but he kept it open long enough to make bacon and eggs for them.

Back at her dorm, Angel re-read *The Bear* while Sharon pretended to study. She watched him all the while, and he knew it. When they went to bed, Sharon stripped to her panties, and Angel stripped completely.

"What a waste," Sharon said, stroking Thor. "Want me to at least make you come?"

Angel shook his head. "I just want to soak up being with you. We're probably not going to get a chance to do this any time soon."

Sharon sighed and rested her head on his chest.

"Angel," she whispered.

"Yes?"

"I think I like you."

Angel smiled. He thought he liked her, too.

Friday
Tripping

Angel rose stiff and exhausted. Sharon slept all night on his shoulder, and he lost feeling in it after an hour. Sharon kissed him and snuck off to the library to work while Angel lay in bed meditating his lot until he thought the dorm might be empty enough to shower.

As he walked into the cold, hard sunshine, he chuckled at the note he had left Sharon. Not that it was funny. He had just said *au revoir* and thanked her. God, that girl could make tapioca hard. Plus, his whole fucking situation was kind of comical.

For instance, he knew he was duty bound to see Cassie. If he didn't, that would be uncivil, even if Cassie never found out that he had been at Smith. He trudged across the mushy grass to her dorm and took a deep breath. He knocked on her door lightly. He didn't know whether to pray she answered or to pray she didn't. Leaving a note would have been infinitely easier.

But, of course she was there.

Cassie didn't even look surprised. She just said, "Hi, Angel," and let him in.

Angel entered and stood indecisively. Did he hug her? Or kiss her? Or sit somewhere?

It wasn't like her to play passive-aggressive, but she did it well, nonetheless and waited for him to speak.

"I was driving up from New York and couldn't drive past without stopping by," he said.

"Why not?

Angel thought briefly of fleeing, but, as he examined Cassie, he felt his eyes watering. Cassie's lower lip was trembling, and her eyes showed pain.

He moved slowly towards her, ready to stop if he saw signs of panic or rejection, and took her in his arms. She embraced him stiffly and shook slightly.

"Are you all right?" he asked.

"I don't know."

Angel nodded and kissed her hair. He sighed, and she seemed to feel him do so and relaxed slightly.

"I shouldn't have stopped by," he said.

"No, I'm glad you did. It's good to see you. But, please, may we skip the 'can we be friends' conversation?"

Angel nodded. Everything about her smelled and felt so familiar. He led her to the bed, and they sat. He put his arm around her again, and she leaned against his chest. They sat that way in silence for a long time.

Cassie broke away and held out her hand. Angel smiled and gave her his handkerchief. She sniffed and wiped her eyes, and then she looked at the handkerchief.

"I know," he said. "You gave it to me."

"Our first Christmas," she said. "You thought it was such a strange gift."

"No, that's not right. I remember opening it and thinking how odd the giver was, and how sweet."

"I read what you wrote about me," she said. "The piece you gave me this past Christmas. I expected it to be maudlin."

"It was, I'm afraid," he said.

"No, it was sweet and true. The whole thing. Even when the Cassie character was thinking about things. It was me. It was exactly what I would have thought or said."

She sniffed and dabbed again, and they went silent.

"I did what you told me to do," she said. "I'm seeing Rob again. Not like us. Just friends. When I first dated him, he seemed so majestic, Harvard and older and everything. He seems pretentious now, but he's kind and attentive. And he's needy. I don't think I would look for that in a man, but, after you, it's nice to feel needed."

Angel smiled. He didn't remember telling her to date Rob. And the 'needy' part was pretty good. There was both a jab at him and a compliment buried somewhere in what she said.

She looked up. "I have to go to class."

"I need to be on the road, too."

"I'm glad you stopped by."

"I am, too." He looked at his hands. "Cassie, I know I shouldn't say this, but…"

"I know. You still love me somewhere deep down."

That wasn't what he was going to say, but he let it linger and echo in the air. It was true.

They stood and went to the door. Angel felt awkward but tender. This was how they should have parted the last time.

He took her to him and held her. She wrapped her arms around him and held her face up to him.

Was it an invitation? Angel didn't know. But he bent to her and kissed her lightly.

She smiled and sniffed and nodded. 'So that's that' she seemed to say.

Angel waited while she locked the door, and walked her to her class. She stood just outside and turned to him, "Ever the gentleman."

"Ever the gentleman," he assented. She blew him a kiss and disappeared inside.

Cassie was right. So that's that. Huh.

He sat in Groucho's car smoking a joint and drinking the remnants of the previous night's coffee and marveled at the variety of feelings that shot through him.

Could he and Cassie ever re-unite? He would have thought it impossible an hour before, but now he didn't know. Maybe in a year. Or, more likely, as one of those happy accidents after a brutal break-up or a divorce when you run into an ex and the stars align.

But not anytime soon.

And he had learned something else, something perhaps more valuable. He didn't love Maggie. That simple knowledge made everything plainer and clearer. If Maggie wanted to date him, he would be happy to do so. But he wasn't getting into any more emotional drama with her.

He didn't have a clue why women did all that shit, anyway. Maggie was at her best when she was with him at Phi Psi. She was relaxed and funny and smart and sexy. More importantly, she was happy.

Why would she throw all that away to have their relationship be something she could describe to her parents and her friends in a single word?

But, if he didn't feel that way about Maggie, why hadn't he banged Sharon? That was food for thought. Oh, yeah. Her period.

He stubbed out the joint and drove towards Hanover. Big doings were afoot. He and the guys were supposed to be doing the Owsley acid Gandalf had sold him. He found a radio station playing *Radar Love* and put the pedal to the metal.

Big doings indeed.

Groucho and Blake were waiting impatiently for him when he got back.

"Let's get this show on the road," Blake said.

They went to Angel's room and, of course, Angel couldn't find the acid.

Shit. Maggie had re-arranged things. So, they went through Angel's desk. Blake pulled a manila envelope from the center drawer.

"Think this is it?" He waved the envelope, marked in big block letters: 'Drugs.' Subtle, Maggie. The cops would never have broken the code.

They each put a tab on their tongues and let it melt. Groucho giggled. Angel put *White Rabbit* on his stereo, and they sat to wait for things to develop.

"Who else is dropping with us?" Angel asked.

"Gandalf might, but he's got his own stash," Groucho said. "Sand and Eddie were supposed to be back, but I haven't heard from them. It might just be us."

"What should we do?" Blake asked.

"Gandalf said its active acid," Groucho said. "I thought we could walk down to Occom Pond and maybe out onto the golf course. We could climb the hills and shit. A Tibetan monk type of trip."

"Oh," Blake said, "and when it gets dark, we could light a fire in the Blue Room and play music."

Angel had a badass idea and disappeared downstairs. He fished in his wallet for the number of Wanda's brother and called it.

Zach, her brother, answered. This was going well.

"Zach, Angel from Phi Psi. Listen, are you guys playing anywhere tonight?"

"No, man. Things have been slow."

"Well a few of us just took some acid, and it would be really cool if you and a couple of your guys would come by and jam in the Blue Room. I could pay you like a hundred bucks or so."

"Will there be beer?" Zach asked.

"I'll order a keg of Bud," Angel said.

Whoa, his head was starting to buzz. The shit was coming on fast.

"What time?"

"I don't know. Eight?"

And before he lost the capacity to do it, Angel called Moe's and ordered the keg. He also put in an order for two for Saturday night. Guys would be coming back early. They always did. There was only so much hometown and parents a man could stand.

Just as Angel hung up the receiver, as if he had willed it into being, the front door swung open, and there stood Ed and Sand.

Eddie swept Angel up in a bear hug, which scared the shit out of Angel.

"Hey, Baby Brother Man, what's shaking?" Ed said.

"Free acid in my room," Angel said. His tongue felt too big for his mouth and he wondered if Eddie would understand him.

"Is there beer?" Sand asked.

"It'll be here soon," Angel said. "Please, don't ask me to speak for a while, at least until I adjust."

"You already dropped?" Sand asked.

Angel nodded. He wasn't kidding. He needed a hiatus from speech. His head was feeling funny. Walking was a good idea. He could already tell it was speedy acid. His neurons were firing like the cylinders in a Porsche at 7,000 RPMs. He could almost feel them flinging their electric impulses madly about his brain searching for a stable epicenter.

He bought a Coke while he was downstairs and went back to his room. Groucho was clearly feeling his head, too. He sat drumming madly on his leg along with The Jefferson Airplane, only he was tapping twice as fast as the Airplane drummer was. Blake Smooth was going through Angel's closet looking for a tripping costume. He pulled a cowboy hat and donned it. He turned to the group, and said, "Eh?"

"It would look better on Angel," Sand said.

"It would look better on a cowboy," Ed said.

Angel turned off the stereo and off they went on their odyssey.

They waited outside Wheeler Hall while Groucho went to look for Gandalf.

Angel took a deep breath. Spring air with a faint taste of cold.

"I swear I can smell Cassie and Maggie," he said.

"Typical," Ed said. "Get Angel's brain swirling and everything smells like pussy."

Angel grinned at Eddie. His lips and cheeks felt like rubber. He put his hands to his cheeks and mushed them around. Yep, rubber. He was rubber-man. Shit, this stuff worked fast.

Groucho emerged from Wheeler with a wobbly and paranoid looking Gandalf.

"He thought someone stole his acid," Groucho laughed, "but he'd already taken it. I'd say he's half an hour ahead of us."

"I hope I don't look like Gandalf in half an hour," Eddie said.

"Fuck you, Sandman," Gandalf said.

"I'm Eddie, you fucked up little wizard asshole," Eddie said.

Everyone found that funny for some reason. A co-ed crossing campus stared at them. Sand ran towards her growling, and she split in a hurry. They all found that hysterical, too.

"You scared that poor girl," Groucho said.

Everyone stared at him and then burst out laughing again.

So, this was laughing acid. That was the best kind. Sometimes, though, laughing acid turned dark later in the trip. Angel made a mental note to be on his guard, but he found that humorous, too. The group alternately walked and danced down Main Street towards Occom Pond. When they reached the bottom of the hill, they saw a group of old, white men circulating in and out of the Occom cabin.

"Trustees," Blake said. "Everybody hide."

Angel hid behind a bush and peered out at the men. Blake tried to hide behind Groucho who hid behind Eddie.

Sand began to sprint towards the golf course, weaving as he went. Gandalf shrieked and ran after him. Soon, the whole bunch was running down the first tee and over to the eighteenth fairway. Blake skidded and slid on his butt from the tee to the fairway below.

"Sleigh ride," Sand shouted, and he duplicated Blake's slide.

"Turn around," Gandalf said. The pair turned and everyone laughed. They were covered with dark mud all down their backs and butts.

But the golf pro appeared on the deck above screaming invectives at them.

Shit. He knew Angel. Mustn't get caught.

Angel began a full-tilt sprint down the eighteenth fairway towards the bridge to the tee.

When he looked behind him, he saw everyone running towards him. Sand and Eddie looked fierce, and Angel freaked.

He skidded when he hit the bridge and almost went over the side, but Eddie caught him and dragged him back to his feet. Once over the bridge, they thought they were safe, so they hiked up the seventeenth hole and walked down the eleventh fairway, which ran adjacent to the highway.

No one spoke for a long time, and each time traveler was left inside his own head.

For Angel, it was traumatic. He couldn't understand why his breathing sounded so loud.

"Can you hear me breathing?" he asked Gandalf.

"Chill, it's from the running," Gandalf told him. Gandalf's cape was moving oddly of its own accord.

"Your cape's moving, Gandalf. Everybody look. Gandalf's cape is alive."

They encircled Gandalf to watch the eerie cape do its magic.

"I think it's from the wind," Groucho whispered.

"Why are you whispering?" Blake asked.

"I don't want to stir up the wind," Groucho said.

Angel put his face up. Groucho was right. A cold wind blew from somewhere to his left. He crossed through the fence and walked up the road trying to find it.

The others followed Angel, curious as to where he was going.

Then Angel saw it: the source of the wind. It blew from a squat building ringed by a metal fence. The initials USACWTL were neatly displayed on the front.

Sand looked at it and turned to Angel. "You're the English major. What's that word?"

"It's word salad," Gandalf said.

"What's that?" Blake asked. It sounded impressive.

"Top secret military stuff. They name shit things like USACWTL to fuck with your mind while they dream up killing shit inside."

Angel stared at the building. He was astonished. "Why haven't we seen it before?"

"Maybe it's not normally visible," Eddie said.

They nodded. That was as good an explanation as any.

"Hide," Groucho said sotto voce. "'The Man' is at two o'clock."

If 'two o'clock' wasn't confusing enough, they saw a large man in a uniform striding deliberately towards them, and he looked angry to boot.

Shit. No time to hide. Act cool.

Angel tried to whistle and shuffle his feet, but his rubber lips only made a sound like 'woo woo' and his shuffle turned into a macabre dance.

"Look at Angel," Eddie said. "That's some funny shit." He imitated Angel's movements, and everyone laughed.

A stentorian voice said in clipped tones, "Can I help you gentlemen?" They looked and saw a giant army man approaching them. So, he was real.

They looked helplessly at each other. Someone had to speak.

Angel would have, he thought, if his lips weren't so gummy.

Gandalf saved them. "We're lost, officer."

"Don't ask him about the top-secret shit going on in that building." Groucho whispered.

Gandalf stared at him.

"Are you boys drunk, by any chance?" Army man asked.

"Yes, sir, we are," Gandalf said. They all nodded.

"And we didn't see your top-secret installation," Eddie offered helpfully. "We didn't see a thing."

The army man looked over his shoulder at the mysterious building and chuckled. "The cold regions' lab? That's been here for years."

"Yes," Eddie said, "but has it been visible?"

The man shook his head and started to turn away. "You boys best move on now."

"What happens in there?" Angel asked. Everyone looked at him indignantly. They were almost free, and he had to ask dangerous shit.

"It's not a secret, "Army man said. "We test how cold a body gets before it shuts down and how to protect soldiers from freezing. Like, say, we're fighting in Russia or at the North Pole. Wouldn't it be good to know how to keep soldiers from freezing?"

Angel nodded. That made sense.

"I'm Army," Eddie said. "I haven't heard a word about any action at the North Pole."

"Yeah," Sand said. "Me neither."

Army man looked at them. "You all go home, now. Go on. Git." And he motioned angrily enough that Gandalf whimpered and strode away briskly, climbing back through the fence and hustling down a fairway.

Everyone followed Gandalf who had no fucking idea where he was on the golf course. That turned out to be a mistake because soon they were at the bottom of the thirteenth hole and trapped in shadow and cold.

"Where are we?" Eddie asked.

They shook their heads. No one knew.

Shit. They were lost.

They turned to Angel who was sitting on the green pretending the flag was a machine gun and making 'ch ch ch ch' sounds as he shot at the trees.

Eddie sat next to him and Sand followed.

"I'm tired," Eddie said. "I don't know if I can walk home even if we find our way out of here."

Blake looked dubiously about him. "It's getting dark already," he said. "We may be trapped down here."

"That's called shade," Gandalf said. "Trees are blocking the light."

Everybody but Angel giggled at that. Angel seemed lost in his own little personal trip.

Blake sat down, too. "Angel, you play golf. Do you know where we are?"

Angel looked around. "We're fucked," he said.

That didn't sound good.

"In what way, exactly, are we fucked?" Eddie wanted to know.

"This hole fucks me every time. I almost lost the Princeton match my freshman year because of this hole and the next one." He shook his head. "This hole is a jinx for me."

"Wait," Sand said, "So, you do know where we are?"

Angel nodded. His head bounced up and down as if it were on a rubber band. It felt funny, so he did it again.

"Can you get us back to Phi Psi?" Eddie asked.

Angel smiled a loopy smile and bobbed his head up and down again. He laughed. It was funny as shit to do that. He bobbed again for effect.

"Will you take us to Phi Psi?" Eddie asked.

Angel nodded.

"Like now?" Sand asked. He pulled Angel to his feet.

"Can we trust Angel?" Gandalf asked. "He seems pretty fucked up."

"What choice do we have?" Blake asked. "I don't want to die in a jinxed place."

So, Angel led them through the woods to the fourteenth hole and, then, to the fifteenth tee. He pointed up a steep hill. "We have to climb all the way up there."

They looked up the face of the hill. It seemed impossible.

And it nearly was. The ground was wet and muddy, and all of them except Angel fell and slid backwards at some point.

When they reached the top, Eddie exclaimed, "I know where we are. That's the ski jump." He pointed to a wooden contraption. It was, indeed, the ski jump. They were saved. They had all watched Winter Carnival events from their current vantage.

Blake looked around. "Where's Angel?"

Angel was lying on the green, curled in a fetal position around the flag. The men went to save him.

"I fucked Maggie right here on this green," he said. "It was phenomenal. It was in the snow, and her ass must have frozen. She has the most beautiful ass in the world, practically. It's so round and munchy."

"It's munchy?" Eddie asked.

"Well, it's kissable, at least," Angel said.

"I'd kiss it," Sand agreed.

"Me, too," Eddie said. "I'd kiss any part of her. I'd flat make out with that ass of hers. Damn fine woman."

They nodded judiciously and repeated, "Damn fine woman."

That made Angel sad. Maggie was disappointed with him because he didn't have the proper emotions, or something. He didn't know what to do about that. People couldn't change their feelings, could they?

Soon, though, the intrepid band was marching back up Main Street to the safety of Phi Psi.

It was getting dark for real by that time, and the gas lamps began to flicker on. It was hard to pass them by without stopping and staring.

They were so beautiful. Like Maggie. Angel felt like crying.

Beware of turning dark inside.

"I will," Angel muttered to himself.

Moe's driver came out of the house as they arrived. Wordlessly he went to Angel and held a piece of paper for Angel to sign. Angel signed it just as wordlessly.

Synchronicity. That was pretty cool.

Synchronicity made Angel think of Rose, and he smiled loopily. Rose. She was so beautiful. She was even more beautiful than Maggie. She was more beautiful than anyone. He would write to her and tell her how beautiful she was and about the keg showing up just as they got home from being lost and finding a secret government lab. Rose would think that was the coolest, and then she would pine for Angel and think he was cool, too.

But the synchronicity had just begun. Sand and Eddie disappeared down the stairs to the bar to try to tap the keg. Angel was glad he didn't have to do that. He was having enough trouble standing upright. His whole body felt rubbery, and he swayed to and fro. While he was focusing on balancing, the front door opened, and Zach walked in, carrying a guitar and followed by three long-haired boys.

"The band has arrived," Zach announced. He took a quick look at Angel and the others. "Man, you guys look fucked up."

Groucho held up a finger as if to say something, but no words came out of his mouth, and he grinned stupidly.

Zach laughed and gestured for the guys to set up in The Blue Room.

Eddie and Sand reappeared, bickering about something, but they smiled widely when they saw Zach and guys.

"Angel, did you make this happen?" Sand said and clapped him on the shoulder.

Angel smiled. It felt like Sand's hand bounced off his shoulder. Ha. That was radical. Eddie and Sand lit a fire. No one was capable of really feeling the chill, but fire sounded like a good thing. Heat and light flickering all over the fucking place. How could you beat that? Soon, they had a blaze going and the band began tuning and discussing what they wanted to play.

"You said a hundred bucks, right?" Zach asked Angel. Angel shrugged his shoulders. He didn't know. Had he?

"A hundred bucks," Sand said. "That's a deal. Everyone chip."

"Why can't Angel just take it from the social fund?" Eddie wanted to know.

Angel shook his head, "Nope. That money is for Green Key weekend, and Zach and the band are getting five hundred bucks, then."

"Chip in," Sand said.

"I've got it," Gandalf said and produced a wooden box from somewhere under his cape. It was like magic, and everyone stared. He sat cross-legged and counted out two hundred dollars. He handed it to Zach.

"This is two hundred," Zach said.

"A hundred isn't enough," Gandalf said judiciously.

While he sat, Gandalf took a juicy bag of pot and a pipe from the box. He stuffed the pipe and handed it to Angel.

"Here," he said. "You look like you need it."

"I'm pretty fucked up," Angel said.

"This will bring you down a bit," Gandalf said. "It will mellow you."

Angel took the pipe, and Gandalf held a lit match for him. Angel stared at the match. He could smell the sulfur. He tried to remember how to inhale but couldn't. Gandalf took the pipe back and showed him. Gratefully, Angel inhaled deeply. He could feel the smoke traveling all the way to his toes. Everyone sat on the floor passing the pipe, a veritable tribe of warriors trying not to let their recent travails harsh their mellow.

"The Animals all right?" Zach asked. Angel nodded, and Zach began a slow, beautiful intro to *The House of the Rising Sun*. The pot began to kick in, and Angel thought his trip suddenly felt manageable.

Guitar notes spread across a college campus in a mysterious way, like a virus crossing the ocean, and, though Phi Psi was about as far off the beaten path as was possible at Dartmouth, people began to trickle in.

In another hour, more than a hundred guys were dancing to Zach's band. Co-eds, too. It was turning into a shit-kicker party.

Gandalf sat on a stool next to the band, and it looked for all the world as if his wizardly smile was mingling with the measures of the music and blessing the dancers with its benevolent beams.

Angel smoked and smoked. He could feel the darkness creeping into his mind which had begun when he had first thought of Maggie's ire. He felt sad, almost Jane sad. All he lacked were the tears and the snot on his face.

That was when Sand and Eddie got concerned for him and began beer therapy. Angel was a wimpy drinker, but the acid trip was turning speedy, and he could feel the tingles beginning in his arms and legs. Even worse, he had begun to grind his teeth. It was the old after-coke, after-speed nastiness, and it would turn him dark faster than anything.

So, Eddie and Sand plied Angel with beers until he was drunker than he was trippy.

It worked for a while, and Angel danced with a co-ed who shouted that she knew him from one of Stone's classes. He smiled stupidly at her and waved his arms above his head.

"You know you're allowed to move your feet," the girl told him. Angel smiled and began to dance all over the floor. He whirled about as long as he could bear it and fell down, a victim of his own excess.

He sat against the wall and watched the flashing lights and the fire and the dancers. He recognized a co-ed, but she didn't see him, so he just watched her hips sway and her buttocks bounce. That made him feel good.

She swayed and bounced and bounced and swayed. Angel was in heaven. He should drink more often. In fact, he felt euphoric. Sand handed him another beer, and someone he didn't know handed him a joint. He sat, pleased, drinking and smoking and watching the strobe light Zach had brought and the dancing flames and Gandalf's waving his arms in time to the music and Zach's groaning into the microphone and the drummer rat a tatting out time, and he got to his feet to dance with all the cool people.

Big mistake.

Angel's stomach curdled and began to tremble. He wobbled towards the stairs, and, with the help of the handrail, made it up the stairs and into the bathroom. There, a girl he had never seen before was giving an enthusiastic blowjob to a guy he had never seen before.

He went to a stall and shut the door. He leaned gratefully against the cool wall but soon slumped until his face was pressed against the even cooler tile. He smiled at the chill on his rubber face, but his stomach began to dance again, and he leaned over the toilet and threw up noisily.

"What the fuck?" the girl's voice said, and a moment later he heard the door open and close. He listened but couldn't even hear anyone breathing. He was alone. He threw up once more, but he had lost his enthusiasm for it, so he stopped.

Angel rose and peeked out of his nice, safe stall. No one there. He wiped off the rim of the toilet, even though it had been up when he barfed, and flushed it again to make even the smell go away.

He stood unsteadily and exited the stall.

The shower stared at him. Of course. A fucking shower. That was just the thing.

He turned the shower on and stood under it until it turned hot. He was cleaner, now.

He pulled his soggy shirt over his head and dropped it to the tile. It was easy to get his boots off, but then his socks got wet and were hard to remove. He sat under the spray and peeled them off. But then he was fucked. He couldn't get his pants off without standing back up. He sighed. So much work. He stood and worked his jeans and underwear off and kicked them away. Some kind soul had left a bottle of Prell in the shower, so he lathered his hair and entire body and rubbed vigorously. He noticed gratefully that his skin didn't seem as rubbery on the outside or as prickly on the inside.

But his stomach began to heave again, so he rushed to the stall again and emptied himself until only bile dripped from his lips, and he was exhausted. He flushed and went back to the still running shower. He repeated his Prell baptism and rinsed off.

He tried to pick up his clothes, but bending over was too precarious, so he said, 'fuck it,' and went to his room.

He couldn't find a towel, (had Maggie hidden them, too?) so he used a tee shirt to sort of dry himself. He sat naked in his desk chair and rolled a poor joint and smoked it. He combed his hair back with his fingers and put Muddy Waters on his stereo. He was getting cold rapidly, so he paced his room smoking until he could feel the pot working.

He sat at his desk. He would write a letter to Maggie apologizing for whatever he had done to piss her off. He couldn't remember what it was, but, somehow, he was a terrible boyfriend.

Then, he remembered Maggie's blowjob and the one he had just witnessed in the bathroom.

He's witnessed two live blowjobs in the past twenty-four hours, and he'd never even seen one before. That was pretty, fucking weird. He would write Rose to tell her about that, too. Synchronicity and coincidence were busting out all over the place. But he was really getting cold, so he took pen and paper and climbed under the covers of his bed.

That was the last thing he remembered that night.

Saturday

Angel woke mid-morning. Someone warm lay behind him with her arms wrapped around him. Angel felt empty and stale. He tried to figure out who was spooning him without looking, but he had no clue. Maggie? She was the most likely candidate, but these weren't Maggie's arms, nor was it Maggie's scent. Jane? No.

Finally, curiosity overcame torpor, and Angel rolled over. Wanda's smiling face greeted him. He smiled back at her and was gratified that his face felt normal. The rest of him felt like shit, though. His head pounded, but that was probably just from the beer. His butt and back hurt. That worried him.

"Hi," he said.

"Hi, sleepy head," Wanda muttered. "Are you alive?"

"I don't know," he said. "My back hurts. My ass, too. You didn't take advantage of my ass while I slept, did you?"

"Maybe," she said.

"Was it good?" he asked.

"You fell in the shower," she said.

"What?"

"Your sore back. When I came up here and found you, you were trying to throw up in the trash can. I took you to the bathroom. You said something weird like 'I love this stall,' and threw up so long I was worried that I should call an ambulance."

"Oh, sorry. I don't think I've ever done that in front of a girl."

"I'm flattered to be your first."

Angel laughed. "And the shower part?"

"Oh, I got you into the shower and cleaned you up. Your clothes were already wadded up there. At least I think they were yours. There were cowboy boots, and you were naked, so I just assumed."

"I think they were mine." He tried to focus. "And you are naked, because?"

She laughed. "I was holding you up in the shower and got soaked. When I leaned over to pick up your clothes, you fell. Well, you more like slipped down the wall, but you landed pretty hard on your fanny and back."

"Oh." That made sense. He looked and saw her clothes draped over a lamp and his desk chair.

"Why didn't you put on one of my shirts or something?" he asked.

"Are you kidding, I finally got you naked, and you expect me to put on clothes?" Angel's eyes widened. "Did we make love?"

"No," she laughed. "I don't even think you knew who I was. You introduced yourself at one point and then face-planted into the bed. I crawled in and held you. You were shivering something awful."

"Oh," he said. "I don't have barf breath."

"I brushed your teeth and made you rinse with mouth wash."

He nodded. "Your brother's band is really good."

"Yes, they are," she said happily.

"They need a name."

"They've had about ten and discarded them all."

Angel thought. "They should call themselves The Waste Land."

Wanda nodded and brushed his hair off his forehead. "I'll tell them."

They were quiet.

"Angel," Wanda said.

"Hmm?"

"Kiss me."

"It won't gross you out? After all the throwing up and all?"

"Kiss me."

"All right." He paused. "You sure?"

She pushed him on his back and leaned over him. She smiled and kissed him. Shit. She tasted good.

She leaned on an elbow and watched him. "Well?" she said.

"Well what?"

"Was that okay?"

"I don't know. I wasn't paying attention. I was waiting until you finished whatever that was so I could kiss you."

"That was a kiss."

Angel shook his head and smiled. "No," he said raising on an elbow and pushing her flat on her back. "This is a kiss." He began with her left breast, pausing to suck on her nipple, and continued to her throat. Wanda moaned and clenched her fists. Angel kissed her mouth gently at first, and then with more urgency. He returned to gently sucking on her lower lip. Then, he lay back.

Wanda didn't move.

"Wasn't that better?" he asked.

"I don't know. I wasn't paying attention," she said. "I was waiting for you to take me like the drunken beast you are."

"I'm not drunk anymore," he said.

"Not much of a beast, either," she said.

"Oh, no?" he asked. He took her hand and placed it on Thor. "We'll see about that."

He rolled over towards her and kissed her again.

And they did see about that.

When they finished, Wanda lay against him. Angel's chest rose and fell with hers as both sought to catch their breath.

"Angel."

"Yes, Wanda?"

"Nothing, I just wanted to hear you say my name. I like the way you say it."

Angel smiled.

"Angel?"

"Yes, Wanda?"

"It's nice being door number one for a change."

When Angel awoke, light flooded his room. He looked for his watch. Shit. It had stopped. It probably didn't appreciate the shower. Stupid watch.

He peeked out his window and guessed it to be about noon. He sat in his desk chair and read the note Wanda had left him.

Dear Angel,

I had to leave after you fell back asleep. I hope that's all right. My parents can put up with my sneaking in at three, but all-nighters freak them out. They are especially wary of Dartmouth men. She seems to think they are all seducers. Gee, imagine that.

But you aren't, are you? A seducer, I mean. I'll bet you don't even try to get girls into your bed.

That was true. He had never thought about it before, but he never sought out girls at all. They just seemed to appear. He had always chalked it up to the fact that most guys made bad boyfriends, so most girls were always at least partially available. And he was innocuous enough not to scare them off.

I hope I'm not being pushy, but I don't have plans for tonight, and, if you want me to, I could come back over. Zach said there's a party tonight. If you have a date or don't want to see me, that's cool. Actually, the not wanting to see me part wouldn't be cool, but I like your friends and Zach thinks you guys are the nicest people on the planet. I appreciate your helping his band out. They work so hard. He liked the name you suggested, by the way, and they are going to use it.

Well, this was awkward. You are sleeping, and, though I know you don't want to hear this, you look sweet and peaceful, like an angel. You can be too guarded behind your cool mask sometimes when you're awake. I promise I don't force myself on boys like this, but call me if it's all right to come over tonight.

Wanda

Huh. So, she had been real and that had happened. He hoped the sex was good but kind of doubted it. They had made love, hadn't they? He wasn't a hundred per cent sure. He remembered little besides her smell and taste and how good she felt cuddled against him.

Shit, yeah, she could come back that night. Maggie had set him free. That was probably not what she intended, but watching her blow Jeffrey provided Angel with a certain latitude in his behavior, and he was just the man to use it. And besides, he wanted to get to know Wanda. She was such an odd creature, all wild eyes and hair. And he had no idea whatsoever what she was thinking at any given moment. He could read Cassie and Maggie easily. Wanda was funny, too. Huh. He couldn't think of a time when he wanted to strip a girl down, lay her in his bed, and ply her with questions, but he could see himself doing that with Wanda. The stripping part was just for visual approbation, like when he studied with Maggie in the fall. It had been dark the night before, and he was curious as hell to find out what her body looked like. He couldn't even remember the size or shape of her nipples, for example. Well, hopefully, these and many other questions would be answered.

He tried to stretch out his back, but it didn't want to co-operate. He found where Maggie had stashed his towels and plodded to the shower for his, what, fifth or sixth shower of the day? He paused before a mirror and turned to look at his back. Impressive. A red line ran almost from his shoulder to the base of his butt and was already turning into what would be a fine bruise. He must have fallen heavily. He forgave the offending shower stall and turned the water to 'scald my ass.' He used the tube of Prell from the night before and soaped with some good smelling shit. When he dressed, he felt pretty fucking spiffy, even if he was old-man creaky.

He called Zach's number and asked for Wanda. An adult female voice answered and said, "Hold on." Hmmm. She sounded none too happy with poor Angel.

Fortunately, that was the last he heard from her, and Wanda picked up.

"Is this Sleeping Beauty?" she asked. God, she sounded chirpy. Where did women get all their energy?

"A piece of him."

"Oh, that's from somewhere, isn't it?"

"*Hamlet.* You are altogether too smart and too cute for my good, and yes, of course I would love for you to come over tonight. But come early, I want to cook for you and grill you. That sounded wrong. I meant grill you as in interrogate you, not cook you, too."

Wanda laughed. She had a natural laugh, not a processed and field-tested laugh like rich girls have. "Okay. Glad to be forewarned. That will give me time to cook up a cover story. Pun intended, ha ha. When do you want me?"

"Wow. That was phrased interestingly? Any time after dark. I have to shop and figure out where my brain went, but I can't wait to meet you."

"Meet me?" And she laughed again.

"We spoke briefly in the fall and then you took advantage of my weakened mental state last night. I know next to nothing about you. Boston College, right?"

"Right. Well, I'll introduce myself tonight. I'll be the one wearing a red tank top and a black mini-skirt."

"Rats," Angel murmured.

"Rats?"

"I was hoping for less."

Wanda laughed. "We'll see, mister."

Angel hung up and smiled. Thank you, Maggie. Thank you for this wonderful and unexpected gift. He would try not to misuse it.

He dressed and went to the kitchen to brew coffee and fry some eggs. He looked, but the bacon had disappeared. Shit. That was his bacon. Probably Eddie. He had bacon thief written all over him. On the way out, he bought a pack of Peanut M&Ms and a Coke, walked past Moe's and down Main Street to the grocery store. He cruised the aisles looking for inspiration. What would Wanda like? He hadn't been kidding. Outside of the fact that she was witty and sexy, he knew little about her. Would she be a vegetarian? No, she liked sex too much for that. He perused the steaks behind the butcher counter, but his stomach didn't feel strong enough for beef.

He settled on a pair of speckled trout with open mouths who sang to him. The rest of the meal revealed itself after that, much like a Bridge hand played well. Everything became more obvious with each choice made. He got some rice and a package of almonds to adorn it. Broccoli sat up fresh and green like a pair of pert nipples. Like Wanda's nipples. The night before was coming back to him. She told him a story while they were falling asleep, and he repaid her by nipping at her nips. They were small and hard. He couldn't tell anything about her areolae in the dark, but they would be light and perfect to go with her reddish hair. Thor was pressing against his jeans, so, to honor him, he bypassed the broccoli and put a handful of asparagus in his basket. Bread? No. Unnecessary. No need for getting stuffed before a party. Mushrooms? Why not? They didn't go with anything else, except the rice, but he was a fan of fungus.

He paid and walked back to Moe's for dinner wine and to get chips and dip delivered for the evening's festivities.

After stuffing everything in the Phi Psi fridge with a sign saying, 'Cane's shit. Steal at your own peril,' he went to the cloak room for M&Ms and a Coke. He stared at the pay phone. Something buzzed in his cranium.

Shit. What if Maggie was driving back to 'talk' to him?

He fished quarters out of his pocket and dialed Maggie's home number.

"Hello?"

"Delilah?"

"Angel. Sorry to disappoint but Margaret's gone."

Angel's heart sank. Shiterino.

"She and mom went shopping for tonight's shindig. My other big sister just finished Med School."

Excellent. He and Wanda could frolic, and he'd get credit from Maggie for calling. Mister Sensitive and all that crap.

"I know why you're calling," she said.

Angel smiled. "Why?"

"You have a chick with you and wanted to make sure Margaret wasn't crashing your little love shack."

Angel smiled even more broadly. God, he really liked this little brat.

"From whence did you arrive at that?" he asked.

"From *Anna Karenina*. If you're cheating on someone, you have to know her whereabouts."

"Smart little booger. You've read *Anna Karenina?*"

"Haven't you?"

Nope, he hadn't. His long-range plan called for Dostoyevsky and Tolstoy the summer after he graduated from Dartmouth.

"Plus," she said, "Every time daddy calls from the city, mama says, 'he's making sure I'm not going to interrupt his sordid peccadilloes.'"

"She actually used the word 'peccadilloes'?"

"Yep, 'sordid,' too. We're not illiterate, you know. Mama was Valedictorian at Bryn Mawr."

"I think I like you, Miss Delilah."

"I like you, too, Angel. You know of course that we're practically twins?"

Angel laughed. "How so?"

"We think alike, nothing bothers either of us, and we're extremely witty. Plus, we both read a lot."

That sounded pretty accurate.

"Want to hear something scary?" she asked.

"Sure."

"Margaret said you're going to be a teacher. Well, that means you're going to have to deal with a whole bunch of teenage girls like me. Well, not like me, but smart and sassy girls who think you're sexy and have crushes on you."

Hmm. "I'm not sexy. Take Jeffrey, for example. Now, he's sexy."

"You take Jeffrey. I'm not interested. Neither is Margaret. She dumped his sorry butt the night you left. I mean brutally. She said something like 'if you've messed things up between Angel and me, I'll kill you. I swear I will.' And I know you're not stupid enough to equate looks with sexiness. You're sexy because you own every room you walk into."

"Wait. Maggie broke up with Jeffrey?"

"Newsflash," she said. "I notice you're not arguing the sexy stuff. Margaret says you don't even try to meet girls. You just wander about being all cool and unconcerned and 'boom,' they take off their clothes."

"Maggie told you she was naked on our first date?"

"Too much information. No, she didn't mention that, but I'm not surprised. Like she says, you kind of exude sex in a wholesome way. I didn't know what she meant until I met you. Like when you broke Jeffrey's finger."

"Shit. I broke it. I thought I dislocated it or something."

"Nope. Broken. He was all 'My parents are going to sue,' and Margaret told him she'd testify that he raped her in her bedroom if he did."

"Shit. I didn't mean to."

"No. That's what was sexy. He threatened me, and there wasn't even a nanosecond before he was crippled. You were like, wham, straight into action. You were all cool, eating your sandwich and making jokes. Then he attacked me, and you went all psycho on his sorry butt. Well, on his finger, anyway. It was super cool. I wrote a story about it right after you left."

"You're a writer?"

"Duh."

"It figures. Well, smartypants, I'll talk to you again if Maggie and I ever reach a truce. Meanwhile, behave."

"You, too, Angel. Wear a condom. I don't want my sister getting a disease because you were lazy."

"You have a mouth on you little girl."

"Apparently, Maggie's is more functional."

Angel cracked up at that.

"Angel, before you go, can I tell you something and you swear you won't repeat it, especially not to Margaret?"

"Of course," Angel said. This should be good. Delilah was an unpredictable little wench.

"Mom and Margaret didn't just go shopping. They went to see Dr. Freeney."

"Who's Dr. Freeney?"

"Their therapist. When I was three, Mama had another baby girl named Jessica. When Jessica was about one, Margaret found her dead in her crib. The doctors called it crib death and said it's nobody's fault, but, apparently, it messed up Margaret and Mama. I was too little to know much, so, to me, it's pretty much just a story."

"Shit."

"Yep. Please don't tell."

Angel was quiet. He realized how little he knew about Maggie. Three sisters? One a doctor and one dead. And the other the delightfully irritating Delilah. Plus, her father was a rich genius and her mother a Seven Sisters valedictorian. No wonder Delilah was so smart.

"Angel?"

"Yep?"

"Just wondering if you were still there."

"I am. I think I love you, young Delilah."

"I don't blame you."

"Can I ask how you got your name?"

"Sure."

There was a pause.

"Well," she said, "go ahead and ask."

Angel chuckled.

"Why Delilah?"

Delilah laughed and laughed. "Because my pregnant mother went to some stupid fortune teller who said I was going to be born a girl and would grow up to destroy strong men." She laughed again. "Mama doesn't even believe in that sort of thing, but I was born a girl with a full head of curls, so, Delilah I am."

"Delilah, you are. And look what you just did to Jeffrey."

"Yep, but I wouldn't be able to destroy you. You're invincible."

"Why do you say that?"

"I don't. Margaret does. She says you don't feel pain. She says you let yourself be hit in the face to meet her and didn't even flinch. Even though you knew some big guy was going to smack you. But, she also says you don't have emotions like normal people, either."

"Well," Angel said. "What's normal anyway?"

"I know I'm not," she said. "Thank God."

"Thank God," Angel assented.

When they hung up, Angel smiled for an hour, though he knew that, like a pleasant nemesis, darling Delilah's words would buzz in his head all night.

Angel showered again just to refresh his head. He rolled a pair of joints for the night but realized he didn't even know whether Wanda partook. Had they smoked together in the fall? He couldn't remember. He made a mental note to ask about her name, too. The Delilah question had yielded interesting fruit for future characters in his novels, and Wanda was an odd name, too. It fit her perfectly, somehow, but he didn't know what it meant. Delilah had chastened him. He made another mental note to begin to find out more about the people in his life. The men didn't matter.

They were born anew every moment, but women carried their pasts in the forefront of their minds all the time.

Angel chose the same outfit he had worn the night he met Wanda, a white shirt and leather vest, to go with his ubiquitous jeans and boots. He couldn't scrounge up any clean underwear, so he went without. With any luck, he wouldn't have pants on long, anyway.

He went to the roof and lit one of the joints. A truck pulled up outside, and one of Moe's minions delivered the chips, dip, wine, and three kegs of beer. Good. Now, all he had to do was to get Eddie to set up the sound system in the Blue Room and Gandalf to decide on a playlist which would encourage dancing and bonhomie. Angel had done it once and been booted from the job. No one danced to his music and everyone complained that it was too bleak. The blues had that effect on some people. Assholes.

He went down to sign for the stuff from Moe's and started cooking in the kitchen. He was low on milk and butter, but he thought there was enough to make a Hollandaise of some sort for both fish and asparagus. There were only two lemons. Shit. He should have bought some. He thought of running to Moe's but decided to make do with what he had.

He had already rubbed down and prepared the fish, pre-heated the oven, and was in the process of making the sauce when he realized Wanda was leaning against the doorjamb, watching him with a smile.

He smiled back at her. In the late afternoon light, her hair glinted red, and the curls in mass profusion reminded him of Delilah's story about her birth. He had never seen Wanda in makeup before, nor had he seen her dressed up.

He took the sauce off the burner and licked his fingers before wiping them on his jeans.

Wanda looked at him shyly. She did, indeed wear a red tank-top, but it was silken, not anything like he had expected, and it was cut low, showing off her *de-colletage*. Her skirt was black and very, very short. She wore heels. Cassie may have been the only other girl in the history of Phi Psi to wear heels. The floors must have been shocked.

"Hi," she said, "I'm Wanda." She blushed as she said it.

"No, you're not," Angel smiled.

"I'm not?"

"No, Wanda is a hippie girl who wears jeans and tee shirts. Wanda is a beautiful girl, but you, whoever you are, put her to shame."

Wanda blushed even deeper.

Angel wiped his hands on a towel and went to her. "Hello, strange girl," he said, and, holding her face in his hands, he kissed her softly. "It's very nice to meet you, but I need for you to show me your driver's license."

"Why?" she laughed.

"It's a precaution to make sure you're not an underage townie or a narc."

"Couldn't a narc or a townie have a fake ID?"

He put his hand out. "Show."

Wanda laughed but reached into her purse and produced a wallet. From it, she handed him her license.

"Wanda Butler Riley?" he smiled. "Could you be more Irish? Butler? Is that a family name?"

"It is. And you know where it's from, Mister English Major?"

"Samuel Butler?"

"Nope."

"Not William Butler Yeats?"

"Yep. My mom is a direct descendant of the Butler clan."

"Get out of here. How did you know I was an English major?"

"Duh, your room is wall to wall books."

Angel nodded. That made sense. Shit. Yeats. "Green eyes?" He looked at her and scowled. "You're a fake."

She laughed. "How so?"

"It says here you have green eyes."

"So?"

"The word 'bewitching' is nowhere on this card. But's that's okay. Maybe it was bad lighting when they wrote that. It says you are five feet two inches."

Wanda straightened.

"This card is absurd," he said. "Nothing about magnificent breasts or the fluidity of your perfect (he put a hand on her waist) hips (he traced the curve of her hips) and long, long (he ran his hand down her leg in in towards her center) legs."

Wanda shivered and laughed. "My mother was right. I do need to be careful around you. Are you, perchance, Mister Angel, trying to coax me into your bed?"

"Perchance," he murmured. "Is it working?"

"I think it's my outfit that's working," she said.

"Rats," he said. "You caught me. And here I thought I was being so seductive."

Wanda kissed him on the cheek. "Cook for me, Angel. Then, we'll see."

Maggie was right. Apparently, he wasn't much good as a seducer. He guessed that was a good thing. At least then he never trapped an unwilling girl into doing anything. And he did like 'willing.' It was an attractive attribute for a lovely woman to have. And he hadn't been kidding. Wanda, his erstwhile tomboy friend, was a truly lovely woman. In fact, what the fuck was she doing with him? Things to ponder.

He smiled and went back to work. Wanda sat at the table with her chin on her hand and observed with amusement.

When everything was ready, they carried food, wine, and glasses to the roof and watched the stars come out as they ate. Angel had stolen hand towels from Groucho for the occasion.

"I don't like paper napkins," he explained.

Wanda just smiled and ate.

"Is it okay?" he asked.

She looked at him sardonically. "You know it is. You're just fishing for compliments."

"I get it," he said. "We're eating trout. Fishing for compliments."

"You're not funny," she said.

"No?"

"No," she said. "You're adorable." She finished chewing a bite and raised her wine glass. "To the first time in my life I realized how beautiful Hanover is."

Angel raised his glass and nodded at her.

He finished his food and put his plate beside him. "Do you mind if I smoke?"

"Are you sharing?"

He smiled and lit the joint. He inhaled and passed it to her.

From below, the house shook as the first notes of music came through the speakers in The Blue Room. Angel listened and smiled. "*Boom Boom*" by the Animals," he said.

But Wanda was lost somewhere in the heavens. "Angel," she said. "Do you remember my asking you if you could point out the constellations?"

"I said I could but didn't."

"You said you were too lazy, but that's not why, was it?"

Perceptive wench. He kept meeting these women who could read minds almost as well as he. "No. I didn't because I was pretty sure you already knew them."

She smiled. "I did. That's when I knew you and I could be good together. You were totally pre-occupied that night, what between organizing the party and door number one's problems, but you were still completely attuned to me. That's your secret, isn't it? You pay attention."

"I don't know. I don't mean to pay attention. In fact, I don't think I do, at least not any better than a normal male, but I do know what women are thinking most of the time. It's not like you hide things very well. And you all operate from the same paradoxical state of mind."

She laughed. "And what, pray tell, might that be?"

"Well, you only want a handful of things. You are all guarded, fearful of being understood. You all see yourself as flawed or even ugly, though in your case I doubt ugly is an operative term, but you also seek men who 'get you,' who understand the secret 'you' that you think no one else understands. That's the paradox, or, at least one of them."

Wanda smoked and watched the stars move in and out of the clouds. "Wine and pot," she said. "I don't think I've ever done both together here in Hanover. There's something about being home where you're treated like a little kid. This seems more audacious than doing it at college. Plus, sex. Good Lord. I am such a trashy girl."

Angel smiled.

"And, of course, what you said makes perfect sense," she said. "It certainly describes my paradoxical desires."

"D.H. Lawrence said all people desire two things: complete privacy and complete immersion with everyone and everything else. The latter is how he explained everything from God to love."

"This is certainly the most intelligent discussion I've had here in Hanover. Most of the Dartmouth guys I've met just want one thing from me."

"Wow. I want a number of things from you."

She turned to him and smiled. "A number of things? Not just conversation and sex?"

"Oh, I must have misunderstood. I want your lips, your breasts, your loins, your sinful ass, your smile, your approval, your company."

"All right," she laughed. "And, I warn you in advance that I am likely to give you all of them, with the possible exception of my rear end. I'm not sure what you want with it, so that will depend. But all the other things I freely give to you."

"Wild, wacky, wicked Wanda. Do you remember what you said to me while we were sitting on the stairs that night we met?"

"That we would be good together. But we won't be, will we? Together, that is."

"Why not?"

She laughed and kissed him. "Because, my dear Angel, I'm in Boston, and you're here. Then, when I'm here, you're in wherever you call home. Where are you from?"

"Florida."

"Florida. My point being?"

"We're a geographical improbability."

"Exactly," she said. "Besides, I'm not looking for a love affair right now. I've had two bad ones in the past two years. One was awful."

Ooh. An opportunity to inquire about a girl's past. Delilah's mocking voice echoed in his head.

"Awful in what way?"

"Let me count the ways. He was controlling. That was the main driver of his dysfunction. He was jealous. He was manipulative. He followed me and checked up to see if I'd been where I said I'd been." She paused. "And, he hit me. I was an idiot and lied to him about where I'd been one night, which was ridiculous because I'd just been studying with a girlfriend. I don't even remember why I told him something else. Just to spite him, I suppose."

"Shit. I wish I'd been there."

"I'm glad you weren't. You'd be in jail, and I wouldn't get to experience Thor again tonight. I think that's what you called him. Anyway, that's not the end of the story. Rorie, that was his name, apologized and pleaded for forgiveness, and I, big stupidhead that I am…"

"Oh, no."

"Yes, I took him back, and shock of shocks, he hit me again a week later. Not once but twice. I got to go to classes with a black eye and a swollen lip. Of course, I was embarrassed and lied about what had happened. But I dumped his sorry ass, which is scary, by the way, and I've been single for a whole, what, three months."

Shit. Angel wished it had happened, if it had to happen at all, at Dartmouth. Justice would have been swift. He and the guys would have fought each other for the pleasure of avenging that one.

"You don't seem damaged," he said.

"I'm not. It had the curious effect of making me less afraid of men. Once you realize they can't hurt you unless they kill you, you feel powerful. That sounds dumb. I mean, I don't go into dangerous situations with men or anything. I know I'm not invincible."

"Like climbing naked into bed with a man you don't even know," he murmured.

"Yes," she smiled, "I'd never do anything that foolish."

They both laughed.

The night was getting cold, so Angel pulled her into his chair and put his arm around her. Wanda sighed and nestled into the crook of his arm.

Angel was glad he had asked her about herself, though her answer was ghastly. This was nice, being inquisitive and shit.

"Tell me about Wanda," he said.

"Okay," she said. "Let's see, Wanda is a bit of a loner, she…"

"No," he laughed. "Your name, Wanda. Everything on your license was Irish. Where in the world did the name Wanda come from? Is that German?"

"Polish," she said. "My mother was an English major at Boston College, hence my being there. She did her thesis on Ouida, a nineteenth century novelist nobody's heard of."

Angel shook his head. He'd never even heard the name.

"Her real name was Maria Louise Rame?"

"Doesn't ring a bell," he admitted.

"Anyway, her penultimate novel was called *Wanda*, and it featured a feisty female heroine named…"

"Wanda," he smiled.

"Yep. When I was little, I don't even know how little, she taught me a line from the novel and said it should be my motto in life: 'I do not wish to be a coward like the father of mankind and throw the blame upon a woman.' Pretty strong, don't you think? I repeated it in school once and was sent to the principal. They said it was blasphemous."

"Catholic School? Our Lady of Perpetual Virginity or something like that?"

"Close," she laughed. "Our Lady on Her Knees So She Won't Get Pregnant Again."

"Is that a blowjob joke?"

"Yes. We had lots. We gave each other knee pads for our sweet sixteen parties. The nuns practically told us that the way to please a man while remaining a virgin was to kneel before him. That's sick."

"You weren't planning on doing that to me, tonight, were you?"

"Someone is presumptuous," she laughed. "But it might happen."

"I'd rather not," he said. "I'm sure you're an expert and all, but right now that's not my favorite method of connection. And please don't ask why."

"Something to do with door number one?"

"No, the other door number one."

"The jealous one whom I passed after I caught you naked from the shower?"

"Yes, that one."

"She's not very good kneeling?"

"I told you not to ask."

"All right." She chuckled and shut up.

Angel took her hand and led her to the roof's edge. He pointed to a constellation. "Do you know that one?"

Wanda nodded.

"What is it?" he asked.

"I'm not telling."

Angel smiled. "That was the right answer," he said, and he took her in his arms and kissed her. He remembered her taste and the pressure of her lips from the night before. He kissed her again just to make sure. He looked down at her, and she stared into his eyes.

"What's wrong?" he asked.

"Nothing," she smiled. "I'm being a woman."

He smiled back. "I know. I miss you already, too. When do you leave?"

"First thing in the morning."

"So, there's absolutely no way you can spend the night?"

Wanda shook her head.

"Want to know something personal about me?"

She nodded.

"I like the time after love-making more than the love-making itself," he said. "If you were staying, I would hold you until you fell asleep and then go to my desk and write about you. I would watch you sleep and marvel at the wonder that you are."

"And I would fall for you and be miserable back in Boston. Maybe it's best I can't stay."

"Maybe."

"Take me inside, lover boy, and dance with me." She put a finger to his lips as he began to object. "I know you can't dance. But you can hold me and pretend, can't you? Then, I'll dance for you. I can be pretty sexy."

"You can't not be sexy."

"Oh, my. I'll bet you don't spout double negatives very often."

"Only for very special people," he said.

They gathered dishes, glasses, and wine and went back downstairs. The music grew louder as they descended, and Angel could feel their private spell being broken. One look at Wanda, though, told him it would be easy to re-establish.

When they entered the melee in The Blue Room, Angel groaned. Eddie was dancing at the front of the room with a microphone in his hand. Angel knew he shouldn't have showed Eddie how to work the sound system.

Gandalf was sitting at a card table playing emcee, which was fine. Gandalf's taste would have amazed and appalled most of the partiers, but he had the good grace to play what people wanted to hear, not what he wanted to play. Gandalf was a genuine weirdo, but he was a good shit.

"Who's that little man in the cape?" Wanda shouted into Angel's ear.

"That's Gandalf. A man of indeterminate gender preference and limitless creativity. He also sells the best acid and pot on campus."

Wanda nodded. Gandalf saw them looking at him and smiled a big, goofy smile. Shit. He wasn't tripping again, already, was he?

Of the hundred or so dancing in The Blue Room, at least three quarters were strangers to Angel. He spotted a group of pimply faced boys huddled in a corner bobbing their heads to the music. Townies.

Angel went to Sand and whispered something. Sand nodded and waved for Eddie to join him. The two men quietly and without much physical damage escorted the townies to the front door and convinced them not to come back.

"Zach wouldn't sneak into Phi Psi," Wanda said. "He really likes you. He thinks Sand and Eddie are about the coolest things going."

She took his hand and pulled him groaning into the crowd and began to slowly move her hips. Boing. There went Thor. That sure as shit didn't take long. The crowd gave her room to dance. There were a bunch of girls dancing, but Wanda was slinkier, or more erotic, or something. Angel shuffled from foot to foot and watched her hips go from side to side precisely with the beat.

Eddie, shithead that he was, stepped up onto the little band platform in the corner and motioned for Gandalf to lower the volume.

"Folks," Eddie said, "I'd like you to give a hand to this evening's host. His name is Angel, and he's responsible for the beer on tap and for getting this shindig together."

Not much of which was true. Angel had ordered beer and food but hadn't done another single thing. No, Ed was up to some of his usual bullshit.

"And he brings with him the lovely, what's your name dear?"

Wanda smiled sardonically at Angel and shouted, "Wanda."

"Wanna? You wanna? Of course, you do. You wouldn't be with Angel if you didn't. He doesn't have much else to recommend him. But what's your name?"

"Wanda!" she shouted, laughing.

"Honda? That's a motorcycle. No, we want your real name, not your stripper name. Come on up here, whoever you are and let the crowd meet you."

Wanda laughed and looked at Angel who shrugged his shoulders. She was on her own.

The crowd parted and cheered as the blushing Wanda stepped up next to Eddie.

"Where are you from, Honda? Angel seems to specialize in Smithies and Colby chicks."

"Boston College," she said. Everyone cheered for some inane reason.

"So, you're Jewish?" Ed said. "Tell us how you met Angel. Was he in the club one night and kept stuffing ones in your G-string?"

"No," she said. "He saw me in *Wanda Does Whomever* and contacted me through my pimp, I mean my agent. He liked it because it was the first grammatically correct porn movie."

The crowd laughed, and Angel shook his head.

"I don't know that one," Ed said.

"Yes, you do. You wrote me a fan letter. Aren't you Short Eddie Salvatori? You and your friend Sandbag," and she pointed to Sand, "inquired about threesomes. You said you got tired of doing each other."

The crowed went truly nuts over that one. Angel shook his head again and sat next to Gandalf. This looked like it could last a while.

Eddie nodded ruefully. He waved for the crowd to quiet and turned to them. "We're going to play a game with the lovely Rhonda. Now, all of you at Phi Psi see a seemingly different woman coming out of Angel's room every ten minutes or so. Those of us who shake our heads at that great mystery have pretty much given up trying to ascertain Angel's attraction. One theory is that women actually prefer tiny dicks."

The crowd chuckled and looked at Angel who smiled and nodded to them. Wanda shook her head and held her hands about a foot and a half apart and pointed to Angel. Then she put them a couple of inches apart and pointed to Eddie. The crowd went apeshit over that. Ed plowed on, nonetheless.

"Pot whores, girls who like to use strap-ons, we've pondered all the possibilities and have, frankly, come up empty. So, we're going in the other direction. If you know Angel, even if you're a fan of his radio show, all three of you, I want to hear from you on this." He made a gesture, and Gandalf cut the music altogether. "Let's try to ascertain what Angel's type is, using the lovely Sondra as our lab specimen. Incidentally, Angel, did that lab specimen come back positive or negative?"

Angel made a thumbs-down gesture.

"That's good. For once, Angel is free of all venereal diseases. Now, everyone look hard at Tawana. What do you think attracted Angel? Remember, you have to have seen at least a dozen of his previous wenches to vote."

A voice shouted out, "She has a nice rack."

Angel stirred uneasily, but Wanda shimmied her chest for the crowd, so, apparently, she was cool with all this.

Eddie nodded. "That's a good start. Could you be more specific?"

"He likes perfect, medium sized chests. I've never seen him with anyone super busty," Gandalf shouted.

"Traitor," Angel said to him.

Gandalf shrugged, "It's true."

"Okay," Ed said. "We're making progress. So, he's not a breast man."

"Not true," Wanda said. "He said mine were perfection and tasted just yummy."

The crowd roared, and Angel nodded. That was true, too.

"Moving on," Ed said, "What about other body parts."

"He likes women with hips and perfect asses," Sand said.

"That's also true," Angel admitted to Gandalf.

"Wanna, turn around for us," Eddie said, and Wanda obliged, wiggling her cute butt at the crowd. "Now for a tough one, most of the chicks have been brunette. Anyone ever seen him with a blonde?"

A chorus of "no's" rang out.

"This one's almost a redhead," Eddie said. "Pretty sexy? What do you think?"

The crowd roared its approval, and Wanda curtsied and hopped down from the stage. Blushing and smiling, she wove her way to Angel.

"Let's give Donna a big hand," Eddie said. General applause. "But, in all seriousness, besides the fact that they're all easy and have nice butts, you have all missed the common denominator. With the exception of Jane, our communal house project, every single girl Angel is attracted to is what?" He held the mike to the crowd.

"Smart," Sand said. "He likes smart chicks with evil tongues. They're all funny. They're all witty."

"And Sandman wins The Golden Testicle Award. Exactemundo. Angel likes witty chicks with a good attitude, and by good attitude, I don't just mean she provides her own kneepads. Thanks for playing, lovely Wanda. Give her a hand, folks." Whistles and clapping. Wanda waved at the crowd and kissed Angel on the cheek, and the place erupted. "Gandalf, music please. Something danceable." And Ed put down the mike and left the stage.

Angel sat smiling with Wanda in his lap. Eddie made his way to them and grinned at Wanda. "You can dish it out, little girl," he said. "Thanks for playing along."

"You know, Eddie," Angel laughed, "You can be pretty fucking funny when you're not shit-faced."

"Seriously, Angel, tell me where I can get one of these?" He smiled his devil smile at Wanda.

"Seriously?" Angel said. "There aren't any more. This one is the prototype." He put his arm around Wanda and kissed her lightly.

Ed shook his head and went in search of another beer.

"Hey Ed," Angel said.

"Yeah?"

"Scope out the bar and get rid of undesirables. I haven't been down to check all night."

"Will do."

Wanda watched him go. "What happens when he drinks?"

"He gets frustrated and angry. Sometimes, he turns mean. I know this is trite, but some of Eddie is still in the jungle."

"Eddie was in Viet Nam?"

"Sandman, too, but Sand's always sweet. It's funny. Sand is the one who looks like he could kill you with a fist, but I've almost never seen him angry. Old soul."

"How did he get that odd nickname?"

"He's the Sandman. If he hits you, you go to sleep for a long time," Angel said.

Wanda clenched Angel's vest and smiled up at him. Her eyes had that moist look they get when they're proud of a guy. She punched him lightly on the chest. Angel knew what she was thinking, that he was the sweet one, not Sand. That was okay. She wasn't going to be around. Let her have her illusions.

Gandalf, ever the prescient wizard, sped the music up as the dancers got drunker and then slowed it down once they began to move sloppily. By sometime near midnight, everything was a slow dance which pleased the lovers and allowed the singles to sway drunkenly in their little, private worlds.

Wanda tugged at Angel. He smiled at her.

"Yes?"

"I've got to go home," she said.

Angel took her hand and led her to the quiet of the library.

"Really?"

"Really," she said. "I was out way too late last night taking care of someone. I don't like to worry my parents. They really have a thing about my being with a Dartmouth boy."

"Why? What do they think might happen?"

Wanda laughed. "Probably exactly what happened last night."

"Oh, about that. I've been meaning to apologize. I'm sure I was terrible. I was still pretty much out of my mind. I was hoping for a do-over tonight."

"Uh huh, well, ain't gonna happen, although I was looking forward to that all day. But you're wrong about last night. You were wonderful."

"Seriously? I don't remember much."

"Angel, you made me come before we even, (she laughed and blushed) before you put that thing in me."

Angel looked dubious.

"Lord knows you don't need a bigger ego, but you pleasured me just using your hands, and I practically exploded."

"I do seem to remember someone making a lot of noise and didn't think it was me. It was good, huh?"

"Yes, silly," she laughed. "It was, what do you morons say, epic?" She turned her face up and her voice got low. "You were wonderful. Where did you learn to do that?"

"I played piano all my young life."

Wanda laughed and kissed him. "Gotta go. Sorry you don't get laid tonight, mister."

"I don't mind. I'm not as hung up on releasing the hounds as you probably think. No, this was a wonderful night. I wouldn't change anything."

"Uh huh, so if I'm not going to stay the night, you don't even care? I see how it is."

Angel kissed her. "Will I see you again?"

"Nope. I drive to Boston early in the morning. You'll just have to suffer. Besides, the real door number one still needs to be dealt with, doesn't she?"

Angel smiled at her. "And what makes you think there's a door number one at all?"

She grabbed the lapels of his vest and shook him lightly. "I'm not blind. When I walked in on you at Thanksgiving, you looked quite nice naked, by the way, very Clint Eastwoody, all lean with those interesting scars on your shoulders and back. You still haven't explained your dermal topography to me. But your room was different back then. Your desk was piles and piles of assorted essays and manuscripts. You had a Smith and Corona typewriter missing keys, and you tossed the towel you were wearing over a chair. Now, there's a brand-new fancy typewriter and no piles of papers. When I showered you last night, I had to search for a towel. There's been a woman at work, one who wants desperately to take care of you and please you."

Angel kissed her. "Maggie. Her name's Maggie. You're not as dumb as I thought, are you?"

"No, Eddie was probably right. You do have a type, smart girls."

"So, no sex, huh?"

She shook her head.

Angel closed the library doors and sat in a chair. "Then strip for me," he said.

"Excuse me?"

"You heard me, missy, take your clothes off. If I don't get sex, I should at least get aesthetics. It was dark last night. I have no idea what that gorgeous body looks like. Strip."

Wanda smiled. "You do know those doors you just closed are mostly glass. I'd be putting on a show for anyone who walks by."

Angel nodded. "Strip, woman."

Wanda smiled again and then slowly pulled her top over her head. She held her arms up with the blouse dangling, a la Marilyn Monroe.

"Nice," he said.

Her face became serious. She unzipped her skirt and shimmied out of it, letting it slide to the floor. She reached behind her and unhooked her bra and removed it, too. She stood before him and shivered slightly.

"Panties, too."

She slowly slid her panties down her legs and stood before him, fully nude. If any passersby were gawking, the two of them were unaware. Wanda went to him and sat in his lap. She kissed him lightly.

"Thank you," he said. His voice was scratchy. "The crowd was right. You are perfect, absolutely perfect. You are misnamed, though."

She laughed. "How so?"

"You should be Eve, God's first attempt at perfect female beauty. I can see Him with a visor and glasses on, fussing over a drawing board. Then, a great smile crosses His features, and He summons the angels to look over His shoulder. 'There,' He says to them. 'Perfect. She's perfect. I'll only make one of her, though. Humanity is weak and couldn't bear more than one.'"

She nuzzled in his neck. "That's what God said, huh?"

"Yep. That's what He said."

"But I'm certainly not perfect. My hips are too wide, and my legs are too long."

Angel laughed. "First of all, legs can't be too long, and secondly, no straight man on the planet prefers a woman without hips. Maybe junior high school boys do, but not men."

"But you do like tiny waists."

"Nope. Waists are like chests and necks. They should be proportional to the rest of the figure."

"But."

"No buts. Women made Twiggy famous and men made Marilyn Monroe famous. And Jane Russell and Sophia Loren."

"What about fashion models?"

"Blech. They're disgusting. They're just clothes hangers who can walk. Men don't care about fashion. Men don't care about a woman's clothes at all unless it hides or distorts her curves. What you were wearing a moment ago was great because it showed leg and breast and didn't have a lot of distracting patterns or pretensions. Simple, clean, nearly naked. The only clothes I really like are the ones you were born in. You can smile at me all you want, but I'm right. There's a whole host of women's magazines springing into being. You know what the women in them do?"

"What?"

"Nothing. They just vamp at the camera. It's pathetic. Men don't want stick figures, but those magazines will produce generations of women who diet and starve themselves to look like eleven-year-old boys. It's perverted."

"And why, oh wise one, do we do that?"

"Because you dress for other women. It's some sick kind of competition among women. And the irony is that the female of the species used to adorn itself to compete for men. Now, they just show off for other women. It's contemptible vanity and it's a mental illness."

Wanda laughed. "You've done some deep thinking on this." She pushed a lock of hair off his face and gazed at him.

"Angel."

"Yes, my lady."

"You have the most singular capacity for making a woman feel that, to you, there's no one else in the world but her, and no other time than the one the two of you are in at that moment. You really focus on a girl. On her. Not on who she has been or who she might become, but on her at that single moment in all of time. It's delicious and unbearable."

"Shit," he said.

She smiled. "Shit?"

"Yeah, shit. Your compliment was better than my Eve one."

She laughed.

"Why am I unbearable, though?" he asked.

"Angel, what you don't seem to understand is that girls can't live in the present as fully as you can. We can feel that it's just a moment, and we know that we will lose it when you aren't with us. That's the fear door number one has."

"How do you know what she feels?"

"First, there's a problem between you two right now or you wouldn't be with me. Second, I can feel that slight panic, too, that I'll miss you, and I don't even pretend to myself that you're mine. Maggie does, though. She's kidding herself, but she does. She thinks she could always feel what I feel right now, this intimacy, this perfect understanding. But, when she leaves, you slip away, and it pains her."

Angel thought about that. He sighed.

"I will miss you, Wanda."

"No, you won't. I will, but you won't. That's where you are a pitiless tyrant. It's the male in you. It's that present moment thing. And she knows that, too." She rose and began to dress.

"Will you come see me when you're in Hanover?" he asked.

She smiled and nodded. "You won't be able to keep me away. Will you come see me when you're in Boston?"

He nodded and gently drew her to him. He kissed her on the forehead. She smiled and left.

Angel sat back down and contemplated his state of affairs. Wanda was a marvel.

But Maggie was unhappy, and that awakened his protective side. He could feel her sway over him waxing as he sat there. There was a poem in all of this somehow. He couldn't hear it or see it, but he could sense it stirring.

Wanda heard the music cease when she closed the Phi Psi front door and walked into the cold. She smiled. How did Angel make talking and leaving seem more intimate than having sex? That conversation and the one on the roof: she had never spoken that way with anyone, much less with a boy. She felt so wise. She went to her car and got in. Parked across the street, a girl sat in a dark car.

Wanda got out and crossed the street.

She tapped on the window of the car, and the girl inside rolled it down.

"Is your name Maggie, by any chance?"

The girl nodded. She had been crying.

"Angel's in there. He'll be glad to see you. He needs you."

The girl wiped her face. "You're the sister of the band leader, aren't you? I've seen you before."

Wanda nodded. "I am. Before you go in there and pester him with questions which will only drive him away, I'll answer them for you. Angel and I are just friends, and, no, we didn't make love tonight. In fact, we were just talking about you not five minutes ago."

Maggie looked distrustful but nodded.

"Want some free advice?" Wanda said.

"Sure."

"Just love him. Don't accuse him of or apologize for whatever's hanging in the air between you. This is probably not in your nature, but try hard to just let it go."

"How can I do that?"

"Do you like Angel?"

Maggie nodded.

"Then he's worth a little effort. Whatever he did or whatever you did, just let it be and enjoy being with him. Because you won't have him forever. You do know that, don't you?"

Maggie nodded. "That's what hurts."

Wanda nodded. "I know. But I know he cares about you."

"Did he say that?"

Wanda smiled. "He didn't have to. I saw his room before you cleaned it. I don't know Angel very well, but I'm pretty sure his writing is sacred to him. And he let you re-arrange everything. Think about that."

She crossed the street and got back in her car. As she drove away, she saw Maggie's door open slowly. She smiled and shook her head. God help that poor girl.

Chapter Twenty-One

A GROWLING SINGER WAILED:

Whoa-oh, tell my baby
Where did ya stay last night?
Why don't you hear me cryin'?
Ah hoo hoo-oh
Ah hoo hoo-oh
Ah hoo.

Angel faded the song out slowly and clicked on his microphone.

That's Smokestack Lighting, and, if you can identify the band, I'll give you a half-consumed bag of Peanut M&Ms. Light up those phones. Well, we only have one phone, but light it up anyway.

Not to minimize the changes at our formerly small, intimate station, though. As you probably know if you listen to me regularly, I wasn't on the air last Wednesday. In fact, no one was. That was the big day when WDCR upped its range by about a thousand per cent. We used to reach the skiway to the north, Woodstock to the west, and Colby to the south. That last one makes me happy because of a certain fan I have down there. Hi Mags. Hope you're listening.

Everyone say hi to Maggie the Cat.

Maggie is my personal heroine. She slipped out of a big party her mother was throwing for a thousand or so close personal friends, way the hell out on Long Island. She just bolted. Threw a bag in her car and drove non-stop until she got to Hanover and Phi Psi. Could have knocked me over with a feather. I don't want to reveal too many personal details, but she was in a, what would be a good word, sultry mood. Yep. Maggie the Cat was smoking. She showed up wearing a formal dress, heels, and enough jewelry to pay my spring tuition. She looked fine. And she was in a fine mood, too. I mean she was sweet.

That's all you get. You'll have to imagine the rest.

But, as I was saying. Now, they can hear my dulcet tones as far away as Smith and Holyoke to the south and Boston to the east. Gracious!

Of course, the increased range makes it more likely the FCC will be eavesdropping, so everyone will have to help me avoid saying fuck or shit, because that's a federal violation, and I don't look good bent over.

Which reminds me of my topic tonight: dating at Dartmouth.

My producer just leaned in and said he thought we had a winner. No, Fred, it wasn't Howling Wolf. Tell that caller 'Good try but to buy his or her own M&Ms.'

Howling Wolf wrote and recorded the song in 1956. Your hint is that this version was recorded exactly ten years later.

Back to dating. It's a new concept at Dartmouth for the most part. Before our co-eds arrived, real dating was rare. Whom could we date? Guys disposed that way could date each other. Guys could date Mary Hitchcock girls or townies. But there were problems with both of those last two. Hitchcock girls are suspicious of Dartmouth guys because they think we look down on them. We're fucking snobs. Shit. You were supposed to stop me from saying fuck! Townies thought the same as the Hitchcock girls and had mothers sheltering them. Both had early curfews by party standards. There were Colby girls, but that usually involved their having to drive home which takes forty minutes or so. As you can tell, I'm drawing a distinction between a date, a one-night thing which might result in sexual gratification but also might just be platonic, and the overnighters we get when hometown honeys or Smithies travel a great distance and spend the weekend. We may call that a date, but it's a whole lot more. It involves expectations on the part of the girl a date doesn't.

But, voila, co-eds. Now, an old-fashioned date is possible, one in which you head down Main Street to catch a flick or have her over to your fraternity house to dance. No expectations of sex. If it happens, it's because you like each other and both of you want to, but, if it doesn't happen, no worries.

I had a couple of dates my freshman year but since then had been in a serious relationship which, unfortunately, dissipated a couple of months ago, so I'm a bit rusty on the whole dating concept. A Hanover girl came over Saturday, though, and we just hung out. We danced a bit. Well, she danced and I shuffled from side to side. We talked a lot and ate some food. That was all. And it was pleasant. Nourishing even. A real-life female friend.

You see, when you just have overnight girls, the getting to know people dries up because you're always with the same girl. One of those weekends and the expectation is that you're a monogamous couple for life. Now, that's wonderful and we all need to develop long-term relationships, but we also need to meet a lot of people. Why? Variety.

And I don't mean that in the shallow sense, like different dishes. I mean that we need to encounter lots of different types of attitudes and strengths and weaknesses. We learn so much about ourselves through contact with others that we even begin to understand whom we really need.

Why am I pontificating about dating?

Because we have co-eds amongst us. There are a couple of hundred fascinating stories to hear. A couple of hundred viewpoints with which to argue. But the co-eds won't even talk to us until they feel safe doing so. The only co-ed I know hates me. She's been in enough of my English classes that I worried for a while that she was a stalker. Oh, that's not quite true. There are two in our fraternity, but they have already attached themselves to two brothers, and I rarely see them.

Isn't that sad, though? Not just the pitiful fact that I don't know many co-eds, but the fact that they don't trust the guys enough to open up.

So, my cure for our divided campus is dating. Talk to a co-ed. Don't be bashful. Ask her out on a harmless date, something like pizza or coffee or a movie. And then don't put your hand in her panties the minute you're alone.

My townie 'date' Saturday told me her mother distrusts Dartmouth guys, so she's not supposed to hang out with them. Really? She's a junior at Boston College. It's okay to wander Boston miles from home, but it's unsafe to walk onto campus and hang out with a Dartmouth guy? We need to seriously re-think our image and our attitudes, guys.

Wait, a message from the booth. Yes! It was by The Animals. Too bad it took so long to get a correct answer. The M&Ms are all gone. But kudos nonetheless.

What was my point in that little quiz? Think about The Animals, a bunch of white punks growing up in Newcastle on Tyne. They began like all those British bands did, playing in a basement or a cramped bedroom, being yelled at by an overstressed mum or a drunken dad. Picture their first gigs playing in dirty smoke-filled shitholes in front of a bunch of alcoholic World War II pensioners just trying to grab a drink with the fellows before heading back to their equally shithole flats. The boys in those bands were fifteen, maybe sixteen, and the average age of the crowd was fifty-something. Not that the band could tell the age of the crowd. The smoke was thick enough and the lighting bad enough that they could have been playing in front of the Queen for all they knew. No one liked their music. It was American, and it was black. That's right. Most of the British Invasion was born on the Mississippi River or in Chicago. Those little English bastards were playing Howling Wolf and Muddy Waters and Lightning Hopkins and a whole host of old black men most Americans had never heard of, and they didn't give a flip whether people liked it or not. They liked it. You can tell when you listen. The sincerity is obvious. Yep, Rock and Roll was derived from the blues, not from the silly pop the radio stations were playing. Please. Franky Avalon? And the pop lyrics weren't blues, they were whiny. 'It's my party and I'll cry if I want to. You would cry too if it happened to you.' Crap. Right?

Ironically, Motown wasn't as directly influenced by the blues as The Animals and The Beatles and The Stones were. Motown is rhythm and blues, which sounds black enough, but their crooner roots owe as much to Sinatra and Dean Martin and the big band sound as they do to Mississippi blues singers playing on a guitar made with a cigar box and a broom stick. Motown may be closer to Perry Como than to Bessie Smith.

Think of the irony: Louis Armstrong playing Big Band tunes written by Johnny Mercer in a glittering ballroom, and The Animals growling out a Howling Wolf song in a dank basement peopled by drunks and losers, those who could feel the blues for real.

So, see, we all bring cool ideas and strengths to the table, even if government or society at large doesn't seem to know it. Remember the story about Elvis getting booed at a show because he was a white guy playing a black venue with a black crowd. By the end of the show, they were digging him big time.

Yeah, that was a sneaky return to my dating nag. Yes, I know I nag. Eat it.

We need to get to know the co-eds on campus and they need to get to know us. But, to gain their trust, we need to take sex out of the equation, not entirely, but as a mandatory thing. So, regain a little innocence. Return to your starry-eyed teens and hang out with a chick. Talk to her. Ask her about her life. She'll dig it. I promise.

I'll close the show with the Howling Wolf version of Smokestack Lightning. Growl that shit out, Howling Wolf. Goodnight Hanover and Colby and maybe even Smith and Holyoke. Rest tight knowing your Angel's playing you some sweet blues.

Fred tapped on the glass and pointed to the phone. Angel smiled. That had to be Maggie, unless Boston or Smith indeed picked up DCR and Sharon or Cassie or Wicked Wanda happened to be tuned in.

Fred handed him the phone and mouthed 'Maggie.'

"Hey Babe," he said. "What are you doing up this late on a school night?"

"Listening to my favorite DJ, and I think he just told the world that we made love Saturday night. Did I get that right?"

"Oops. Did I reveal too much?"

"No," she laughed. "My dormmates are jealous. They were curious about your 'date.' I told them you were just friends and didn't have sex that night."

"That's the God's honest truth. We just hung out. In fact, we talked about you a lot. She helped me clear my head and get some perspective. She's a good shit. You would like her. You have a lot in common."

"I know nothing happened that night, Angel. Wanda told me."

Angel was silent trying to figure out what that meant. He had a vision of a tortured long-distance call between the two women wrought with jealousy, accusations, and denials. Shit.

"Um."

"Relax, Angel. Wanda was leaving and saw me sitting in my car. She's the reason

I had the courage to go in and face you. She's also the reason I didn't try to talk about 'us' the whole night. She said to just enjoy being with you, and that's what I did."

"And you did that very well. Twice, if I remember correctly."

Maggie laughed. "Anyway, thank you for the sweet shout-out to the whole state. It gave me goosebumps."

"So, you're not jealous about Wanda?"

She laughed again. "Men are so stupid. Of course, I am, but I'm not going to let that ruin things between you and me."

"That's how I felt about Jeffrey. I'm not made of stone. I was angry and jealous. That's probably why I broke Jeffrey's finger. But that doesn't mean I don't want to see you."

"The version I heard was that you broke his finger because he threatened Delilah. At least, that's Delilah's story. It's the one she proudly told at school the next day."

"That, too." There was a comfortable silence. Then, "Are you still coming up this weekend?"

"That's part of what I called about. I can't. I have to drive to Smith and Holyoke for interviews. I don't think I'm going to get in Dartmouth. You were right. They only admit Seven Sister girls."

"I will miss you this weekend, Sweet Pea."

"Hmm. I doubt that. Jane will probably show up, or someone else will appear." She paused. "Angel, this is all hard for me, but I'm trying."

"Me, too."

"Promise?"

"I promise," he said. "Next weekend is Green Key. You've got to be there for that."

"I'll be there with bells on," she said.

"What does that mean?" he asked. "I never understood that saying."

"Good night, Angel."

"Good night, Maggie, my sweet."

He tripped over the 'my sweet,' and Maggie picked up on it.

"You almost said 'Maggie, my love,' didn't you?"

"Maybe."

"Hm. Maybe. We'll see about maybe," she said.

"Mags."

"What?"

"Good luck with your interviews. Want me to come with you? We could stay in a motel, and I could help you prepare."

"I'll bet you could. My mother will be staying with me, and she snores. Would that keep you awake?"

Silence. Angel could almost hear Maggie smiling on the other end of the phone.

"Okay, fine, but I'm not doing your mother. That would be weird."

Maggie laughed.

"Oh, Angel, you are a mess."

"Yeah," he smiled, "but I'm your mess."

They hung up. Angel and Fred set programming on the feed they shared with affiliates late at night, and DCR ran on auto pilot until the morning weather and sports show.

Angel walked back to Phi Psi under a waxing moon humming *Smokestack Lightning* and feeling pretty good about life.

Ah hoo hoo-oh

Ah hoo hoo.

Chapter Twenty-Two

Friday April 9, 1971
Blood and Barf

MAGGIE, PURSUED BY AN ANNOYED AND AMUSED ANGEL, staggered and face-planted as she ran across The Green.

Angel helped her to a sitting position, from which she spat out grass and mud. "Ptui," she said.

Angel sat next to her. The ground was still wet, but it was no longer cold. Spring had hit Hanover, and Maggie was officially plastered.

"So, this is what you're like when you're drunk," Angel said.

"Yep."

Angel stood and helped her to her feet. He wasn't completely sober, either, but he had gotten stuck on the *Heorot* pool table long enough to have avoided being plied with drinks every ten minutes. Not so, Maggie.

She had been dancing with Linda, Sand's girl, and with Jane. That improbable trio was the hit of the dance. *Heorot* had good bands, and the girls got tired of watching Angel shoot pool and Sand and Eddie play high stakes Bridge with a pair of *Heorot* super-nerds.

Linda and Jane were mildly miffed with Maggie because she received nearly all the attention for her dancing and had been rubbed up against and offered drinks by nearly every single guy there.

Angel had finally lost and surrendered the pool table, and, when he found Maggie, she had a guy in front of her and a guy behind her. The guy in front had his hands on her hips and the guy behind was smack up against her sweet ass with his hands around her ribcage, cupping her breasts. The trio swayed together in a sex sandwich. Maggie held her hands high above her holding her drink and shouting 'whoo!'

When Angel saw the scenario, he grinned. He pushed through the throng, took Maggie's hand, and pulled her to him. The two boys thought about complaining, and one even reached feebly to drag her back, but his companion recognized Angel and hauled his disbelieving friend away.

Maggie threw her arms around Angel, spilling most of the drink down the back of his shirt. The music slowed, and Angel pulled her to him and held her head against his chest.

When the music ended, Angel kissed her and said, "Let's go home."

"Home," Maggie said. "I like the sound of that."

But, the minute they cleared the *Heorot* threshold, Maggie had taken off running and laughing. Periodically, she would stop to taunt Angel who strode smiling behind her.

But the face plant demanded more than a smile. It was hilarious. Maggie's face was covered with mud and bright green grass which shone under the gas lamps and the just waning moon. Yes, spring was upon them, and Maggie wore it beatifically.

Angel dabbed at her face with his handkerchief but gave up and put his arm around her waist.

Just outside Phi Psi, Maggie broke loose and bent over with her hands on her knees. But nothing came of it, and she straightened up and smiled, "False alarm."

Once back in his room, Angel undressed her and tossed her clothes in a muddy heap. Maggie stood swaying and humming with her hands over her head.

She looked down at herself. "I'm all naked."

"Yes, you are, dear." Angel stripped and grabbed a pair of neatly folded towels. Together they stood under the shower's hot spray while Angel soaped her off.

"Angel, this is gross. You know I'm on my period."

"I don't care. You're still muddy."

"You've got a Mister Boner," she laughed and grabbed his shaft.

Angel turned her around and cleaned her back. He rinsed between her cheeks and asked, "Do you need to take that thing out before I clean you?"

"Yes," she said meekly. She trotted to a stall and closed the door. Angel heard a flush and she reappeared in the shower. "This doesn't gross you out?"

"Maggie, do you know how to tell when a man cares about you?"

"He tells you he loves you and stops diddling other women?"

Angel smiled. "Yes, those would be indicators, but I meant something more psychological."

"What, then?"

"He sees you when you're sick or puking or on your period or in a terrible mood and still likes you."

"Oh," she said. "Then you must really care about me right now," and she rushed towards the stall again, skidding on her own puddles of water and nearly falling.

Angel let her throw up for a moment and washed himself off. He toweled and knocked on the stall door.

"Who is it?" Maggie squeaked.

"A big, bad wolf."

"Oh, I was hoping it was Angel, because I don't feel so good."

"Open up, Maggie."

Angel heard a bolt slide and saw Maggie with her face on the side of the toilet seat. She looked as if she were holding on to the rocking mast of a boat.

"Everything's spinning," she moaned.

Angel sat on the floor of the stall and pulled her to a sitting position before him and held her. She began to shiver, and he knew that her nausea was gone for the moment.

He pulled gobs of vomit from the tips of her hair.

Maggie began to cry.

Angel helped her up and back to the shower, turning the water to lukewarm so as not to heat her up again, which would start another wave of puking. He washed her hair and soaped her all over. He toweled her and led her back to the stall where she sat. He wrapped a towel around her and asked, "Where are your tampons? In your purse?"

Maggie nodded abjectly, and Angel padded naked to his room, encountering Jane as she entered Groucho's room. She looked at him and smiled. "Everything all right?" she asked.

"Sick girl," he said and disappeared into his room. When, he returned to the bathroom, Maggie was leaning sideways against the stall. He kissed her forehead, handed her a tampon, and left.

He heard a voice asking, "Do you just wander around naked and hard?" It was Jane again, about to go down the stairs.

"Pretty much," he said. He smiled, "And you of all people should know that this isn't fully hard."

She cut her eyes down at him and then back up. "I think that's changing as we speak."

Angel looked down. Rats. Thor had a mind of his own, as fucking usual.

"Angel, I do need to talk to you this weekend," Jane said.

Angel nodded gravely. "Of course. You okay?"

"Not really."

"Are you staying in Groucho's room?"

"Yep. But I'm going to watch some movie with the guys in the tube room. *Dr. Strangelove*?"

"Okay. Go. I'm going to put Maggie to bed. I may try to find you later."

"Thanks."

"Jane, I know I'm a nag, but I don't think you need any more alcohol tonight." She smiled and went unsteadily down the stairs.

Angel watched to make sure she made it and went to his room, where he pulled on jeans and a tee shirt. He grabbed a long-sleeve shirt for Maggie and went to retrieve her. She was still sitting on the toilet leaning against a wall. She mutely handed him the wrapper from her tampon and tried to stand. Angel gave her the shirt. "Put this on," he said, and he gave her his hand and led her to his room.

Maggie flopped on the bed, and Angel sat beside her. She took his hand and said, "You're so sweet."

Angel went to his heap of clothes and pulled a roach from his pants pocket and lit it. He sat back beside Maggie. "Here, smoke a little of this. It will help with the nausea."

Maggie inhaled and held her breath. She looked like a little kid trying to smoke her first cigarette. Angel smiled and brushed the wet hair from her forehead. Maggie exhaled and tried to smile back. Her effort was pitiful and Angel laughed.

"You are a mess," he said. He bent and kissed her forehead. He got her brush from her purse and made her sit up while he brushed her wet hair.

"I guess I drank too much."

"You think?"

"Are you mad at me?"

Angel responded by holding her hair up and kissing the back of her neck. She began to shiver again so he put the brush aside and lay her down, putting his arms around her. He held her head against his chest and stroked her hair.

Maggie's breathing grew slower, and she became still. Angel thought she was asleep until she said, "That's true, what you said in the shower, isn't it?

Angel smiled at her. She sounded so serious. What had he said in the shower? He raised his eyebrows in a shrug.

"About seeing people when they're not perfect?" she said.

Angel nodded. "Yep. I really believe that. When someone falls for you, it has a miraculous effect. It's so affirming. It says, 'Someone got to know me and saw me without my makeup and when my complexion wasn't perfect and when my hair was a mess.'"

"And when I was puking and when he had to clean blood off my thighs," she groaned.

"That, too," he agreed, "and he still liked me."

"God, I was sure I'd be through with my stupid period before now. My mom would die of shame to know that you have seen me this way."

"I know. I'm thinking about dumping you this instant," he smiled.

She put her arm on his. "You're a good man, aren't you?"

"I'm a work in progress, just like you."

"So," she asked, "does a breakup tell you the opposite?"

"Uh huh, that's why they're so earth-shattering, especially to girls. They say, 'A guy got to know me, really know me, and he didn't like what he saw. He only liked me when I looked my best and behaved.' That's a soul sucking lesson."

She was quiet for a moment. Then, she sighed. "Did you have fun at *Heorot*? I don't remember much. Were we dancing?"

"No," he laughed. "You were dancing. You had a guy grinding your ass and feeling you up while another in front of you had his hands on your pelvis."

"Shut up," she protested. "Oh, shit, I did, didn't I? Are you angry?"

Angel shook his head and kissed her. "Yuk. Someone needs to brush her teeth."

Maggie blew in her hand and sniffed. She made a face and got out of bed. She rummaged in her bag and found a toothbrush and toothpaste and fled towards the bathroom.

Angel lay on the bed with his arms behind his head. He had to admit, this was way better than dating. He liked taking care of Maggie. She was a sweet drunk, unlike too many of his friends.

Maggie returned and put her toothbrush on his dresser next to his. She scooched him over and slid under the covers.

"Why aren't you angry?" she said.

"Jeeze, you can't let anything go, can you?"

Maggie shook her head.

"Would you be angry if you saw a girl pawing at me?"

"Not at you. I'd be mad at the girl, unless you were enjoying it too much or provoking it. Oh, shit, was I enjoying it?"

Angel nodded and smiled. "I was glad to see you enjoying yourself. I would have been pissed at the guys if I thought they knew you were with me, but they were younger and ran away when I got there. They were just being lonely guys. Besides, if I didn't know you and saw you dancing like that, I would have been all over you, too."

"You would, would you?"

"Definitely."

"Try the kissing stuff again," she said.

Angel smiled and kissed her. "Much better. Now you just taste like period."

"What?" she laughed and hit him on the chest. "You're so gross."

"No," he said. "It's true. You taste different. Metallic, sort of."

"Are you making that up?"

Angel laughed. "You know I'm not. It's not bad different, but it's different." He kissed her again. "See, I don't mind."

"Hmm," she said. "I can't decide if you're a pervert or a sweetheart."

"Can't I be both? In fact," and he slid his hands under the covers and caressed a breast, "I don't mind love-making either. In fact, it's kind of nice."

"Okay," she laughed. "I'm not that evolved, yet. Jeffrey would have died even knowing I was on my period. If I said the word 'menstruation' he would have run from the room."

They both laughed but grew quiet.

"You know, Mags, I can talk about things like you and Jeffrey. If you want to."

Maggie looked thoughtful but shook her head. "No, I think I get it. Delilah explained it to me. She's a smart little witch."

Angel smiled and relit the roach. This should be good. Delilah. What a piece of work.

"Delilah said you weren't jealous because you were secure enough to let me have my freedom and that it didn't mean that you didn't like me."

Ha. That wasn't bad.

"She also said that if I don't go slow with you, I will lose you," Maggie said. She looked at him. "Is that true? Would I lose you?"

"I don't know, Maggie. I'm not exactly cognizant of how my inner-dealings work. I just kind of go on instinct. But my instinct tells me that I just got out of a long relationship and shouldn't jump into another one too quickly. A little panic button goes off."

"That's what Delilah said, too." She sighed. "So, does that mean you want to date other girls?"

"No, not if date means seeking out new people. I'm perfectly happy with you."

"When I'm with you. What about when I'm not with you?"

Angel thought about that. How honest could he afford to be?

"I don't know Mags. I'm just kind of making it up as I go."

That was true. He hoped that she wouldn't ask about sex with other women, because Wanda and Sharon were never far from his febrile brain. But she didn't.

"Why don't you nap and I'll get some writing done?" he said. "All right?"

Maggie nodded. She stroked his face. "Delilah said I should be patient. She said that you're worth it."

Angel had no response to that. He wasn't sure that was true at all. But he kissed her eyes and told her to sleep. Maggie nodded and turned towards the wall.

Angel spooned her until she stopped wiggling happily and dozed off. He crept out of bed and went to his desk, but he didn't feel like writing, so he watched Maggie sleep.

He had a feeling that he and Maggie had weathered their crisis too easily, but he wasn't about to poke a hornets' nest with a stick, so he determined to let it lie. His dating others was sure to come up again. Or maybe not. If Wanda didn't appear, he would probably be monogamous enough. He did like having the illusion of freedom for a while, though.

He pulled on his boots and snuck out. He found Jane in the tube room eating popcorn and watching *Dr. Strangelove* with Groucho and Blake.

Sand and Eddie were playing bridge again, this time against the SAE assholes who had almost beaten them for the Dartmouth championship.

Eddie rose. "Gotta take a leak and eat. Angel, sit in a hand for me."

Angel nodded and plopped in Eddie's seat.

"If you're going to the kitchen, make me a bacon sandwich." Eddie gave him a thumbs-up and disappeared. Angel pulled the score sheet to him. Hmm. Both teams were vulnerable, and Eddie and Sand must have gone down at least once because they were points in the hole. It was Eddie's deal, so the blonde guy to his left shuffled and Angel dealt.

He looked at his hand and bid quickly. "Two clubs."

Sand stared at him and put out his cigarette. He tapped on the table.

The SAE guys looked at Sand.

"New system," Sand said. "We're playing Italian Blue Team. You're going to need alerts on every bid unless you know the whole system, and Angel just opened with a doozy."

"We don't know it," the pretty blonde guy said.

"Two clubs means Angel's got between eighteen and twenty-one points. He's asking for my aces."

Blondie looked at his partner. "Pass," he said.

"Two hearts," Sand said.

"That means he's got one ace," Angel said.

"Pass," the long-haired guy said.

"Three clubs," Angel said.

"He's asking for kings," Sand said.

"Pass," Blondie said.

"Three diamonds," Sand said.

"That means he's either got all of them or none of them," Angel said.

"Pass," long-hair said.

They all stared at Angel.

Shit. He was missing an ace and a king. Eddie would kill him if he blew this hand. It was an easy game winner. He could bid four spades and they would win the set.

"Are we playing for money?" Angel asked.

"Yep," Sand said, "but bid the hand. Don't worry about the money."

Angel looked at the score pad again. If he overbid and then SAE won a game, Sand and Ed would be screwed, financially. But, if he bid four spades and made a small slam, Ed would castrate him. He decided death was better than castration.

"Six spades," he said.

"Is that an artificial bid?" Blondie asked Sand.

"Nope. It means he wants to play spades. He must have a long suit. At least six of them. Maybe seven or even more."

"But he hasn't even mentioned spades," Blondie said. "How does he know you have any at all?"

"He doesn't. It's a math based system designed to tell the opponents almost nothing about the hands. All I can tell you is that Angel thinks he can take twelve tricks."

Blondie stared at Sand and then at Angel. He looked at his partner who shrugged. "Double," he said.

Sand looked long at his hand and then long at Angel. Angel was impassive. It would have been cheating to give anything away. Sand glanced at the score pad and leaned back.

"Redouble," he said.

"Pass," said Longhair. He looked dourly at Blondie.

"Pass," Angel said.

"Pass," Blondie said with a smile.

Angel smiled. These fuckers gave away too much information. Sand's redouble told him that Sand had some spades, and Blondie's double meant that he probably had both the missing ace and the missing king. It was a dumb double, but Angel would have had to play the hand the way he was about to anyway, no matter what he thought Blondie had or didn't have. Angel led the four of hearts almost before Blondie had finished bidding. Sand laid his dummy hand down. Sand had the ace and queen of hearts. Blondie stared at the four and at Sand's hand and put down the Jack of hearts. Angel smiled at him and played the Queen from Sand's hand. Longhair looked disgusted and threw down the two. Blondie sat back angrily. Angel played the deuce of Spades from Sand's hand and the Ace from his own. Then he led the King of Spades. There, trump were all gone. He played the three of hearts. Blondie played a ten. Angel played Sand's Ace and then led the six of hearts back to his hand. Longhair played the nine and Angel trumped it with a low spade. Blondie angrily threw down his now useless King. "Shit," he said. He really was a pissy, pretty boy.

Angel played the Ace and King of diamonds from his hand and then ran the rest of the spades. His last card was a club and Blondie futilely won it with his Ace.

"Six spades, mucho points, and that's the set," Angel said. "You boys are down a ton of money. You might want to think of calling it a night." He rose and stretched.

Eddie came back with his bacon sandwich and handed it to him.

"What's happening?"

"Angel just made a small slam missing an Ace and a King," Sand said. "And we're rich."

"Good man," Ed said.

"Good sandwich," Angel said and left munching on it. He bought a Coke and stuck his head in the tube room again. A commercial was on, and he caught Jane's eye. She nodded and followed him to the library.

They sat in the pair of red leather chairs in front of the Dickens collection. Angel waited for Jane to speak.

She didn't seem to want to at first and just stared at her hands. Finally, she looked up.

"I don't know why I'm bothering you with this," she said.

Angel smiled at her. "Just tell me."

"All right," she said. "I haven't been having any thoughts about killing myself since I saw you in the fall."

"That's good."

"My parents finally saw my wrist and my stomach, though, and want me to start therapy again."

"Your stomach?"

Jane nodded. She pulled her skirt down, and Angel saw three distinct lines across her abdomen just above her panty line.

"You're cutting yourself?" he asked.

She nodded. "I did the first one over Christmas. The other two are Spring Break. You haven't seen me in a while. We haven't, you know, since Thanksgiving."

Angel ran his fingers over the cuts. They were barely raised scars. They were precise and thin, like the cuts a razor might make.

"Were you home for those holidays?" he asked. "I mean, is being home what does this to you?"

Jane nodded. "I did the one at Christmas because my mother and father were yelling at me all the time. I don't know why. My grades were good. But they were yelling at each other, too. They pretty much hate each other. My dad doesn't exactly treat my mom like you treat me. Like everyone here treats me." She paused and looked to see what Angel's response was. His expression must have been re-assuring because she went on, "I didn't bother you with the Christmas one. I didn't even do it to myself. My friend Krista did it for me. She does it all the time. And things were fine when I got back to school, but then Spring Break, and, well, here I am."

"And you want advice?"

Jane nodded.

"Sounds like you should move in here and sleep with me every night."

"You're joking, but I wish. That would make things so much simpler."

Angel thought. What the fuck did he know about female neuroses?

"What do you think you should do?" he asked.

Jane's face fell. "I guess I should start therapy again. But then it just puts off graduation even longer, and it doesn't make me feel any better. I don't know."

"My first thought would be to avoid your friend Krista. Is she at Northeastern with you?"

"No. She's at home."

"Good. Stay the fuck away from her and from any other self-destructive friends you have. In fact, stay away from home as much as possible." Angel sat pensive. "Are you still pre-law?"

"Yes."

"Try to get a summer internship in Boston. Want me to see if I can find a lawyer you could work with?"

"I can probably find one, but thanks, I may call you."

"And get your cute little ass up here any weekend you want to. You can just stay here and study if you want. I can get you library privileges at Sanborn House. That's the English library. The woman who runs it likes me."

Jane smiled. "Why am I not surprised?"

"She's like sixty."

"Hmm."

"Have you gone to the Northeastern psychologist or psychiatrist or whatever they have there?"

"No."

"Try that. Then, school wouldn't get interrupted. Plus, they're on your side. The ones at home try to be, but they're being paid by your parents. I'm serious, though. Hang out here whenever you can." Angel took Jane's hands in his. "Look at me, Jane." She looked up at him. "You're fine. You're nutty, but everyone is. You know what the best things for depression are?"

She shook her head. "Pills?"

"No," he smiled. "Friends, the good kind, that is, and work. I'll bet you're fine when you're working, aren't you?"

She nodded. She looked up at him again. "You can't make love to me anymore, can you?"

"I don't think Maggie would appreciate it."

"Maggie doesn't know how therapeutic your hands and that other thing are, then."

He smiled at her and pulled her into his lap and cuddled her.

"It's not fair," she said.

"You're such a pussy," he said.

She laughed at that. "No, I'm not. And I'm doing better most of the time."

"Are you kidding? You're so much saner than when I first met you, it's ridiculous."

"How am I saner?"

"Well, you're much more trusting than you used to be."

"That's you guys," she said.

"And, you now seem capable of having fun. When we met, you were pretty much a downer."

"I was, wasn't I?" she said. She kissed him and hopped up. "Thanks. That was exactly the talking to I needed."

"I didn't do anything. In fact, I can't do anything. People cure themselves," he said.

"When they're in places they feel secure. Shouldn't you be getting back to Maggie?"

He nodded. "And you should get back to *Dr. Strangelove*. It has the best ending of any movie ever."

"Of any movie, ever?" she mocked.

"See, you can be funny when you're not being solipsistic."

"Okay, I don't know that word."

"Funny? It means…"

"I know that word. Eddie's right. You're a douchebag."

"Nice mouth. Solipsistic means you think you're the only thing in the universe. Total self-absorption."

"Oh, well, it's no wonder you know that word."

"See," he said. "That's funny." He patted her on the butt. "Get back to your movie."

Angel closed up the library and locked it. The next night would be chaos, and he didn't need idiots rummaging through the Phi Psi collection. A lot of the books were more than a hundred years old.

Sitting on the bottom of the stairs was Maggie the Cat, wrapped in a blanket. Angel sat next to her. "Hi there. Feeling any better?"

Maggie had tears in her eyes, and Angel brushed them away.

"Hey," he said. "Are you upset that I was talking to Jane?"

She shook her head and leaned against his chest. He put his arm around her.

"No," she said. "I heard pretty much the whole conversation. I'm so proud of you. You really are a good man. I know that embarrasses you, but it's true."

Angel lifted her chin until her shining eyes faced his. He kissed her lightly.

"So, you told Jane you can't sleep with anyone but me?" she said.

"Did I say that?"

"Yep."

Angel smiled. "When was the last time anyone carried you to bed?" he asked.

"I don't know. When I was five, maybe."

Angel stood and cracked his knuckles. He bent and lifted the laughing Maggie like a child.

"God, you weigh a ton," he said.

Maggie laughed and hit his chest. "Unhand me, you brute."

"I don't think so," he said, and he carried her up to bed.

Chapter Twenty-Three

Saturday April 10, 1971
Union Village Dam

CANE AND EDDIE CARRIED THE KEG DOWN THE STEEP, muddy hill to the watering hole at Union Village Dam. Twice, Eddie slipped and skidded, dropping his end of the keg.

"Christ, Eddie," Cane said. "Quit fucking around." Shaking his head in disgust, Cane shouldered the keg and carried it the rest of the way himself.

Angel and Maggie followed them, holding hands and laughing at their clownish friends.

Maggie had never seen the falls before, and she was excited. The sound the water made crashing onto the rocks was immense, and, by the time they reached the bottom, it was deafening.

Cane dumped the keg in a shallow pool.

"Who's got the tap?" he asked.

"Sand," Eddie said.

"Where the hell is he?"

"He's coming."

Angel took off his boots and rolled his jeans legs up. Maggie did the same and stepped into the water. She hopped back immediately.

"Oh, my dear Lord, that's cold," she said.

Angel tested the water and agreed. "This is the earliest I've ever been here." He pointed above the rock which cleft the waters in two and created the twin fifteen feet falls which roared their displeasure at being interrupted in their race down the mountainside.

"That, my dear, is all melted snow from the White Mountains," he said. "It's cold even in the summer. But, it's in the seventies, the sun is hot, and we are going swimming."

"Oh, no we're not," she laughed.

"You don't have to skinny dip," Cane said. "It's not that appealing anyway to see a woman on her period."

Maggie howled and punched Angel. "You told them?"

"No, I swear," Angel laughed.

"I saw a couple of tampons in the bathroom trash," Cane said. "And you've been crabby all weekend."

"I have not," Maggie said and punched Cane.

"See?" he said.

Maggie laughed and hit him again. For good measure, she hit him a third time.

"Having fun?" Cane asked.

"I am," she said, "I've been wanting to do that since the first time I saw you. You guys are seriously twisted. And, for the record, I finished last night. If there's skinny-dipping happening, I'm in."

"Thought you weren't swimming," Angel mocked. "It's too cold. Waah."

"I'm certainly not letting you be the only one naked with sights like the one coming down the trail available."

Angel looked up the hillside and saw six girls slipping and sliding down the hill wearing shorts and bikini tops. He recognized two from campus as co-eds. Behind them, Sand and Linda picked their way down the trail.

"About fucking time," Eddie shouted. The girls thought he was talking to them and looked startled; the one in the front tripped and slid on her rear end at least fifteen feet down the trail. She got up rubbing her ass and laughing.

"That's the one I was referring to," Maggie said. "She has the biggest breasts I've ever seen in my life."

Something besides lust bounced around in Angel's cranium. A faint recognition? No, he'd probably just seen her on campus.

Eddie offered a hand to the girls as they reached the stream below the falls and stepped from stone to stone, heading towards a large boulder. The girls gave Eddie their towels and bags and clambered up on the rock, offering Eddie a prime rear view. He turned to Cane and raised his eyebrows appreciatively. The last girl kept slipping, so Eddie thoughtfully put his hands on her butt and gave her a push.

"Thank you," she said blushing.

"Any time," Ed said. The other girls burst out laughing.

Ed waded back to Cane and Angel, smiling broadly.

"You guys," Maggie said.

"You have to admit that girl has an amazing body," Eddie said, looking over his shoulder at the big-breasted one. She turned and brightened when she saw Angel. She waved and mouthed 'Hi.'

Angel smiled goofily and waved back. Maggie swatted at his arm.

"That girl does not have an amazing body. She's fat," Maggie said.

"That's an uncharitable view," Cane said. "From where I sit, she looks like Filet Mignon."

Maggie laughed. "I know, women made Twiggy famous and men made Marilyn Monroe famous."

"That's pretty astute for a broad," Cane said.

"Angel said it, not me."

"Sure sounded like you said it," Cane said.

"I heard her, too," Sand said as he and Linda reached the party.

"No, you idiots, he said it the other night," Maggie laughed.

"That's a woman for you," Cane said. "Angel says something, and it bounces around in a chick's empty skull for weeks. She opens her mouth the next day, and it flies out."

"Is it true?" Maggie asked.

"That chicks have empty skulls? Yeah," Cane said.

"No," Maggie said. "The part about guys liking thick girls?"

"Well, Angel likes you, and you're pretty thick in the head."

"Cane, I'm going to punch you in the balls," she said.

"Go ahead. It'd probably be the best sex you had all weekend. Oh, I forgot, you were hosting the Rhine River and probably didn't get anything last night."

Sand twisted the tap into its slot until it clicked and straightened up from the keg. "And we have beer."

Eddie waded a few steps towards the co-eds who were sunning and pretending not to listen to Cane's idiocy. "Hey, ladies, we have beer and cups. We do have cups, don't we Sand?"

"Shit," Sand said. "Be right back." And he began the trek back up the hill to his car.

"Is there enough for everyone?" a petite cutie asked.

"Quarter keg, that's eighty-eight and a half beers. I'd say we have enough," Ed said.

"We'll be there in a while. Let us sun and get hot first."

Ed waded back to his group. "They look pretty hot to me already."

"Enough," Linda said. "You're all perverts who objectify women. All of you."

"Objectify women?" Eddie said. "Is that Women's Liberation-speak? What the fuck does that even mean?"

"Like those girls over there," Linda said. "You just see them as bodies."

Eddie glanced at the girls on the rock. "Of course, we do. We don't know them, so all we can do is see them. They are, technically, visual objects like the falls. The falls are beautiful. There, I said it. I objectified them. So, sue me."

"People are not objects of nature," Linda said. "Maggie, back me up."

"I'm not sure I'm with you," Maggie laughed. "Angel doesn't see me as an object, do you baby?"

"Well, you do have nice tits and a wonderful ass," Angel said. "I think I plead guilty."

"See?" Linda said.

"No," Maggie said. "He's teasing. So is Cane. You probably don't know how I met these two. Cane, tell Linda why you chose me to assault out of all the girls crossing the quad that day."

"You were the alpha leading a likely looking group of girls."

"Why did you think I was the alpha?"

"I don't know. You just were."

"Was it because of my tits or ass?"

"No, it was the way the group responded to you."

Maggie turned to Linda. "See? Cane's first reading of me was about strength and personality. Cane, why do you tease me all the time?"

"Because you're funny as shit. Because you dish it out. You dig trading gibes with me, you know you do."

"Maggie's right," Eddie said. "When those girls come over here, we'll get to know them, and they will cease being visual objects."

Sand slid the last fifty feet down the hill with two sleeves of cups. "What did I miss?"

"Maggie and Linda were having a cat fight," Cane said.

While everyone lined up for beer, Angel quietly stripped and waded, shivering, into the water. When he was knee deep, he did a shallow dive and came up spluttering.

"Is it freezing?" the busty girl from the rocks asked.

"Nope," Angel grinned. "It's bracing."

When Sand finished pumping the keg, he poured a cup of foam and dumped it. "Beer's on," he said.

Eddie filled a beer and sipped. "Man, that's frosty."

Sand was next. He filled a cup and handed it to Linda.

Maggie looked agonizingly at Angel who was motioning her to join him.

She stripped and stepped in the water. Immediately she backed out and shook her head. "It's too cold."

"Come on, sweetheart. I'll make it up to you tonight," Angel said. He ducked back under the water to prove it was bearable.

Maggie shook her head but stepped back in. She waded, wide-eyed until the water was almost to her waist and dove. She came up laughing and screeching.

Soon, the busty co-ed and the small one were down to their panties and wading in. Sand climbed to the ledge beside the falls, beat his chest, Tarzan style, and leapt into space.

He hit the water in a cannon ball and came up roaring. He beckoned Linda who shook her head. "Let me get some beer in me first," she pleaded. Sand shook his head and swam towards her.

The other four co-eds descended from their rock and lined up at the keg.

Maggie swam to Angel who treaded water in the deep basin carved by the falls. Angel took her hand and pulled her towards the falls. Off to the side, the water was shallow enough for him to touch bottom, and he stood precariously and held her in his arms. He kissed her.

"You taste good," he said.

"No period taste?"

"Nope," he laughed. "Just my sweet girl."

"What does a period kiss taste like?"

"You must know," he said. "You taste it too. It's hard to describe."

"You taste good, too," she said and kissed him back.

"Are you freezing?" he asked.

"I don't mind," she said. "Just hold me."

"Wanna see something cool?"

Maggie nodded, and Angel drew her to a boulder and bade her climb with him. Together, they ascended to a flat place near the top of the falls. The sound redoubled, almost like chords, as the water rushed down the hillside and was forced abruptly into two separate streams. From that point, it encountered a granite rock which looked as if it might be the model for Henry Moore's *Knife Edge*.

From there, the rushing waters dropped twenty feet into the pool Angel and Maggie had just left. The sound reverberated from the hillside and from the boulders encasing the falls on either side of the divide. It then crashed into the basin below, where it sounded a series of angry bass notes loud enough to be heard a mile away.

Angel sat on the rock adjacent the cleft and clutched a shivering Maggie until the sun warmed them both. The boulder shuddered from the ferocity of the cascading water as if its atoms were trying to burst from their bonds.

"Angel, why didn't we wait another month to come here? The water and the air would have been warmer."

"Because this is the most dramatic time, when the snow is melting rapidly and the falls are the most volatile," he said. "And because it's about to become a new Phi Psi Green Key ritual," he laughed. "Besides, look, the place is almost empty."

Beneath their feet, the falls stirred the pool and then slowed until, a hundred or so feet to the south, the water became one of those bucolic New England streams, replete with rocks and gurgling sounds.

They watched the co-eds mingling with Eddie and the guys. The busty one and her friend had given up on wading in the frigid water and joined the party. Eddie stared, seemingly incapable of speech.

"Check out Eddie," Maggie said. "He's trying so hard not to look."

Angel smiled and lay back on the rock. The sun felt good, and his chill was dissipating on the hot granite.

Maggie lay back, too, and Angel drew her to him.

"Mag," he said.

"Uh huh?"

"You still haven't said anything about your transfer applications. How did your interviews go? Did you like either school?"

Maggie stretched and turned towards him. "I think I liked Holyoke better," she said. "Maybe I just didn't like Smith because you store your women there."

Angel smiled.

"I liked my Holyoke interviewer, too. She's a writer, Joyce Oakes. Ever heard of her?"

Angel shook his head. He was getting drowsy in the sun. Especially after the cold.

"We talked about books and writers. We talked about my family. It was nice."

"What about Dartmouth?" he asked.

"They didn't even offer me an interview. You were probably right. They only consider Seven Sister schools."

"Which means you could transfer to Dartmouth for your senior year?"

"After you're gone? What would be the point?"

"I don't know," he said. "I just can't see you at a school comprised entirely of women. What a waste." And he traced a line from her throat between her breasts and to her navel.

"You don't have to stop there," she said.

"You don't mind people watching?"

She shook her head. "It's amazing what I no longer mind," she said. "This is the first time I've ever been naked in front of other people. I've never even been topless in a crowd."

"You're so selfish," he murmured. "Think of the joy you've denied hundreds of guys."

"Hmmm."

"I'm serious," he said, rolling towards her and leaning on an elbow. "Look at you. I love the way your breasts fall sideways when you're on your back. If you sat up, I would love the way they hang. Your nipples are, I don't know what they are. I don't have a word good enough for them. When they're cold like this, they point and say, 'bite me.' They're like the eyes in those paintings that follow you everywhere you go." He ran his hand over her hip bones and towards her pubis. "And the flattened area between your hips, oh my dear sweet Lord." He bent over her and kissed just below her navel. "And, I've seen your *Mons Venus*. They can't from down there," he said gesturing to the crew below them, "because it's cleverly disguised with a beard, but I know how lovely your lips are and how sweet your juices are."

"Okay," she said. "You can stop now. You're actually making me wet, and you're getting hard."

"I was born hard, baby," Angel said with a smile.

"Hmmm. You know, I'm smarter than you think."

"That's unlikely, especially since Delilah told me about your brilliant sister and mother. And since Delilah is a petite Einstein in a devil's costume."

Maggie ignored him. "You were paraphrasing *The Canterbury Tales*, weren't you?"

"I was?"

"*Mons Venus*? Who says that besides the Wife of Bath? And the beard part was from *The Miller's Tale*."

"'What's this? A woman hath no beard,' quoth Absalom. You are adorable, aren't you?"

"I am." She lay back on the rock and soaked in the sun while Angel contemplated her. She knew he was watching and smiled, an arm across her brow.

"What else did she tell you?" Maggie asked finally.

"Who?"

"Delilah. What else did she tell you about our family?"

Ahh. He was trapped.

"Did she tell you about where Mama and I were Saturday when you called?"

"Shopping?"

Maggie paused. "She didn't tell you about my other sister, the one who died?"

Angel was silent.

"It's okay. I wanted to tell you, but it's kind of hard to weave into ordinary conversation," Maggie said. "It's just a part of me that you need to know."

"Why do you go to a therapist?"

"That's mostly for Mama," Maggie said. "Sometimes, though, especially when I feel lonely, I think about my sister. And, sometimes, I have these dreams. I don't know how to describe them. They're not exactly nightmares. They're strange."

"She's just kind of there, not really doing anything special? Just inhabiting your head."

"Yes, how did you know that?"

"I don't know. I just know you. And I've watched you sleep. You and your mother both blame yourselves, don't you?"

Maggie nodded, "But I don't want to talk about her. This is too perfect an afternoon." She sat up. "Sand jumped from here. Is it safe?"

Angel nodded. "It's deep enough to dive if you want to."

"I want to dive, and I want you to dive, too."

Angel smiled and shook his head. "Not gonna happen."

"You know those lips and juices you were raving about?"

"Yeah, I get it. If I don't dive, lips and juices won't be available later."

Maggie smiled and stood. "I think we understand each other." She took the band from her ponytail and re-tied it tighter. Angel watched, wondering why girls did that. She stuck out her tongue at him and did a swan dive into the frigid basin beneath her. The force of the falling water jolted her sideways under water. She must have come up ten feet from where she entered the water.

She turned on her back and stuck her tongue out again, mouthing the word 'pussy.' Then, she swam to the shallows and stood. She walked away without even turning towards him, her beautiful ass swinging from side to side as she stepped over or around rocks.

Angel sighed. He guessed he was going without later, because he sure as shit wasn't diving. He might jump, but that was about it. She knew he was afraid of heights. Crap.

Angel watched Maggie sit on a rock next to Cane. He said something, and Maggie looked up at Angel and laughed. Cane rose and went to the keg to get her a beer.

Sand and Linda were wading, and Sand pulled Linda into the deeper water. She squawked but went with him, and they paddled about contentedly. Linda was good for Sand and he was good for her. They made Angel happy.

Eddie was gesticulating madly at the co-eds as he tried to reinforce some point he was making. Angel smiled. It looked to be quite a diatribe, but the four co-eds sitting with him seemed enthralled. Probably some arcane army shit, like a story about driving his ambulance up the Ho Chi Minh trail to rescue guys from a fire-fight gone wrong. Ed had a zillion of those, and they were all good. That they were true was even more impressive.

It was funny, though. Sand never told Viet Nam stories.

Busty and Petite were climbing the rocks towards Angel's perch. Petite was cute, but Angel couldn't make his eyes leave Busty's chest as she labored upwards. Her breasts swayed and swung and bounced and did nearly everything Angel could imagine breasts doing during her climb. And Maggie hadn't been exaggerating. They were impressively immense.

When they got to the top, Busty introduced her friend, "Angel, this is Denise."

"Hi," Denise said. Her voice was perky and matched her compact frame. "I've heard stories about you."

"That's enough," Busty said. "Don't give him any hints. I want him to figure out who I am. He obviously doesn't remember me, and, no, we haven't slept together. I know that panicky thought was crossing your mind."

"I'll let you two catch up," Denise said and leapt from the rock.

Shit. Even little people weren't afraid of that plunge.

Angel eyed Busty who smiled enigmatically at him.

"But I do know you, right?"

She nodded happily. At least she was having fun.

"From a class?"

"Nope," she said.

"From sometime in the past?"

She nodded. Angel was warming to her. She seemed a sweet-natured girl, even if she was enjoying his discomfort. He looked at the group below. Maggie sat on a rock smiling at him. She looked entirely too satisfied. She made a diving motion with her hands and then spread her legs. Cane watched the exchange and cackled. He made a jerking-off motion to Angel.

Ha ha. Funny people.

Busty leaned back on her elbows. Rivulets of water ran from her hair and then mingled to slide between her massive breasts. Her nipples were huge, perhaps the diameter of a baseball, and light cocoa colored. Angel watched the drops race past her belly and get caught and funneled again by her hips. They then disappeared into the light brown jungle at her center.

"Did I see you at a strip club?" Angel asked.

Busty snorted and shook her head. "Do I look like stripper material to you?"

"Yes," he said.

She snorted. "Maybe about fifty pounds ago."

"You're wrong," he said. "Every part of you is proportional. Your body is perfect."

Busty blushed, seemingly to her feet. "No, it's not, though I appreciate the compliment. You always were sweet. And you don't have to pretend. I don't mind your staring at my chest. Boys have been doing it since before Middle School. That, by the way, was a definite clue to my identity."

"I wasn't staring."

"I see that thing of yours sticking out."

It was true. Angel was as hard as the granite they sat on. He looked again at Maggie who narrowed her brows but laughed silently at him. She glanced at his middle to let him know she saw.

Angel looked at Busty's face. Something flickered dimly.

"Ah, the chest thing was a McGuffin. We knew each other a long time ago, didn't we?"

"A McGuffin?"

"That's what Alfred Hitchcock called something he placed in a movie to divert attention from what was really going on. Like the suitcase full of cash in *Psycho*."

She laughed. "No, my chest is an integral part of our relationship."

Angel was buffaloed.

Busty laughed at him. "I'm Louise," she said.

Angel looked confused but then smiled. "Louise Baker. From Scarsdale Middle School."

Louise laughed. "That's right. I was Billy Pardoe's best friend."

Angel smiled. Billy Pardoe. He hadn't thought about her in years. In the summer after fifth grade, Angel used to ride his bike to Billy's house and make out with her under an Elm tree in her front yard. The tree was big enough to hide what they were doing from Billy's mother.

"How was your chest a clue?"

"Tommy Ritter?"

Angel shook his head.

"I got these," and she gestured towards her chest, "way too early. Tommy Ritter and the Martin brothers used to call me Big Tit Mama and lots of other things."

"And I beat Tommy Ritter up. I remember now."

"You went berserk. You practically launched yourself at him. He was surrounded by about eight friends who could have killed you, but you didn't care. They had to drag you off Tommy. You sat on his chest and punched him in the face over and over."

"And I got suspended for two weeks. What a good way to begin Middle School."

"You were my hero. Plus, the math thing with Muffy."

"I don't remember that," he said.

"Base five?"

Angel shook his head.

"First day of school? The homework was to come the next day and explain how one plus four could equal ten?"

"Oh, yeah. I played with that all night, but Muffy figured it out, too."

"She just looked it up in the book."

"Oh," he smiled. "I never knew that."

He sat, pleased by the memories.

"You can put that thing away, now," she said, pointing to his dick.

"Sorry, it's on auto-pilot. It's listening to your body, not to my orders."

"Tell it that I play for the other team," she said.

Angel looked at Thor. "Louise isn't interested."

Louise leaned over Thor. "I'm a lesbian. You don't impress me." She looked back up at Angel. "Actually," she whispered, "I should have just said that it doesn't interest me. It does, however, impress me. So does that giant guy's thing."

"Cane?"

"That's Cane? The basketball player?"

"In the flesh."

They both cracked up at that.

"I'm jumping," Louise said. "It was great to see you again. I listen to your radio show and wondered how many non-Hispanic Angels there are, but, until I saw you, I wasn't sure it would really be you. I mean, that's a big coincidence, us being at the same college and all." She flicked his dick. "Goodbye big boy. Take care of that brunette who spread her legs at us. She looks yummy." And she jumped into space and hit the water with a splat.

Angel looked down at Thor. 'Yeah, yeah, I know. If I don't dive from this rock, you don't get to muff dive later. You don't really think she means it, do you? I mean, she'd lose out just as much as you would.'

Thor mutely projected into space. Even to Angel it looked as if he was pointing to the edge of the rock. Jump, Angel, he seemed to say.

Angel looked at Maggie. His exasperation must have been evident. He pointed at Thor and shook clenched fists. Maggie spread her legs again and blew him a kiss.

Angel looked down at Thor. 'Fuck you, Thor. I may just go down on her or use my hands. See how you like that.'

But he edged forwards until his toes were over the ledge. His stomach churned. He said 'Om' a few times to relax and then dove, arms outstretched in perfect form, into space. Somewhere in that space, though, he flattened out, because he hit the water with a womp.

Maggie saw it happening and grabbed Cane's arm while Angel was still in midair. By the time Angel came up gasping for air, the rescue team was there. Cane pulled Angel to the shallows while Maggie swam after, laughing the whole way.

"That was the best bellyflop ever," she said.

Angel followed her ruefully and lay backwards on her towel.

Maggie stretched out next to him and poked his ribs. "So, what was all that between you and your stacked girlfriend?"

Angel sighed and stretched. "The usual. She wanted to give me a blowjob, but I told her I had that covered. She said, 'you mean the scrawny brunette? She looks like one of those stuck-up bitches who acts like everything she does is a favor.' I said, 'Yeah, pretty much.'"

"Uh huh." She poked him again. "You aren't ticklish, are you?"

"Nope."

"That's unfair." She lay beside him and ran her hand over his chest. "What did she really say?"

"Her name is Louise, and, apparently, I was her hero in sixth grade. I beat up a boy named Tommy who used to tease her about having giganto tits. Plus, she thought I was a genius."

"No, really, what was that long conversation?"

Angel laughed. "I just told you. Ask her, woman, if you doubt my veracity." He raised himself to an elbow and grinned at her. "And someone owes me some pussy."

Maggie kissed him and lay back in the sun. "We'll see."

When the sun got low enough to cast them all in shade, Eddie broke away from his two new friends and went to Sand and Linda who were in the shallows skimming rocks.

"Hey, it's getting late. Are we bagging the chariot race?"

"Yeah, probably," Sand said.

"Fuck it," Angel said. "Let SAE win something."

"Cool," Eddie said. "But I'm getting hungry. Anyone else feel like heading back?"

"Ooh, me," Maggie said. "I'm cooking dinner for everyone and still need to shop. I'm freezing anyway. Aren't you guys cold?"

Cane poked at the keg. It bobbed on the surface, a sure sign it was at least halfway kicked.

So, they dressed and packed. Sand lugged the keg up the hill while Eddie carried everything else. The co-eds waved goodbye to Eddie. Louise sought out Maggie. "I'm Louise. Did lover boy tell you that we go way back?"

"I'm Maggie, and yes he did. So, he was saving girls way back in sixth grade?"

"The summer before, actually. Ask him about Billy Pardoe." She gave Maggie a hug.

"What was that for?" Maggie laughed.

"I figured you'd need it with that guy," Louise said. "See you two tonight. Eddie has invited our whole dorm to your dance."

"You won't be disappointed," Maggie laughed. "It's a bizarre crew."

Back at Phi Psi, Maggie made a beeline for the shower. Groucho and Blake were already in two of the stalls, but Maggie didn't care. She was frozen. She hogged the hot water while Angel stood behind her, content with catching the warm spray from her body. He didn't mind. At least the view was divine.

She finally turned to him. "Your turn." She wrapped in her towel and hurried away.

Angel laughed as he watched her go. Not very romantic. He showered quickly and toweled. He found her under the covers in his bed with nothing but her head peeping out.

"Get in," she said. "I'm still freezing." Angel slid next to her and held her. He was burning from the shower, and together they generated enough heat to melt her frozen marrow.

She snuggled against his neck. "I don't know why I'm so cold. I drank a lot of beer."

"That's a myth. Alcohol doesn't keep you warm."

"Really?"

"Really."

She burrowed against him. "This is nice."

Angel squeezed her. She was right. But, he had work to do and so did she, so he kissed her and got dressed. He pulled on his jeans and sat on the edge of the bed, facing away from her, putting on his socks and boots.

She watched him intently. "I know most of the scars on your back are from motorcycle wrecks, but I don't know what any of the others are from."

"They're all from different things," he said. "The football shaped one is from getting knocked off the highway going about eighty. I slid a long, damn way to earn that one."

She traced a scar which went around his right shoulder blade. "This one?"

"Uh huh. The one on my right side is from a stupid crash. I was drag-racing a guy in a Corvette and hit a block of wood in the road. I hit on my left side and bounced all the way to my right. It snapped my left ankle and made those marks."

She traced the lines.

"The star-shaped ones, they're puckers of skin. When I was ten, I leapt to catch a fly ball in my back yard and got impaled on a chain link fence. That was amazing. I can still see my mother's face. The other, smaller ones, are from a variety of childhood things." He turned to face her. "This one," and he pulled back his hair to reveal a small, horizontal scar, "is from rock fights we used to have when I was six or seven. This one," he indicated a circular scar on his ribcage, "was from a chest tube. I broke some ribs and punctured a lung skiing. You knew that one. They put a tube in my side to suck out the blood."

"What about this one?" She touched his right cheek.

"That's from a guy's ring. A guy was hassling a girl, and I intervened. He cut me open pretty good with a giant class ring or something like that. The rest you pretty much know. I get my nose broken pretty often and bust ribs a lot. The scars on my knee are from a pair of surgeries. Nothing very interesting. Football stuff."

Maggie touched his cheek and his nose. She held her face up to be kissed, and Angel obeyed. Maggie pushed the covers back and pulled him down until he was lying on his back. She kissed each scar on his chest and side, and worked her way to his middle. She unbuckled his belt and pulled his jeans down to his knees. She took his shaft in her hand and stroked it, watching it grow as she touched it. She leaned over him and kissed the head and shaft, moaning slightly as she did so. She cupped his balls in her hand and kissed them, too. She tongued the underside of his shaft and took him in her mouth.

"Maggie."

She looked at him. "Hush."

She straddled him and began to work on him in earnest, stroking him faster as she sucked on the tip. Angel grabbed a handful of her hair and arched backwards. Oh, God. He thrust lightly in and out of her mouth and, when she took him fully down her throat, he thought he would go mad. He felt the rictus grabbing his body and let go of her hair, straining his head backwards with his eyes closed while his inner scream neared full volume. His hips shook, and Maggie squeezed him as hard as she could. It seemed to last forever, and then he lay flat and empty while she knelt over him, victorious.

She lay next to him and kissed his chest. He pulled her mouth to his and kissed her. She seemed startled but kissed back.

"Angel," she began.

"Shh. I'm trying to get my breath and brain back."

She smiled and was silent, but she began to stroke Thor, and soon he was hard again.

"My my," she said.

Wordlessly, he rolled on top of her and entered an inch at a time. Her eyes widened with his incursion until he was fully in her, and she wrapped her arms around him. They lay, thus, for a moment, and then he began to slowly move in and out. Periodically, he withdrew completely, and, when she looked questioningly at him, he plunged into her again. Then, he sped up slightly. Then he slowed. He smiled at her and brushed hair from her head.

"Angel," she began again, but he kissed her into silence. She threw her arms around his neck, and he began to thrust harder and harder until she held on as best she could and their bodies rose and fell as one. She could feel her body shaking, and she began to repeat 'Oh God,' 'Oh God' as if it were a mantra which might save her. When her body shook violently, Angel raised up on his arms and thrust as violently and rapidly as he could. Maggie covered her face with her arms and began to writhe and shake. Angel's hips spasmed, and Maggie screamed as she came. But Angel didn't stop, and her orgasm gave way to a series of after-shocks. When he finally rolled off her, she lay mute.

Maggie put her hand sideways onto Angel's chest which rose and fell violently. As she felt his heart slow, she knew that her own was doing the same. With her other hand, she pulled the covers over them.

"What did you want to say a moment, ago?" Angel asked.

"I don't know," she said. Then, "Why are you so silent when we make love?"

He smiled. He had no idea. "I'm concentrating on you, I guess."

"I'm your piano?"

"You're my masterpiece painting."

"Can I tell you something, and you won't get mad?"

Angel smiled again. One of the dumbest questions people asked each other. But he nodded.

"I like that you don't hold my head and force it onto you when I'm, when we're, you know."

"I seem to remember grabbing your hair."

"But you don't push my head down on you. What you do is more like my digging my nails into you when I'm climaxing."

"Oh," he said. "Well, I'm glad you like my manners when I'm receiving a blowjob."

She punched him. "You're not funny." She lay her head down on his chest again. "And you always kiss me after."

Angel laughed. "I kiss you all the time. Why in the world wouldn't I kiss you after you'd just been so generous and technically proficient?"

Maggie punched him again. "You know what I mean."

"Yes, Jeffrey didn't kiss you after."

"No one ever has," she said.

He looked wryly at her. "Gracious, have there been that many?" This time, he grabbed her fist as she tried to hit him. "Why do girls hit me so often? Did you hit Jeffrey as often as you hit me?"

"Okay," she said, "I regret bringing up the subject. I don't want to talk about Jeffrey, and, no, there have only been two, but neither kissed me. And no, I never punched anyone I dated before. So, it must be your fault."

"My fault, huh?"

"Yes. You are an aggravating man. You never stop teasing me."

Angel nodded. That seemed fair. Every girl he had ever dated had hit him, usually, but not exclusively, after sex. Maybe he should be nicer to women?

Nah.

"Maggie, have you noticed that we can mention Jeffrey without your freaking out?"

"No, I'm freaking out internally. You just can't see it."

Angel laughed. "Fair enough."

Maggie sat up. "Well, I'm supposed to be shopping and cooking, and someone's kept me from doing either."

Angel shook his head. She was a piece of work.

Maggie dressed, kissed Angel, and left. Angel lay on his back with his jeans still around his knees and Thor perking up again. Angel stared at him. 'What? You think there's more on the horizon? Think again.' But Thor, as usual, ignored him. Like a bored dog, though, he eventually looked about him and lay down. Rest time.

Angel pulled his pants up and buckled his belt. He chose a shirt, buttoned it, and went downstairs to ready the house for the evening's debauch. There wasn't much to do. Sand and Eddie were setting up tables in The Blue Room, and Linda was covering them with tablecloths. Groucho and Blake brought chairs up from the Chapter Room in the basement. The Waste Land wouldn't begin playing until after dinner, so he didn't have to worry about them. He wondered if Wanda would show up.

He went to the cloak room and bought a Coke and a pack of peanut M&Ms. Maggie and the cold water at the falls had conspired to deplete his energy: they had sapped his vital fluids. Angel smiled at the *Dr. Strangelove* reference. He was a witty son of a bitch. Munching gratefully, he called Wanda's number to make sure Zach's band were still planning to play.

Zach's mother answered.

"Hi, I'm calling from Phi Psi," Angel said. "Just making sure Zach and the guys are still coming tonight."

"Is this Angel?" she asked.

Gulp. "It is."

"My daughter has a crazy crush on you," she said.

Angel didn't know what to reply to that. 'Oh good' or something like that?

"She's a good girl," she said. "I don't want you to hurt her."

Angel smiled. "I'm sure she told you I would never do that."

"She did. But she trusted that boy at Boston College, too, the one who mistreated her."

Angel felt almost grateful for that last comment. It gave him a surge of adrenaline just thinking about finding the guy who had hit Wanda and beating him unconscious. Like Tommy Whatshisname and Louise in fifth grade.

Now, he was in party mode, ready to scour the partygoers for socially maladjusted Dartmouth men, ready to defend or avenge, whichever seemed necessary. Pow. Lower the boom on that motherfucker. Yeah.

He locked the library. He didn't need anyone messing with the books, and he removed the lamps from every room and stored them in a closet. The pictures were already more or less permanently gone from the walls. They had been forced to survive too many parties and flying objects, and the night promised lots of good-natured property damage.

He wandered the house looking for something to do until go time.

Freak was in the card room playing chess with a guy Angel had never seen. It was pretty cool watching them. Freak with his Einstein hairdo and his opponent with his swarthy beard and Rasputin eyes and attitude. Freak's eyes were watery, as if he were about to nod off, but Rasputin stared at the board like an angry hawk, wary that the pieces might move about all on their own. They played with a timeclock, and their moves were almost precisely thirty seconds apart. Angel couldn't tell from the board who was winning. Freak had a habit of pulling his wiry curls skyward when he thought, and he was tugging hard enough to be bald by game's end. Angel didn't know whether that was good or bad. Angel sat on the arm of a chair to observe, but Rasputin raised his glare until it burned a hole straight through Angel's head. Angel took the hint and slunk off.

Cane came in with his friend Tim, a giant Indian with long, black locks. They disappeared upstairs with Groucho trailing behind them. Drug run? Since when did Cane do any kind of drug besides alcohol?

Angel gave up and lay down in his room. He bounced a baseball off the wall and tried to decide what to do about Maggie. She clearly wanted to be an exclusive couple, but every atom in Angel's body resisted the notion. He wasn't sure why. Maggie was smart and funny and sexy. Best of all, she really dug Angel.

Something, though, he didn't know what, held him back. She had a strong jealous streak in her which was annoying but wasn't all bad. Had Cassie been more demonstrative about her feelings, Angel might have been less promiscuous when they were a couple. But jealousy meant proprietorship. Angel had a problem with any kind of authority, but being solely owned like a holding company didn't appeal to him.

Or was it just the Wandas and Sharons of the world who held him back? Was he a 'yes, I love you, but I'd really like to fuck these other women' kind of guy?

He smiled. That sounded about right.

Shit.

Groucho interrupted his reveries to tell him that Maggie was back and wanted help in the kitchen.

He pulled his boots on and went to see what she needed.

"Hi Baby," she said and kissed him. "Would you get the rest of the stuff out of my car?"

Angel smiled and went outside. It was pitch black but still smelled of first spring, which made him think of Cassie for some reason. He had no idea why. God, his mind was all over the place. Focus, dipshit. Big doings tonight. And a fine woman with whom to do the doings.

Sand and Eddie passed him carrying boxes of wine and bags of groceries.

He almost laughed when he got to Maggie's car. In the back seat were three gigantic pots and two more bags of groceries. He carried the pots inside, juggling and almost dropping them. Maggie took one from him, and he put the other two on the kitchen table where they joined six bags of groceries. Sand went back outside for the last two bags.

"How many people are you cooking for?" Angel laughed.

"How many Phi Psi brothers will be here?" she asked.

"Probably thirty or forty."

"Well, that's just about how many Colby girls will be here."

Angel smiled. "You invited your dorm sisters?"

"Of course," she said. "Did you think I was going to let you go down there, get hit by Cane, and meet someone new? Now, get to work."

"Yes, ma'am. What do you want me to do?"

"Cut up some onions and mushrooms and start browning the meat," she said. "You're cooking all this."

"I thought you were."

"Nope. Your recipe. You cook. I'm going to get prettied up for you. I'll be back to make the salad." She kissed him and left him there.

Groucho leaned against the wall and chuckled. "Need any help?"

Angel looked at him. "Yes, a big fat joint would be a big help."

"Righto," Groucho said and disappeared.

"And a beer," Angel shouted after him.

"Righto," Groucho said.

Angel emptied the bags on the table. She had enough onions and meat to feed a hundred people. He sighed and began to peel and chop onions. When he had a dozen ready, he put the ground meat in one of the pots and mixed in onions and mushrooms.

Groucho came back in with his beer and a lit joint. He held it for Angel who had onion and beef fat all over his hands. Angel took a long hit while he washed his hands.

"You cook the onions with the meat?" Groucho asked.

"Yeah, the onions sweeten everything." Angel dried his hands and took the joint from Groucho. "Thanks," he said. He offered it back to Groucho who waved him off.

"Keep it," Groucho said.

Angel lay it down and sipped the beer. Man, it was cold and good.

"That's the tail end of the keg from Union Village," Groucho said. "Moe's delivered eight kegs. Is that right?"

"Yep. Gonna be a howling at the moon night. We'll need all the towels and bandages we can muster."

Groucho chuckled, nodded his head, and disappeared, leaving Angel to his cooking. He was glad to have something to do.

He broke the meat up with a wooden spoon and stirred until it was all browned. Then he put that pot and Maggie's three new pots on the stove top and turned the burners to low. He drained the meat and divided it up into the four pots. Then, he made the sauce. He opened and poured the cans of tomato sauce equally into the pots and chopped tomatoes and added them. Next, he chopped the garlic. Shit. He should have done that first. He always forgot how long it took to peal each little bit of garlic. He sprinkled those in and added salt and pepper. He stirred and drank his beer and relit the joint while the sauce simmered. He tasted it. Preliminary tasting was a crude measure of what the final would be, but he knew he needed more tomatoes, so he chopped the rest of them and dropped them in. He opened one of the boxes of wine and took out a bottle. Chianti. That would do. He liberally poured some wine into each pot. He chopped and added a Jalapeno pepper to each pot and stirred again. Time for his secret ingredient. He looked down the hall to ascertain whether any spaghetti spies were lurking, but they weren't, so he ladled nearly a cup of sugar into each pot and stirred. He turned them up and finished his beer while they came to a near boil. Then, he turned them all back down and left them to simmer uncovered.

Cane and Tim poked their heads in.

"Thought I smelled your spaghetti," Cane said.

"Smells good," Tim said.

Angel started. He had never heard Tim speak.

"It's an old Indian recipe," Angel said.

"Really? What tribe?" Tim asked. Tim was three quarters Lakota, and he wanted everything to be about his tribe.

"Arapahoe," Angel said.

"Oh," Tim said.

Cane looked at Tim dubiously. "He's shitting you, you dumb fuck."

"Oh," Tim said, and the two left.

Angel washed his hands and the knives he had used and went back out to check on things. Wiley, the drummer of the band walked by and nodded at him.

Oh, shit. Way too early for the band.

Angel went to the Blue Room and found Zach.

"No, no, no," Angel said. "You don't want to set up yet."

"Why not?" Zach asked.

"Because your instruments and amps will get covered in food, that's why."

"Oh," Zach said. "Okay." He motioned to the guys to stop what they were doing. "Have you talked to Wanda? She's here somewhere."

Oh, shit.

"Kidding," Zach said. "You should have seen your face. Wanda told me to do that."

"Wanda's hysterical," Angel said. "Tell her I'll get even with her."

"She'd like that," Zach said. He nodded and went to explain to the others that they needed to pack up and leave.

"When do you want us back here?" he asked Angel.

"About nine. Just peek in. You'll know."

Zach nodded and carried his mike stand back outside.

And then it began.

Maggie looked like a Roman goddess in her toga. She had gold dust sprinkled in her hair, and he had never seen her in so much make-up. Angel stripped to his shorts, and Maggie fastened a sheet around him. She safety-pinned it so well he thought it might never come off.

The Colby girls poured in wearing a variety of colored togas. There were pink ones and purple ones and creamy ones. Maggie's roommate Lucy looked diabolical in a black toga with black make-up.

The Phi Psi guys, by contrast, looked as if they had just wrapped sheets around themselves and tied knots to keep them on for as long as possible. Or as long as necessary.

The spaghetti sauce had been poured into large plastic punch bowls purloined from the dining hall. The pasta and salad were done the same way. The only utensils in sight were the ladles for the sauce. There were no forks and no napkins. Forty-eight bottles of wine were uncorked or unscrewed and placed randomly on the tables. Eddie and his new love, his microphone, sat at the head of the table. All in all, there must have been eighty diners. Many were forced to share chairs. Some sat on empty kegs. Eddie sat royally in one of the leather chairs from the tube room.

The hubbub drowned out the music which poured from the amplifiers on either side of the fireplace. A blaze lit the room and bounced from the mostly ruined chandeliers whose few remaining pendants attempted valiantly to diffuse and re-direct the light from the fire. When dinner was about to commence, Sand cranked the sound up and turned on the strobe lights.

Eddie stood, holding his mike and a bottle of Chianti.

"Everyone raise a glass, well, a cup, anyway, of your blood red wine to celebrate Dionysus, the deity who presides over our spring fling. Men of Dartmouth, women from wherever, join me in thanking the unfairly pneumatic Mary Margaret Miller who paid for all of the food and wine, freeing our social budget for beer and bands, and to our own fallen Angel, Mary Margaret's debaucher, who cooked all this shit."

"Your first name's Mary?" Angel whispered to Maggie who elbowed him in the ribs.

When everyone was standing and the red cups were lifted aloft, Eddie finished his blessing, "Let the games begin."

Great handfuls of pasta were heaped on paper plates and great glops of sauce were ladled atop the pasta. The Colby girls and the various other small groups of Smithies and Holyokies screeched delightedly as they tried to eat with their hands. The beauty of the Colby togas didn't last long as everyone began wiping spaghettied hands on each other's attire.

Wild Thing blasted over the amplifier, and it wasn't long before the wine and the joints making their way around the tables began to further suspend the rules of decorum. Soon, there were two distinct groups of diners, the guys who leaned over the plates and devoured the spaghetti, their faces practically in their plates, and the girls who trilled at impossibly treble octaves their amazement at the mess they were making. Angel wiped his hands on Maggie's toga to take a joint from Groucho. Maggie screeched her dismay and shoved a tomato in his face.

Dates became napkins, and it wasn't long before those who were unattached got into the act.

When the sauce bowls were nearly empty and the salad all but gone, Eddie rose and announced, "In time honored tradition, we of Phi Psi have voted, well, not really voted, Sand and I picked, Cane to throw out the ceremonial first pitch."

Cane rose to applause from the brothers and polite clapping from the uninitiated. He smiled as he circled the tables.

"What is he doing?" Maggie asked.

"He's choosing."

"Choosing what?"

"Shh," Angel said. "You'll break his concentration."

Gandalf put *Inna Gadda Da Vida* on the stereo, and Cane circled for what seemed an eternity. The tension built. Cane nodded, "In the tradition of Green Key Weekend, the official kick-off to spring in Hanover and all the renewal it promises, we honor Dionysus by choosing the Spring Maiden." He circled once more and stopped next to Maggie.

Maggie looked at Angel who shook his head and buried his head in his hands. "Angel?"

"It's too late. You've been chosen."

Cane proffered his hand, and Maggie took it uncertainly. He helped her to her feet. The Phi Psi brothers roared and the Colby sisters screeched their approval.

"Yay Maggie," the girls shouted. "Woo hoo!"

Cane lead her to the front of the room and bade her step up onto a chair and then onto the head table. Eddie graciously gave way.

"Congratulations," Eddie said. "And bravo. You are an excellent choice."

Maggie smiled and colored, but, holding the fold of her toga, she climbed up on the table and waved to the audience.

"And now, in honor of a new season, I hereby dedicate the first pitch to our Green Queen," Cane said.

The room grew quiet. *Inna Gadda Da Vida* was reaching its drum solo zenith. It was time.

Cane, without further ceremony, picked up a large handful of spaghetti from Eddie's plate and hurled it at Maggie. It splatted on her shocked chest, the pasta sticking to her lovely protuberances, and the sauce sliding down her belly and loins.

As one, save for Angel, the brothers arose and began pelting Maggie with spaghetti and salad.

Maggie shrieked with laughter and doubled over, trying unsuccessfully to cover herself from the onslaught.

Then, the guys turned on each other and on the other girls present. Maggie pointed a finger at Angel who shrugged. She picked up a handful of the gooey pasta and hit Cane squarely in the face.

As *Inna Gadda da Vida* reached its shuddering climax. the air filled with flying edibles. When the song finished, almost before the last notes had died away, Gandalf removed it and once again put the needle down on *Wild Thing.*

Maggie climbed down from the table and made for Angel with laughing menace in her eyes. He put his hands up in mock surrender. Maggie grabbed a handful of food but, just before she got to him, she slipped on loose salad, and her lovely ass hit the floor and skidded.

Pandemonium reigned as food flew, and the Phi Psi satyrs chased shrieking nymphs about the room. It was a scene straight from *Satyricon*. Boys chased their dates. Howling girls chased other howling girls, and the music and the strobe light chased everyone.

Togas began to come apart. The boys' sheets were mostly just wrapped and tied to them, so they fell apart rapidly. The girls' togas were mostly pinned, so they fared better, but it wasn't long before the room was filled with women in bras and panties running after or being chased by boys in their underwear.

Maggie cornered a protesting Angel. "Why didn't you warn me?" she laughed at him, pelting him with salad. Angel defended himself by pulling her to him. He shut her up by kissing her, and soon, they stood, wrapped about each other like a Rodin sculpture while the rest of the room was all motion and laughter.

Angel picked Maggie up and carried her from the room and up the stairs.

"Eek, sir, unhand me," Maggie laughed. Angel dumped her on her feet when they got to his room and ripped her toga from her. She was braless and wore the smallest panties he had ever seen.

He pulled his toga over his head without unpinning it, and Maggie dropped to her knees and tore down his shorts. She pushed him backwards on the bed and, almost as an afterthought, shoved the door closed with a foot.

With Angel on his back, Maggie knelt between his legs and stroked his dick. She bent to kiss it, but Angel suffered her mouth for only a few moments before he grabbed her hair and pulled her up to him. She lay flat on him, holding his face with her hands and kissing him madly.

He rolled her over until he was on top and kissed his way down her. He was rough with her. He crushed her right breast with his left hand while he took her left one in his mouth and sucked hard. Maggie moaned and clutched his hair. He kissed the inside of each hip bone and then followed their motion with his tongue down to her pussy. He spread her lips with his fingers and licked her lightly. Maggie moaned again and pounded the headboard with her fists.

He stopped abruptly, and Maggie opened her eyes and looked at him.

"Flip over," he said.

"What?"

"Flip over. Ass in the air."

Maggie paused, confused, but then did as he asked. With her face in the pillow and her rear up, she offered herself up to him. Angel roughly pushed her legs farther apart and then went back to work on her. He ran his fingers over her clit while he licked around it. Then he thrust first one, then two, then three fingers into her pussy. Maggie made an inchoate noise and clutched the pillow tight. She wriggled her ass against his onslaught. He worked his fingers in and out of her while he licked her. She trembled and then began shaking. They were accompanied by music and screams from below them which, though they couldn't distinctly be heard, could be felt because of the bass beats on the floor of the room.

Angel's hand and tongue left her, and she felt herself being penetrated by him. "Oh, God, yes," she groaned.

But that didn't last long, either. He withdrew abruptly and asked. "Is this okay?"

Maggie laughed and pulled on her own hair. "Yes. Yes. Fuck me, you asshole."

"Funny that you should mention that," he said, and Maggie felt his finger circling her rear opening.

God, it was so sensitive. Then his thumb was back in her pussy and his fingers were on her clit. As she trembled and began to build again, she felt his tongue tickling her ass.

That was all she could take, and she exploded, nearly shredding the pillow with her hands and teeth. In the middle of her convulsions, Angel rammed Thor deep into her, and her head snapped back. Angel grabbed her hair and pulled it even farther back as he pumped her. She shrieked her pleasure and came and came and came.

Angel stopped before he came. He withdrew slowly and then kissed her on each cheek.

"You certainly have a beautiful ass," he cooed.

Maggie slumped flat and lay there, trying to breathe or think. She didn't know which.

Angel sat on the edge of the bed and pulled matches and a joint from the nightstand. She watched incredulously as he lit it and took a deep drag.

"What are you doing?" she asked.

"Taking a break," he said and smiled at her. "You don't want me all worn out this early in the evening. I'm sure you'll want more when we go to bed later tonight."

Maggie buried her face in the pillow and screamed. She came up laughing.

"Kiss me," she said.

Angel put the joint down and lay beside her. He stroked her hair gently and bent over her. He kissed her long and sweetly.

"Like that?" he asked.

"Yes," she whispered. "Just like that."

"Do we taste good?" he asked.

Maggie nodded.

Angel lay beside her and held her.

"I always want you to kiss me after you've been down there," she said.

"Down where? In the Blue Room?" he asked.

Maggie punched him.

"Is that like kissing you after you blow me?" he asked.

She nodded. She covered her eyes with her hand and laughed. "Aaaaagh," she said. "The things you do to me."

Angel lay silent.

"You knew I just finished my period."

Angel nodded.

"And you still…"

Angel nodded. He rolled to her. "You always taste like Maggie."

Maggie began to cry softly against him. Angel smiled and held her tighter.

"Angel, don't be angry with me." She stopped and wiped her tears away. She laughed at herself and sniffed. "But I love you."

Angel smiled. He squeezed her and said, "I love you, too, Maggie."

"Truly?"

"Truly."

She searched his eyes as if looking for something, and then lay back against him.

"Oh, my God," she said.

"Yep."

They lay silent after that, listening to the beat of the music change at least three times. A slow song was playing.

"Dance with me?" Angel said.

"Do we need to talk about what we just said?"

"If you make me talk about it, I'll take it back," Angel said with a smile.

She searched his eyes and kissed him lightly. "Then, dancing it is," she said.

"Good."

Maggie got up and began to dress. She pulled her panties on and pulled a dress from her suitcase.

"Nope," Angel said. "It's a toga party."

"But my toga was half off and covered with food."

"Sorry," Angel smiled. "Everyone else will be half-naked and dancing. You can wrap your sheet around your waist if you want. But no fair dressing."

Maggie sighed. "What do you want me to wear?"

"Panties."

"Okay. What else? I can wear my bra, can't I?"

Angel smiled wickedly. "Panties."

Maggie went to him, and he put his arms around her. "Kiss me, then, and give me some of that joint. I'm not sure I have enough wine in me for this."

Angel kissed her. He re-lit the joint and they smoked. He kissed her nipples while she smoked, and she giggled. "That tickles."

Angel knelt and pulled her panties down. He nuzzled the down between her legs.

"No, Angel."

"No?"

She laughed, "You are incorrigible" and caressed his hair.

He rose and took her hand. She gave it gladly and went with him downstairs to face the mob.

The Blue Room had been cleared of tables. Chairs lined the walls and food was still everywhere. The walls looked like demotic, three dimensional, Kandinsky paintings. The Waste Land had set up and were playing *A Whole Lotta Love*. Zach even looked like Jimmy Page. His hair had gotten longer and his face had matured in the few months since Angel had first seen him.

Angel spotted his busty friend Louise and the same gang of co-eds who had been with her at Union Village. She saw him, too, and waved. Angel smiled and nodded. Louise made a 'come dance' gesture. Angel returned it with a 'maybe later' shake of the head. She stuck her tongue out at him and returned to her friends. Angel wondered if Eddie had seen them yet. He had been doing pretty well with the skinny, intense looking one.

Maggie saw Angel's exchange with Louise and punched him in the ribs.

"What?" he smiled. "She's a lesbian."

"Uh," Maggie said. "And you believed her? Why would a lesbian transfer to Dartmouth?"

Angel hadn't thought of that. Good question. He would have to ask Louise that later and maybe get another peek at her creamy white bosom. And those huge areolae and nipples that whispered, 'bite me.' He sighed.

Angel led Maggie to where Gandalf and Freak sat in the corner. Both looked completely gone. Billy sat next to him, smiling the blithe smile of the pleasantly drunk.

"Hey, Billy," Angel said. "You remember Maggie, I'm sure."

Billy nodded. "She's my girlfriend."

"Hi, Billy," Maggie laughed. "I hope Jane and I didn't get you into trouble with your parents."

"Are you kidding?" he said. "My mom drank herself silly. She didn't remember enough to be scandalized, and Dad probably went to the bathroom and jerked off. He thought you were great."

"I'm glad," she said, laughing.

Angel lifted one of Gandalf's lids and peered at his eyes. "Are you tripping?"

Gandalf smiled and nodded slyly. He looked so elfin when he smiled like that. Freak shook his head to the music, ignoring Angel and Maggie.

"Is anybody else?" Angel asked.

"Yup," Gandalf said. "And there's something bad going around. Mescaline or something. Two guys looked spooked and snuck out of here a few minutes, ago. Bad juju."

Angel nodded grimly. Shit. As he led Maggie to the dance floor, she asked him what Gandalf had said. "Bad what?"

"Juju," he said. "It's like an evil presence. There's some bad shit circulating. Do you see your girls?"

Maggie searched the crowd. She only saw about a dozen of her friends. Most were nearly naked and dancing madly.

"They seem happy," she said. "One of them is with Eddie. Is that all right?"

Angel nodded and pushed her backwards into the mob. "Dance for me, wench."

Maggie smiled and began to move her hips seductively. The music slowed during a long, improbable guitar solo, and Maggie danced to the guitar notes. Angel was mesmerized.

As, apparently, were several couples around her who gave way. Two of Maggie's friends broke away from their partners and joined her. The three began a dance routine they had clearly rehearsed, though probably not to Led Zeppelin. The crowd around them began to clap rhythmically, and Zach modified his solo and motioned for the drummer to do the same. The beat shifted to a simple four-four, and the girls really began to get down with it.

The tall dark-haired girl who had worn the black toga, worn being the operative term, because now she was clad only in black panties and a black bra, was clearly the best dancer. But, as she had been at Colby when Cane had first seen her, Maggie the Cat was the queen bee. Her body flashed in the strobe light, and her dark nipples exaggerated the movement of her breasts. The other girl, one of the originals Angel had seen her with at Colby, was a stubby blonde who struggled to keep up, but the wine was strong in her, and she danced well enough.

All Angel could see, though, was Maggie. Sand handed him a beer and clapped him on the shoulder. Angel smiled at him without his eyes leaving Maggie's or hers leaving his.

Sand and Linda hit the dance floor, followed by Eddie and a Colby chick, and the crowd filled in around the nubile trio.

Three or four beers later, Angel tried his best to dance with Maggie, who compounded his sense of awkwardness by laughing at him. Angel felt a tug at his arm and turned to see Gandalf beckoning him. Angel made a 'just a minute' gesture to Maggie who nodded and kept dancing. He needed to keep an eye on her. She had been drunk the night before and imbibed her share at Union Village. Now, she was downing wine with her friends at an alarming rate. Maybe she was dancing it off?

He lost Gandalf in the crowd but saw him in the hallway outside the Blue Room and followed him to the relative sanity of the tube room where Johnny Carson gave his monologue to an empty set of chairs.

"We have a situation," Gandalf said.

Angel peered at him. Gandalf was in some other galaxy. Angel smiled reassuringly. Never freak out a tripper.

"No," Gandalf said. "This is for real."

"Okay," Angel smiled. "What's up and why are we being so furtive."

"We're being furtive?"

"Never mind. What's up?"

"That bad juju I told you about, it's here."

"Ah," Angel said.

"There are two girls being attacked by it."

Angel's antennae trembled. "Where?"

Gandalf took his arm and led him to the card room. He pointed. Two girls sat at the card table in a single chair. One had her arms wrapped around the other to still her or comfort her, but both girls shook badly.

Angel turned to Gandalf. "Get Sand and Eddie."

Gandalf nodded and vanished.

Angel went to a chair across from the girls and sat. "Hey, girls. Are you all right?"

The black girl who was holding the other girl stared at him. Her eyes were super wide. She was clearly freaking out.

"What's your name?" Angel asked her.

"Marilyn."

"What's your friend's name?"

"Sarah," Marilyn said. "You're Angel, aren't you?"

Angel nodded. "I am. Tell me what's happening Marilyn. Did someone here hurt you? Or threaten you?"

Marilyn shook her head. "We drank something."

Angel nodded as if he understood. "With something in it, you mean? Like a drug?"

Marilyn nodded. Sarah raised her head. She looked absolutely terrified. "My head won't shut up," she moaned. "Make it stop."

Sand and Eddie showed up with Linda and Maggie in tow.

"They took something," Angel said.

"What?" Sand asked.

"I don't know. I'm working on that now," Angel said. "Sarah, what did you drink and who gave it to you?"

"A girl gave it to us. We thought it was wine. She was with a guy."

"Would you recognize her?"

Sarah cringed and shook, but Marilyn said, "I would."

Angel went to them and knelt before their chair. "Sarah, I want you to go for a walk with these two girls." He pointed to Maggie and Linda. "Maggie, put on a jacket and take Sarah for a walk."

"Where?" Maggie asked.

"Not far. Maybe to The Green and back. Try to get her outside her mind. We need to get their trip turned positive. Point things out to her. Make her look at things."

Maggie approached the girls. She took Sarah's hand and helped her off Marilyn's lap.

"They're both fully dressed, so they must have gotten here after dinner," Eddie said.

"Yeah, so they couldn't have taken anything more than an hour ago," Sand said.

"Somebody go find Gandalf," Angel said.

"I'm right here," Gandalf said peeking around the corner. Freak stood behind him.

"What do you think they took?" Angel asked. "Marilyn, tell Gandalf what you feel like."

Marilyn stared at Gandalf and Freak. She didn't look re-assured. "Is he a wizard?" She pointed to Gandalf.

"Yes," Angel said. "He can help. He knows magic potions and all sorts of things."

Gandalf approached her slowly. "Are you paranoid?" he asked. "Does everything seem dangerous or scary?"

Marilyn nodded.

"Do you feel speedy?"

"Speedy?"

"Jittery, antsy, like when you take speed to study for a test?"

Marilyn nodded. "My skin kind of crawls like there are bugs underneath it."

"Does my voice sound normal?" Gandalf asked.

"Yes."

Gandalf turned his back to her and whispered to Angel. "They're rushing pretty hard. Whatever they took is potent. It's bad shit, obviously cut with speed or arsenic or something. The good news? They're not getting sick. The bad news? This is probably something like cheap mescaline. They're probably looking at two hours or more of strong effects and another couple of afterburn."

"Shit," Angel said. "That's what I was thinking, too." He turned to Marilyn. "Marilyn, walk with me. See if you can point out the girl who gave it to you. Okay?"

Marilyn nodded. When she rose, she swayed as if dizzy.

"How much have you drunk?" Sand asked.

"Kind of a lot," she said. "Is that bad?"

"No," Angel said. "That's good."

He took her hand and led her to the Blue Room.

"Do you see the girl or the guy?" he asked.

Marilyn took a moment. She was clearly having a tough time focusing. Then she pointed to a girl leaning against the wall.

"Anybody know her?" Eddie asked. Angel and Sand shook their heads.

"Okay, Angel, you take Marilyn. Sand and I will get her out of here and find the guy."

"Eddie," Angel said.

"Yeah."

"Don't hurt the guy until you're sure he did something on purpose."

"I wouldn't dream of it," Eddie said.

"I'm with him," Sand said. "He'll behave."

Eddie smiled evilly, and Marilyn smiled goofily at him. Angel shook his head. Shit.

Angel grabbed a coat from the cloak room and put it on.

"Do I get one?" Marilyn asked.

"No, I want you to get cold," Angel said.

"Why?"

"It will make your head feel better."

"Angel," Gandalf said.

"Yeah?"

"No coffee or Coke. No stimulants."

Angel nodded. He gave Marilyn his arm, and they went outside. "Let's find Sarah," he said.

Marilyn nodded. She looked scared to go outside and dug her nails into Angel's hand.

They met Sarah, Maggie, and Linda at the base of the driveway.

"Sarah wanted to go back inside," Maggie said.

Angel nodded. They turned to go back in, too. Sand and Eddie emerged, roughly escorting the drug dispensing girl outside.

"We're going to Richardson Hall," Sand said.

"The guy's from there?"

Sand nodded. "I think I know the guy. We'll be back soon."

"Or in jail," Eddie said.

"This isn't a combat mission, Eddie," Sand said.

"You never know," Ed said darkly.

Sand shook his head. "You're seriously demented, you know that?" He kissed Linda and off they went.

"Do you feel any better?" Angel asked Sarah.

Sarah shook her head. "My skin hurts."

"The trees were scaring her," Maggie said.

"Take them to my room and play some Moody Blues or Procol Harum or something," he said.

"Where will you be?" Maggie asked.

"I'll be there in a minute. I just want to check and make sure there aren't any other fucked up girls wandering about."

Maggie nodded.

Linda and Maggie each took a girl and led her inside and up the stairs. Angel hung up his jacket and checked the house. He went down to the bar. No problems there. A game of bar bottles was raging and the floor was covered in broken glass, but it was quiet and, other than a passed-out Colby girl on one of the benches, everything looked fine. He peeked into the grotto. A group was playing beer pong, but, other than Erin, Blake Smooth's co-ed, there weren't any girls there, and no one looked completely fucked up.

"Beer pong?" Smooth asked Angel.

"Can't. On patrol," he said. Smooth raised a beer and nodded.

"You owe us your spring dues," Angel told Erin. "So does Meredith. I gotta pay for these shindigs," he said. Erin raised her beer and nodded in imitation of Blake.

Cute, Angel thought, but you still got to pay your fucking dues. Chicks.

Things had calmed in The Blue Room. Everyone had reached that point of maximum drunkenness when giddiness recedes and exhaustion begins to take its place. Zach and his guys were doing some weird take on *My Baby Done Left Me*. Angel kind of dug it and nodded to Zach. He scanned the crowd, but no one looked to be as zonked as Marilyn and Sarah. All he saw was a normal looking bunch of drunks. A pair of Maggie's friends made their way across the dance floor to him.

"Where's Maggie?" the stubby blonde asked.

"She's upstairs taking care of a pair of sick girls," Angel said.

"Can we help?"

Angel pointed to the stairs. "First door to the right."

The girls dutifully climbed the stairs and disappeared.

Gandalf tapped Angel on the shoulder. How the fuck did he always appear from nowhere?

"I need to get Freak back to his dorm," he said.

Angel nodded.

"Would you take us?"

"You mean like drive you?" Angel asked.

"No. Walk with us. Freak hasn't said a word in an hour, but I'm getting pretty heavy hallucinations," Gandalf said.

"Sure," Angel said. He motioned to Lucy, Maggie's friend in black, who had ditched her bra since he had last seen her.

She smiled and slunk over to him. God, she was fucking hot. Her breasts were twice what Angel expected and stared impudently at him.

"Yes, sir?" she said.

"Would you tell Maggie I'm walking these two losers home?" he said, pointing to Freak and Gandalf.

Gandalf smiled toothily at her. Freak just gawked at her bosom.

"Where is she?" Lucy asked.

"Upstairs, first door on the right."

"Like what you see?" she asked Freak.

"If he doesn't, I do," Angel nodded. "Ardently."

"Ooh, ardently, that's an odd compliment," she laughed.

"Sorry, I don't even know what that meant, and your matched set deserves more praise than I can muster this late in the evening."

"Yes," she said, glancing down at him. "Your master seems impressed, too."

Angel glanced down at the bulge in his underwear. Fuck, Thor, can't you keep any opinions to yourself? Angel nodded at her.

His eyes followed her out of the room and up the stairs. World class tits and ass. Superb attitude. And he had told Maggie he loved her because, why, exactly?

Because it was the truth, dumbass.

Yes, but tactically stupid.

He sighed for so much beauty.

He put his jacket and boots on and escorted Freak and Gandalf to Wheeler Hall where he deposited them, safe, sound, and trippy. They had hours of bliss ahead of them.

"Stay put," he told them.

"We will," Gandalf said. "We'd get lost if we went out on our own."

"Any other tips for dealing with those girls?"

"Bad trips usually mean bad stuff in the drug. Arsenic or something. Get them to smoke. It might bring them down a little. If distracting them and entertaining them doesn't work, try a warm shower. There's always Sand's kung-fu treatment, too."

"Kung-fu treatment?"

"He'll show you."

Angel plodded back across campus. The warmth of the day had been replaced by a decided chill. He shook briefly. It felt good, though, and it cleared his head.

People were trickling out of Phi Psi when he got back. Several Colby girls passed him, giggling and waving. He hoped they were fit to drive home.

As he climbed the stairs to his room, he could smell the pot from the hallway.

Inside, Maggie and Lucy were sitting on the floor talking to Marilyn and Sarah in hushed tones. Maggie's other Colby friends were gone. Rod Stewart sang *Maggie May* on his stereo. God, he hated that song.

Maggie went to Angel and whispered in his ear. "See if you can get them to smoke some pot. Lucy and I tried but failed. Lucy keeps rolling joints, and she and I just keep getting more stoned."

Angel smiled. "*Maggie May*?"

"Hey, it was their choice."

Angel nodded. He sat in front of Marilyn and looked at her eyes. She was still pretty far gone. Sarah was worse, though. She had terror and paranoia etched in her pupils.

Maybe if he could get one to smoke, the other would follow suit.

"Marilyn, remember me?"

"Sure, you're Angel. I love your radio show," she said. She made a pouty face, "You left us."

"I'm back. How do you feel?"

"Creepy. My skin still feels bad."

"Would you like to smoke a joint with me?"

"I don't smoke pot."

"Okay. Just try it this once. It will counter the bad juju inside you."

He lit a joint Lucy proffered to him and took a deep drag.

"Have you ever smoked a cigarette?" he asked.

Marilyn nodded.

"Same thing. Here." He handed her the joint, but she trembled and withdrew. "Okay," he said. "We'll do it a different way. Just pretend you're going to kiss me." Marilyn looked confused but nodded. Sarah watched them closely. Angel turned the joint around until the lit part was inside his mouth. He leaned forward slowly. Marilyn met him, and he shot-gunned a stream of smoke into her mouth. She looked startled but covered her mouth with her hand and tried not to cough.

"Hold it," Angel said. He smiled. He could hear himself using his radio voice. Mister Dulcet Tones. "Okay, now just let it escape." Marilyn opened her lips and a stream of smoke leaked out. "Good," he said. "Now, again," and he repeated the process.

He sat back and took a hit for himself. It tasted good, not Maggie good, but pretty damn fine. It really had been a long day. "Now, just listen to my voice and see if you don't feel better." Marilyn sat back against the bed, and Sarah leaned against her.

"Two of my friends went to find out what you took and to punish the guy who did this," Dulcet Angel intoned. "You're fine. You feel bad, but you'll feel good soon. Are you and Sarah both Dartmouth students?"

Marilyn nodded.

"Are you roommates?"

She nodded.

"It's nice that you are taking care of Sarah even though you don't feel good. I'm proud of you. What schools did you go to before Dartmouth?"

"I went to Smith. Sarah is from Bryn Mawr."

"Nice. Sarah, I've heard Bryn Mawr is beautiful."

Sarah huddled tighter against Marilyn.

"Marilyn, I practically lived at Smith the last couple of years. I was in love with a Smithie. I still know several people there. What is your major?"

"Political Science."

"To be a lawyer?"

Marilyn nodded.

"Did you ever have a course with a professor named Spencer? I don't remember her first name."

"Uh huh, Babs."

"Pardon?" Angel said.

"Babs. Her first name is Babs. I took two courses from her. She's the one who told me to apply to Dartmouth."

"She's really good. I sat in on a bunch of her classes my freshman year." Angel reached out and caressed Marilyn's cheek. "Do you feel any better?"

"Some."

"You know what would feel good? A shower. It might make your skin feel more normal."

"Okay."

Angel turned to Maggie. "Feel like helping Marilyn with a shower?" Maggie nodded.

"No," Marilyn said. "You."

"Me?"

"You help me."

Angel looked at Maggie who shrugged and nodded. He got a fresh towel and took Marilyn to the bathroom. A pair of guys Angel didn't know were snorting some coke from off the edge of the sink.

"You guys," Angel said. "Out."

The two looked startled. "What the fuck?"

"Out. Now."

They stared at Angel for a second but left. When they were gone, Marilyn held her arms out like a little kid waiting for mommy to undress her. Angel unbuttoned her blouse and removed it. Her arms were still out, so he unhooked her bra and took it off, too. She had soft, lovely breasts and the darkest nipples Angel had ever seen. The only black girl Angel had ever slept with was more mocha colored than Marilyn and not nearly so beautiful. Thankfully, Thor didn't awaken to check out the scenery. Angel turned the hot water on in the shower and finished undressing Marilyn. He motioned for her to get in the shower.

"Come with me," she said.

Angel sighed. The things he did out of duty. Well, a man's gotta do what a man's gotta do. So, he stepped with her into the water.

She stood facing him under the shower with her eyes closed.

"Too hot?"

She smiled and shook her head.

"Turn around," he said, and she did so. He took a handful of shampoo and gently kneaded it into her hair. He rubbed her scalp and then the back of her neck. He moved to her shoulders and back. "How does this feel?"

She just nodded.

Angel soaped her back and her arms and gently rubbed. He turned her to rinse and tried to deal with her front without touching her chest or her middle, but he couldn't stop his eyes from caressing her. Marilyn opened her eyes and caught him looking. She smiled. He smiled, too, and motioned for her to rinse. She did so and immediately turned to him again.

"Do my face," she said.

Angel lightly soaped his hands and began to lave her forehead. He massaged her temples and Marilyn moaned. Shit. Her moan and the view had finally awakened Thor.

The curtain pulled back, and Maggie stood there. She saw everything at once and her eyes tightened.

"Sarah's freaking that Marilyn's not with her," she said. She gave Angel a look and left.

"Rinse your face," Angel said. She let the stream bounce off her face and smiled again. "This feels so good," she said.

"No more pins and needles in your skin?"

"No, you made them go away."

"I'm going to take care of Sarah," he said. "Are you okay by yourself?"

"There are spots you didn't wash," she said.

"Uh huh," he said. "Well, you can do those for yourself."

"It's not the same," she said.

Shit. Was every girl he met a minx?

He tried to dry with as little of the towel as he could so she wouldn't have to use a sopping one, but Maggie re-appeared with another towel. Angel smiled at her, and she returned a tight-lipped smile.

"Will you stay with Marilyn?" he asked.

Maggie nodded.

"Mags, I swear," he began.

"Go. I was just fucking with you," she said. Angel gave her a kiss and went to deal with Sarah.

Sand and Eddie had returned, and Sand was ministering to her. Sarah shook even worse if possible.

"Did you find the guy?" Angel asked.

"No," Sand said. "We got to The Green and the girl bolted. Eddie was too lazy to chase her."

"I'm lazy? You could have chased her."

"I was tired," Sand said.

Eddie looked at Sarah's eyes. "Do we need to get her to Dick's House?"

"I don't think so," Angel said. "Sand, Gandalf said something about some kung-fu thing you do. Do you know what he's talking about?"

Sand nodded grimly. "Let's get her down to the bar."

"She won't go anywhere without Marilyn," Lucy said. "She won't even let me touch her."

"Who are you?" Eddie asked.

"I'm Maggie's roommate."

"I'm Eddie," he said and offered his hand. She shook it.

"For God's sake Eddie. This isn't pick-up time," Sand said.

The door opened and Maggie and Marilyn walked in. Lucy wrapped a blanket around Marilyn who smiled goofily.

"Well, it looks as if there is life after whatever they took," Eddie said.

"Yeah, all we need to do is get Angel naked with Sarah and have him rub her all over," Maggie said.

"That was nice," Marilyn said.

Everyone looked at Angel.

"What?" he said.

"Marilyn, help us get Sarah downstairs, okay?" Sand said.

Marilyn nodded and enfolded Sarah in the blanket with her. The whole gang went down to the bar. Thankfully, it was empty save for the smell of beer and all the shattered glass on the floor. Clearly, beer bottles had been the bar game of the evening.

"Ed, kill the music," Sand said. Eddie nodded and went behind the bar and switched off the stereo. It got eerily quiet, and, with the damp, cold granite walls, it felt sepulchral. "Anybody need a beer while I'm back here?" Ed asked.

"I do," Lucy said. He poured one for her and one for himself.

"Okay, Ed, you know the drill," Sand said. Eddie nodded and motioned for everyone to sit on the benches beside the bar.

Sand went to the far end of the room and turned to face them. Sarah sat between Marilyn and Maggie. Everyone watched Sand. Angel had no clue what was about to happen.

Lucy sat next to Ed, sipping her beer. She looked faintly turned on by the whole thing. Ed took her hand. "Watch this," he said. "This is cool."

Sand sat on a bench and spoke softly while he removed his combat boots and shrugged off his coat. "This was taught to me by a pair of Buddhist monks I saved in Hanoi. They were being bullied by some drunk G.I.s. We became friends, and they taught me meditation. This is from a Tai Chi breathing drill. Sarah, I want you to watch everything. Don't look at just my eyes or my feet. Expand your vision. Watch all of me." Sarah glanced at Marilyn but nodded. "I want everyone to breathe with me. In," and he slowly breathed in and raised his arms. "And out." He lowered his arms as he exhaled. "In. Out. In. Out." When he had created a rhythm and everyone was breathing with him, he began his dance. He carefully placed a bare foot in front of him and slowly shifted his balance to that foot. Glass crackled beneath him as he stepped. Sand slowly went through what looked like a martial arts exercise, except it was totally rhythmic, with every movement matching his breathing.

He crushed glass with each step and each turn, but his face showed that he felt nothing. He looked seraphic, and Angel could almost feel the intensity of his concentration. Angel turned to watch Sarah. She was mesmerized. Her breathing matched Sand's movements, and her pupils had lost their fearful edge.

Sand danced his way to them and then back. He did it once more. He was so deliberate, that it must have taken him five minutes or more to dance the fifty or so feet. Maggie nodded to Angel that Sarah's body was, indeed, relaxing.

When he finished. Sand sat on the floor in the classic Buddha pose, legs crossed and arms at his side with his finger forming a circle. He began to chant his personal mantra.

Angel chanted Om with Sand, and soon, the room was buzzing with the mantra.

Then, Sand stopped. He looked at Sarah. "Better?" he whispered. She nodded mutely. Sand gestured with his eyes to take her away, and Maggie and Marilyn led Sarah back up the stairs. Angel and Eddie arranged chairs around the dying fire in the Blue Room, and they sat contemplating the splattered food and spilled beer cups.

"This must have been quite a party," Marilyn said.

"About typical," Eddie said. "I need some air. Anyone feel like a walk?"

"I do," Lucy said.

"I do, too," Sarah said. Everyone looked at her. It was the first time she had spoken of her own volition. She had a funny, squeaky voice.

Angel re-lit the joint and passed it around. This time, Sarah partook on her own. Marilyn took it and inhaled. "I think I have a new vice," she said.

Maggie gave her a dark smile which said, 'You better be talking about pot and not about my man' in girl language.

Everyone but Angel and Maggie put on coats and left.

Maggie kissed Angel.

"I swear, Maggie," Angel began, but she put a finger to his lips and smiled.

"I know," she said.

Angel looked about him. "Maybe if we wait until morning, this mess will clean itself up."

Maggie nodded. "You go on up to bed. You look exhausted. I'm going to check on Sand. I'll be up in a minute."

Angel nodded. She really was a good girl. He rose and groaned. He was getting too old for this shit. He smiled at her and went up to his room.

Angel lay on his back for what seemed an eternity, staring at the ceiling in the candlelit room. Maggie came and went twice, getting another towel each time. Finally, she crept back in and slid under the covers next to him, shivering.

"What were all the towels for?" he asked.

"Sand," she said.

"Sand?"

"His feet were slashed to bits. You didn't think he was doing some Shaolin magic trick, did you?"

Angel nodded. He had.

"Why didn't Linda take care of him?" he asked.

"Linda's been asleep for two hours," she said.

"Oh."

She cuddled against him. "Interesting evening," she said.

He smiled. "Like Eddie said, pretty typical."

She kissed his chest. "Is that what you do all the time?"

"What?"

"Run around taking care of people and righting wrongs?"

"Pretty much."

She pondered that. "Your world is very different from mine," she said finally.

"Sorry," he said and caressed her hair.

"Sorry? It's invigorating," she said. "My world, at least when I'm home, is pretty much all vanity and narcissism. Things are different when you grow up surrounded by nothing but females."

Angel smiled.

"Angel."

"Hmm?"

"We're not going to make love again tonight, are we?"

"Probably not. I'm pretty beat. I'll try if you're feeling neglected."

She squeezed him. "God, no," she said. "I'm the opposite of neglected, whatever that would be." She chuckled. "Taken care of, I guess. You make me feel so, I don't know what."

Angel said nothing. He drew his Buddha on the wall with his fingers.

"Angel."

"Hmm?"

"Did you mean it?"

Angel leaned on his elbow and kissed her. "I think so."

"But you hadn't thought about what it meant about our future when you said it, had you?"

"No," he said truthfully.

"Does that scare you?"

He smiled. "No. Not much scares me. Heights are about all I can think of."

"I'm serious," she said.

"I am, too."

"Say it again, then," she said.

"Nope, too tired," and he flopped back down.

It was Maggie's turn to lean on her elbow and look at him.

"Say it," she said.

"Not gonna happen."

She poked his ribs. "Say it."

He turned away from her. She dug her nails into his ribs. "It really pisses me off that you aren't ticklish." No response from him. She balled her fist and pounded his back. "Tell me you love me."

"I'm sleeping."

She punched him again. He turned and grabbed her arms, pinning her to the bed. He kissed her and looked her squarely in the eyes.

He smiled broadly and whispered, "I love you."

He kissed her again and then turned away from her. As she spooned against his back, she kissed his shoulder blade and silently mouthed,

"I love you, too, Angel."

Chapter Twenty-Four

Sunday April 11, 1971
Easter Sunday

ANGEL FELT SOMETHING TICKLING HIS EYEBROW AND flicked at it. Whatever it was went away for the moment and he rolled over. But there it was again. He opened his eyes grumpily to see Maggie beaming at him.

"He is risen," Maggie chortled.

"Not hardly. I'm still asleep," Angel groused. "And that's sacrilegious."

"Not you, sleepy head. Him," she said and grabbed his dick.

Angel looked down. "That's a peehard."

"A what?"

"It's a fake erection because I need to pee," he said. He groaned and slung the covers from him. Maggie sat nude next to him, her lovely bosom dangling close to his face. He was tempted to take a nip. That would teach her to interrupt his beauty sleep. "What time is it?"

"I don't know," she said. "Noon, maybe. I've been watching you sleep for hours. You snuck out of bed while I was asleep. It was nice to see you finally sleep."

Angel pointed to his desk. "I wrote last night."

"I know," she said. "I read it. Somebody was in a romantic mood."

Angel sat up. The evening's shenanigans were coming back to him, including the 'I love you' stuff. He rubbed an eye and kissed her. "Come on. You can help me pee."

Angel trod naked to the bathroom, and Maggie followed in one of his Harley tee shirts.

Angel went to a urinal. "You hold it."

"What do I do with it?"

"Aim it at the urinal."

Maggie looked dubious but took hold of his shaft and aimed for the center of the urinal. "It's pretty hard. Are you sure this isn't for me?"

"Nope. You'll see."

Angel leaned his head back and let go of his pent-up urine. Aaah, it felt good.

"I can feel the pee running through it," Maggie said.

When the stream stopped, Angel told her, "Now, shake it."

Maggie did. She flicked the last lingering drop off with her finger.

"Now, lick it," he said.

"Ugh. Really?"

"No. Just kidding."

Maggie gave him a bold stare, leaned over, and kissed the tip. Then she kissed him. "There," she said.

Angel turned on the shower.

"I take it we're showering?" she said.

"I don't know about 'we,' but I'm showering."

Angel felt the temperature and climbed in to purify his soul. Maggie wasn't far behind.

"Someone's a grouch," she said and kissed his back. "Are you regretting last night?"

"No," he said. "I'm glad we helped those girls, and that really was a great party."

Maggie slapped his butt hard. "No. You know what I'm talking about. Do you want to take it back?"

Angel turned to her and pulled her under the hot spray. He kissed her softly. "Not a chance. You, my lovely lass, are doomed. Why, are you thinking of taking it back?"

"Nope. I'm in for the whole ride."

"Hmm," he said. "The whole ride, huh?"

He dunked her head under the shower and began to shampoo her.

"This feels good," she sighed. "I'll bet the black girl last night enjoyed it, too."

"Marilyn," Angel murmured. "She did. I think she came twice."

"Ha ha. You're so funny," she said. "I've never done that before. It was kind of fun."

"You've never watched me cleanse a Nubian princess? Well, I can arrange another performance. I think Marilyn and I bonded."

"No, silly. I've never held a man's thing while he peed."

"Oh. And that's a big deal because?"

"It was intimate," she said. "The whole weekend was. Do you remember how it started?"

"You almost caught me banging Jane?"

"No. Somebody's really full of himself this morning," she said. Angel pushed her under the water and rinsed her hair as thoroughly as he could. She laughed and pushed him away to do it properly. Men. "I was on my period. That's how the weekend started."

Angel watched her squeeze water from her hair. "So?"

"So? You are a nincompoop. To a girl, she's gross then. For days before, you feel swollen and bloated, and then, you feel like your insides are going to drop out. It's gross. You certainly don't want to be doing things with a boy, because then he'll think you're gross, too."

Angel kissed the back of her neck. "You're never gross to me."

"I know. That's what's so romantic. You really believe that Walt Whitman 'the body is pure' stuff."

"Mags, you're going to have periods. Am I supposed to lock you in a closet or make you walk twenty paces behind me? It's no different than your having a cold or something. I'm going to love you all the time."

"Angel, you just don't know how odd that is to a girl. Like holding you while you peed. Most people would thing that's gross. You make it seem intimate."

"Well," he smiled. "You have to admit, it is intimate."

"It is. You're right. But we're not trained or conditioned that way. Even showering. You showered with that girl."

"Marilyn."

"With Marilyn, and it was no big deal to you. To a girl, showering is so private," she said. "I've never showered with a boy before."

"I didn't know that," he said. "I would've been gentler."

"You laugh, but I'm serious."

"I'm not laughing," Angel said. He pulled her to him.

She looked up at him. "This is all new to me, and you have no idea how scary it is. Like the word 'love.' You think I wanted you to say that to me?"

"Didn't you?"

"Yes, but it terrifies me. I've never had a boy say it to me and mean it before." She gripped his jaw. "You did mean it, didn't you?"

"Well."

"Oh, God. You're going to take it back, aren't you?"

"No," he laughed and kissed her. "I was going to tell you that while I watched you sleep, I tried to look up a line from D.H. Lawrence. I pawed through *Women in Love* and *Sons and Lovers* but couldn't find it. One of his male characters tells a woman he loves her and immediately thinks, 'the moment I uttered the word it began to cease to be true.'"

"Angel?"

"Hush and let me finish. I kept waiting to feel that way, or, at least, to have some doubt, but I never did. I just watched you sleep and wrote sappy poetry. Look at me

Mags," he said and tilted her chin upwards. The spray of the water formed a kind of wet halo around her hair. It got in her face and she laughed and shook her head. "Mags, I have said it to another woman, and I meant it then, and I mean it now."

She searched his eyes and seemed satisfied by what she saw. She leaned against his chest and sighed.

While they dressed, Maggie chattered happily. Angel barely listened. His mind had moved to Faulkner. His class had finally gotten around to *The Sound and the Fury*, a novel which took place, appropriately, on Easter weekend.

He sat at his desk and opened the book. This was going to be epic. Maggie made his bed and began to pack.

"Are you leaving?" he asked.

"Did you hear anything I just said?" she laughed.

"No. Was it important?"

"Evidently not. I'm going back to Colby. I need to read *One Flew Over the Cuckoo's Nest*."

"Come to Sanborn and read with me."

"Oooh. Your holiest of places. Okay."

As they crossed The Green, Angel veered to the right.

"Where are we going?" Maggie asked.

Angel pointed. "Rollins Chapel."

Maggie tightened her grip on his arm.

Angel tugged open the thick wooden door, and they entered. The atmosphere was somber. Specks of dust drifted desultorily in the light slanting through the stained-glass windows. Angel thought of Quentin Compson watching the accreted dust swirl in *Absalom, Absalom*. That was good. His Faulkner mood was reviving.

Maggie gasped and went to the great sculpture in the outer chamber of the old church. Angel followed her, smiling. "Angel, it's Noah's Ark."

Sculpted in dabs of iron, the ark stretched some ten feet or so, with its finely fashioned pairs of animals huddling together in terror as the old vessel struggled against the ferrum waves.

Angel watched Maggie circle it. He could feel the holy hush of the old tragedy in the darkened place. Maggie touched a bird lightly and then wandered into the main chapel. Her eyes reached up to the Romanesque wooden beams. She turned to Angel with tears in her eyes.

"I thought you might want to pray," he said. "It's Easter. The particular moment which augurs our eternal series of resurrections into new and better selves."

"Will you pray?" she asked.

Angel shook his head. "I don't know how to explain this, but my whole life feels like prayer. That's what my books are, meditations on the sorrows of the world and gratitude for the courage and strength to turn grief into unspeakable beauty. Like this chapel. Martin Luther King preached here. But it's also used for Jewish services. This is the spiritual epicenter of the college."

Maggie looked long at Angel. Then, she approached the altar and knelt.

Angel watched her and marveled. She wasn't as cute and full of life as Wanda. Nor was she as intellectually inspired as Cassie. No, Maggie's beauty was old and Catholic. Her dark hair and dark eyes, her long, lean, abundant form. Angel thought her the most beautiful woman he had ever known. And her beauty had never seemed more profound than when she knelt in the old chapel, praying for what? Eternal love? Thanks for all her blessings? He didn't know. But she looked lovely when she was thus consumed.

When she rose, she again had tears in her eyes. Angel wiped them away and kissed her. He took her hand and led her back out into the light. Resurrection had never seemed so real as it did that day, walking from the old gloom into the green and blue of a Hanover spring. He could practically smell the grass growing.

Later, as they sat reading in Sanborn, chairs turned outwards facing The Green, Angel broke from his Faulknerian trance to watch her again. She read with her legs pulled up almost to her chest, playing with a strand of hair as the words wove their magic. She had her lips slightly parted, as if she were about to speak or sigh. At one point, she darted a quick glance at him and caught him watching her. She smiled and reached to him, squeezed his hand, and returned to Kesey.

Mrs. Sellers brought him another cup of coffee and a pile of chocolate chip cookies.

"Would your lady friend like anything? Some tea, perhaps?" she whispered.

"Mags."

Maggie looked up, startled.

"Yes?"

"Coffee or tea?" Mrs. Sellers said.

"No, thank you," Maggie smiled shyly and returned to her book.

The two read until the day darkened. Angel filled pages with notations and page numbers, but Maggie hadn't lifted her eyes from her book except to make sure that Angel was real and hadn't vanished. That this life was really hers.

Finally, Maggie closed her book and looked outside.

"I have to get back," she said, taking his hand again.

"Can't you stay and drive back in the morning for class."

"No. I have a chemistry study group."

"They won't miss you," he said.

"They might. I'm the leader."

"Of course, you are," he laughed. He made to get up.

"No," she said. "You stay and work."

"I should walk you back to Phi Psi," he said.

"No," she said. "If you sit in your chair and keep on reading, it will be as if this day never ended."

She rose. He pulled her face down to him and kissed her softly. She caressed his face and left without a word. Angel watched her walk the length of The Green which was lit only by gas lamps. The moon hadn't made an appearance yet, so Maggie walked from light to shadow and back into the light again. Angel smiled and took a sip of his now cold coffee.

He shook his head and picked up *Absalom*. He flipped to the part he sought. Henry faced Bon for the zillionth time at the Sutpen gate.

Time for a death, Angel thought. His mind re-entered nineteenth century Mississippi, and he, too, stood watching and waiting, just as the now never to be married Judith must have done inside Sutpen's crumbling mansion.

And Henry and Bon stared at one another in their fatal moment, just as they stared on the stage of Angel's brain two hundred years later.

Chapter Twenty-Five

ANGEL SANG THE FINAL VERSE WITH THE RECORD. WHEN it finished, he lifted the needle and clicked on his microphone.

Yep. 'The women going crazy' about that cocaine. That was Spoonful by Charlie Patton. I know you're used to the Cream version with Clapton on the guitar, but Cream was covering old Charlie. Sorry it was so scratchy, but that was recorded in 1927, so we can just be grateful to hear it at all. The miracles of modern technology.

I picked a drug song because that's what I wanted to rag about tonight. We had a situation at Phi Psi last weekend, and I'm still pissed off. Two of our co-eds, remarkably comely co-eds, I might add, had their drinks spiked by a guy and a chick not from Phi Psi. Now, I know that's the topic of fun in current drug movies, but, in real life, it's serious shit. Seems this weasel put some cheap mescaline in these chicks' wine. They freaked, and it took hours to chill them out. We nabbed the girl who handed the wine to them, but the guy got away, and, when the girl was leading our posse to find the guy, she bolted, never to be seen again.

If you're that guy, we will find you, and it won't be pretty. If you're that chick, and you're a co-ed, remember that there aren't that many of you, and we'll see you crossing campus one day. I know, FCC and all that, you can't threaten bodily harm over the airwaves. But I am doing exactly that. I most certainly am.

We will teach you the first drug rule: never, ever, give anybody anything she didn't ask for. Not under any circumstances.

And we'll brand it on your scrotum with a hot poker.

My second topic is connected, but it's a lot cheerier.

We have a couple of co-eds who are social members of Phi Psi. I'm planning on inviting a bunch more to join.

So, I put forth a simple question: why don't fraternities open their doors to co-eds. My fraternity consists mostly of nerds and social losers, but we have chicks, black guys, Asians, an Indian, and a couple of guys of mysterious sexuality. I think they're queer, but they may not know themselves. They mostly hang out in the tube room screaming answers to Jeopardy.

Which is a discussion for another day. Do we have to make it so tough for homosexuals to admit to the world who they are? I know their families make them suffer. I have a good friend trying to tell his folks, and it's debasing. Do we have to be rough on them, too?

But, back to fraternities. I don't even think the Afro-American house is welcoming co-eds. Everybody wants chicks at parties. But don't you also want them around to talk to? To study with? To just hang with? A couple of my closest friends in high school were chicks. Did I bang them? Sure, but they were friends first. The rest was just dessert.

So, local houses, open yourselves to the co-eds. Invite them to join. Oh, I hear the gnashing of alumni teeth from afar. Two hundred years of tradition down the drain.

Yeah, well screw you. We're starting a new two hundred-year tradition. How about that?

And, finally, bad news for those of you who suffer through my rants. I've been asked to do programs three nights a week next year. I haven't decided what I'm going to do, yet, but only Wednesday will be a Blues night. The other two would be my choice. Any ideas? (Other than the usual 'get off the air. You blow.') Call the station with your suggestions and votes. Anybody want a jazz hour? Or a guitar night? Or a female vocalist night?

Oh, that reminds me. I want to apologize for that Motown came from Perry Como comment. Apparently, that riled a bunch of brothers up, and my buddy JB has threatened to beat me senseless unless I apologize. So, here it is. Mister Como, I apologize.

And we're ending this set with the Dope Head Blues by Victoria Spivey and Lonnie Johnson. Victoria will be the one singing. It's from 1927 and even scratchier than Spoonful was.

Enjoy. Love you guys. Love you girls more.

Everyone say Hi to Maggie the Cat. I hit her with the L word last weekend. Hope she hasn't panicked and bolted.

Angel clicked off his mike, took a sip of Coke, and dropped the needle on the record. He lit a joint and sat back to listen to Victoria, who sang 'Just give me one more sniffle, Another sniffle of that dope....'

Chapter Twenty-Six

Friday April 16, 1971
Practicing the Dark Arts

ANGEL WAITED LONG BEFORE ANSWERING. HE WANTED TO get it right.

"No," he said. "Brooks is wrong. Caddy isn't the center of the novel. For starters, the book is 'a tale told by an idiot', but 'signifying nothing' isn't true. Faulkner reveals himself as the tragic ironist he is when he picked the title. Macbeth was howling at his own impotence to order his world. Shakespeare certainly wasn't a nihilist. Nor was Macbeth, really. His was an emotional outburst at the death of his wife and at all the blood he had waded through. *Macbeth* isn't a nihilistic play. It is more a grinding away of falsities, like *King Lear*, until nothing but the raw nerve is left."

"So, Cleanth Brooks and everyone who knew Faulkner personally and wrote on him are wrong about Caddy and wrong about *The Sound and the Fury*?" Cara said. Her tone exuded contempt.

Angel stared at her. "Yes," he said. "They were all wrong."

"They spoke with Faulkner. They knew his intent in writing the book," she said.

"Careful," Professor Stone said, smiling. "You're giving Angel ammunition."

Angel looked briefly at Stone and then back at Cara. "Professor Stone means you are offering up the stalest of tropes. You do know of the intentional fallacy?" he asked. "That it doesn't mean shit to a tree what the author intended."

"But it's his novel," Cara said. She looked abashed. She did know the term and was caught in an Angel trap.

"No," Angel said. "It's the reader's novel. If he meant for us to like a character and we don't, tough shit. Faulkner's dead. The novel is sitting in my hands speaking to me."

"And it says?" Stone prodded.

"It says that, like the title, it begins and ends with the inchoate voice of Benjy, the idiot. His section and Jason's, a different type of idiot, and Dilsey's become brackets around Quentin, not around Caddy. Even Caddy knows the world and the novel are Quentin's. She names her daughter Quentin for that reason. It's not Quentin who is obsessed with Caddy. It's the other way around."

"But Quentin tells father the exact opposite," Charles Dell said. Charles was a thin, sensitive Lakota from some polar region in North Dakota and was smart as shit.

"Again, who cares what Quentin says?" Angel asked. "Polonius says lots of intelligent stuff in *Hamlet*, yet we know him to be a fool. You can't believe a character's interpretation of things around him. No, Quentin's lament to his father isn't nihilistic or sacrilegious or even tragic. Like Macbeth's outburst, it is more like raw synapses sending messages to the mouth to scream. That's why his father doesn't take him seriously."

"If the book isn't tragic, then what is it?" Professor Stone asked.

"I said Quentin's comments weren't tragic. I didn't say the novel wasn't. It's not, though. It's what Polonius would call tragic irony. It feels the absurdity of a world which would sell off the family lands and whore out its only daughter to pay for Quentin's year at Harvard, a year punctuated by his suicide. Now, there's a return on investment for you. But the novel's not about absurdity, either. It takes a lot of things quite seriously. Dilsey, for example. Her offspring and their offspring are comic buffoons, but Dilsey represents Faulkner's hope for humanity. He said of her, 'she endured.' 'Endured.' That's the same word he used in his Nobel acceptance over and over, again. It's his hope for society, that, as in *King Lear*, we will live long enough for all this shit to wear away, and man will emerge as truly human.

Nor is this Quentin's book. It's just the set-up for the true book of Quentin, *Absalom, Absalom*, the ending of which, as well as much of the middle, is the finest writing ever done by an American, maybe the finest writing of all time."

"I don't think many in the class have read *Absalom*," Professor Stone said.

"Then they didn't prepare for class properly," Angel said. His tone had become bitter. "Reading *The Sound and the Fury* without reading *Absalom, Absalom* is like reading the first chapter of a novel and then proclaiming your understanding of the whole. You need to read before you can read," he said. "For instance, Father is clearly an ironic version of Mr. Bennett in *Pride and Prejudice*. Caddy is a *Moll Flanders* stuck in the south."

"How does seeing Father as Mr. Bennett help?" Charles asked.

"Because then you see him as partly comic," Angel said. "Otherwise, you're tempted to see him as a seer. He's not. Like Mr. Bennett, he retreats into his library and does nothing while the family lands are lost. He may be smart, but he's impotent. He's Quentin's father in that they are both smart and helpless, but Quentin is a much grander figure, a Prufrock writ large. Mother is a Mrs. Bennett, too, although it's pretty obvious that she's a silly piece of shit."

"Back to this novel," Professor Stone chided him gently.

"Okay, the tragedy of the novel is not that Benjy nee Maury was born with a mental incapacity. The tragedy is that the brightest of the bunch, Quentin, can be destroyed so easily by his neuroses. We see him in other Faulkner novels. He's Darl in *As I Lay Dying*. He's Uncle Ike, the dispossessed possessor in *Go Down, Moses*. He's Prufrock in T.S. Eliot. The tragedy is that the most exceptional modern men can't survive either in the old, bigoted dispensation, nor in the new vapid world of Oxford, Mississippi owned by people like the Snopes."

"And we'll stop on that note, class," Professor Stone said smiling. "I want everyone to run right out this weekend and read all of Shakespeare and Austen and Eliot and Faulkner. See if you can be ready for Angel's fireworks display on Tuesday."

As the class filed out, Angel sat feeling truculent. He didn't know why he was so angry.

Cara plopped next to him. "You all right?"

"Sorry," Angel said. He unclenched his fists and tried to breathe. "It's Faulkner. He does this to me."

"Everyone seems to do this to you," she said.

"No," he smiled. "Just Faulkner."

"And Shakespeare and Joyce and Eliot and Whitman and a bunch of lesser luminaries."

Angel ducked his head and tried not to laugh. He sighed and turned to her, "Cara, I've been wanting to ask you this all year. Why do you dislike me? Did I insult you somehow?"

Cara put a hand on his arm. "Dislike you? I like you a lot."

"Then why do you argue with everything I say?"

Cara laughed. "Oh, so in your world I am the one doing the arguing? You practically accuse me of stupidity or sloth every time you open your mouth. Did you notice that I'm the one who just sat down to cheer you up? I think you're a conceited asshole, but I also think you are brilliant and interesting. I'd date you if I didn't have a better boyfriend already."

"You would, huh?" Angel said laughing.

"I would." Cara laughed, too.

She rose. "Buy you a cup of coffee at Larry's? I'm sure you have some cheap little hussy lined up for tonight."

Angel stood. "Coffee sounds good. And I had designs on a really, easy slut, but she just told me she has a boyfriend."

"Oh, so that's how it is?" she laughed. They left Sanborn together to find Marilyn and Sarah waiting for them.

"Surprise," Cara said. "They're the ones taking you to coffee. I don't want anything to do with your sorry butt."

Angel smiled and kissed her on the cheek. The three watched her walk off.

"Hi," Marilyn said shyly. Sarah stood mute.

"Hi," Angel said. "Are we really going for coffee?"

"I'd like that," Marilyn said.

"I just wanted to say, 'thank you' for helping us Saturday night," Sarah said. "I don't remember much, but Marilyn says you and your friends saved us. You two go on ahead. I'll head back with Cara." And she abandoned them.

Angel and Marilyn crossed The Green in silence.

Finally, Angel said, "How do you know Cara?"

"She's in our suite. She's been talking about you all year. That's why we were at Phi Psi last Saturday."

"And that's how you knew who I was?" he asked

"Um hum. Partly. Plus, I've been listening to your radio show all year."

"Oh," he said. "Sorry about that."

Marilyn laughed.

"That was nice what you said Wednesday night," she said.

"What part?"

"All of it. I liked your lecture on not giving girls drugs, but I think all of us appreciated the 'let the girls join the fraternities' part. You've been a big supporter of the co-eds all year. Sometimes you sound like a male chauvinist pig, but most of the time you've been on our side."

Angel smiled. "I didn't know there were sides. And when am I a pig?"

"Oh," she laughed. "You know. Like when you're making little comments about sex. You kind of have a one-track mind."

"Hmm." Her rich voice sounded his bass notes, and her eyes made Thor's interest flicker. He guessed that proved her point.

At Larry's, they sat in the window. Marilyn drank tea and laughed at the way he took his coffee.

"Mister macho cowboy likes a lot of sugar and cream," she said.

"I'm not macho."

"Oh? I heard you and your friends are the place to go on campus if a guy has wronged you. I heard you beat two boys' heads in last fall."

Angel smiled. "Oh, that."

Marilyn smiled.

"Were you serious?" she asked.

Angel raised his eyebrows.

"Would you like to see us at Phi Psi, the co-eds, I mean?" she asked.

Angel sipped his coffee and nodded. He made a face and turned to Larry. "Larry, using turds for coffee beans again?"

"I'll brew a fresh pot," Larry said.

"Would you?" she said.

"Of course. I don't know about Sarah. She seems a bit delicate. We're not the most sophisticated guys on campus," he said.

"Yeah, you're kind of the losers' fraternity," she said.

"I wouldn't say losers," Angel smiled. "Less socially adept, maybe. Nerds and misfits, maybe. The Debate Team guys are members, and they're national champions."

"Ooh, the Debate Team. Hold me back," she laughed. "Would you like for me to come by tonight?" Shit. Was she asking him for a date?

"My girlfriend is coming tonight," he said.

"Your girlfriend?"

"Maggie. Long dark hair. You met her."

"Oh," she said and ducked her head. "Now I'm embarrassed."

Angel was silent.

"You showered with me," she said. "You saw me naked, and your hands touched me."

"I was trying to make you feel better. You asked me to. I didn't even undress all the way."

"I was naked. I've never showered with a boy before."

Wow. Where did all these sheltered women come from? He'd been showering with Cassie since high school. And he'd gone skinny-dipping in eighth grade.

"Marilyn, I'd love for you to come by. Bring Cara. Bring Cara's boyfriend."

Larry plopped a fresh coffee in front of Angel. "Your highness," he said.

Marilyn took it from him. "Let me," she said and spooned in five sugars and poured cream on top. She stirred and licked the spoon. "That's pretty good."

"I know, right?"

"Can we start over?" she said.

"Please," he said.

"Thanks for the other night," she said.

He smiled. "You're welcome."

"I enjoyed my shower," she said.

"Not as much as I did," he said.

"Yes, you looked, what would be the word, engaged."

"Did you say engorged?"

Marilyn laughed. "Yes, in fact, I did."

"That would be an accurate assessment. Have you really never showered with a man?"

"Never."

"Well, you did it very well. Do you remember what you said to me?"

"What?"

"You said there were other places I could wash if I wanted to," he said.

"Oh, God. I did, didn't I? I'm such a slut."

"Okay, I'm going to say this, and if you repeat it to Maggie, I'll beat you with a stick. I've showered with a lot of women, and you are by far the most beautiful."

Marilyn ducked her head and smiled. "See," she said.

"I know. One-track mind. You started all this."

Marilyn smiled. "So, how serious is this girlfriend thing?"

"Deadly. Oops. That sounds like *rigor mortis*." He put his hand on hers. "It's pretty fucking serious, I think."

"You think, huh?"

"I think. You know it's awfully hard to think or speak with you sitting there all bosomy and smiley."

"Oh, it's hard?"

Angel cracked up. He pulled his wallet, but Marilyn stopped him. "I've got this," she said.

She eyed him. "Friends, then?"

Angel nodded. "Friends."

Marilyn finished her tea and put a bill down on the table. She got up to leave.

"Oh good," Angel said.

"You're glad I'm leaving," she said.

"I'm glad you're leaving first."

"And why is that?"

"I'm betting you make a lovely exit."

She shook her finger at him. "One-track mind." And she sauntered away, swinging her hips as if to taunt him.

Angel looked down at Thor. "Did you see that?" he said. Thor nodded. He certainly had.

As he approached Phi Psi, Groucho was leaving. "Call Maggie," Groucho said. "She's called three times."

"Groucho," Angel began.

"Yep. It's on your dresser. You can pay me later. I haven't paid Gandalf yet."

Angel bought a pack of peanut M&Ms to wash down the coffee and dialed Maggie's dorm. Maggie's roommate Lucy answered.

"Hi Angel. Hold on. I'll get Maggie."

He heard her click down the hall and then click back a moment later.

"She's coming. Hey, great party last weekend. Will you tell me something honestly?"

"Sure."

"Your friend Eddie asked me out. Is he an okay guy? Maggie said 'yes' but seemed a bit ambivalent."

Angel smiled. "Eddie is just exactly how he presents himself. He was in Viet Nam and is a bit tightly wound, but you can trust him with your life."

"Cool. I may see you tomorrow night. Here's Maggie."

He heard her tell Maggie, 'If you dump him, I want him.' Then Maggie's bright voice greeted him.

"Hi sweetheart."

"Hi Babe," he said. "What's up?"

"Well, I'm going to have to bail tonight. I'm having a tough time with that *Cuckoo's Nest* essay. I'll be up tomorrow if that's okay, and I have some big news."

"What?"

"I'll tell you tomorrow," she said.

"Tell me now," he said.

She paused. "Okay," she said. "I decided where I'm going to college next year."

"Cool. Where?"

She paused for effect, "Dartmouth College," she said.

"No shit?"

"No shit," she laughed. "I'm so excited. Please tell me you're glad."

"I am," he said. "How did that happen? I thought you said they only took Seven Sisters girls."

"That's what they said. So, tell me, my Angel man, what did you do?"

"What did I do?"

"You helped, didn't you?"

Maybe. He had tried to call in a favor with Dean Hall, but he wasn't sure she had any sway over admissions.

"Not me," he said.

"Uh huh, well, I'm in anyway. So, you're going to have to put up with me every day."

"Does that mean you can room with me?" he asked.

"We'll see," she said. "Maybe if you're really nice this weekend and beg a lot."

"Ha," he said. "Why don't you come here and I'll help you with your essay?"

"Because you'd end up writing it."

"What's it on?"

"I don't know. I was going with the metaphor about mind control, you know, the Control Panel and the drugs and shock therapy and all that, but I just keep going around in circles."

"Can I ask a question?"

"Okay, but no telling me what to write."

"I promise," he said. "What is the source of Billy Bibbitt's problem?"

"His mother," she said.

"Uh huh, and Harden's?"

"His wife."

"And Chief Broom?"

She sighed, "His mother was white and sold off the tribe's land. His father drank himself to death after that."

"McMurphy's?"

"Okay, I see what you are getting at, but McMurphy doesn't fit the mold. He just wants to get out of doing field work in jail."

"Yeah," Angel said. "But what does he tell the Doctor when asked what his problem is?"

"I don't remember."

"He says he 'fights and fucks too much.' What does he fight over?"

Maggie chuckled. "Women. So, you're saying my thesis is that women are the root of all evil?"

"No, I'm saying the book is misogynistic. The whole book is anti-female. Even the Big Nurse is described as uber-female. When McMurphy attacks her, he rips her bodice open, exposing?"

"Her huge, maternal bosom."

"Right, and who are the only good women in the novel, the ones who make the men actually feel good instead of crappy?" he asked.

"Candy and her friend, the other hooker. I get it. So, you want me to write an essay saying the book is bigoted towards women? That the only good women are prostitutes? I have a male professor. He won't like that."

"Your duty every time you speak or write is to tell the truth. Fuck your professor. Scratch that. It came out wrong. You'd probably do it."

"He is cute," she cooed. "Okay, I'll work on that. You work on staying out of every woman you meet tonight."

"I'll try. It might be hard. I just saw Marilyn, and she said she and some friends might drop by tonight."

"Who's that?" she asked.

"She was one of the tripping girls Saturday."

"Oh, yes, the one you showered with."

Angel laughed. "Yes, that one. Drive up if you finish early. Otherwise, see you tomorrow. If I'm gone somewhere, I'll leave you a note on my desk. Love you, Baby."

"You just made my heart stop. I love you, too, Angel. See you tomorrow."

Angel hung up smiling. Maggie had gotten into Dartmouth. That was so cool. She could live with him, and he could write each night watching her sleep. He couldn't think of a better life.

Back at Phi Psi, he flopped on his bed and bounced his baseball off the wall trying to decide whether to nap or shoot pool. He hopped out of bed and went to the pool room, but no one was there, so, a nap it was. He stripped and climbed in between the sheets. He thought about jacking off since Maggie wasn't coming. It wasn't a bad idea.

He let his mind wander over Marilyn and Wanda and Sharon and everyone he could think of, and soon, Thor was into the game and wanted to play. Thor watched Marilyn walk away from him with glee and felt her mocha skin in the hot, pounding shower. Angel settled into his nap on a warm, sticky sheet, happy with the universe.

Angel awoke to total darkness and took a moment to adjust and figure out what was going on. He sat, groggy, on the side of his bed and waited for his brain to function. When he was pretty sure it wouldn't, he grabbed a towel and headed for the shower. As they almost always did, the scalding needles benefitted his soul as much as they did his brain and body. He soaped and shampooed and then just leaned against the wall while he was pounded. This was the same stall he and Marilyn had been in, and the thought gave him a boner. Angel looked down and admonished, 'best think of Maggie,' but to little avail.

He pulled on fresh jeans and a white shirt. He put on his luckiest pool-shooting vest and headed downstairs to reconnoiter the area. Things had begun to hop in a minor-league way. The tube room was jammed with the social members who only came over on the weekends or for the beer on tap during the week. Freak was playing chess and pulling on his hair in the card room. Someone had set up the sound system in the Blue Room, hoping for an impromptu dance. Angel was pretty sure that wasn't going to happen. All the big houses had bands that night. He and Sand had discussed going to Sigma Nu to crash their party, but neither felt up to fisticuffs.

No, it looked to be a tame evening which suited Angel fine. He made a peanut butter and jelly sandwich and bought a pack of M&Ms and a Coke and headed back to his room. He sat at his desk, eating and listening to Miles Davis. It was a *Bitches Brew* kind of night. He picked up the pot Groucho had left him. It was a pretty hefty ounce. He opened it and smelled it. Fresh, too. He looked for papers but couldn't find any, so he padded next door and purloined a pack from Groucho's desk.

He lit a joint and inhaled. Now, that was damn fine. He bet Faulkner would have made a good stoner. He might have lived a lot longer with more pot and less alcohol. He wondered if anyone had bothered to look into reefer use in Mississippi at the turn of the century. He was fairly sure the entire black population toked. Drugs were in almost every blues song they wrote, and that was all Mississippi Delta shit. Maybe that was his thesis topic: *Did Faulkner Get High and How Did It Affect the Imagery in Absalom, Absalom?*

Nope. He was sticking to his plan. He would write about *Ulysses*. He had been planning that for over a year. He had only gotten on his Faulkner kick to keep him away from Joyce. *Ulysses* was like the hot girl you know you need to avoid until fucking time. She would rip you up if you were around her too much.

Half an hour later, he was high on Miles Davis and Groucho's weed, too high to shoot pool against Eddie. He could probably hold his own against Sand, though, so he climbed to the pool room. Sure enough, Eddie was playing a guy from Beta and berating him the whole time.

"Oops, dumb leave. You left me the whole rest of the fucking rack. Boom, there's one and a leave. Cross-side. Boom. Suck on that Buddy. Seven in the corner. Boom. How's your pride taste going down? Four in the side. Boom. Rack 'em and stack 'em. Fast Eddie's on a roll."

Cane and his buddy Tim poked their heads in.

"Just tapped a fresh one," Sand said.

Cane nodded at Angel. "No chick tonight?"

"Nope," Angel said. "Might be a couple of free-lancers coming, but nothing right now."

"Priest go five on one," Cane quoted and left cackling at his own wit.

"Already done that," Angel called after him.

Angel watched Eddie play. They were at least five racks from finishing the match, so Angel went out on the rooftop. Sand followed him. They sat in lounge chairs and enjoyed the chill.

"You know we might get snow this week?" Sand said.

"Yeah, I heard," Angel said. "That's late, even for Dartmouth."

Sand nodded, and the two fell silent for a long time.

Eddie leaned his head out. "Hey Angel, visitors."

Angel turned to see Marilyn and a girl he didn't know stepping onto the rooftop.

"Is this safe?" the other girl asked.

"We're not sure," Sand said and rose to greet them. "Hi, I'm John," he said to the new one. He nodded to Marilyn. "I'm glad to see you looking sane."

Marilyn laughed. "We were out of our heads, weren't we?" She gestured to his feet which were still bandaged. "Is that from us? From walking on the glass?"

Sand nodded. "I'll bet you thought I was some eastern mystic or something."

"I did," Angel said. "You fooled me."

"Me, too," Marilyn said. "This is Ivy. She said she knows a guy here. Is there someone called Freak?"

"There is," Sand said. "Are you a chess player?" he asked Ivy.

"No, I'm a violinist," Ivy said. "Freak sits next to me during orchestra. Is he like a genius or something?"

"More like an idiot savant," Sand said. "He's helping write all the computer code for Kiewit. He plays chess against the computer all day and gets class credit for it."

"Kiewit?" Marilyn asked. "We were connected to Kiewit at Radcliffe."

"Yep, we're the computer hub for the whole northeast. MIT just formed their own web last year," Sand said.

"So, what are you guys doing tonight?" Marilyn asked.

"This is pretty much it," Angel said. "Last weekend was our big bash. But you know that. You were here. That is, if you remember much."

"I remember taking a shower," Marilyn said. Her voice dropped an octave when she was being sultry. Angel smiled. Ivy looked confused.

"Anybody want a beer?" Sand asked. "Ivy want to see the bar and get the grand tour?"

Ivy nodded.

"Ivy," Marilyn said. "You're wasting your time with that one. He has a girlfriend."

"I do," Sand said. "But she trusts me to get beers for girls and talk to them."

Ivy laughed. "He looks pretty safe to me."

"He's not," Angel said. "Ask him how many men he killed in Viet Nam."

"Ooh, really?" Ivy asked.

"That would be zero," Sand said. "I was an M.P. I mostly dragged soldiers out of bars."

"Yeah," Angel said. "Because walking into a massive brawl to arrest fully armed soldiers just back from the killing fields was a completely safe endeavor."

"Do you have stories?" Ivy asked.

"Eddie has better ones, and he likes to tell them. I don't."

The two climbed through the window and disappeared.

Marilyn sat in the chair Sand had vacated. "This is nice," she said.

"Yep. It's bucolic. All you see are trees. You wouldn't even know there was a campus if you couldn't see the Baker Tower."

"I study upstairs in Baker," she said.

"What's your major?"

"Well," she said. "It's math, but I'm switching to electrical engineering. I'm going to Thayer. That's why I came to Dartmouth."

"Oh," he said. "I thought it was to meet real men. We must be a shock after those pusillanimous Harvard types."

Marilyn smiled. "Have you read *Last of the Mohicans?*"

"Of course."

"The women came from hothouse lives in England and found themselves in a savage place. Hawkeye asks her if she's appalled by New England and all the violence. Do you remember what she says?"

"She says she found it thrilling. So, you're comparing us to the Mohawk nation during the French and Indian Wars?"

She laughed. "If the shoe fits."

"Better than you think. Hawkeye and Uncas went to Dartmouth."

"What? You're making that up," she said.

"Hawkeye said they went to Dr. Wheelock's School for Indians. That turned into Dartmouth. Do you know when we were founded?"

"No."

"1769," he said.

"Right after the French and Indian Wars" she finished. "You are a font of information."

"So, they say. Actually, most say I'm a tedious and arrogant know-it-all."

"Who says that?" she laughed.

"Your friend Cara said it today."

They were silent.

Angel sat up. "Marilyn, you may be the first woman who ever heard me ask this, but do you want to go dancing? There's a killer band at Sigma Nu."

"Why Angel, are you asking me to step out with you?"

"That's the worst southern accent I've ever heard, even from a black chick."

She laughed. "Okay smartie, where am I from?"

Angel thought for a moment. Her accent said New York, but it was more cultured than Brooklyn or Queens. "Scarsdale?"

Her face soured. "You shit. Somebody told you that."

"There's another girl from Scarsdale here," he said. "Her name is Louise. Do you know her?"

"She's the busty one? We met. I think she was hitting on me. Is she really from Scarsdale?"

"Yep."

"I don't remember her. I went to boarding school practically my whole life, though."

"There's another Scarsdale kid here," Angel said. "He's supposed to be a super stud."

"Ooh, introduce me. Wait. Are you talking about yourself?"

"Yep. Fifth, sixth, and part of seventh grade. And then a shithole in Jacksonville, Florida. My high school was completely segregated."

"No way," she said. "I thought that stuff was gone."

"It is, now. Not then. Robert E. Lee High School. The Fighting Generals. Our school color was gray."

"You're making this up," she laughed. "I thought you said you'd been with a black girl before."

"I have. Her name was Jewel, believe it or not. We met at a dance. The Swinging Medallions were playing, and she wasn't put off by my stunning incapacity on the dance floor. In fact, she seemed amused, as if I was trying to look klutzy on purpose. God, she was a sweetheart. Too fidgety during sex, but her mouth tasted so sweet."

"Did you date her after that?"

"Just once. Then her giganto boyfriend paid me a visit."

Marilyn laughed. "And he was persuasive."

"I didn't get much of what he said. My head was too busy exploding while he beat me. Luckily, I was out as soon as my head hit the sidewalk and didn't feel much pain. That was too bad. I really liked her, and she really liked me back."

"Well, I don't have a huge boyfriend."

"See, my timing just sucks."

"Or mine does," she said.

"Okay," he said, smiling. "Stop that."

"Stop what?"

"Being all cute and sexy. You know what I mean."

Marilyn laughed.

"I think I will take you up on that dancing. I want to see you do something badly. You seem like an overachiever."

"Hah," he said. "Hardly."

He led her back inside and stopped by his room. Marilyn gravitated immediately to the bookcase. She ran her hand over a row of books. "I wanted to look at these Saturday night, but I was too messed up." She sat on the bed. "You really are a nerd, aren't you? Cara says you've read everything and think everyone who hasn't is stupid."

Angel sat at his desk. "Not true. I think English majors should read, that's all. And, if they haven't, they should keep their mouths shut." He dangled his new bag of pot and raised his eyebrows.

"Sure," she said. She went to his side while he rolled and picked up a sheaf of papers. "May I?"

Angel nodded and smiled. She was holding a sex scene with Maggie in her hands. Marilyn leaned against his desk and read. Angel finished rolling and lit the joint. He took a deep hit and held it for her. She took it without raising her eyes from the page and toked. She choked briefly but held the smoke in. Her eyes widened and she exhaled. "Oh, my," she said. And then, "Oh my dear Lord."

Angel smiled. Nothing like watching a girl read about cunnilingus. Marilyn arched her brows at him. She fanned herself with the pages and went back to reading. Angel laughed and took the story away. "Enough," he said. "So, what do you think?"

"I think your description of sex is graphic."

"Graphic good or graphic bad?" he asked.

"It's so," she searched for a word, "real."

"So, that's good?"

"Yes, unless it makes you faintly jealous."

Angel smiled. "Fair enough. Let's go dancing."

"Should we tell Ivy?"

"If you want, but I'm sure she's fine. She's totally safe with Sand. He wouldn't cheat on Linda for the world."

But they didn't see Sand or Ivy when they went down to the bar, so Angel bought a Coke and they headed outside.

They didn't get very far.

There on the steps sat a sobbing Jane, drenched in her tears and snot.

Angel had seen this before.

He sat beside Jane and put his arm around her. She bawled into his shirt.

"Marilyn, I'm going to have to take a rain check. Jane, this is Marilyn. Marilyn, Jane."

Jane looked up. "What happened to Maggie?"

Angel smiled. "Nothing happened to Maggie. Marilyn and I were just going dancing. She's a friend."

Jane looked at Marilyn distrustfully. Then she turned to Angel. "I can sleep in Groucho's room, but I do need to talk to you sometime tonight."

Angel smiled at Marilyn. He poked out his lip and made a frowny face. She smiled back and nodded, her 'it's okay' look.

She sat next to Angel and Jane. "Jane," she said. "Go talk with Angel. It's all right. Really."

Jane stared at her. "You can sleep with him later. I just need to talk to him."

"Girl," Marilyn laughed. "You think I'd sleep with him? You're crazy."

Angel made a face at her. He dried Jane's face with his handkerchief and took her inside. Marilyn followed.

"If you were Sand and Ivy, where would you be?" Marilyn asked.

"Oh, I know that one," Jane said. "In his room. He loves to show people his business projects. They're kind of boring, but he's so sweet and excited while he shows you."

"Past the bathroom on the right," Angel said. "If they're not there, go back up and check the poolroom. If that fails, the bar."

Marilyn saluted and took off up the stairs. Angel followed her sweet ass wistfully.

He turned to Jane. "Have you eaten anything?"

"Not in a couple of days."

Angel nodded. That figured. Depressed women either ate constantly or not at all. The skinny ones like Jane were particularly susceptible to the latter.

"But I'm not hungry," she said.

"You're going to eat something, or I won't talk to you," he said firmly. He tried to shake the vision of Marilyn's rear from his mind's eye, but it wouldn't leave.

Angel half-dragged Jane to the kitchen. "Bacon and eggs?" he asked.

Jane nodded glumly and sat. "Who's the new one?"

Angel smiled. "Marilyn? She's a rescue project."

Jane sniffed. "Sounds about right. That's what we all are to you, isn't it?"

"If you're going to be an asshole, I'm not going to be nice to you," Angel said and set a plate of food in front of her. "Eat."

"Kiss me first."

"Nope. Eat then kiss. And I shouldn't even do that. My big news is that Maggie and I have gotten serious. Last weekend, to be exact."

Jane digested that while she ate. Angel watched her for clues as to how to deal with her. She was pretty obviously depressed, but she seemed more manic and angry than she had the first time he met her. There seemed to be less self-loathing going on, but the fear of something inside her almost gave off an odor.

Jane finished and held up her plate. "Good enough, or do I have to lick it clean""

"Lick it," Angel said. "That should be erotic."

Jane stared blankly for a moment, but then slowly ran her tongue across the plate, keeping her eyes locked with Angel's the whole time and moaning. A mischievous smile lit her face up.

"Ah, a smile and a sense of humor," Angel said. "That's good. Ready to tell your sad tale?"

"Kiss first, then tale," she said.

Angel pecked her lips and pulled her towards the stairs.

"Real kiss."

"I told you," he began.

"I know, Maggie. She's not here and I won't tell. Real kiss," she said and held her face up.

Angel took her face in his hands and kissed her gently and sweetly. "How's that?"

"More."

"Upstairs. My room. The telling of the tale is about to commence," and he chased her up the stairs spanking her cute butt as she ran squealing.

Once there, she flopped on his bed and sighed. Angel smiled, put The Moody Blues on, and rolled a joint. She was nuts, and God hadn't graced her with beauty, but she was kind of cute when she wasn't covered in snot. Angel lit the joint and sat by her. Jane took it gratefully. She looked around her and lay back down. She blew smoke towards the ceiling and looked meditative.

"Maybe I'll just move in and live here," she said. "Would that be all right? I could sleep in Groucho's room when you have a girl here."

"Yeah. That would be great," he said. "It might get crowded, though. Maggie's moving in next fall."

She punched him. "What? She got in Dartmouth. She told me she didn't have a chance. Good for her. I don't even feel sad enough to tell you what's been going on now."

"Tell me anyway," he said and ran his fingers through her hair.

She sighed. "How do you make problems seem so trivial?" She thought for a moment. "I guess the first part of the story is that I met a guy. He's a grad student at Northeastern and is from my hometown, although I'd never met him before. He went to Lawrenceville. Plus, he's three years older. I think you'd like him. Scratch that. You wouldn't." She sighed again.

"So, you met this guy," Angel said.

"Uh huh, and for a while it was great. He's in International Law which is what I want to do, and it seemed like we had a lot in common."

"Is he good in bed?"

She laughed. "Way better than you, no offense."

"None taken. Tell me how and maybe I can improve."

She leaned on an elbow. "Well, for one, I turn him on. I always feel like I'm a pity fuck to you."

"Ouch."

"I notice you're not denying it," she laughed.

"Nothing to even bother denying. It's absurd. I'm just not very good in bed."

"You know what you are good at? Cuddling. Cuddling and showering. Your hands are amazing in the shower."

She paused.

"And, thus, begins the sad part of Jane's tale," she said. "I tried to re-create Angel in the shower with him. Bad move. He saw where I had cut myself, and I had to tell him my whole sordid story."

Jane's eyes filled with tears, and Angel pulled her head to his lap.

"And he didn't react well," Angel said.

"He didn't react at all. We made love that night like always. The next morning, he kissed me and left. That was the last time I saw or heard from him."

Angel stroked her hair but said nothing. He was sure there was more, and he wasn't wrong.

"Angel, I really liked him. I mean, I thought he was, you know."

"The one."

"The one," she echoed. "That sounds stupid, doesn't it?" She looked up at him. "You're the one. I know we wouldn't ever love each other in a romantic way, but if I were with you, my life would be mellow and content. You'd make me feel good about myself. You would, wouldn't you?"

"I'd try. I wouldn't have to do much. There's nothing wrong with you except for your propensity to tear yourself down."

"Yes, but I'm an expert at that." She frowned. "I tried to contact him, of course, but his roommate said he went home. This is all last weekend, by the way. Not a word since. Then, I got crampy, and my mood tanked. I mean tanked hard. I could feel all the old, bad, creepy shit in my head, so I got in my car and drove here. Not much of a story. Sad girl loses chance at love and gets sadder."

Angel lay beside her and pulled her to him.

"Straight talk?" he asked.

Jane nodded.

"Jane, you know I dearly love you?" She nodded with a rueful smile. "Okay, here goes. Jane, you are all of the Janes. The scars and the bad periods and the mood swings are all Jane. So is the sweet smile and the wicked sense of humor and the way you kiss and cuddle. You said I cuddle well. You know the rule of cuddling, don't you?"

She shook her head.

He smiled. "It takes a good cuddler to recognize a good cuddler. And you're an expert."

"I'm just the right size for you. We fit."

"We do fit," he said. "But part of good Jane is only there because of bad Jane. You're a whole person, not an essay which can be refined. My reading and thinking comes with an unhealthy dose of arrogance, but I'll gladly accept that to get to do all the mental shit I get away with. And I bond easily with women, which tends to screw up my relationships. Everyone gets jealous and angry with me eventually. But I can't stop reacting to women the way I do. It would be like asking me to grow six inches."

"Wow," she said. "You'd be too long then. You wouldn't fit in me."

"You are a foul-mouthed wench, but that's what I mean. You're funny and clever. I don't know how to tell you to do it, but moods are like colds. You just need to rest and wait them out. And your scars are just that, scars. They are tissue art to remind you not to go to that place again."

Jane snuggled against him. "Do you think I'll meet a boy who doesn't run when he sees them?"

"Did I run?"

"No. But let's face it, Angel, you're not quite right in the head. And you're not exactly boyfriend material."

"Oh? And why not?"

"You just said it, silly," she said and poked him. "I'd come home one night after a long day's work. 'Did you feed the children' I'd call out. There would be no answer, and I'd go to the bedroom to find you making love to some harlot while *Boom Boom* by the Animals plays."

"Hm. You're seeing the long picture. I guess my scars are all in front of me. At least yours are from the past."

"Yes," she said, "But what do I do when you're not here for me to run to?"

He held her. "I'll always be somewhere waiting for you. You just may have to travel further."

She looked at him. "Really?"

"Really," he said. "Friends for life."

Jane snuggled back against him. "All right, then."

"All right, then." He kissed her hair and held her.

"Your bed smells like sex," she said sleepily. "Are you sure you weren't boffing the cute black chick before I got here."

"No," he laughed. "I entertained myself this afternoon."

"Oh. Why do boys do that all the time?"

"We don't have a choice. It's like peeing. When you have to go, you have to go. Women connect sex to feelings. Men see it as a biological necessity."

"So, you don't feel things during sex?"

"That's not what I meant," he laughed. "I know I do. For me, sex is like a language. I use it to communicate my affection for a woman. Jerking off is like reading. How did we get on this subject?"

"I don't know," she said. "Do you mind if I take a little nap. Crying makes me sleepy, and I haven't slept much all week."

"Okay," Angel said and kissed her hair.

"Hold me till I fall asleep?"

He pulled her against him and kissed her neck. Jane sighed and squeezed his arm which was around her.

Angel lay as still as he could and thought about what it would be like to be subject to moods. It didn't sound like much fun. He knew he rarely had much more than a pulse except for his periodic bursts of anger. But those were like outlets on a steam valve, and they were usually directed towards appropriately assholic people. Like guys who needed a fist in the mouth.

Maggie was pretty level, but she was moody, too. Cassie had been a champ at never taking her feelings out on him, even if he had caused her pain through his fuckups. But Maggie was getting better. Her only flare-ups came when her jealousy button was pushed. That was rich, given her Yalie blowjob right in front of him. She could protest all she wanted, but it didn't look to Angel as if she were doing that against her will. No, she had been into it. And Jeffrey wasn't queer. He may have been a freethinker about that sort of thing, but he wasn't into men exclusively. He was digging what Maggie was dishing.

Shit. This was a dreary avenue of thought. Best say fuck it and move on.

He could tell from her breathing that Jane was probably out, so he unwound his arm from hers and separated himself from her gradually. She didn't stir. From long practice, he was adept at getting out of bed without disturbing Cassie, but he was pinned against the wall, so this extrication was trickier. He scooched towards the foot of the bed and climbed off. Jane still didn't register any awareness of his absence. He sat at his desk and put his boots on. He would go to the pool room and see if he could get a game.

But he never left his room. Instead, he picked up the stuff on Maggie that Marilyn had read and started to go back through it.

It wasn't half bad. Angel hit a key on the typewriter and watched Jane. No reaction. He wrote a sentence. Still nothing.

So, he put in a new piece of paper and began to write. He wrote for a long time. He didn't know how long.

He stretched and went downstairs. There was singing down in the bar, but the rest of the house was quiet. Even the tube room was empty.

He went outside and smelled the night sky. It was cold and smelled of snow. Perhaps the forecasts were right. Perhaps there was a late snow brewing somewhere to the north.

But the sky was cloudless and moonless, so the stars shone brilliantly. It was his kind of night. A girl asleep in bed and prose pouring from his fingertips. It might be the wrong girl, but the writing was the real deal. His chest swelled with gratitude.

This was his life, and he loved it.

Chapter Twenty-Seven

Saturday Morning April 17, 1971
Oh Well

ANGEL WROTE UNTIL THE SUNLIGHT ON HIS WINDOW glared and hurt his head. He pulled the curtain and looked over at Jane. She was still out cold. Good for her. It wasn't easy being Jane.

He took a quick shower to clear his head, dressed surreptitiously, and snuck out. The day was gorgeous, which was sometimes an ominous sign in Hanover. The best days often began in a mist. When the mist burned off, the sky would be high and a dark New England blue.

He went to Lou's and read the paper another early riser had left behind while he ate pancakes and bacon. Vermont syrup. Simply the best. He drank two cups of coffee, but his head still felt like the mist he had been hoping for outside.

When he got back to Phi Psi, Jane was gone. Her bag and clothes were still there, so he guessed she was eating breakfast or showering or something. He was too tired to care and climbed into bed.

He was out almost instantly.

When he woke, he had that odd sensation of not remembering where he was. He rubbed his head and looked about him.

Maggie sat in his desk chair staring at him. He gave her a big, goofy smile.

"Hi Mags. You're a nice surprise."

Maggie didn't answer. She looked cold and was shaking slightly.

"You okay?" he asked.

"You shit," she said. "You absolute shit."

Angel sat up. His manuscript lay open on his desk. Had she been reading it? Had he written something which pissed her off?

"Did I miss something?" he asked.

"Well, for starters, you just missed Jane dressing here, in your room. When I walked in, she was completely naked, just the way you like your women. You missed her gathering her things and sneaking out. You missed me sitting here for an hour trying to decide whether to leave or kill you."

Angel pulled the covers off and sat on the edge of the bed. He chuckled. "You think Jane and I had sex?"

"Go ahead, Angel. Lie to me. Try to talk your way out of this. I caught you redhanded. Gee, naked Jane. The whole room smells like sex. What could that mean?" she asked. He had never heard that petty tone from her. She sounded vicious and petty.

"Jane and I didn't do a thing," he said. "She came here needing to talk. She fell asleep in my bed. I wrote all night. That's the whole story." He rose and headed for the door.

"Where do you think you're going?" she asked. Now her tone was shrill.

"I don't think I'm going anywhere. I know I'm going to pee."

"I may not be here when you get back."

"You know the way out," he said and went to the bathroom. Angel peed and washed his face. He looked at himself in the mirror. His face was puffy. He needed more sleep. What he didn't need was Maggie's bullshit.

But his petulance melted away quickly.

Maggie was hurt. It didn't really matter that he hadn't done anything. What mattered was her pain.

On his way back to his room, Jane stuck her head out of Groucho's room.

"Maggie's here," she said. "She's really pissed. I tried to explain, but she didn't want to listen to me."

Angel nodded and smiled. He pushed her head back into Groucho's room and pulled the door shut.

Not Jane's problem.

When he re-entered his room, Maggie was still there. That was a hopeful sign.

He sat on the bed and patted the spot next to him. "Come here, Mags."

"I'm fine over here," she said.

Angel wished she was crying. He looked at her eyes but didn't see hurt in them. He just saw anger. He sighed.

"Maggie, I'm going back to sleep. I've only slept an hour or two, and I don't need this shit."

Maggie came out of the chair. "You fucking asshole. You fuck that ugly little piece of trailer trash and then lie to my face and it's somehow 'shit?' Saturday, one week ago, you told me you love me, and then you pull this?"

Angel stared impassively at her.

Just let her vent until she runs out of oxygen.

"You're right," she said. "This is my fault. I knew you couldn't be trusted. I met you on a lie. Protecting me? No. You were just picking up chicks. That's your job. No, that's your whole fucking life, isn't it? Picking up chicks and pretending you've saved them or care about them. I can't believe I trusted you."

Angel watched her sit back down. Maybe that was all.

But no.

"I have the worst taste in men. I mean, look at this place. A world-class collection of idiots and losers. The whole building looks like it might fall down."

She fell silent. He guessed it was no fun if he didn't put up a fight.

Angel detested passive aggressive people, and he would have said something if he could have thought of anything.

"You through?" he said, finally.

"How could you do this to me?"

"If you don't have any more clichés to hurl in my direction, get out," he said.

"What?" she said.

"Cliches," he said. "That's when nothing you say is original."

"You son of a bitch," she hissed.

"See?" he said.

"I hate you," she said.

"No, you don't," he said, "But I'm getting sick of your shit pretty quickly, so get out."

"Oh, no, mister. You don't cheat on me and then tell me when to leave."

"Maggie, get the fuck out of my room. I didn't cheat on you, and you called me a liar. If you were a guy, I'd have already beaten the shit out of you. Now, leave my shitty falling apart house full of idiots. You're a petulant, spoiled brat and not worth arguing with. Go, leave."

"Angel, you've had sex. I can smell it."

"Yes, I had sex."

"You admit it?"

"Yep. I had a threesome."

"There was someone besides Jane? God, why does this not surprise me?"

"Jane wasn't even here. The threesome was me, myself, and I. I jacked off. I jacked off almost every day this week, because every time I thought about you I got a hard-on. I couldn't stop thinking about you. I was so fucking happy. I wrote all night about you. There, it's on the desk behind you. It's a bit romantic, but it's pretty good, I think. But I won't jack off over you anymore because I'll probably always hear that bitch voice you've been using. That's a real turn-off. You ought to work on that. If you want to make a guy feel crummy in the future, try crying, not bitch voice. Because all I want now is for that voice and that face you're making to get the fuck out of my room."

"Angel," she began.

He rose and walked towards her. Her face turned white with fear, and she rose, too. He took her arm and dragged her towards the door.

"You've called me a liar and accused me of being the kind of guy who might hurt you. Get the fuck out and don't come back unless you can figure out a way to apologize and make me forget what you sound like when you're a raving bitch."

He pushed her out the door and slammed it.

He stood for a moment and then sat down on the edge of his bed. He rubbed his temples.

Fucking bitch. Never tell a woman you love her. Especially not a spoiled rich kid. One week. A new record for futility. Shit.

Angel lay in bed and tried to nap. He must have fallen asleep eventually, because he heard a tapping at his door.

"Come in," he said. His voice sounded thick with sleep.

Jane poked her head in.

"Not now, Jane," he said.

"Do you want to talk?"

He smiled at her. This was ironic. He shook his head. "No, I'm fine."

"You're not fine," she said.

He thought about that. No, he was pretty sure he was. He had seen the face of the gorgon and survived. He was lucky.

Jane came in and sat on the edge of the bed. "I'm sorry, Angel. This was my fault."

He sat beside her and put his arm around her. "How is it your fault that Maggie's a bitch? She called me a liar. Can you believe that?"

Jane nodded. "Jealousy turns people into monsters. That wasn't her talking."

"Good. But whoever's inhabiting her body needs to leave soon."

"You joke and say you're fine, but you know what you've got to do," she said.

"I do?"

"Yes, you need to find her. She goes to Colby, right? Is that far?"

"No. About forty minutes away."

She patted his leg. "Clean up and go to her. You can do this, cowboy," she said firmly.

Angel smiled at her. "I thought you were depressed."

"I thought so, too, but I've thought about Ron, that was the man I was dating."

"And?"

"And, I think I'll give him time to realize he was an idiot and call me," she said.

"And if he doesn't?"

"Then, fuck him," she said.

Angel laughed. "So, if he comes back, you fuck him, and if he doesn't, fuck him?"

Jane laughed. "You're not funny. Now, shower or whatever and go see Maggie."

"You wouldn't say that if you knew the things she said about you," he said.

"If I was in her position, I'd calumniate me, too."

"Calumniate, huh?"

"Yes. I'm not stupid, Angel, except when it comes to men. And look at you. Sometimes I meet a good one." She pecked him on the cheek. "Now, go get her."

"I'd rather stay here and fuck you," he said.

"Go. If you're still single tonight, maybe I'll reconsider, but I doubt it. You're damaged goods."

Angel groaned, but he rose, showered, and dressed again. His head ached and he wasn't into the whole enterprise, but he knew he was expected to at least try.

He made a pitcher of coffee and poured it into a thermos. He bought two bags of peanut M&Ms and went to his car. Jane walked out with him.

"Whose car is this?" she asked.

"Mine."

"I didn't even know you had a car."

"Yep. It's been out of commission all winter. I couldn't afford getting it fixed. Turned out all I needed was a new battery and a rebuilt alternator."

"What is it?

Angel pulled the top back and fastened it down. "It's an Austin Healey 3000."

"Wow. It's nice. I like the blue." She peeked inside. "Stick shift?"

"Of course," Angel smiled.

"Is it safe?"

"Are you safe?" he asked and pulled her to him. He kissed her lips. She molded herself to his body and offered her face up for more. Angel kissed her again.

"You know," he began.

"I know. If you weren't my therapist, we could date." She smiled. "Lucky for me, you're not really my type."

"Oh, what type is that?" he asked.

"You know. Good looking. Sexy. Unattached."

"Uh huh," he said. He kissed her again and climbed over the door and plopped in the seat.

"The door doesn't open?" she laughed. "Classy."

"Wish me luck," he said and drove off.

Jane waved and mouthed 'good luck.'

The sun was hot but the air which flew past him was chilly. Both sensations were good for his head, and, by the time he parked at Colby, his head felt remarkably good. He thought long about what he should say or do.

He was wrong to be angry with her. He probably looked undeniably guilty from her point of view. And she had been sitting in his chair simmering while he slept.

That couldn't have been good for her disposition. Maybe she had cried and been all girly and loving for a while but had gotten bitter and distrustful afterwards, and all he saw was the bile.

So, no accusations. No defensive behavior. He would be sweet, and she would see the error of her ways.

But, even if all that worked out, did he really want to be back in the love trap with her. She sure got jealous quickly, and jealous people were annoyingly insecure.

Come on Angel. Be a grown up. Even if she's pissed at you, even if she calls you a liar, you can make things right, can't you?

Angel smoked an old roach he found in the glove compartment. Thank God for honest mechanics.

Thus bolstered, he climbed out of his cockpit and crossed campus. Saturdays at Colby were quiet. Most of the girls were somewhere else or studying. Angel went to Maggie's dorm and asked the dorm mother to send someone for her. He sat in a chair and waited.

He saw Maggie's roommate Lucy trotting down the stairs. Wow. She looked completely different when she wasn't dressed like Lucifer's sidekick. She looked almost sunny.

Lucy sat in the chair next to him.

"Hi Angel. Maggie's not here. I thought she was with you at Dartmouth. She left this morning."

"We had a fight, and she split. I assumed she was heading back here."

"Oh, no. What did you do? She was in such a good mood when she left."

"Nothing. Absolutely nothing. She thinks I cheated on her, but I didn't." Angel sat and thought for a moment. Where the fuck was she? Now, he was the one inventing jealous scenarios. He sighed. She could be anywhere licking her wounds and crying. Or she could have driven to Yale. But, what if she did? He couldn't blame her if she had.

Oh, Maggie. You dumb fuck.

"Can I leave her a note?" Angel asked.

"Sure. Come on up to the room."

Lucy gestured to the matron that they were going upstairs. The woman nodded stolidly. Angel wondered if the old lady suspected hanky panky every time a guy went up the stairs. He smiled at her. She grimaced in return.

Lucy gave Angel pen and paper. "I'm heading to the library. Just leave the note on her bed." She took a step towards the door. "Angel," she said. "You really didn't do anything?"

He shook his head. "Scout's honor."

"Shit," she said. "I think I believe you."

"Maggie should have, too," he said.

She looked as if she was about to say something else, but she shook her head and left.

Angel stared at the blank piece of paper. Surely, she would be cooled down by the time she got home. He wondered briefly if he should be worried about her, but he shook it off. Maggie was a big girl. She was all right. He took up the pen and wrote:

Mags,

If this is goodbye, then I say this with love, goodbye. I said I loved you, and I meant it.

That was nice. Slip in a past tense.

You know, or you should know, that I wouldn't lie to you. I didn't do a single thing with Jane. I haven't cheated on you with anyone. Not once. Not even close. Yes, I am cavalier about my dealings with women, but I would never, ever lie to you. Shoot, I wouldn't lie to anyone about anything. It's never worth it, and it's just not me.

Your distrust pained me, but I know you were jealous and not yourself.

That was good. Faintly accusatory but not brutal.

I don't know where you are right now, and that scares me. Even if you never want to see me again, please call Dartmouth and tell me you are all right.

I hope this all passes. I am sorry you are hurting. Please look into your heart, though. You will see there that I am being truthful.

This pains me to say, but I have to say it. If you need to fight more, I don't want to see you. Nothing good ever comes from arguing. People just say things they can never retract. If you want to be my lover, I need for you to try to honor that. You said things today I will have a difficult time forgetting or forgiving.

Shit. He was getting angry. What was with him? Was he having a man period or something? He had been irritable in class, too. This wasn't working. He tore off a strip from the bottom of the page and wrote, *'call me and let me know you are all right. Angel'* He wadded the rest of the sheet up and threw it into the trash can.

Fuck this. Fuck telling a chick you love her because she wants for you to say it even if you're not ready to say it.

No. Fuck being in love. Fuck Colby and fuck Maggie and fuck Lucy for even asking him to repeat his innocence. Fuck anyone and everyone who didn't trust him.

He didn't need this shit. He would do fine on his own. There was a shitload of fine women in the world. He could think of several who would immediately offer comfort and affection without calling him a fucking liar and insulting his friends.

Maggie was a stuck-up Long Island bitch who blew a guy right in front of him and didn't even have to suffer a reproachful word.

Angel put the strip of paper on Maggie's bed. He felt like whipping out his dick and peeing on it.

But he didn't. Instead, he sat at her desk and smoked a roach until his temper passed.

This was what fucking love did to you.

On a notebook atop her desk were a bunch of cryptic notations. He picked it up.

Shit. It was a playlist of the blues songs on his show, and it went back to before he met her.

He took a final hit on the roach and stubbed it out. Maybe if he just sat there, she would walk in and fall into his arms weeping. That would be sweet. It wasn't going to happen, but it would be cool.

The day had started so well. He had written through the night about Maggie. It was an extended love letter in novel form.

And he had to admit, he was glad to have his car back. Groucho was generous, but Angel just wasn't an Impala guy. The ride down had felt like he was back in the saddle, car-wise. He put down Maggie's playlist. On her desk was a copy of *Absalom, Absalom*. There was a marker nearly halfway through. She was reading that to please him. He lay on her bed face down. Her pillow smelled like her.

Oh, Maggie. Figure out a way to make us whole again, because I don't have a clue what to do.

Chapter Twenty-Eight

MARILYN'S TEETH CHATTERED AS SHE AND ANGEL FLEW home with the top down. The day had been hot and the rocks hotter. Lying in the sun on a hot boulder made the chill from the water seem as if it had dissipated. The falls at Union Village dam roared with snowmelt, and the water was still icy.

Leaning on an elbow and running his fingers over Marilyn's breasts and teasing her cold, stiff nipples until she swatted at him had been wonderful.

Two townies had pointed and said laughing, "That guy's got a boner."

Angel had smiled at the boys. Indeed, he did have a raging pole. Marilyn was a walking, talking boner.

But the sound of the falls brought back both Cassie and Maggie, a personal failure for each exploding slue of water, and Angel was melancholy during the ride back to campus.

Marilyn's chattering teeth made him laugh, though, and he shook off his mood.

He dropped her at her dorm, and she leaned over for a kiss.

"Are you ever going to ask me what I'm doing tonight?" she cooed.

"Nope. I'm working tonight. I'm trying to nail down an essay while it's still making sense in my head."

"Guess I'll have to find my entertainment elsewhere," she said and sashayed off.

Man, she did a fine sashay.

Back at Phi Psi, he took the steps two at a time. He needed to pee, and he and Marilyn weren't to the point where he could pee in front of her so he had been holding it. He hopped in the shower and turned it to skinscald. The medicinal spray drove away the bite from the cold waters.

He was dressing when Freak called up the stairs, "Angel, phone."

Angel pulled on his jeans and went downstairs. Freak looked petulant when he handed Angel the phone. "I was in the middle of a game," he said. Four games were set up in the card room, but Angel didn't see an adversary. "Playing myself," Freak said. Angel nodded. He had never heard Freak speak a whole sentence before.

"Hello," he said.

"Angel?"

"Wanda?"

"The one and only. I'm sorry to bother you, but can we talk? Is this a good time?"

Angel slid a quarter in the candy machine and pulled the lever for a pack of peanut M&Ms.

"Of course," he said. "Come on over. I'm not dressed, but that never seems to bother you."

Wanda laughed, but her voice sounded tight.

"No, I'm in Boston. It's just that…" She paused. "Angel, I have a problem and there's nothing you can do about it, so I don't know why I'm bothering you."

"Slow down," he said laughing. "Breathe. Just tell me what's going on."

There was dead silence on the line for so long that Angel thought she might have hung up.

"Wanda?"

"I'm here. Remember I told you about a boy I was dating?"

"The one who hit you." Angel's voice grew cold.

"Uh huh."

"Did he hit you again?"

"No, not exactly. He's kind of stalking me."

"Stalking you? Like following you? Or threatening you?"

"Both. He seems to show up everywhere I go, and he brushes past me sometimes with little warnings, like 'watch your back, bitch.' Things like that. He's scary."

Shit. Angel couldn't see Wanda as easily intimidated. This guy must be a royal prick.

"Have you done anything about it?" he asked.

"Yes. That's the part that infuriates me. I went to the campus police, and they said they'd talk to him. I told them he hit me, but that was months ago, and I couldn't prove it. They came back and said they were sorry, but it was a 'he said, she said' situation and that I'd need proof. I told them he follows me around. They said, 'it's a small campus, and we're bound to run into each other.' I mean they were polite and apologetic, but they basically told me I was on my own."

Angel could feel the familiar heat rising in him. The hair on his arms tingled.

"Will you be around tonight?" he asked.

"Yes. Wait. Angel, you're not thinking about driving here are you?"

"I'm leaving in ten minutes," he said.

"No. For real, no. I just wanted to talk to you and get some advice."

"Fine, I'll give it to you in person."

"No, Angel. That's silly. And I don't think Maggie would appreciate your driving here to see me."

"No more Maggie."

"What do you mean?"

"Maggie and I are over. I mean, really, really over."

"Oh, Angel. I'm so sorry."

"Yep. It was your fault, too."

"Mine? How? Now I'm really sorry."

"Boy, are you easy?"

"You were kidding?"

"Yes, Wanda, I was kidding. Not about the breaking up part, though." He paused. "So, you really don't want to see me, huh?"

"Of course, I want to see you. It's just that it's stupid to drive all the way here. There's nothing you can do about Rorie. That's his name, Rorie. My stalker."

Angel chuckled. "I'll be there in about three hours. I'll call for directions when I get to campus."

"Angel, there's no purpose in coming. You can't help."

"That's okay. Maybe I'll find something else to do when I get there."

"Oh," she said. He could swear she said the single syllable as if she were blushing. "Well, in that case, I guess I'll pretty up."

"Don't go to any trouble on my account. I don't even care if you're wearing clothes."

"You are a bad man," she laughed.

Angel hung up and munched on an M&M. He peeked in the tube room, and Eddie and Sand were both there. He plopped in a chair. He glared at a sophomore social member. "Leave," he said. The kid got up and scurried away.

"You guys up for a road trip?" Angel asked.

Sand looked at him. "Can't. You know that. We have a bridge tournament in Montreal."

"Oh," Angel said. He had forgotten.

"Where were we going?" Eddie asked.

"Boston. There's a guy there who needs some advice on how to deal with women," Angel said.

"Like a lesson in manners?" Sand said.

"Exactly," Angel said.

"Well, that sounds like fun," Eddie said, "but we can't. Is it just one guy?"

"Yeah, I think so."

"Well, then you can deal with him on your own. Advice?" Eddie asked.

"Please," Angel said.

"Be resolute. Go after him hard and don't let up until there's no way he can fight back."

"He's right," Sand said. "If he's bigger than you, use anything available. If you're on his turf, look about you for potential weapons."

"I doubt this guy has knives or guns lying around his dorm room," Angel said.

"Anything can be a weapon," Eddie said. "Lamps, books, trash cans, chairs."

"That's not just so you have weapons," Sand said. "You need to be aware of what's available to him. You may be wailing on him, and, if he hits you with a lamp, you're fucked."

"Got it," Angel said. "Go hard. Look around me."

"You know who wins a fight, don't you?" Eddie said.

Angel smiled. This was going to be some *Art of War* shit.

"The guy who doesn't mind getting hurt," Eddie said. "If pain bothers you, don't fight."

Angel smiled. "I think I'm good on that count. And I can box. You've seen me."

Sand laughed, and Eddie shook his head. "Angel," Eddie said, "Sand or I could beat you to death in five minutes. You're not that tough. I mean, look at you."

"What's wrong with me?" Angel asked.

"You're scrawny," Eddie said.

Cane walked in. "He's right, Angel, you're a scrawny little fuck."

"I'm lean," Angel said. "Like Clint Eastwood."

Cane barked his laughter. "Who told you that? Maggie?"

Sand shook his head at Cane, a 'we're not mentioning Maggie' look.

"What? So, now, Angel's so fucking sensitive a name would bother him? Have you seen that hot black chick he's banging?"

"Yeah," Sand said. "Marilyn. What's up with that? Are you two boyfriend-girlfriend?"

"Yep," Cane said, "and Angel's the girlfriend. She could beat the shit out of him, too."

"You guys are so fucking funny. I wish I could stay here and laugh all fucking night, but I'm going to kick a pervert's ass while you two go play bridge. Who's the pussy, I wonder?"

"You, definitely," Cane said.

Angel shook his head and headed upstairs. He finished dressing and threw clean underwear and a shirt in a bag and went to the bathroom for his toothbrush. He rolled four joints and tucked them in his underwear.

He brewed a pot of coffee and bought M&Ms for the road.

He smoked the last of a roach while the coffee percolated. He filled his thermos and headed for his car.

He was excited. There was shit that needed doing, and a road trip beckoned. He thought briefly about calling Maggie lest she show up while he was aiding another woman but thought, 'why bother?' Maggie hadn't contacted him since their fight except to tell Groucho that she was back at Colby safely. And that had been three weeks earlier.

The ride was pleasant but uneventful. He lost WDCR long before he approached Boston, and the Boston stations all seemed to suck. There was supposed to be a good Harvard station, but he couldn't remember what it was. So, he turned off the radio and listened to the wind hum in the niches of his ears. The engine sounded good. The Austin Healey wasn't powerful, but the exhaust made a pleasant, throaty sound.

It was a pity. Before I-89 was finished, the Boston drive must have gone through mountains and small towns. Now it was just interstate. It was pretty, but banal. Trees and curves stretching monotonously for two hours.

He had no trouble finding Boston College. He just took a right onto Commonwealth and followed signs. He was surprised how far it was from downtown Boston, but the campus was bucolic and peaceful. It seemed an unlikely place to harbor stalkers and girlfriend beaters.

Wanda sat on the stoop outside her dorm and waved gaily when she saw Angel drive up.

She ran to him and leaped on him, wrapping her legs around his waist and her arms around his neck. Angel laughed and spun her around.

When he put her down, she held her face up to him, and he kissed her. God. She tasted so sweet.

"Um, wow," he said. "Someone's in a good mood. I had this image of your hiding and trembling in your room."

Wanda laughed a tinkly laugh. Who was this bubbly, excited creature? The Wanda he knew was Miss Cool. Always ready with a verbal jab.

She hooked her arm through his and took him to her room. It was part of a suite of rooms joined in the middle by a common area. She even had her own bathroom. Her room had real furniture and paintings hanging from the walls. There were books and folders everywhere, and the clutter went well with the rich furnishings. A circular rug with a bright peacock held it all together.

"This is nicer than I expected," Angel said. "I take it Jesuits aren't very monastic these days?"

Wanda laughed. "This is the nicest dorm on campus. Sit. Talk to me."

"Are your roommates around?" he asked. He could feel the blood in his throat thickening his speech.

"No," she said smiling. "Why, whatever did you have in mind?"

"Actually, I was hoping they were." he said, "To protect me from your wiles."

"You are so bad," she said. But she sat on her bed and patted a spot next to her.

"I think I'll stay over here," he said and sat at her desk. A *Bhagavad Gita* sat on a pile of notes. It had about a million bookmarks sticking out. He flipped it open and smiled. "You read Sanskrit?"

"I'm learning," she said.

"So, what's the deal with the criminal justice system here?" he said.

"It's not their fault. If I had gone in originally with a bruise on my cheek and a black eye, they might have been able to help. But Rorie and I were alone, so I didn't even have a roommate to back me up." She went to the window and gestured. "He stood right there last night. He must have seen my light and known I was here. He just smiled up at me and drew his finger across his throat. I don't think he'd do anything. He probably just gets off scaring me." She pointed, again. "His dorm's right there, so he can see my light from his room. That's kind of creepy. I've stopped walking around nude."

Angel got up and stood behind her. "Which dorm is his?"

Wanda pointed.

Angel put his arms around her waist. "Okay," he said. "You wait here. I'm going to visit Rorie. What's his room number?"

"Seven. It's that window in the middle on the first floor."

Angel nuzzled her neck, but she felt tense and didn't return his affection. She turned to him.

"Angel, what are you going to do?"

"Talk to him."

"He won't listen to you. He's a rich, spoiled brat who thinks his father can get him out of anything."

Angel chuckled. "Rich, spoiled brat. Seems like I've heard those words recently. Ah, the irony."

"Angel. Be careful. He's bigger than you, and he wrestles. Don't try to start anything. You'll just get hurt, and then I'll feel worse."

"Relax." He kissed her neck again, and this time she sighed and melted a bit. "I can be very persuasive."

She turned and put her arms around him. "Thanks for coming. I really appreciate this. And if you were serious about Maggie being a thing of the past, I may reward you for your efforts."

"No," he said. "It's the other way around. I needed this, and I may reward you." He kissed her softly. "God, you taste good."

Angel crossed campus knowing her eyes were on him as he walked. His back tingled from her presence.

He hadn't been kidding. This was exactly what he needed, muscular release and getting the hell off the Dartmouth campus. Even the Boston springtime air smelled different. There were huge trees everywhere which were partially leafed. They were ahead of the Hanover trees, but not by much. He knew to savor northern springtime. In a few weeks, he would be home and driving daily to the paper mill, where the air was like a furnace and the odor like a sewer. But the work always pleased him. There was no need for thought. His muscles just repeated whatever work they were asked to do. It was Zen-like.

And, of course, Wanda was learning Sanskrit. Every surgeon needed to know Sanskrit, didn't she? He laughed. Smart girls warped his orbit. That was for sure.

He thought about Eddie and Sand. Be resolute. Go full blast. No doubts. Look for weapons. Got it. It was shitty that the guy was bigger than him and a wrestler. This might get painful. That was okay, though. Pain had a way of clarifying the mind and reminding it to return to basics. He had a Faulkner essay to write. He needed to try to be as basic as possible. He and his class had fought again that week. They didn't appreciate his little disquisition on Einstein and relativity. He had been trying to tie relativity to the fractured points of view in *As I Lay Daying* and *The Sound and the Fury*. Charles had been the only one on his side. Stone probably agreed with him, but it was evident that Stone was weary of his showboating. It had been funny, though, when Stone sighed loudly while Angel was talking. Cara caught that. She smiled ironically at Angel. See, her smile said, even Stone thinks you're a dick.

That was okay. And now he was going to be a big dick, or at least to swing one at Rorie's head. Was everyone Irish at this school? Joyce went to a Jesuit school, though Angel doubted it was as nice as Boston College.

When he got to Rorie's room, he wondered whether he should have a plan. It was pretty late for that, though, so he just knocked. He had seen Rorie's light on as he neared the building, so he was reasonably confident Rorie was at home.

Oh, shit, what if he has a roommate? Angel hadn't thought of that.

The door opened, and a taller, slightly less lean version of Angel stared at him.

"Are you Rorie?" Angel asked.

"Yeah."

Angel hit him in the solar plexus as hard as he could. Rorie staggered backwards and went down hard.

Then, Angel fucked up. He fucked up bad.

Instead of just taking advantage of the fact that Rorie had no wind and was choking practically to death, Angel did the TV talking bad guy thing.

"I'm told that you've been a bad boy, that you've been hitting and terrorizing a chick named Wanda."

Rorie struggled to sit up. He didn't look as if he had heard a word Angel had said. Angel leaned over and grabbed Rorie's hair. "Hey, fuckball, I'm talking to you." Rorie gasped and choked, but he wouldn't look at Angel or respond. Then Rorie lashed out with his right leg, connecting with Angel's bad knee and making him topple backwards. Angel felt and heard his skull make an ugly crunching sound when it hit the edge of a dresser. Rorie got to a knee. His breath was coming back, and Angel was dazed. Angel stood and looked for one of Eddie's weapons, but Rorie tackled him, driving him back into the dresser again. Both men fell to the ground, and Rorie grabbed Angel's left arm and tried to bend it into a half-nelson. Angel kicked at him and hit his chest. Angel got to his feet, but so did Rorie, who came at him again. Angel hit the same fucking dresser for a third time, and this time he felt his ribs explode. Angel turned away and grabbed a tiny, souvenir baseball bat on the dresser. Rorie punched Angel in the kidney, and Angel slid to a knee. Rorie grabbed him by his collar and swung him, face first, into the door. Angel slumped to the ground. Rorie staggered, but came after him. Rorie reached for Angel's shirt and dragged him to his feet. Angel kicked at Rorie's knee and missed, but Rorie backed up a step, and Angel swung the bat, catching Rorie on the left side of his face. Rorie went down as if he had been shot. Blood spurted from the gash on his face. Angel leaned over and hit him on the back of the head. Rorie made a grunting sound and stayed down this time. Angel looked in the mirror. Shit, his right eye was busted open again, the same brow he had split boxing in the fall. He dragged the semi-conscious Rorie to his desk and plopped him down in his chair.

"Now," Angel said. "I want you to write a note to Wanda. Write exactly what I say, word for word."

"Go fuck yourself," Rorie said.

Angel smiled. Tough son of a bitch.

Angel glanced at an open note-book on Rorie's desk. The letters slanted the wrong way. He was left-handed. Angel grabbed Rorie's right arm and slammed it down on the desk top. He took the bat and brought it down hard on Rorie's right hand.

Rorie made a muffled screaming sound.

"Shut the fuck up or I'll break the other hand, too," Angel said. He placed a pen in front of Rorie and pulled a cream-colored sheet of paper from a stack. Rorie turned, and Angel hit him on the head again. The bat made a satisfying cracking sound when it hit bone, the same sound it made when hitting a baseball solidly. Blood oozed from the wound.

Rorie picked up the pen.

"Write 'Wanda, I'm sorry I hit you. The first time I just lost my temper. I have no excuse. The second time was because I thought you were cheating on me. I can't believe I did that. I've never even gotten angry with a girl before.'"

Rorie wrote. Angel watched grimly.

"Write 'I know you think I'm stalking you, and I guess I am. I don't mean to. I come by your room sometimes thinking we might talk and get back together. But you hate me and that makes me crazy. The throat slitting gesture was wrong. I apologize for that, too. The Campus Police came by and talked to me. They made me aware that what I'm doing is not only wrong but illegal. I promise you I'll never come near you again. If I do, you can give this letter to the police. What I'm writing protects you from me, but it will help me keep my distance because I know what will happen if I don't. Again, I'm so sorry for hurting you. Rorie.'" Angel looked at it. "Good," he said. "Now, date it yesterday and put your hand down on the page, flat."

Rorie looked puzzled but did as he was told.

"Fingerprints," Angel said.

Rorie nodded. "Nice touch."

"I thought so. Now, I'm going to walk out of here and give this to Wanda. I will check with Wanda periodically and with the Campus Police. If you go near her or she's scared of you, or, if something happens to her, I'll come back. And it won't just be me, next time." He looked at Rorie. "We cool?"

"No," Rorie growled. "You're a douche."

Angel went to the door and turned. "You're a lot tougher than I thought you'd be."

"Gee, thanks. Come over here without that bat and show me how tough you are."

Angel stared at him. He could feel his eye swelling shut and taste the blood as it dripped onto his lip. He smiled and dropped the bat.

But Rorie didn't move. Angel held up the letter. "In case you get some wild hair about beating Wanda into giving this back to you, she won't have it. I will. It gets forwarded to the police if something happens to her." He folded the letter and put it in his pocket.

"Behave," Angel said. "Find a girl who likes pain."

"Are you fucking her?"

"Wanda?" Angel asked. "I don't even know her. I'm a friend of a friend."

Angel was glad for the cool of the evening air. His adrenaline ebbed as he crossed campus, and he knelt by a tree to vomit. Afterwards, he walked about thirty feet and sat under another tree, trying to catch his breath. His knee hurt, his ribs screamed, and his face throbbed. He had glimpsed enough in the mirror to know he needed stitches. Shit. Wanda was going to be pissed.

Why did chicks get pissed when guys got hurt defending them? It was a mystery.

He was right. He was barely inside her room before Wanda began chiding him. 'Stupid' seemed to be her favorite word. Angel got the gist, so he stopped listening.

"You're going to need stitches," she said. She was cute and funny when she tried to sound fussy. "What are you smiling at?"

"You."

"Men. You're proud of yourself, aren't you? How did your getting beat up help the situation?"

"Beat up?" Angel said. "I won." He grimaced as she poked at his ribs. "They're fine. Leave them alone."

"They may be broken."

"They're just cracked. Ow. Quit poking me woman." He pulled the letter from his pocket and handed it to her.

Wanda took it. "What's this? Your will?" She opened it. Angel watched her eyes widen as she read. "Angel, did Rorie really write this? How on earth did you convince him to write this? He admits hitting me and stalking me."

"I told you. I'm very persuasive," he said. "Ow. Leave my ribs alone, woman. Give that letter to a roommate. Tell her to use it if he comes near you." He grabbed her wrists and stopped her prying hands. "Wanda, he won't bother you again. I promise."

Wanda pulled him towards her bathroom and began wiping his brow clean. "We're going to the infirmary," she said. "This won't close. You need stitches."

"No infirmary."

"Why not?"

"Because Rorie will be there."

Wanda took a step back and looked at him. "Angel, what did you do?"

"Nothing. We had a scuffle. I kind of broke his hand. And he probably has a concussion. And his face is pretty fucked up."

"Angel."

"'Angel,'" he mocked. "It wasn't my fault. He was tough. Now, find a sewing kit and stitch my eyebrow."

"Angel, I don't know how to do that."

"Have you ever sewn on a button?"

"Yes."

"Same thing."

Wanda laughed. "It is not the same thing, but all right. I can't believe I'm mixed up with hooligans."

Angel smiled. He was a hooligan.

"And stop smiling at me, Angel. You're sweet, but you're not funny."

His grin got bigger.

"Okay," she said laughing. "What?"

"I'm gonna get me some," he laughed.

"Hah. We'll see about that," she laughed.

"Nope. I am. I'm very persuasive," and he ran his hand up her thigh.

She slapped at his hand and then disappeared. Angel looked in the mirror. Yep. It was the exact same spot as before.

Wanda reappeared in the bathroom with a small bag and her desk chair. "Sit," she said.

Angel sat and smiled up at her.

Wanda fiddled in the medicine cabinet and found a bottle of hydrogen peroxide. From her kit, she took needle and thread. "White or black thread?"

"Black." That would look badass.

Wanda shook her head and tried to thread the needle, but her hands weren't steady, and she kept failing. Angel took it from her and put the thread through the tiny loop.

"And you're sewing me up?" he said.

"Shut up." She poured the peroxide over the needle and waited till it stopped bubbling. She put the needle to his brow, and he howled. She jumped back.

"Just fucking with you," he said. "Do it a little closer to the cut. You don't want it to bunch up. The scar would look ghastly. We're going for cool, not ghastly."

"Do you want to do this?"

"Shutting up."

Wanda put the needle to his brow again and slowly poked it through the skin. When the world didn't end, she gathered courage and began to sew. "I have no idea how far apart to do these things," she said.

"I think the rule is the closer the stitches the less scarring. Just pull together gently. Don't make them pucker."

"Like this?" she said. She pulled the thread through both sides of the cut and pulled lightly. She stood back. Angel looked in the mirror.

"Perfect," he said.

"This doesn't hurt?"

"Of course, it hurts," he laughed. "Come on. Finish up. I want to get some food and then play with you."

Wanda shook her head but went back to her surgery. She worked slowly and took forever, but, when she finished, the stitches looked pretty good. She pulled tiny scissors from her kit and cut the ends after knotting the thread.

"Close your eyes," she said and poured peroxide over the stitches. She patted it dry and did it a second time. She used the wet cotton balls to clean his cheek.

"Do you have another shirt?" she asked.

Angel nodded. "In my car."

"Where's that?"

"Out front. The blue and white Austin Healey. The tops down. The bag's in the back seat."

"You have a sports car?"

Angel nodded.

"Cool. You may get lucky tonight after all. I had you figured for a motorcycle guy or something."

"That's at home in Florida."

"Of course, it is." She went to the door. "Anything else I need to know about Rorie?"

"Nope. He's got a broken hand which will require surgery and several nasty knocks on the cranium."

"What did you hit him with?"

"A small baseball bat. A Red Sox bat. Serves him right for following the Sox. Oh, and I told him you don't know me. I'm just a friend of a friend."

She shook her head and left. Angel gingerly unbuttoned his shirt and removed it. It was covered in blood. He smelled rank. The fighting, he guessed. He stripped the rest of the way and got in her shower and washed everything but his face. While he was in the shower, he heard music playing and saw Wanda put his bag down, but she disappeared again, so he showered to the beat of the bass and drum. He stepped out, soaking wet, and reached into his pants pocket for a joint and matches. He lit it and stepped back into the shower. He leaned against the wall and let the water and smoke unknot his muscles. The joint tasted good but made him aware his lip was sore, too. He must have busted it on that fucking dresser which kept rising to meet him. That thing was a bitch.

He took inventory of his ailments. His ribs looked raw, but he pushed and nothing squished, so he must have been right when he said they were just cracked. The damage seemed to be in just two of them, not that the number mattered. Cracked ribs meant difficulty breathing and sleeping and pain during sex. He had seen Wanda's body, though, and knew she would be worth it. His knee worried him. It had been operated on twice and looked like shit in an X-ray. He hoped it was just sore or twisted.

He stubbed out the joint and called Wanda.

She came quickly and handed him a towel. "Try to get as little blood on it as possible," she said.

"Wow. Your gratitude is touching."

Wanda laughed. She touched his ribs again. "How are they?"

"Fine."

She bent slightly and touched his knee. It looked raw and swollen. "How's your knee?"

"Fine."

But Thor was looking her in the eye and asking, 'what about me?'

Wanda stroked his shaft. "And this bad boy?"

"Now, he's going to require some serious attention. He's all stressed out."

"Hmm," Wanda said. She knelt in front of him and kissed up and down the shaft, murmuring 'poor baby' as she went. Angel leaned against the sink. Now they were getting somewhere.

But Wanda just patted Thor and rose. "He'll have to wait."

"Say what?"

"I need to bandage your eye. I stole Merthiolate and bandages from Julie, my roommate." She dabbed the red liquid over the stitched area. Angel winced. "Putting needles through your skin doesn't bother you, but Merthiolate does?" she chuckled.

"It stings," he said.

"Aw, does it hurt his little brow?"

But her face was too near his to resist, and he took it in his hands and gazed at her intently. Her eyes changed as she read his meaning, and she tilted her head back to receive his kiss. He kissed her long. When he finished, she stood in the same pose for a moment before opening her eyes. "Um, wow."

"Yeah," he said. "I was just thinking the same thing."

"You taste like pot."

"I do," he said. "Want some?"

"I think I need some," she said.

Angel lit the joint for her and went to dress. "Now," he said, "where can a man get a good meal around here?"

Wanda posed in the bathroom door and raised her skirt with one hand. She looked very Veronica Lake, if Veronica Lake had had freckles across the bridge of her nose and had asked a man to eat her.

Angel smiled. "I missed you, Wanda. I didn't know how much until now."

She cackled. "Is pizza okay?"

"Pizza's fine."

Angel sat at her desk and pulled on socks and boots. "Sanskrit," he said, shaking his head.

They walked hand in hand to Queensbury Street and sat outside a little pizza joint. The food was slow and the service almost non-existent, but Angel didn't care. For the first time in weeks, Maggie was gone from his head. He had been right. He needed to hit somebody, and he needed to get hit. Both were cathartic.

Wanda surprised him. He had thought her a chatty type because they had talked so easily and intimately the few times they had been together, but she was content to sit sipping her beer and holding his hand. They watched college couples walking up and down the street, and, from time to time, Wanda would invent a scenario which explained them.

"See the cute girl with the really nerdy guy?" she said. "She's always been into jocks, but she got tired of how shallow they are and latched onto that guy. He has no clue how he got lucky. Well, he hasn't actually gotten lucky yet, but he thinks tonight might be the night."

"That's why he looks so fidgety?" Angel asked.

"Uh huh," she said. "She's already tired of him, though, and she's about to break his heart. She thought he was going to be a rich doctor."

"He's not?"

"Nope. A biochemist. And they don't make much money. Plus, they always have that lab smell on them."

They grew quiet. Angel poured Wanda another beer.

"Now do us," he said.

"What?"

"You're that girl that just walked by. What would she have thought about us?"

Wanda knit her brows. "She probably thought I was babysitting Frankenstein's monster."

Angel laughed. "No, seriously. Pretend I'm not banged up. What would someone see?"

Wanda looked at him. "They'd probably see a girl with a super crush on a man who knows she has no chance."

"No, for real," he said.

"For real."

"And why doesn't she have a chance?" he asked. "She's lots better looking than he is."

"True, but no one has a chance with him. He'll just hurt her eventually, and she's had enough of that."

Angel sat silent.

"You sound like Maggie," he said finally.

She took his hand. "Oh, honey, I'm exactly like Maggie. I knew when I met her that she needed a man like you, but that she couldn't handle what she was getting into. No one could."

"Why? What's wrong with me? I'm nice."

"You are a super sweetie," she said. "But you are super sweet to every girl. What did you do to drive Maggie away?"

"Nothing. She came to my room, and she saw that Jane had stayed there. She assumed I had banged Jane. I hadn't. I didn't even sleep with her. She passed out in my bed, and I wrote all night. I didn't climb in bed until Jane was already out of it."

"Oh, Angel, you are so stupid."

But finding out exactly why he was stupid would have to wait because their pizza arrived.

Angel eyed her quizzically while they ate. He winced when he bit into a jalapeno with his sore lip, but he was starving and ate with relish. He poured each of them another beer and watched her eat. She really was a fine girl, albeit an odd one. Humor and brains mixed with some stubborn Irish sense of self. He didn't know what she was going to tell him about Maggie, but he was sure it would be interesting and that she wouldn't pull any punches.

Wanda excused herself to go to the restroom, and he watched her walk away. My

God, her body was even better than Marilyn's. Marilyn's was close, but her waist was thicker. Maggie's figure was pretty damned fine, too, and her ass was spectacular. He loved to watch Maggie read in bed. When she lay on her side, he would watch the sine curve of her body flow downwards over her hips and then taper forever into her long legs. Wanda's body, though, screamed sensuality. It said, 'I'll never need you, but while you're here, I want you to fuck me until I come over and over. And watch out, I'm a biter.' Wanda's breasts were full and heavy, a perfect match for her hips and ass. Every curve complemented every other curve. He watched until he saw her walking back towards him. She sat and smiled.

"You were eating me up with your eyes," she said.

"God was kind when he created you," Angel said.

"You're silly," she said, but she blushed and ducked her head.

They walked back to her dorm in silence. Rorie's dorm light was out. Perhaps he was still getting medical treatment. Perhaps he had fled the country.

Back in Wanda's room, Angel pulled the curtain so Rorie couldn't aim a telescope at them or something. They undressed shyly. He removed her clothes and she his. Angel felt like a first-timer. He didn't know why. There was just something about Wanda. Her sensuality had morphed into a kind of still grace. In the darkened room, her freckles disappeared and her hair seemed darker.

They climbed in bed together and pulled the sheets over them.

"Wanda, do we need to finish the conversation about how impossible I am before we do this, or would it just spoil the love-making?"

She leaned on an elbow and pushed the hair off his forehead.

"No. I can tell you." She looked at him sadly. "You really are a sweet man, and you're a natural protector, but you cheat on whomever you're with all the time."

"I never cheated on Maggie."

"Oh, baby, you cheated on her with me, with Jane, and probably with half a dozen others."

"Our definition of cheating must be different," he said. "I never had sex with anyone else while Maggie and I were in an official relationship."

"Listen to you," she said. Her voice had taken on an Irish lilt. "An official relationship. Did you sign papers or something? No, that girl has wanted you since she first laid eyes on you. I know because I felt the exact same way. But, sweetheart, you give all your humor and tenderness to every girl you're with. You may not put your penis into them, but, to Maggie, it's the same. You cherish girls, just as right now you cherish me. I see the look in your eyes. Women seek that look their whole lives. It's a look that says, 'you are the finest woman ever, and I'm so glad I'm here with you and nowhere else on the planet.' Being with you is remarkable, because it's simultaneously humorous and sexually charged. A girl can relax and laugh and just be herself. Plus, she knows she gets an orgasm later. You're in love with lavishing affection on girls. Maggie knows that, and it drives her crazy. I know it. That's why I never made a play for you. Being with you is amazing. Being away from you is sheer torture. No, baby, you cheated on that poor girl, and she was right to be hurt."

Angel absorbed all that as best he could. The little boy in him kept screaming 'not fair' and 'I didn't do it' but the man in him knew it to be true. At least from the woman's perspective.

"But, if I'm supposed to appreciate how a woman feels and thinks, why doesn't she have to do the same? Why doesn't she have to know that I mean well and that I'm not, in my heart, being disloyal to her?"

"Oh, sweetie, it doesn't work that way. Maggie didn't hurt you when she accused you. She may have angered you, but that's completely different. No, with you, it will always be the woman who feels pain."

Angel stared at the ceiling. Shit.

"If you don't want to make love any more, I'll understand," she said. She ran her hand over his chest.

Angel took her hand and squeezed. "You think I would take a beating without a whimper and then be hurt by the truth? I'm sure you were right about all of that. There was a girl named Cassie before Maggie, and I'll bet she suffered for three years. I've probably caused a lot more pain than your friend Rorie has."

"Oh, Angel. I didn't say all that to make you feel bad."

"I don't feel bad. Not for myself, anyway. I can't change who I am. I don't feel any guilt. But I feel bad for Maggie and Cassie."

He stopped and thought.

"Wanda, do you know why guys like to fight?"

She looked at him with a raised eyebrow. "All right. I'll play. Why do men fight?"

"I didn't say that. We fight for a million reasons, for everything from a brutal nature to self-defense. I asked why you thought we enjoy fighting."

"Because it makes you feel manly?"

"Partly," he laughed, "But also because it's completely true. There's no bullshit. You hit me and I hit you. Pow. Bam. It's real, and that makes us feel pure."

Wanda smiled. "Well, that explains football and rugby and boxing and a lot of things," she said. "I'm not sure how we got on the topic."

"Because when you talk to me, it always seems real. There's no bullshit with you. You're honest and direct."

"So, you're complimenting me for my judgmental rant about you?"

"No, that was a thank you, and an honest assessment of what I like most about you," he said.

"Why thank you, sir. I'm not sure men always appreciate my frank nature, but I'll take it."

"Here comes the complimentary part," he said. "Actually, more like the adoration part. And, since you know me so well, you'll know I'm telling you the truth. Ready?"

Wanda laughed. "I don't know. I guess."

"You're the finest woman ever," he said, "and I'm so glad I'm here with you and nowhere else on the planet."

"Oh, shit," Wanda said. She kissed his chest and lay her head on it. "I think I just melted."

"That's okay," he said. "I think my resolve stiffened even as we spoke." He took her hand and put it on his shaft. Thor bobbed in acquiescence. It was go time.

Wanda put a hand on his chest. "Angel, I just wanted to tell you I've never done this."

Angel smiled. "You don't even know what we're going to do. I don't even know what we're going to do."

"No, I've never made love to someone I wasn't in a relationship with."

"Wanda, we've already had sex, before."

"Yes, that was sex. This feels like more. I don't want you to stop. I just want you to know this is special for me."

Angel grabbed a handful of hair and pulled her face upwards towards his. "We've been in a relationship since we sat on the Phi Psi steps, and we both know it."

Wanda didn't answer, but her eyes teared. Angel kissed her softly. She threw her arms around him, pulling him down to her, and he kissed her more fiercely.

And it was as if his fight with Rorie had been foreplay. His pent-up world seemed to explode in him, and he wanted Wanda more than he had ever wanted anyone. He kissed her mouth and moved to her throat. He crushed a breast in his hand and then took it in his mouth. He sucked hard, as if trying to get the whole breast in his mouth. His hand found her pussy, and he rubbed the heel of his hand up and down, pressing hard.

He moved his mouth down her belly and roughly jammed two, then three fingers in her.

She gasped and arched to meet his fingers. Without removing them or slowing their invasion, he moved between her legs and took her clit between his teeth. Wanda arched her back again and grabbed huge handfuls of his hair.

Angel removed his hand from her pussy and forced her legs backwards until they were almost by her head.

"Oh, God," she moaned. "What are you doing to me?"

"Hold your legs there," he commanded. Wanda grasped her ankles and held herself wide open for him.

Angel stopped licking and rubbed her clit with his hand. He put his face to her again and re-inserted his fingers. He worked her faster and faster while she went berserk. He circled her ass with a finger and then slowly inserted it. She came with a gush and screamed 'fuck, fuck, fuck' loud enough to summon Rorie from across campus.

Angel straightened to his knees and leaned over to insert himself into her, but she said 'no' and pushed him off her.

"I want to be on top," she said.

Angel lay obedient to her will while Wanda straddled him and lowered herself onto him. "Oh, my God," she said as she took all of him into her. "Oh, my God."

She put her hands on his chest and began fucking him, but when she saw the pain on his face, she said, "Oh, your ribs," and moved her hands to the bed. Angel was fascinated. Wanda simultaneously fucked him and kind of slid upwards. He could tell she was rubbing her clit against him with each motion. It felt different from anything he had ever experienced. And he was fascinated by her face. He thought he had seen every kind of fucking face, from the ones who looked in agony to the ones with closed eyes and looks of rapture. He had even seen frightened 'what am I doing?' faces. But Wanda leaned slightly forward and stared into his eyes the whole time she fucked him. It was so, he didn't know what the word was, personal, maybe. Intimate. Direct. It was just so fucking Wanda. He watched the freckles on the bridge of her nose and the heaving of her ridiculously gorgeous breasts. Her body was nearly parallel to his with each stroke, and her breasts hung straight down, emphasizing their weight and shape. He grabbed them and squeezed hard. Her eyes widened and a smile crossed her face, the kind of smile he offered up during a fight. Her breathing got heavier, and he took her left breast into his mouth. She bent to leave it there while she finished fucking him. He could feel her body convulsing as if she were having a massive stroke. All her muscles gathered, and her eyes, though they never left his, became glazed and dim. He could tell that she had gone inside herself, sensing the eruption which mounted and attacked her from within. Then she came. Her smile became a grimace, and she finally closed her eyes. She silently mouthed, 'Oh, God' several times and collapsed against him.

His ribs were on fire, and his sore knee seemed to be cramping, but he put his arms around her and caressed her hair as she lay gasping on him. When she finally rolled off, her chest still heaving, Angel grit his teeth and tried to hold off the paroxysm of pain which gripped his chest and knee. He tried breathing the pain away, but there was little to do but focus on Wanda and wait for it to subside. It felt as if a rib had broken in half and penetrated a muscle. The pain was excruciating.

He reached sideways and ran his hand over her face and then grabbed her hair.

"That was amazing," he said.

Wanda chuckled, "Yes, it was." But when she looked sideways at him, she saw his agony and rolled towards him. "Oh, Angel, did that hurt you? I didn't think about your ribs."

"I'm fine. Just give me a minute." He lay until his breathing slowed. Wanda watched him intently.

"Angel, did you even come?" Thor was bobbing 'no' at her.

"I didn't have a chance," he said. "It's all right. It's almost as if, the better the sex is, the less likely I am to come. It's a paradox."

Wanda put her hand on his shaft. "May I?"

Angel smiled and nodded. "Yes, please. I love a polite woman."

Wanda bent over him, careful not to lean against his sides and inflame his ribs. "Yum," she said. "Is this what I taste like?"

"Probably. I'm not licking my dick, so I'm not exactly sure what you're tasting."

"If you're going to get mean and gross, I'm going to stop."

"Sorry. Yes, if it tastes like honey with a drop of vinegar, it's probably all you. Nice, huh?"

Wanda gave him an evil smile and then ran her tongue the length of his shaft to his balls. She tickled his balls with light flicks and then went back up to the head.

"Seriously, Angel, why didn't you come? You didn't like what I did?"

"I loved what you did," Angel said. "I've never experienced anything like it."

"You're making fun of me," she said. "You've never had a girl on top?"

"I have. I've never had a girl so adroit at rubbing herself against me. I've never had a girl stare me down while fucking me. Mostly, though, I'd never had Wanda doing any of those things," he said.

Wanda laughed and went back to work. She took his head in her mouth and ran her tongue over it. Then she tried her best to take all of him down her throat, but choked and gave up laughing. "You, sir, are too long."

She gave Thor a final pat and rolled off him. He cradled her head, and she cuddled against him.

"This doesn't hurt?" she asked.

"No," he said. "It's my left side that hurts. You're fine. To answer your earlier question more seriously, I don't come when I'm on my back. If I'd been standing when you ministered to me with your mouth like you just did, I'd have come like a volcano."

"Why?"

"Gravity, I guess."

"Oh," she said. She kissed his cheek. "Then why don't you stand up? I can play good Catholic schoolgirl for you."

Angel smiled at her.

"No," she said. "I'm serious. Stand up."

He did. And she did. And he did.

His drive home was peaceful and uneventful, and when he got back to Phi Psi, he went gingerly up the stairs to his room. No one seemed to be around except for the tube room geeks. He remembered that Sand and Eddie had gone to a bridge tournament. The house was dark and quiet. Angel was glad. He could lie in bed and fantasize about the evening's events in peace.

He flipped the light switch in his room and stood still. Shreds of paper were everywhere. He picked up the pieces nearest him and realized they were all from the novel he had begun about Maggie. He went to his desk and picked up the sealed envelope which sat next to his malevolently beaten typewriter.

Angel looked around to see what Maggie would have used to destroy a typewriter. A bent golf club was halfway through the plaster above his bed.

Shit. The girl must have been pissed.

Angel went downstairs and got a Coke and a bag of peanut M&Ms before he returned to the carnage. He rolled a joint and sat at his desk contemplating the letter and the scene.

Groucho poked his head in the door.

"Maggie came by," Groucho said.

"I see that," Angel said.

"She asked me where you were."

"And?"

"You know me, Angel. I can't lie to anyone. I told her you went to Boston, but I told her it was just to help Wanda out and not for a romantic interlude."

"A romantic interlude, huh. Since when do you sound like Tennessee Williams?"

"Anyway. She seemed calm and thanked me. She closed the door. I thought she was just going to wait for you." Groucho looked at the destruction. "Guess she got tired of waiting."

"You think?"

Groucho nodded and left, closing the door behind him.

Angel smiled. Groucho was a funny fuck. There wasn't a kinder, gentler person around.

He lit the joint and leaned back trying to guess the contents of the letter.

Oh, Angel, I've seen the error of my ways and want you back.

Unlikely.

Angel, you are the biggest shit that ever walked the face of the earth and I hope you die in agony. If you come near me again, I'll kill you or have you arrested.

Much more probable. Of course, she should've said 'who ever walked,' not 'that ever walked.' 'Who' is for people; 'that' is for things. Why did everyone mess that up?

The first response was closer to the truth, but Maggie wouldn't know that. The second would be what she thought she felt. Angel sighed. Some protector he was. He opened the envelope and read:

Dear Angel,

I'm sorry for ruining your things. I've calmed down now. I guess violence can be therapeutic. Who knew? Is that why you fight? I'll bet it is.

I'm not even angry any more. I see now that it was a mistake for us to be together. I know you meant it when you told me you loved me. It's just that you aren't capable of love. Your Faulkner characters are more real to you than I am, or anyone else for that matter. Oh, we're real enough when you are on top of us, but we cease to be when we drive home.

I just re-read that last part, and I know it sounded angry and accusatory. I didn't mean it that way.

You are a wonderful man, and I wish you well. You just aren't the type of man I need. I need someone who can commit to me. I know that sounds jealous and weak and needy, but it's true.

So, keep on making everyone you meet happy and no one feel truly loved.

Don't get me wrong. I know I gained a lot from you this year. I am stronger and more confident. I am definitely more sexually daring. I now smoke pot. Not sure if that's a good thing. I'm also more intellectual. I used to study hard to make good grades. Now, I actually care about what I learn, and I think much more analytically. So, you see, I can say good things about you. And you are a wonderful lover, sexually. I know I like my body a lot more than I ever did before.

You are smart and funny, too. So, now, I just have to find a man who's smart and funny and actually cares about me, even when I'm not nearby. How hard can that be? Probably, really hard. I've already met someone who may qualify. He took care of me the night you told me to 'fuck off and get the hell out.' He's been kind ever since. He goes to Dartmouth, too. You would probably like him.

I will be at Dartmouth next year, so if you could keep your distance, that would be nice.

Shit. I'm getting angry again, so I'll stop and say goodbye.

Maggie the Cat

P.S. I tore up your Maggie script, because you no longer have the right to dissect me or praise me.

Well, shit.

Angel put *Baby Please Don't Go* on his stereo and re-lit his joint. He smoked and munched M&Ms among the ruins of his room.

Much of what Maggie had written was true, but the rest was the result of being in pain. And he, dumbass that he was, had done the hurting. It didn't bother him much. He couldn't have done anything very differently. Not without being another person. The Angel Maggie was attracted to was the same Angel who hurt her.

No, what bothered him was what Wanda said.

He wasn't sure if he would ever be able to hold onto a lover without her becoming jealous. His treatment of women was purely involuntary. He liked almost all of them. That was one of the problems. And he liked making them feel good. The combination was very *Tom Jones* deadly.

What he wanted most to do was to drive to Colby and scoop Maggie up in his arms. He wanted to protect her from the bad man who hurt her.

That would be him, though. A paradox, as it were.

He smiled. He still amused himself. That was good.

He searched the meager inventory of his feelings. Did he actually love Maggie? Sure. Of course, he did. He didn't know why. She was too needy. That was a shock. Fall for an Alpha and find a Beta. He guessed she was right. She was an Alpha around the girls at Colby. She even was when jousting with Cane and the guys. But she turned Beta the minute he kissed her or cooed into her ear.

Wanda would be the better match for him. Their wild romp that night had the best sex he'd ever had. Well, maybe. It was hard to tell, coming as hard as it did on the heels of a good, old-fashioned cock fight. His adrenaline and testosterone had been up and kicking.

Still, Wanda was magnificent. So, why did he prefer Maggie? Was it precisely because she was needy? Wanda had needed his muscle, but she didn't need him. She didn't need anyone. She was a self-sufficient cutie pie.

Angel put out the joint and sipped his Coke. He stared philosophically at the can, and it spoke eloquently to him. It said, 'why do you prefer me to Pepsi?'

The can was right. Taste couldn't be explained by looks or any other objective metric.

The reason he loved Maggie was because he loved Maggie.

He would tell her so.

But not in a way which would imply that he wanted her back. No, she wanted away from him, so let her go. If she wanted him back, they could talk.

Never, ever, pursue a girl. That was high on his list, right after 'never fuck a girl when she's drunk or high.' No, you had to wait until she didn't want to talk about feelings any more. Otherwise, you were just leaping back into a bowl full of vomit.

Oh, Maggie.

Angel went to his dresser and searched for aspirin. He hurt everywhere. His knee and ribs and face, especially, but his head and the rest of the body had joined in. He lifted his shirt and looked in the mirror. There was an angry red mark across his back from one of his frequent encounters with Rorie's fucking dresser.

He thought about the fight. That had been fun. Rorie was a tough son of a bitch. Angel wasn't sure he would like a fair rematch. But Rorie was an evil shit, and Angel played the sound of the bat hitting Rorie's head and crushing his hand over and over in his head.

He changed the record and put *Beggars Banquet* on. Nothing like old school rock and blues for post-fight, post-fuck meditations.

He was pleasantly stoned, sore, and tired, but the writing itch was strong, so Angel went downstairs and brewed a pot of coffee. He stirred sugar and cream directly into the pot and took the whole thing upstairs.

He picked up a Maggie fragment and read it. That was a good place to start.

Maggie could be pissed at him and tell him to stay away, but, by God, she couldn't tell him what he could or couldn't write.

He lay on his bed and bounced a baseball off the wall (waiting for the coffee to kick in.) He would take a shower, drink some more coffee, and then write all weekend.

Shit. Marilyn would almost certainly come over Saturday night. Contrary to the Phi Psi banter, Angel and Marilyn hadn't yet fucked. Well, that would change. Angel was a free bird.

He closed his eyes and listened to the Stones and to Wanda's words in his head. God, he liked talking with her. She was a kindred spirit. He had been telling the truth when he told her that they began fucking the minute she sat on the stairs next to him. And she had been right to say Maggie's jealousy was earned. Angel felt as if he had always known Wanda. Just as he felt about Rose, his buxom physicist.

Rose. How had he forgotten Rose when he was thinking Wanda had the best body of any of his women? Shit. Rose made them all look as if God had used up his supply of pulchritude.

He wondered if Rose would come back to the states over the summer. If she did, he would be all over her.

The summer beckoned and excited him. All he had to do was work and read and fuck whomever came his way. Life when it was honest. Yep. He would sweat all day at the paper mill and then shoot pool with his redneck buddy Wayne. And read and fuck, of course. He wished he had a good picture of Wanda to show Wayne. He would practically drown in his own drool.

He sat up and thought of showering but lay back down. He could still smell and feel Wanda, and he didn't want to lose that.

What an amazing night. Maggie's visit put a perfect coda on it. If he had been home, would they have cried and reconciled? Maybe.

It was better this way, though. Maggie could take whatever she had gained from him and then test drive it on her own. She needed to grow. She was, he was, they were all just fucking kids when it came right down to it. Everything they experienced was new.

Take Wanda that night. All in all, that may have been the best night of his life. Even the pizza and beer were good. Rorie was great, and Angel would always be thankful to him.

But Wanda was the star. Dear Lord, what a magnificent beast she was. Angel felt his life overflowing with joy again.

He sat up. He would shower the night off and write the new. He needed to share this joy with Maggie, if not right now, then later.

But he knew *The Book of Maggie* was not yet written.

Chapter Twenty-Nine

Saturday May 29, 1971
Agenbite of Inwit
Setting: Colby Junior College for Women

ANGEL LEANED AGAINST HIS CAR AND STUDIED THE SKY. IT seemed too early to be this steamy in New Hampshire. He lit a joint and took a hit. He peeled off his long sleeve shirt and reached into his bag for a tee shirt. It was going to be a long, hot drive to Florida. The air smelled like rain, but he didn't see any sign of it in the heavens. Rain would lengthen an already twenty-two-hour drive. Rain would be good for thinking, though, and he certainly had plenty of that to do.

Angel smiled. He was in a mood. Pussy, he told himself.

He exhaled and watched the smoke dissipate into the gathering breeze. Rain might slow him enough that he would miss the next day's shift at the paper mill. That could be a good thing, though. He was exhausted. Between his sore ribs and twisted knee, he hadn't slept well since the beating Rorie gave him two weeks earlier. It would be okay, too, to put off the snide looks the Palatka men gave him. City boy. Ivy leaguer. He was shit to them.

Angel heard a voice say, "You can't smoke that stuff here." He turned to see a graying, bespectacled man.

Angel smiled. "Professor Hetherington?"

"Yes. Do I know you?"

"I heard you read your paper on Milton at Boston University two years, ago. I was with Professor Hart from Dartmouth. My name is Angel. We talked afterwards."

"Yes. I remember you. You wanted to discuss Blake's Satan."

"Yes, sir, from *The Marriage of Heaven and Hell*," Angel nodded. "Your talk was immensely influential on my thinking about Satan. I quoted from your paper when I wrote on Ahab as a Byronic hero. That was from your take on Milton's Satan."

"And now, here you are," Hetherington smiled. "Like a vaporous emanation into our little Eden, bringing drugs to the girls."

"And sex, too," Angel laughed. "But you don't need to worry about this." Angel held up his joint and took a drag. "It's all been approved," he said, and exhaled through his nose. "Fine stuff. Just got it from a wizard."

Hetherington blinked. His eyes looked watery when he was confused.

"Better to reign in hell than serve in heaven, right Professor?" Angel said and winked.

Hetherington smiled weakly. "Ah," he said, "I catch your drift. I implied you were Satan, and you…"

"Yes, I got it," Angel said.

And the good professor ambled off. Angel watched him go, his feet hitting the ground at odd intervals. He has bad knees. Certainly, not from football or any other sport. He's awfully young to be falling apart. Angel took another hit. The pot was good. It wasn't soporific, which would have been really shitty on a long drive.

Then, Angel saw Maggie and a girl he vaguely recognized come out of the library and begin to cross the quad. The other girl laughed at something Maggie said and walked towards their dorm. Maggie stood still.

Angel followed her gaze and saw a guy walking towards her. Was it Jeffrey? No, he was the right height and build, but he didn't have Jeffrey's mass of curls. Plus, he was dressed in standard Dartmouth gear, jeans and a tee shirt. A Yalie would have been in slacks or something less rustic.

Maggie lit up as the guy approached her. Unlike Hetherington, Maggie's boy moved athletically. Swimmer? Runner?

They hugged briefly when they met. Angel smiled. Maggie had given him a side hug, not the full-frontal hug which would have mashed her breasts against his chest. He said something, and she laughed. Again, though, he fancied it was her artificial Long Island laugh, complete with a head flip. It wasn't the way she laughed at Angel. When he cracked Maggie up, her laugh exploded spontaneously and was usually accompanied by a punch to his arm or chest. She wasn't beating on whoever the new guy was yet.

Angel took a last hit of his joint, crushed it out between his fingers, and pocketed it. Still leaning against the Austin Healey, Angel crossed his arms and willed Maggie to look his way. Maggie did another cutesy thing with her head and took the guy's arm. They began to move towards her dorm, but she stopped at something he said. She smiled and shook her head. A gust blew her hair, and she turned towards the breeze to put the wandering strand back in its place.

And she froze. She put her hand to her forehead and gazed into the lowering sun. Her body language was unmistakable in its anguish.

She had seen Angel.

Angel straightened when she looked his way and raised his hand.

Maggie stood still for a long time, so long that the boy looked to see what she was staring at. She turned to him. She put a hand on his chest and said something. The boy glanced in Angel's direction and nodded. Maggie said something else, and the boy smiled at her.

She walked slowly towards Angel. He tried to gauge her body language. It wasn't an angry walk. No, it was more the 'going to the guillotine gait' that he imagined frightened French royalty must have employed.

As she neared him, Angel shifted slightly so Maggie wouldn't have to face the sun as they spoke.

Maggie stopped. She seemed unsure what to say or do.

Angel felt a wave of remorse go through him. He shouldn't have come to see her. It had seemed like such a good idea back at Phi Psi. Eddie and Sand had counselled him to leave her alone, but Angel said he knew her better than they did.

And that was true. He knew Maggie better than anyone did.

"Hi Maggie," Angel said. He spoke so quietly that she seemed to barely hear him.

Or, perhaps, the whole thing seemed unreal to her.

Shit. Angel knew better than this. Girls liked to be forewarned about things. The last thing Maggie needed was to face Angel unprepared. Angel didn't know how one went about preparing emotions, but he knew girls attempted to do just that all the time.

Angel watched her curiously. What would she say? Something trite like 'Angel, you shouldn't be here' or something self-pitying like 'Angel, I can't deal with this right now.'

But she said neither.

She just said, "Hi, Angel." There seemed a hint of a sob behind her words, but he didn't see it in her face.

"I'm driving home," Angel said, "and I wanted to respond to your letter. I tried writing you about thirty million times but tore them all up. They seemed inadequate."

"I know," she said. Something in her voice said, 'I thought of calling you every day,' but she didn't say it aloud.

"I miss you," Angel said.

"I miss you, too," Maggie said. Now there was a definite catch in her throat, and she labored to breathe normally.

"That wasn't what I meant. I wasn't trying to get you to say that back to me. I do miss you, but what I really wanted to let you know was that you're wrong about me. I can miss people. You do exist when we're not together. More than my books. More than anybody else in my life."

She didn't respond, so Angel stumbled on. "I talked to my analyst earlier this week, and she told me you're no longer angry with me."

Maggie smiled slightly. "You mean Delilah? She told me you called her. You are so odd sometimes, Angel."

"And you almost smiled. Then you know what Delilah told me. Was she right?"

Maggie looked downwards. "She probably told you that I still love you."

Angel waited, but that ended Maggie's response. "No, she told me that you have the maturity level of a fifteen-year-old."

"That sounds like Delilah. I should probably kill her."

"Don't do that. Then I'd have to break your finger," Angel said softly.

Maggie tried not to smile.

"I'm not going to say I still love you, Angel."

"I don't care. Remember, I'm the one who thought loving was doing, not saying."

"Angel, I've got to go."

"Please hear me out. This will probably be the most female thing I've ever done in my life, but I've kind of rehearsed an entire speech. I don't know which of us it's designed to make feel better, but I need to say it."

Maggie looked at him quizzically, but she didn't leave.

"You're not the least bit jealous of the man I'm with, are you?" Maggie said.

"No, but not for the reason you think."

"Oh?"

"For one thing, you didn't hug him straight on?"

"What?" she laughed.

"Chest to chest. Girls hug sideways when they don't want the man to interpret the hug sexually. And you gave him your fake laugh. So, I know you two haven't made love."

"You don't know that. We might have."

"You might have had sex, though I doubt it, but you haven't made love," Angel said. If possible, he spoke even more quietly. "You've never made love with anyone but me. Not in your whole life. Somewhere, deep inside, you're worried that you never will again. Not with the same intensity."

Maggie turned slightly pale, and she cast her face down.

"Maggie, I just wanted to apologize to you for a bunch of things. First and foremost, I said you were a spoiled rich kid."

"I am," Maggie said without lifting her face.

"No, you're not. You may have been acting like one when I yelled at you, but you aren't one. And I said I hadn't cheated on you," he said.

She looked up at that, and her nostrils flared.

"I didn't have sex with anyone while we were a couple. I really didn't."

"I know. Delilah told me. She's a true believer."

"But I cheated in a million other ways. The night you came to see me and tore up my room," he began.

"Oh, Angel, I'm so sorry I did that."

"No, that was fine. I told the campus police a vandal tore up my typewriter, and insurance got me a new one."

"But I tore up your writing," she said.

Angel looked at her. "Because you were hurt. Because I hurt you. Me, the guy you should have been able to trust more than anyone on the planet." He sounded subdued. "I went to Boston to help Wanda," he said. "I know you know that. Groucho said he told you. Wanda was hit by a guy and was being terrorized. She went to the police, but they couldn't or wouldn't do anything."

"Why is she your problem, Angel? Everyone is your problem. Look at Jane. Don't they have counselors at her college? Doesn't she have friends? Why is it always you, Angel? And why does it only seem to be women?"

"It is mostly women, but that's because they're the only ones who ask for help. That's not true. I've been an emotional lifeline for Billy, too. But guys would usually die rather than ask for help. They want to go down on their own. Sweetheart, look at me. I'm a mess, and I wouldn't ask anyone for help."

"Not even me?" she said.

"I think I'm asking you for help right now," he said. "I'm asking you to listen to me, even though I know you hate me."

"I don't hate you," she said.

"Yes, you do. You love me, too. It's all connected."

Maggie didn't reply to that. She bit her lip and bowed her head again. Angel took her hand, and she didn't withdraw it.

"Sweetheart, Wanda told me that I cheated on you over and over. I didn't understand what she meant at first, but then I realized that it's cheating for me to shower affection on other women. I use intimacy to connect to women all the time. I've kissed girls and thought nothing of it. I let Jane know that she's always welcome and always safe. Wanda and I have an amazing connection. You don't even know about this one, but I've been exchanging letters with Rose, a girl in London, and they have all been flirtatious."

"I know," Maggie said. "Rose Bird at London University. I read one of her letters."

"Uh, huh. That's what I mean, though. What I've discovered is that I crave intimacy. It's my life-blood. It means more to me than my books or my writing. I know that when you see me with another girl, you can feel my connection to her. I thought I wasn't cheating because I didn't sleep with Jane. But I know now that, to you, I was, even though I didn't touch her. What I'm trying to say is that I know how I hurt you, and I don't blame you for not wanting to be with me."

"Angel."

"Sweetheart, let me finish. I'm kind of on a roll here." Maggie had tears in her eyes, and she was looking at him now. "I'm not saying I'm going to change my evil ways. I don't think I can. I may outgrow the need to bond with every woman who enters my sphere, or they may stop seeking my help, but, I understand now why we can't be a couple."

Maggie choked.

"You need someone who will only see you, someone who will adore you and make you feel secure. I'm not that guy. Maybe he is." Angel pointed to Maggie's new guy who looked impatient. "But I need someone who will trust me. Someone who can see me smile at another girl or help her out and not feel threatened. I need someone who will always know that she's the only one I love and care about."

"Angel, what would happen to the Janes and Wandas if you didn't take them under your magic cloak? Really, what would happen to them? Would they just die for lack of Angel's magic touch?"

"I don't know. Jane might kill herself. Wanda would probably be fine. I went there as much to fight Rorie, that's the guy who was stalking her, as I did to help her out. You and I had broken up, and I needed to hit someone. He sounded like a good candidate."

"Is that what happened to your face?" Maggie asked and touched his brow. Wanda's stitching had left an imperfect scar which was still red and raised.

"You should've seen Rorie," Angel said wryly.

"I'll bet. What did you do to him?"

"I broke his hand and maybe his wrist. I mean I smashed the bones to bits. And I'm pretty sure I gave him a nasty concussion. It was kind of epic," Angel said.

"Good grief," she said. "What did you hit him with?"

"A baseball bat." Her eyes widened. "Just a little one, one of those souvenir bats."

"What did he hit you with?"

"A dresser. He hit me with a dresser and a door."

Maggie shook her head and sighed. "You guys."

"I know. We're morons."

Maggie touched his brow again and then saddened. "Angel, Delilah's right. I am emotionally still a kid. I have trust issues. I should have known you cared for me. That should have been enough."

"But it wasn't."

"No."

They were silent. Maggie snuck a look over her shoulder and raised her hand in a 'wait a minute' gesture to her guy.

"Anyway," Angel said, "I just wanted to say all that and to give you an early birthday present."

"You don't know my birthday," Maggie said.

"June fourth. Delilah told me. Delilah told me your whole life's history. Apparently, I was your first real love."

"That's true."

"So," he said and reached into his car. "I made this for you." He handed her a package.

"You wrapped it in the Sunday comics?" she smiled.

"It seemed appropriate, given my moronic nature," he said.

"Should I open it now?"

"Well, it's pretty obvious what it is," he said.

"A manuscript"

"Yep, I re-wrote what you tore up. You are holding a chapter from *The Book of Maggie the Cat*."

"A chapter? It feels like a whole book."

"I think it's eighty-two pages. It's not like the other stuff I wrote. Unlike the old stuff, this chapter hasn't happened yet. In it, you go on a motorcycle ride out west with a lean, rangy cowboy type."

"Ooh, I like that type."

"No, you like country club boys, and that's all right."

"You're wrong," she said.

"I wouldn't let the new guy read it. You have a lot of sex with your cowboy motorcycle friend."

They were quiet. It was nice.

"Maggie, are you still going to Dartmouth in the fall?"

"I am."

Angel was silent for a moment. When he looked up, he sought her eyes.

"Maggie, I'll stay away from you next year and give you all the room you need. I won't even speak when we pass if you don't want me to. But I want you to know that I'm still your best friend. If you ever need me, I'll be there for you. If you're sad or lonely or just want to hang out, everyone at Phi Psi would be glad to see you. Bring your friend over there if you want. I promise to be nice to him and appropriately jealous." Maggie looked dubious. "You think I never get jealous, but I do. When I walked in on you and Jeffrey, I was, I don't know how to describe it. It's not jealousy the way you feel it. But remember when you came downstairs?"

Maggie nodded.

"I made jokes because I didn't know what else to do. I felt bad for you and for Jeffrey both. For you because I knew you were humiliated, and for Jeffrey because I knew you no longer cared for him. I knew I was your guy. What you were doing with Jeffrey was separate from that. I thought you were probably trying to break up and didn't know how to do it. That happened at Christmas with Cassie. I wanted to break up with her and ended up having sex. It was cruel and unfair to Cassie. But I trusted that you cared more for me than you did for Jeffrey. And part of me truly didn't care. If you want someone else, if someone else makes you happier than I do, I want you to be with him. I really do.

But always remember this. I know you, Maggie. You, the odd, individual you. No one else does. I hurt you repeatedly, and, for that, I apologize. When you were with me, though, your life was vivid. You felt smart and sexy and brave. You'd never been happier in your entire life. And you were so funny. We laughed all the time. That's how I know we're over, now, because I don't think we can make each other laugh anymore. Laughter should be an official litmus test for relationships. It should be in the psych manuals.

So, please don't avoid me next year. I am your true friend and will be forever. And now I'm going to kiss you goodbye. Don't pull away. You know that it's a more fitting way to part than torn books and hurled recriminations. Don't worry about your guy over there. If he likes you, he'll get over it. Besides, he needs to know about your baggage. We always need to know a lover's history to see what the trajectory of our relationship might be. And we all have baggage. You knew all about Cassie when you fell for me."

Maggie moved closer to him and raised her face.

Angel took her face in his hands and kissed her gently. Her lips tasted sweet but for the salt which ran from her eyes.

He caressed her hair and kissed her again.

"Goodbye, Sweetheart," he said.

He climbed into the Austin Healey and started it.

Maggie still held the manuscript to her chest. Tears ran down her face. Angel smiled, reached into his back pocket, and handed her a handkerchief. She looked at it and chuckled. "Of course," she said. She looked at him as she dabbed her eyes. "See," she said. "We can still laugh."

She turned and walked slowly back to meet Dartmouth boy.

"Mags," Angel called. Maggie turned. "My address and phone number are on the manuscript in case you are traveling south or need to talk this summer. I won't be home much. I'll be working double shifts at the paper mill and reading. My monastic summer."

She smiled, turned away, and began her walk again.

Angel watched her go.

Man, she had a really fine ass.

He put the Austin Healey into gear and let the clutch out. He didn't want to see the guy embrace Maggie and ask her what was wrong.

At a red light, he reached into the little ice chest on the floor of the passenger seat and got out a Coke. He pulled a hit of speed from his vest pocket and took it. He chased it with the Coke and settled back for the long ride.

Angel turned up the volume as *Baby Please Don't Go* began and listened to Van Morrison belt it out.

Perfect song to kick off a long ride.

He wondered briefly what Maggie was thinking and feeling. Kissing her had probably been cruel. She would think about him all day. That was okay. She would be in his head, too. Angel relaxed and gave way to the beat, Groucho's super-mellow pot, the speed, and the sweet, sharp bite of his Coke.

He turned south on I-91 and punched it. The little car growled and leapt into action.

He tried to envision Maggie's cute rear crossing the quad. Why didn't it bother him more that it was probably already in another man's hands?

Angel knew why, though. That was his ass and she was his girl, no matter what. And he knew that Maggie knew it too. It had been in her kiss and in her tears and in her voice. It had even been in the lilt of her hips as she left him. Women know when they're being watched.

Thor perked up at that, and Angel settled into a comfortable fantasy. In it, he sat writing at his desk, and Maggie slept on her side with that delectable rear end of hers facing him. He turned back to his work. He knew that when he finished, that sweet ass and everything attached to it would conform to his body and be one with him.

Thor growled to let his presence be known, a sound which said, 'I'll be waiting.'

-Finis-

Cue the Howlin' Wolf version of *Smokestack Lightning* and turn it way the fuck up...